West End Quartet

A FIVE DIRECTIONS PRESS BOOK

West End Quartet

FOUR NOVELLAS

ARIADNE APOSTOLOU

ISBN-13 978-1947044005
ISBN-10 1947044001

Published in the United States of America.

A Five Directions Press book

Cover photographs: Ansonia Hotel © Gregory James Van Raalte/ Shutterstock; Nafplio, Greece, via Pixabay (no attribution required).

Book and cover design by Five Directions Press
Five Directions Press logo designed by Colleen Kelley

FIVE DIRECTIONS PRESS

DEDICATION

To you, people of the Peloponnese in the precious Arcadian villages that include the hamlets of my grandparents. Your humanistic worldview, your collective wisdom that takes the long view and your willingness to laugh more than cry affirm life. You inspired the ideas, incidents and characters of these novellas.

To you, Manhattan and your infectious, fighting spirit.

To you, revolutionaries of Nicaragua, Cuba and Granada with vision for the empowerment of women and the necessity for literacy, and to those who died to vanquish oppression. You are remembered.

To you, my daughter.

"The novellas that constitute *West End Quartet* collectively tell the story of four idealistic women who join together in 1980 to fight nuclear power and other destructive forces before going off in different directions to live out their lives. What's striking here is not so much the concept as the author's ability to devise plot nuances that are both unique and intimate and to acquaint us with characters that are every bit as alive and intriguing as any of the real people in our lives. The combination makes for a thoroughly enjoyable, thought-provoking reading experience, along the lines of Jane Smiley or Louise Erdrich."

—Joan Schweighardt, author of *The Last Wife of Attila the Hun*, *The Accidental Art Thief*, and other novels

"Taken together, these poignant, complex stories create a redeeming vision of love, loss, remembrance, and friendship. The nuanced plot of this wonderful book flows naturally from the plight and inner life of each finely wrought character. The characters in this work, both adults and children, will live on in the reader's mind long after the back cover is closed. I usually have a favorite. In this case there were just too many good choices."

—Rocco Lo Bosco, author of *Ninety Nine* and *Buddha Wept*

Five Directions Press publishes contemporary
women's fiction, historical fiction, science fiction,
fantasy, and memoirs.

For more information, see
www.fivedirectionspress.com.

FIVE DIRECTIONS PRESS

Contents

IT'S BEEN QUITE A LONG TIME SINCE THAT BLACK DAY SITTING ACROSS *from each other over brunch, you bursting with the news that destroyed me and ended our friendship. I wanted to rip that elation off your face. What right to happiness did you have, when I had suffered so much more than you even knew? I had never been so angry. I actually scared myself. And you never doubted I'd be overjoyed at your newfound "purpose," as you put it. You would adopt a baby. Impossible at your age, Kleio! Who did that?*

Ageism be damned, you enthused. Yes, there were age restrictions for international adoptions, but what gave men the right to stamp motherhood with an expiry date? We—you and I and Group—fought for women's rights. For equal rights. Freedom to adopt in middle age was a just cause, you insisted. You believed I'd help you. You believed without question that I would support you. It was at that moment that I actually felt molecules beading within me, forming a thin stream of envy to poison my blood. I remember shaking. No, I could not. If your age was not an impediment, then your bout with cancer! It could return at any time. It was a selfish whim, a cruel joke to play on some orphan child for you to meet an early death. Of course, I could not support such irresponsibility. It was so American of you to think it was a good idea. I could not.

After that, I made excuses. I blocked you. You called the others, asking them to give me messages, and they did. I kept my silence. I could not explain my disapproval. I went on with my life, and I became the success my father would have lauded, acting on behalf of my government, regularly quoted in the Financial Times. *You'd not recognize me today, Kleio. Long gone is the Bolshie-politico of yore. I* became what Mum and Dad had hoped: conventional. Settled, though not well, alas, as envy is an empty vessel; it holds no happiness, no peace.

In the old days, we would say friendship among women was a precious commodity, using a Marxist economic construct, as if it were a bar of gold to be collected and stored, traded or sold. Now I know that friendship is no commodity but exists in the willingness to see through another's eyes, to understand the other as much as one can. It is empathy, for me hard won. I beg your forgiveness for my cold desertion in your time of need. I let my envy shut you out. I did not want to open up grief that I had packed away. If I could have, I would have told you what a child meant to me. We would have held each other, cried together, mourned together. I would have healed my own suffering. We would still be friends. I would have helped you.

I remember you used to say that the Greek language had two words for time: chronos was for time counted and measured. The other word, kairos, you said meant "the right moment" and was known by intuition. It was elastic, unmeasured and felt. It came upon a person as a heightened state, and that was the time to act. When it was no longer felt, the time for action was over. That's how it worked, you insisted. We thought you were daft, but I've come to see that there is a kairos and it has urgency. This is my kairos, Kleio, my time to break the silence and tell what transpired in Nicaragua. It's my time to tell you and the others the entire story which I've kept a secret for three decades. Would you see me now? Would you forgive me?

And this, my time, coincides with a child's time, a child I've come to love and for whom I seek your help, a suffering child at a critical juncture. Could you open your heart and your home to her this summer? Have her know you, and your daughter? You heart was always big, Kleio, and full of empathy. Can you spare some room for us, me and this child I very much love? She is Mina's daughter. Her name is Skye.

Mallory

How to Change the World

Mallory, 1980–1981

"What was is now no more; and what was not has come to be;
renewal is the lot of time."—Ovid

Manhattan, October 1, 1980

EMERGING WITH THE THRONGS ONTO THE PLATFORM AT CANAL Street Station, bumping her way past pushing bodies—"so sorry," "beg pardon," "excuse me, please"—Mallory twisted a path through the sensible people heading home and stole a glance at her Rolex. Precisely 5:46 PM. Damn. He'd said meet him at Paco's *a las cinco en punto,* 5 PM sharp, ever intolerant of her lack of Spanish. Should she continue? Would he even wait for her?

Mal just hated Love, her taskmaster. It had her chasing all over creation in search of a Miskito Indian from her economics seminar who flirted with danger and dangled her like an afterthought. Juan Xochitl Davila of subterranean politics and dubious revolutions—entangling her in situations her London circle would deem reckless. Love, dammit, had plonked unpredictability onto her thoughtfully planned future.

If she could only spot the farthest exit sign above the sea of heads—Americans were so massive and she was so petite— she would surface at the edge of the meat-packing district. She would have to sprint in her new platform shoes, because Paco's El Burrito Bar was centered in the second long block of Canal Street. She'd go anywhere for Juan, deliriously happy that he had called after four months of silence. She perspired in the warm October rush hour. Air. Air. She needed air.

So very tardy! Not finding her there, he may have already bolted. Waiting for any period of time was apt to spook him. He saw CIA operatives on every corner, heard the click of bugged phones—things she had never thought about. She should dash. Impossible to second guess him.

Mal flew up the exit stairs, adroitly dodged a lump of doggie-do in the gutter and burst into a run, full-throttle. Such a help, truly it would be, if Juan would explain why he was a target. *Safer for you not to know, querida.*

Most likely true. With the Sandinistas gaining ground in Nicaragua and the Republicans running America, both CIA and FBI freely stalked the campuses, so students were mindful. Now even her women's collective, Group, took care to avoid detection.

She ran. Love you, yes, but a commitment had better follow your vanishing act, Juanito, she thought murderously.

Her heart thumped. At least she need not worry that he was wasting away in Guantanamo, the least menacing of the scenarios his sister, Mina, had dreamed up. Oh, what a devil he was to enjoy those frissons of competition between sister and girlfriend, now that Mina had joined Group. *Mal, she takes care of herself, but Jasmina, mi manita,* his little sister—*she needs protection.* Well, Mal was equally entitled to protection and had threatened that if he offered no proposal by graduation, she'd return to London—weeping about her bad American romance. Her pouty outburst had only amused him. *Let us see, let us see what the future will bring.* And soon after, he disappeared.

Truth was she missed him desperately—even his machismo, his surety, the magnet pulling her along, screaming and kicking.

Had she packed her diaphragm in her rush to leave uptown? She slowed to feel for it in her knapsack then scrunched her nose at the thought of his rattrap tenement ruled by brazen, black creatures that scurried over unwashed pans in the sink. *Cucarachas, querida; they coexist with the poverty.* Two years later, and she coexisted with it all.

Just keep running. Almost there.

The sun dropping quickly beyond the Hudson River elongated the shadow she chased, attached to her shoes. The streetlamps popped on. Canal Street soon would be deserted and the dreaded Crazies would emerge.

She hyperventilated. The Burrito Bar façade was visible—dark, of course, where Juan's dodgy *hermanos* often congregated in the back room to argue their tactical fantasies till all hours. Up front, Paco placidly assembled burritos for the double-parked coppers while humming "*mucho trabajo—y poco dinero.*" Too much work, too little pay.

It drove her mad, having to sit at the counter with "the fuzz"—smurfs at home, the *tongo*, the *yuta*, whatever were their Spanish names—the enemy, in short. And her, the Bad One: *Mal*. Juan's old lady, the unfortunately named white girl out with the *tongo*. Juan's so-called brothers sniggered—she knew—no idea that she was Lady Mallory Tame. Clearly that was why she favored Paco, from an Argentine family of means who understood what titles were.

Mal stopped short, breathless before the barred window and banged on the metal-sheeted door, her heart racing.

Damn. Just as she'd feared: no Juan in wait with open arms.

Peering through the bars, she made out the contours of counter and stools. She squinted for a line of light beneath the breakroom door, none. Pointless to go back uptown. Best to catch one's breath and wait—though he should have arrived by now. Latinos were not famous for punctuality, another of their irritating habits. Their political activities were not unlike the game of Clue, so it was plausible that someone, Paco himself, might materialize to direct her elsewhere.

Paco, *muy* sexy. Where had Paco, Group's communal heart-throb, gone to? Paco flirted with the commune women like the other Latinos, but only he applauded Group's efforts to draw attention to the oppression of girls and women and agreed their cause had as much urgency as Fidel's volcanic revolutions currently erupting across South America.

Her commune was duly impressed that she'd snagged an itinerant fugitive to share his horror stories about women's conditions in Bolivia and Peru. Proof she excelled at her job as education director and commune leader, by bringing in the direct evidence, the first-hand reports.

But her frustrating Prince Charming? Nowhere to be found: a snapshot of her future with him? No future at all was the downside of loving Juanito. Life is a test, he would snap. *Accept me as I am, or leave me!*

Now it began. The vagrants who belonged in hospital wandered about, shouting obscenities at the cars whizzing toward the Holland Tunnel. Why did the city allow this?

She pressed herself inside the door alcove. Definitely out of place in bell-bottoms, and even worse was her absinthe-hued choli, chosen for its sheen, which reflected her silver locks but exposed her midriff. Mum's lecture on forethought came to mind. The countess asleep in London would think it a nightmare: her daughter waiting on a dodgy street for her brown-skinned *enamorado* who might not even show.

Safer, perhaps, to wait with the petrol station chaps across the street, the well-mannered Sikhs. "Like Queen Elizabeth you speak," one actually had said when she'd gone in search of Juan, who was never one to miss a sympathetic jaw with The Worker and lend an ear to the endless whinge: *mucho trabajo y poco dinero—*

The screech of a taxi cab jolted her. A split second then to recognize the man in gray camo with backpack and beret. Juan. Thinner, glowing, his gorgeous smile aimed at her, his arms opened wide.

"*Querida! Mi amor!*" His sloe-eyes on her were full of tenderness and tears.

She ran to his embrace, laughed and kissed him and held him tight. Unbearably handsome was her Juanito, exotic, thrilling—his good-feeling hold on her again, his foreign smell of vines and earth and animal fur.

They sobbed and laughed and spoke at once.

"Nicaragua!" he said, releasing her, wiping her tears. "Where did you think? Back home, of course! Paco came with me. I just dropped him off, so I am late, and you don't like late. *Ya!* Are you hungry? I ate nothing—all the day on planes. Come! We go to El Cid. It's close by. They did not permit me to disclose this trip. Not to you, not to Mina. I was so sure you would guess it. So your famous intuition has failed you, *Chiquita?*" Chuckling, he pinched her cheek and kissed her.

"They invited me to see the progress of the revolution." He splayed his fingers at her face. "These! They felt the bullet holes that pepper the walls of Estelí, of Matanzas and León! The photographs of all the dead—little children, women, even *abuelitas*—are hung like art gallery pictures in the town halls. *Presente!* They write this word in black across the faces who witnessed the terrible birth of freedom. *Presente! Presente!* I am here! I cried to see them. But you, *mi amor?* How are you?" He kissed her as they walked, bumping knees, hugging, laughing.

"Me? Happy and relieved at last. You are alive and safe." She squeezed his arm.

"*Ay, qué bien!*" He hugged her. "The Sandinistas introduced me to the future leaders. I tell you a secret: Father Ernesto Cardenal—the press calls him the poet-priest—he will address the United Nations. He invites me as his guest. He, and Danny Ortega and the Chamorros: what they will do for Nicaragua! *Ay!* And I shall join with them—*mestizo* that I am, I am useful to the revolution."

It was disorienting to take in his words, to make meaning from them and his excitement, and at the same time, to depress her inner ache and anger. Four months of numbing herself to dire scenarios only to learn he'd simply gone home! A nascent rage fought her desire for him. *Let's do an about-face, let's go uptown to my bed,* she wanted to interrupt him. Physical expression would sort her jumble of emotions.

But they were already at their old haunt, El Cid, before she could speak. Through the window the small restaurant glowed; the checkered tablecloths and candles beckoned. He opened the door for her, and its familiarity calmed her; their life from before he had disappeared was apparently resuming. They sat in the red leather banquette, the one they favored. Their bodies touched wherever possible.

"And you, *mi vida, mis ochos.* Tell me about you, now."

My life and my eyes. How she had missed his endearments. Even so, she knew her impotence to nudge him from his world of magical names, his newest heroes. Come back here, to this table on Canal Street, to me!

"Juan. We were so worried all this time! Look here: you should have rung, if not me, then Mina. They have telephones, right? We thought you could be dead! Do you understand how desperate it was for us—you simply vanishing? You might have sent some sort of word."

"Sure, sure, I see it, but we were obliged to be covert, *querida,* because of who I am and what they want of me—"

He was impossible. She wanted remorse, not reasons.

He cast around the sparsely peopled restaurant, drew her to him tightly. His gorgeous eyes narrowed and looked intently into hers. "I have something to tell you."

"Okay, tell me." She began to trace his lips with her finger. She loved the otherness of him. She touched his cheeks, the epicanthic folds of his eyes. His appearance spoke of other worlds she yearned to enter. In Chipping Campden, one never saw Miskito Indian eyes, the gift of his mother along with the Mongolian Spot, he'd explained proudly when Mal had discovered the brown dime-sized circle on his backside. Mina lacked his Indian traits, he'd said, physical proof of their inherent differences.

"What is it?" She wanted him to ignite from her heat. She felt the warmth of his tawny skin, its energy. She removed his beret and stroked his blue-black hair, grown now to shoulder length, and pushed it behind his ears.

"Listen carefully." He took her hands to still them.

Undaunted, she snuggled into his delicate frame, a match for hers. His patina of swagger, renewed by the home visit, was such a turn-on. Juan was perpetual conflict; how could she cling to outrage and want him so powerfully?

"I have a secret mission from the Leaders. They will create a big role for me in the new Nicaragua if I succeed."

Mal started. "A mission? What role is this? Who are *they*? Really, Juan, did no one consider the beastly agony that being *covert* creates? Did *you* think about it?"

"Yes, of course. But so it had to be, *mi amor*. It will not happen again, leaving you like that. I see the restaurant is clean—no *federales* followed us in. I have been checking. So, it is safe to say this: in March I will return to Nicaragua—but with you. Together we will work for the revolution—as teachers. The Sandinistas plan a rapid campaign for the *inalfabetizados*—the millions of adults who do not read—to make them literate in one year. We will surpass the Cubans, who needed two years. You and I, we shall not be apart. *Te amo, mi amor.* You know it. I was desperate for you the entire time. But it is my country, and I was born for politics. You understand this is the legacy from my father. I must do it, contribute to the historic change. War wages for the soul of Nicaragua. I was absent for its liberation but am spared to rebuild it, to be *presente* my own way. In Managua they support me—" He covered the question she was about to ask with his hand. "Safer for you not to know their names."

Mal froze. Stunning this, his highjack of her life without even the offer of a choice. She shook her head in disbelief. This was giddy Sandinista oratory speaking, macho guilt for sitting out the war. Lady Mallory spirited away to a Third World country? No thank-you.

"I'm at a loss for words, Juan."

"You know how we are, *querida,* you and I, two halves that make a better whole. With you beside me, I will succeed, Mal. You have the cool head that calms my passions and the good judgments for my impulses. We balance each other. Just think! To shape the future of Nicaragua! One day, you might become Mrs. *Presidente.* Surely you would like that. The new future has begun. My beautiful country will charm you, I promise." He kissed her forehead.

Tread carefully, avoid confrontation. His allegiances fluctuated with the wind: *compañeros* one day became *enemigos* the next. Yes, she knew how they were together, compatible one day, arguing the next. Unless, unless... Not exactly how her fantasy went: down on a knee and the offer of a sparkling diamond. But was it the revolutionary's round-about proposal of marriage?

"There is much to know and understand." She kept her voice bright to encourage communication. "But please, not at your flat, Juanito. The cockroaches!"

"But not uptown at *el Grupo,* either: your female tribe! They will argue it down. It is big, I know, what I ask of you, want from you. As for Mina, I will visit her in the morning. And for tomorrow night, I invite all the Talk-Talk Liberation Ladies to a Nicaraguan fiesta to celebrate our new Manhattan cell." He leaned back against the padded seat and watched her response.

The game of Clue was now a game of chess.

"All right, Juan, fair point. You wish to avoid the commune. I know why, because of Kleio. I can't take arguments tonight, either. Shall we go to a hotel then, to celebrate your return? My treat?"

He beamed. "*Que bien!* First, we celebrate with dinner. I am so hungry, and very defeated by rice and beans."

He had foisted that unpalatable dish on her often enough. "*Paella*, then? *Tinto*?"

"How well you know my heart, *Compañera Mallory!* We are made for each other."

The mood slipped easily into what she loved best, distanced from the naysayers that populated their respective worlds, the mismatched two together against all odds, cuddled up in an intimate restaurant at the bottom of Manhattan, a bottle of wine before them. She glanced at their reflection in the long mirror above the bar, the light and dark couple, always, the frisson;

behind their images, cars raced home. Her home was Juan Xochitl Davila.

As they spoke of neutral subjects, she became the girl etched in gold on the cinnamon-colored cover of her childhood adventure book, a gift from her father. The girl sat in a tree house hugging a book entitled *The People of Other Lands*. Lord Tame would surely say, if he knew of Juan's plan, *better to embarrass me by burning bras than by traipsing about the jungle like a camp follower behind a pied piper who never worked a day in his life*. But Daddy never would. Because she would never walk into a civil war with someone so unreliable as Juan, even if he should propose on bended knee and cover her knuckle with a behemoth diamond ring. She would not go. But her turmoil was better left unvoiced until she'd heard him out.

Over dinner she described the changes she was making to Group. She had ejected two roommates he had never liked and was about to replace them with one more manageable. She preferred the naïve enthusiasm of the new candidate over their snarky cynicism, she explained. She had advertised the availability of space in a feminist commune on the Upper West Side in the NYU student paper, and yesterday, before his call, she had interviewed a candidate she liked, a bit of an innocent but game to try it. They'd discussed feminism and had seen eye to eye. "This Gwen actually clapped her hands when I said empowered women empower those they love."

Juan listened with interest.

"I explained that the FBI pays women to infiltrate communes like ours. It issues propaganda that feminism is socially subversive. So we are cautious. We will interview her tomorrow night. And we will decide."

Juan nodded approvingly, looked serious. This was so unlike him, to listen without a running commentary of pot-shots and jokes.

"Juan, something is going on with you. I'm waiting for your jibe that *el Grupo* isn't radical enough to attract the FBI.

Where is the boast that *your grupo disidente* was hauled to police headquarters in a paddy wagon? Come, Juanito. Where is the teasing, the jokes? I'm waiting..."

He smiled and kissed her forehead again, began rubbing her back. "I am thinking you won't be in *el Grupo* that much longer."

She stopped short, unwilling to agree or disagree. She said instead that in his absence she had been feeling ambivalent about Group, that she had even considered disbanding it, thinking perhaps that their activities were becoming too dangerous in the current political environment. But in the end, she had decided to persevere.

"I would have loved to talk to you about it. I missed your perspective...," she said.

Juan nodded. "And me? I missed your ideas. So, you told this *chica*, Gwen, that empowered women empower those they love. I am thinking about that. Because, just so it will be, to empower your Nicaraguan sisters, to make them literate. You will empower their children, who are the future of Nicaragua. That will be your most effective 'hands-on feminism,' as you call it."

Mal started. He'd turned her words back on her, the fox biding his time to pounce.

"You know full well my opinions about 'my Nicaraguan sisters,'" she snapped. "Those gum-chewing molls of your mates. They reek of garlic and cheap perfume. I reject them as 'sisters' because they are unenlightened in every sense!"

He shook his head and smiled to demonstrate his infinite patience, another tactic of his. He never raised his voice.

She changed tack. "Teaching is not my bag, darling, least of all teaching grammar—and Spanish grammar at that. Spanish is impossible. How often have you accused me of being the Slowest Learner of Spanish in *el mundo*? Teachers must communicate with their students, sweetheart."

He kissed her. "We cannot discuss the 'how' tonight, *querida*, but we will find it. As I see it, your wish to change the composition of *el Grupo* arises from frustration. But changing one *chica* for another does not change the core. This commune business, all the talk-talk you do together, it is too small a playground. It is not enough. I present you more meaningful work. More than half of my people are illiterate. More than half, Mallory! And these illiterates have told us that to learn to read and write is more valuable to them than food or work. You, *mi amor,* have advanced consciousness. Logically, it is your next step."

He was serious and she was stunned again. "What can I say? I must think, Juan. There are many considerations. I require some time to decide."

"Take time, yes, but not too much. And promise me: do not tell the others about this. *Claro?*"

"Of course."

They finished the bottle, and Mal ordered a split more to mute her growing anxiety. Despite all her own fine political talk, he was the true revolutionary, the authentic activist. He wanted her to be like him, to force change.

They ordered flan and Sambuca with coffee beans that she rescued from the sides of her drained glass with a finger. Wobbly, they hailed a taxi and tottered into the lobby of the Waldorf Astoria.

After they made love, she cried softly, unable to sort the sources of her grief. One thing was clear: to love him was to want what he wanted, that she go with him to Nicaragua.

—⁓—

In the morning Juan left for the West Side to visit his sister at the commune. Mal headed to her classes at NYU. It was possible, she still hoped, that in returning to his pals and student life he would rethink this daft idea.

The morning air was chilly. She needed a jumper and hadn't carried one. She would have to wear the bellbottoms and choli to class. Oh well, it was NYU and it was the times; once she got there, she'd look unremarkable, just another student.

Crossing Washington Square Park toward her classroom building, she marveled that the hot-dog carts set up their yellow and green umbrellas so early. White-haired men were already at the chess tables by the Arch. She loved it here. It even looked like London. Across the street, the row of Greek revival townhouses, columned and stately, that faced the square echoed the grand versions at home on which they had been modeled. The morning roller-bladers swirled paths around and behind her, swooping toward the central fountain. There were guys already strumming guitars, a mime chalked up in white was feeling his way out of an imaginary box. And the people walking dogs—so many dogs! The pétanque area was still empty. She often stopped to watch the game because it resembled British lawn tennis but was played in the heart of noisy, sooty Manhattan. Students milled about, headed to classes; friends chatted, book bags were scattered everywhere. She felt happy to have chosen New York University for additional graduate studies after Oxford, grateful for what it gave her, the gift of an urban life, the privacy to explore, the wealth of varied friends. And Juan, of course.

The morning sun splayed long shafts of light across the square. There was life in the shouts and barks and honking traffic. Why would she forsake this for a jungle of scorpions and monkeys? Because she loved him.

In class, as morning progressed, she realized she could not trust herself to keep the silence she'd promised Juan. The longer she sat in Statistics, staring at equations, the more she dwelt on her indecision. She longed to sort it out with Kleio's help.

Kleio would approach it logically, after flipping out at first. Level-headed Kleio was a real friend, and even if her emotions got the best of her at times, in the last analysis she was fair. She could see all of Mal's points of view. It had been thus from the beginning of their friendship. It was Kleio she was desperate to see, not Mina. Not Juan.

Increasingly inattentive to equations, she mulled over a middle ground position, such as occasional visits and long separations. But left to his own devices, would he not be lured away by a local *Nica-chica* bit oozing availability? Would he forget her? Would he never return?

In Latin American Economics and Public Policy class, where she ought to have paid attention given Juan's demand, she drummed her pen on a notepad and tried to imagine living in a state of contradiction: the backwardness of illiteracy and the forwardness of revolution. The problems her professor described, of banks restructuring to promote sustainable development, fought mightily with her vision of jungle life with Juan. She had him virtually swinging from vines, while she struggled to roll her R's in that god-awful tongue with nary a consonant within earshot, her hair dented into permanent frizzles, barefooted, dodging snakes. No more glad rags from Madison Avenue, no more cute shoes. A headache lurked. To go with him was dangerous, life-altering, and a derailment of everything she'd set for herself, long before she'd ever met him.

At day's end, before heading uptown to meet with Gwen, the new candidate, she and Juan rendezvoused at a coffee-shop in the Village. They sat opposite in a small booth and ordered tea. She recognized his look of impatience. She caught him studying her eye movements for indications of a decision reached. "Not yet."

It irritated her that he urged her to be quick. She would not be rushed. This decision would affect her future, their future. And what was it, exactly, that he proposed—a lark for six months? A lifetime together? Marriage? She needed to know.

"What I said last night!" He was exasperated. "We will be together in Nicaragua to support the revolution. I love you. But if it makes you feel better, see it as an experiment in living and working together. Let us see how we manage that much. We will know when the experiment ends and what the next step will be. Maybe we marry. Maybe we part. But do not mix apples and pears. Our joint venture is for the revolution. For us as a couple, we go a step at a time. Who knows the future, Mallory?"

"But it is about *us* that I care. Our *future!* It is too open-ended, for my liking. An 'experiment' is not a commitment."

He argued that the experiment was *also* a commitment. Just like Group.

In that case, she needed Kleio to talk it out.

"No," he countered, "a poor idea. Think for yourself, Mallory, so you know that whatever you will decide, it is your choice. All the consequences are on you. No third party–neither parents, nor friends—has a say in what concerns only us: my position. End of discussion."

She bristled and said no more. She wasn't asking his permission. She *would* tell Kleio.

"*Bueno*. A stalemate. Let us talk no more of it now. Instead, listen to my first day back in New York. This morning I saw Mina. She was surprised and, like you, relieved. I told her that I would take you to Nicaragua. She said it is exciting. She will say nothing to Kleio who, she agrees, will influence you not to go. I visited my advisor to inform my intention to withdraw at end of the term. He accused me to be 'Aye-wol.' What is that? Attending classes is required to get my degree. I argued: to participate in economic strategy as it develops on the ground is superior knowledge. He said I need theory, that I am a smart-ass." Juan chuckled.

Mal winced. "That was foolhardy, Juan. Arrogant. You must go back to apologize. If you rethink this and decide to stay, he'll not support you. You said in essence you care neither for your degree nor for his good opinion."

"In essence, *si, Señorita*. You are correct. I take the finals for the classes I missed. Then I leave. I do not need a degree to help my country."

Her insides tightened. He was simply naïve about the world's workings. She argued this was his time for education, not revolutions, the reason why his uncle had sent him to university and saved his skin in doing so. Nicaragua was unsafe for impressionable, rash boys.

As she spoke, he wagged his index finger back and forth in disagreement. "You all do that," she accused. "You Nicaraguans. To control the space between us. No!" She grasped his finger.

"No, *chica*. It is you who wants to control all the space. You want the degrees. You want the wealth. You want the world to bend your way."

And why not? She wanted a degree. It opened doors, networks. She did not intend to quit. Everyone wanted the world to bend their way, even the Sandinistas. Why was that exceptional?

"*Ya!* So let's go. I give you a deadline—the end of the term. Your choice: by then, you can arrange for a leave of absence, or double up on courses, even transfer credits to Managua, if degrees are so important to you. Or, you can decide not to come with me. But if you decide that, know that I will leave anyway, and we will part for good to prevent my heartache of wanting to return to New York, to you. A clean break. You see my problem? I love you, Mallory. I expect you to come with me. A split will be brutal for us both. But for me, better to be finished clean—*acabo*—than to desert my destiny and return to you."

"You can't mean that, Juan! That's bullying me! There are legions of consequences I must consider—what I will give up— my studies, my own political work, my friends, my parents, my career. Do not push me like that!"

"*Ay mi vida!* The choice is so simple if you love me! But okay. You take the time. I give it to you. But decide without *el Grupo*. Your women do peanuts compared to what you can do for my people. How can *el Grupo* change America when Big Money works against everything? You know it is futile."

Mal scoffed. "You sprinkle the revolution with airy-fairy dust. Do you honestly believe Big Money drives *nothing* down there? Really? They are *that pure*? Sweetheart! It's *all* about the money. The revolution included."

Mal was furious enough to spit. She couldn't stand to be near him another second and stood up. He was so naïve. He was crazy, impulsive. Her rage at his political proposal without a marriage clause burned red-hot all the way uptown.

—∿∿—

Letting herself into the flat, Mal felt torn to shreds. She foresaw the discomfort of sitting across the table from her friends, wishing she could blurt it all out and keeping silent. Her dilemma was consuming. She wanted sympathy. She wanted advice. She did not want to lose him. And she did not want to go.

She poked her head into the rooms. Kleio was not home, yet. She stormed around the kitchen to prepare for the meeting, pulling food from the refrigerator, hardly noticing it. How cavalier she'd been about his political dreams, underestimating him, thinking that he playacted The Revolutionary with his far-fetched, grandiose aspirations: president of Nicaragua! He was, indeed, intent on soaring. She, for one, preferred to be on the ground to do what could be done reasonably, then move on in politics, economics, the lot. She feared she was about to lose him. She had to tell Kleio she was in a pickle. Why must Kleio be late tonight of all nights?

—∿∿—

Everyone arrived together in a clatter, talking at once, shouting and giggling. Mina and Kleio had discovered Gwen at the elevator pressing the seven button. The three had introduced themselves and laughed the whole way up, they explained to Mal in the foyer.

Before long they were seated at the round oak table that Mal had prepared with a bottle of wine, glasses and nicely chopped crudités, chattering in anticipation. Mal listened to the chatter, pleased to be with her friends, pleased that they liked Gwen. Her intuition had been spot on. The girl was clean, not an agent. She caught Kleio's laughing eyes and they smiled at each other.

Mal used her most serious tone. "Gwen, we expect to hear all about you shortly, but first, there is something Kleio should know. It's that Juan returned—just last night. From Nicaragua, as it turns out. Where he's been these last four months, studying the revolution first-hand."

Kleio already knew, she said. Mina had called her at work and told her.

"Well, good, then. Let's move on." Mal wished Mina hadn't called Kleio. She picked up from her tone that Kleio expected Mal would have called her with the news. *Trouble. Right here in River City*, she thought. Tread carefully.

"Juan invited us to a fiesta later tonight to inaugurate the newest cell of Casa Nicaragua. I understand important guests are expected. It might be fun to go as Group. Show our support. Learn what's happening. Quite a lot, it seems. Mina and I are definites, yes?"

Mina nodded, her long curls bobbing on her shoulders, a finer texture than Juan's aniline-black hair. "Always up for a fiesta! Juan told me who's expected. Really important people. I'm stoked. The Sandinistas are being taken very seriously."

Kleio said, "For sure, it's a relief he's back in one piece. But at the risk of shocking Gwen with my true opinions about Juan, I'll leave it that he was absolutely despicable to disappear on his sister and his girlfriend without one word! Next time I see him, I'll certainly make that clear. Sorry, I won't join you. I've got an early morning. You'll tell me all about it. What is a Casa Nicaragua cell, anyway? Wouldn't they be better off tackling their social problems, instead of riling up outside support? Typical male thinking to expand power, instead of aid."

Gwen perked up. "Well, that's rather intriguing, Kleio. Please, if I'm going to live here, could I be filled in? I don't really understand what you mean, or about Juan. I guess I'll meet him."

Mal's anger at Kleio's bias was instant. "Oh yes, do continue, Kleio," she said icily. "We know, so no worries offending us, but do share with Gwen your honest opinion of Mina's brother and my boyfriend." She looked daggers at Kleio. It would be impossible to tell Kleio, rationally, about Juan's ultimatum after that. She poured wine for everyone and glared.

"Well, I don't intend to be mean, but it just sucks the way he disrespects women—like we don't count. He knew you'd wait compliantly for him—as you have, of course, Mal—it's your life, so I have no right to comment, but it's Juan's egregious disrespect for our commune that bothers me. You know what he did last spring, Gwen? He turned our sofa-bed into a safe house without our knowledge or permission—to help out a Sandinista buddy who was traveling around. Illegally."

She turned fully toward Gwen. "Juan slipped this guy into our apartment late one night, because he had Mal's house key. The guy was gone by the crack of dawn, and Juan told us in the morning, like it was a big joke—just a riot that he had pulled it off without our knowing. In reality, Juan had endangered us. He even bragged that both the Somosistas and the CIA were chomping at the bit to assassinate that guy. What if they'd raided us and killed us? Arrested us for harboring a terrorist? Deported Mal? We were lucky. Because of that escapade, we created two House Rules, both of which will apply to you, Gwen. First, no one is allowed to give Juan our house keys. Second, no one may bring in anyone new without all the women being briefed in advance and agreeing the person is welcome. If even one woman objects, the guest may not enter. Got that?"

Gwen, her gray-blue eyes wide, nodded.

"Kleio exaggerates, just a tad." Mal suppressed a smile as she remembered that morning: Juan, his bad boy, sheepish grin, eyes a-twinkle. Fetching, he was. She had hardly kept from laughing herself. *What you gonna do,* muchachas! *Se fue. Gone! So rejoice! Even in your sleep you support our revolution! The brother just needed a good night's rest. Your house is clean as a whistle; that's why I brought him here. You were never in danger.*

Mina added, "Well, I've already scolded him about disappearing and freaking us out, and he apologized. He had some security reasons."

Mal smiled at her. She liked Mina, in fact. Juan had only reconnected with Mina a year ago, when she entered Barnard. He had begged Group to rescue his sister from her dormitory, to teach her political consciousness. They had welcomed in Mina, the youngest. They liked the animation and energy she brought to the group.

Mina wanted to go to the fiesta because Paco was back and would be there. "He's really hot," she told Gwen, fluttering her fingers from her wrist, the Nicaraguan way. Gwen wished to go, too, even dressed as she was. "Your world—the commune world—is so expansive! It's like a door opening for me."

"Well then. We'd better hear about you, hadn't we?"

Gwen happily "shared" as she said, beginning with her nervousness of the afternoon before, walking into 7G and meeting Mal, and when she left, deciding that living with them was what she wanted. She was curious about them as individuals, and how they managed to cooperate, being so different, how they overcame feminine jealousy and cat fights. From Mina, she hoped to learn about the Sandinista revolution of last year. And with Kleio, she already felt an affinity because of Ari, the Greek sculptor she was dating who wore his feelings on his sleeve, as Kleio seemed to. Mal had told her that Kleio was of Greek descent. Displays of emotion were refreshing to her, coming from a buttoned-down family. Ari was super-opinionated about politics, which was exciting, too, since she was so ignorant.

"Cool," said Kleio, on her second glass of wine. She acted out an arm-waving Greek, with an exaggerated accent, stating improbabilities that caused Gwen to burst into laughter.

"Yes! That's Ari! Exactly! He's so funny!"

Mal said, "Okay, let us switch gears, shall we, and discuss the mechanics of moving you in, Gwen."

"Wait a sec!" Kleio jumped up. "Now we are four! I have a bottle of champagne in the fridge for just this moment. Congratulations, Gwen. We want you in Group!"

"And just in time for next month's rent payment, too!" Mina laughed.

Afterwards, as Mal and Mina cleared the table, Mal sought a moment to pump Mina about her visit with Juan earlier that day, but Gwen was with them. It was not the time.

⸻

Walking up the flights of tenement stairs, the home of the newest Casa Nicaragua cell, Mal knew Juan would be upstairs and hoped to assure him that her rage of the afternoon had faded. She wanted to explain that the idea discombobulated her. In fact, she felt calmer, grounded, despite speaking to neither Kleio nor Mina about her concerns. She was certain she would resolve it. She wanted desperately for him to know, in case he was giving up on her.

The *fiesta nicaragüense* was loud and late in starting, much like others Mal had attended in different flats and social halls. The ceiling was decorated with streamers of the flag colors, blue and white, and cutout letters were strung across the far wall, spelling CASA NICARAGUA NUEVA YORK 1980. She and Mina would look for Juan and Paco in the crowd by standing near the door. Gwen ventured forth in search of beer. Mal needed to be by the door. She felt self-conscious among the Latinos, aware of her incongruous white hair and fair skin. She was an anomaly— *la blanca*—she often overheard the word in the Spanish babble. How would she fare in a country of Nicaraguans?

She could see that Gwen, the other *blanca*, blonde ponytail bobbing flirtatiously, used her difference to advantage, striking up conversations at the table of food and drink, laughing with whomever stood near, swaying to the beat of merengue. So, if her prematurely white hair and English skin were not the cause, why did she feel so different?

"Look over there. Gwen is totally at ease not speaking any Spanish," Mina remarked.

"Because *she* wants to learn it," said Mal. "*She* wants to be part of this."

They spotted Juan at the far end in the center of an animated group of guys. Paco was yet to be seen, and Mina was scanning every pocket of people for her newest crush. Mal smiled tightly at the *hermanos* with their sex-pot women when they stopped to chat with Mina and nodded at her. The language was painful to her ears, so harsh and loud.

Mina translated overheard snippets and rumors. A member of a prominent newspaper family that had flipped pro-Sandinista would be present with a newly appointed minister whom Juan had met as well. Mina pointed them out as they were enveloped by crowds. A Sandinista politico representing openly socialist Nicaragua at the next UN General Assembly was rumored to be on his way with the film star, Blair Beaufort. Oh yes, Mal knew of her. Lady Blair. Wasn't her father a duke? She and Blair had attended the same public school, Blair being some years ahead. Her Nicaraguan mother had been a model. Mal was interested to see her.

Merengue and salsa from the amps quickly overpowered the laughter and talk. To Mal, the women dancing looked like Gauguin's languid Tahitians. She lacked their sinuous grace. She did not belong either there or in this room. Mal felt herself fade. Yes, she and Juan should break up. This was not her world.

Just then the music was cut, and voices hushed. Mina nodded toward the door as Blair Beaufort paused at the entrance, her entourage behind her. Her eyes flashed at the crowd; she smiled and held her arm up like the queen. The room erupted with clapping and shouts of *viva Nicaragua!* She was stunningly chic in a short red skirt and the plunging white blouse that put a glow on her coffee-colored skin. She had an aura, style and class, nothing like the *chicas* here. Mal could easily identify with her.

People began moving aside for Juan at the far end of the room as he began navigating toward Blair. Reaching her, he kissed her cheeks and cheers arose. They touched each other's arms and laughed together at something he said. Mal envisioned her dad, a hereditary earl, awkward and reserved as a peer in the House of Lords. In similar situations, he mumbled and lowered his eyes, kept his distance, avoided a fuss.

Juan, it was obvious now, was plugged in at a powerful level and could work the room. It was his path. He was born to this. Commitment to the Sandinistas would be his best entry into Nicaragua's political arena, his driven desire since she'd met him. Focused, as he was now, he had it in him to lead. Someday it could be Juan Davila addressing the UN on behalf of his country.

He had begged so earnestly and sincerely for her help; he acknowledged and appreciated her steadiness and good sense to guide him. How shocked and fearful he had been that she even hesitated. It was what women did for their men, he insisted. They would be a team, as Mum had been with Dad, no hesitation. Her parents had meshed their interests, as adults committed to one another did. Yes, have your personal freedom, Juan had argued, but not to the exclusion of who you love. That was adolescent behavior. Personal freedom derived from the security of being part of a team, he insisted. We both make trades to be together. Look: what was Group but a team? Double-talk, she had snapped, perhaps hastily.

"She's lovely, isn't she?" Mina sighed. "I'm jealous."

Blair Beaufort was surrounded, while Juan took up with one of her entourage. Fascinating. Here was a woman of standing at home, transformed from actress to advocate for justice in her mother's homeland. Mal could imagine herself transformed, too, even as a future First Lady of Nicaragua, if she took this first step with Juan.

The chatter resumed; the decibels of static and music increased. Mina shouted in Mal's ear, "So, will you do it? Will you go?"

"No decision yet," Mal shouted back, "but an intriguing concept. I vacillate. If I went, at least I'd find out if Bluefields, where Juan was born, is actually blue. Maybe I'll go just to know. I hear you think it's a good idea."

Mina shouted, "Of course it is! I was born in Bluefields, too, you know. It's not blue, just a typical jungle town. You'll see. Do it, Mal. He needs you. You love him, right?"

"Yes. But, the war—it's scary, somewhat more than I bargained for in life. I'm not very courageous. I'd like to discuss it with Kleio, who knows me so well."

Mina nodded. "Sure you do, but don't. He doesn't want her involved. Those two are oil and water. I cannot believe what Kleio said to Gwen tonight about my brother!"

Mal nodded. From a distance Juan caught her eye and winked at her. They watched him approach through the crowd, glad-handing and back-slapping the brothers in his path, accepting their congratulations on his witness to the revolution, Matanzas, Estelí, León. She divined his words through the noise like a bell.

At that moment Paco appeared before them, greeted and kissed them both. She was pleased to see him again. She'd missed him, too. He spoke and she nodded, but she could not hear him. He put an arm around Mina and they left, leaving Mal to smile into the air in embarrassment, a single foreigner in this sea of Nicaraguan couples.

Juan had been turned around by the swell of people and headed away from her. Wherever the crowd took him he went without a qualm. She was an afterthought once more. Could she trust him to protect her there? Did he protect her here? Did he ever see things from her point of view? Why must she always take care of herself?

When the evening was done, Juan would come uptown to her, or maybe he would not. She could not rely on him. And for the moment, she didn't care. She wanted to leave. What was here for her? Nothing.

Perhaps that other *gringa,* Gwen, was ready to share a taxi uptown where she'd been invited to stay until her move-in on the week-end. But Gwen, Mal could see, was bent in conversation with an older man, the new minister, Ernesto Cardinal. She might join Gwen to meet this latest diamond in Nicaragua's crown. She might introduce herself to Blair, chat about London and the society they would know in common. She saw Juan, now in serious conversation with Paco and Mina: she might join them. They would switch to English for her and repeat their *bons mots* that always translated badly, requiring her to laugh. Her self-consciousness would be followed by awkward silence until they reverted to Spanish, easier, they would explain, by way of apology.

No, she was tired of heat and incomprehension; more than tired, she was quite angry. At Juan.

He should have come to her immediately, taken her around with him, made introductions to Blair and everyone else. These Nicaraguans—upstarts—paled against the Tames who had for centuries dedicated themselves to the common good. These *poseurs* did not deserve her presence. Tossing her hair, she turned and walked out the door.

Down on Avenue A it was blessedly cool and quiet at 1 AM, no one in sight. She glanced up at the second floor windows clouded with condensation. Goodbye and good luck; she smirked and flagged a cruising taxi.

Uptown, in the silence of her own bed, with Kleio asleep down the hall, she was at peace.

—~~—

A week later, at 10 PM, Mal waited for everyone to gather at the oak dining-table for Gwen's first house meeting. Mal had managed to avoid the flat for most of the week by studying late at the library and spending nights at Juan's—fairly moved in with him, going round and round with him about her concerns. They were getting along well despite her lack of resolution.

She never did talk to Kleio. She tried to avoid her by zipping uptown at midday to change clothes while Kleio was at work. Kleio would have noted her absence, as it was unlike them to go for days, let alone a week, without communication, usually at breakfast or late at night.

In midweek, Kleio had left for work later, and they met, inadvertently, in the kitchen. Mal said she had no time to chat, because she'd added an extra course for the term. Kleio raised an eyebrow. Why? Mal promised a full account at the house meeting on Thursday and hurried out, ignoring Kleio's incredulous expression.

Gwen had moved in her suitcases and book cartons as scheduled and made the original maid's room her own. Mal, in her midday visits uptown, noted that Gwen had stocked her assigned refrigerator shelf with health food brands and organic products. All seemed to be going smoothly.

Gwen sat down next to Mal. Kleio and Mina were still in their bedrooms.

"How goes it, so far?" Mal asked. "Sorry not to be here much since you moved in. I suppose we were last together at the fiesta? You were chatting up the new minister when I left. You know who he is, right? What did you talk about?"

"Poetry, since I'm a literature student. He explained that Nicaraguans enjoy their poetry set to music. He recommended Carlos Mejia Godoy and Ruben Dario. Do you know them? I found tapes of their music. So lovely! Mina's been translating some for me, and she's lent me a CD of Silvio Rodriguez, the Cuban New Wave singer? Do you know him? Political music seems so interconnected. I intend to learn Spanish, if only for the poetry."

Mal squirmed. She called toward the bedrooms. "Mina? Kleio? Shall we get on with it?"

This house meeting might not go swimmingly. Staying with Juan had put her out of touch with the group's dynamics. But she had needed time with Juan to talk about her concerns about the war, and what she would tell her parents. He had answers for everything, and she felt increasingly pressured to go.

Tonight, as part of the house meeting process, Mal intended to tell Group her problem. On a weekly basis, they discussed the personal issues that confronted them, and tried to help each other with ideas and suggestions. They usually ended feeling close and bonded, even if there was no immediate solution. She had been silent an entire week, and it was enough. *Nebbish,* that Manhattan word, described her: meek in the face of Juan's insistence. She felt annoyed at herself.

Mal played with a pencil, tapping it on one end and then the other.

Gwen picked up yesterday's *Times.*

Mina appeared and apologized, kissed them both on the cheek and sat down. Her energy was high and her mood sunny. She began a conversation with Gwen, called out for Kleio, and in mid-sentence, pointed at the wine bottle for Mal to open.

With the two chatting, Mal realized she should reconsider her idea of talking to the group, having overlooked how new a member Gwen was. Was it really prudent to expose Juan's political aspirations and activities to the new woman? What if Gwen moved out next week and palavered about Juan to others—to her mad sculptor friend, for example—and information found its way to the FBI? Should she wait to talk to Kleio and Mina alone? But what divisiveness—to withhold information from one member? How daft she'd been not to have thought this one out! Her hands began to shake as she uncorked the bottle of Bordeaux and poured into the four stemmed glasses intended for white wine. Mum would certainly have something to say about *that* faux pas.

Kleio entered and sat next to Mal, smiled pleasantly at everyone. "Mother was on the phone. Couldn't just hang up." She winked at Mal: no hard feelings.

Mal smiled back. Estrangement from Kleio had made her lonely. They were true blue underneath it all. Juan could be a divisive prig.

Mina was telling Gwen about her trip to Cuba on the previous Christmas holiday as a member of the Venceremos Brigade to harvest sugar cane, and about Fidel's three hour rant to thousands of cheering Cubans in which he predicted that Central American uprisings against American imperialism were eminent. Gwen listened in astonishment.

Kleio waited for a pause. "Gwen, tell us about your first week with us. What's it been like?"

Gwen smiled. "I really feel at home. It's fun. I'm getting to know you. I loved that party last week! The apartment's great. It's all great—"

"Good. Glad to hear that." Kleio cut her off. "Usually we begin our house meetings with house business—bills and money stuff. But I propose that tonight we first hear from Mal who has been mysteriously absent all week."

Mina and Gwen nodded. Mal studied her wine glass.

"We'd love to hear from you, Mallory, now that Juan is back safe and sound. I guess you've been with him. But I feel something going on that Mina seems to know, but she won't say. Am I being kept in the dark?"

Mal's face reddened. This had to be how others felt when she put them on the spot. She wondered what to say that would not incriminate Juan, yet sound plausible.

"Wait," said Mina. "Let me tell, because Mal promised Juan to keep it quiet. She can keep her word to him if I tell instead. I promised too, but I'm so mad at my brother for making us promise to keep a secret from Group. Stupid of us both but let him be mad at me all he wants. Too bad."

Mal shook her head. "I'd rather you didn't, Mina. I can speak for myself." A long pause followed as she considered what to say.

So Mina jumped in and told.

"What?" Kleio turned her shock toward Mal. "You have been harboring an idiotic plan to move to Nicaragua with that macho bird-brain and you said nothing to me! Me? I can't believe you, Mallory Tame!"

Mal's eyes quickly filled with tears. "Because I had promised. How could I break my promise? Except one week was long enough. So I did intend to tell you all, tonight. It's been intolerable for me. I honestly don't know what to do, Kleio. I really would like to hear what you think."

"You know *exactly* what I think! You shut me out. How am I supposed to feel about that?"

Mina raised a hand. "Okay! Stop it, ladies. I can fix this." She took the phone and dialed.

"No! Don't do that!" Mal reached out to stop her. "Please don't call him! He really needn't know. Let's discuss this amongst ourselves. Please, do leave him out of it."

Juan answered and Mina began a tirade in Spanish that Kleio translated as needed. Mina interrupted whatever Juan replied and kept it going. The siblings went back and forth, escalating their anger.

Kleio stopped translating and laughed. Ridiculous, she mouthed to Mal. Mal laughed, too. Totally absurd. Why reprimand Juan at the moment Mal needed to talk? "Hang up!" Mal whispered several times, but Mina would not. She kept shouting until Juan hung up on her in the middle of a tirade of name calling. There was silence. Mina exhaled, looking wild-eyed.

Kleio spoke quietly. "Well, now, Mina, I'm sure that feels better, getting it off your chest. But let's help Mal now. Except, Mal, it does hurt that you didn't trust me and you listened to him, instead. It sucks. But I can understand."

"It does suck, and I understand, too. I'd really appreciate it if we could entertain some options for me. I need help sorting it out. I'd like not to act from emotion. I've been upset all week. My options boil down to: go with him to Nicaragua or lose him. I don't know what to do."

"Really? You don't know?" Kleio was incredulous. "Why? Have you lost your marbles? Of course you can't go! You can't go with that sociopath to a war zone!"

"What did you call my brother?" Mina's hackles were up again. "I've had just about enough of your name calling, Kleio! And what do you mean—*of course* Mal can't go? Nicaragua is way too dangerous for Juan to be there alone! Mal *absolutely* should go and watch over him. Help him! *He needs her.*"

"Sure Mina, but what about the danger for *me*? How would I help him? I don't even speak the stupid language. There's a civil war on. I can be killed as easily as Juan." Mal heard her own voice rise an octave, American style, sounding whiny and helpless, which she hated. She accused Mina of being self-serving, and her brother of pomposity. He *was* macho. Kleio was right there, and it was not too cute.

Gwen excused herself suddenly and stood up. She had early class in the morning. She picked up her wine glass to take with her.

"I apologize, Gwen." Mal laughed as Gwen paused at the door. "This must seem silly to you. We're not often like this. Emotional display is rather an embarrassment, too American for my taste. Though, I must say, it was rather a liberating sensation just to listen to Mina have at it."

Gwen waved good night to everyone from the door and went to bed.

Kleio continued. It was *idiocy* to believe Juan was worth dying for.

"Hey! Juan is *my brother!*" Mina exclaimed. "He *is* worth dying for! Kleio, you need to stop with the attacks on him. Even if his idea is crazy, at least it comes from a selfless place inside him. He is a *good person*! Mal knows that. You're just mean because you don't have a cool boyfriend like Mal!"

It was going nowhere. Juan had been quite right in predicting that.

—*∿*—

As Mal prepared for class in the morning, everyone stumbled sullenly around in the kitchen, getting coffee. Gwen had already left for NYU. Mal smiled at that. Such a smart girl to remove herself.

In her own classes, Mal remained distracted. How upset she'd gotten! How angry at both Kleio and Juan, how torn she'd felt. Ironically, she had agreed with everyone in turn, then disagreed as well. She imagined herself marching into a Government seminar on the floor below to announce that democratic principles—conflict resolution through discussion— were naïve. Her group proved that the democratic process, free speech, had a downright ridiculous side, did it not?

Most worrisome was Kleio's threat to telephone Lord and Lady Tame to come take their daughter home, if Mal went through with it, and to report Juan to the FBI for deportation. The CIA, the KGB and the Stasi had nothing on Comrade Kleio. The woman was utterly determined to prevent Mal from joining the revolution.

After classes Mal wandered in the library among the back carrels, exhausted, sighing, avoiding anyone she knew, wondering where to go. Thanks to Mina's call from the house meeting, Juan felt betrayed and refused to speak to Mal until such time as she agreed to go with him. Only then would she be welcome to stay with him. Go back to your Talk-Talk Ladies! Live with the enemy! Taste life without me! He was no less dramatic than Mina. They were peas in a pod.

What path to take? She could run back to her parents—a spot of drama of her own, she readily admitted. She was unused to having her back against the wall, unused to being the object of wrath, unused to being so confused. Reflux burned and seared her stomach. Call Mum on this one? But was Mal's situation even comprehensible to a woman living such a different reality, in such a different time zone? With such a different worldview? After all, Mummy was rooting for Ronald Reagan to win the American election in November. Mum and Dad sided with the CIA-backed Contras. They would never understand.

—⁓—

Rather than return uptown, Mal checked into a midtown hotel for the night. She needed space. She notified no one of her whereabouts. Let them worry, if they even cared. She was capable of sorting it out in peace and quiet, just as Juan had asked of her, with no one to blame but herself if it all went badly down the road. She was no victim.

She drew a bath and settled in for a long soak, letting her mind rest on different subjects. What did she truly think about Nicaragua? The confusing political groups, in reality, bored her, all the Arguing Hermanos, dull and duller. Only Blair Beaufort had sparked her interest. And a good thing it could be, teaching literacy to women: she believed in that as a cause. Blair would certainly agree.

Group, the collective she had organized and nurtured, had its limitations, and had let her down by not getting beyond petty personal issues. Theoretically she was a superior analyst and better read than any of them. There was little real privacy in Group, as she had just experienced. And the idea of "sharing" was at odds with her innate, introverted self. Indeed, was it not tiresome to live in a relentless good mood, hiding one's impatience with annoying clichés and bad grammar? She could find better political expression than Group.

And anyway, her consuming passion was, in fact, Juan. Che had been her original darling. To Che, a revolutionary meant sometimes having to do things one mightn't do otherwise, all things being equal. One took the action required by the situation. But one must believe the situation needed changing. She did believe that mindless domination of the weak by the strong needed changing. She had been raised not to ignore injustice. She was a Tame. One had to ask, as Lenin had, what is to be done? There was never a lack of something to be done. Consider Dad, who served with what was available to him— the House of Lords, his inheritance, his good name. Juan, too, had opportunity to matter to his country, even if he risked his life. Juan believed in acting justly. It was now or never, he had assured her. Do it with me. Pondering these things, she felt calmed enough to sleep.

——

Mal returned uptown to the flat the next morning and found Kleio in the kitchen waiting for the Chemex to filter the coffee.

"Oh, goody. I'll have a cup, too. How are you, Kleio?"

Kleio turned to face her, and Mal watched her tight mouth soften into a smile. She hugged Mal. "I'm so sorry," she mumbled. "Sorry for getting so mad when you need help. I'm just so scared for you, Mal. This is big time stuff you're dealing with. It could change your life, dramatically. You could die."

Mal nodded and sat down at the dinette table while Kleio rummaged for mugs. "You're quite right, and I appreciate your concern, Kleio. You're on your way out, I see, but I've come to a decision and would like to tell you."

Kleio immediately took a chair across from her. So disciplined, Mal thought; Kleio was nothing if not responsible, so committed to her children's museum of screaming kids.

"At some point, you must catch me up on museum doings. I'm quite out of touch with what's been happening there for you."

Kleio waved the topic away and poured them coffee. "Tell me. What did you decide?'"

"I am committed to him, Kleio. Not your favorite revolutionary, I know, but he is my favorite. I shall go with him to Nicaragua. I can only learn from the experience, see what he sees there. Help out. Learn their damned language. That night at the fiesta—which I detested—Blair Beaufort showed up. The actress. Her courage impressed me, to abandon the good life and advocate for her people. My politics are at a crossroads. I could stay here, finish my degree, research endless corruption, play the feminist. Or, I could actually do something meaningful, and help the man I love. Help women learn to read and write. I'm ready for a bigger purpose. In the long run, won't it be for good? The future? Ours, too? For the children you and Mina plan on having to raise here communally someday?"

Kleio exhaled. "That's the mature way to see it, I guess. Illiteracy is a problem for many of my Bed-Stuy kids. The parents don't read English or anything else. The kids do everything. Illiteracy is destructive. I see it infantilize the parents, erode their dignity. Their kids become the adults. To have adult responsibility, pay the bills, the taxes, the conferences with teachers—it robs them of childhood, I get that. It *is* good. I support you in that."

Mal felt a surge of relief that Kleio had come to her side through reason and heart. She reached out her hand.

Kleio clasped it. "But it's so dangerous, Mal! Mina says so, and she knows. She reads the Managua paper all the time. She knows Juan, too—his limitations. He could dump you there. Find a cutie to shack up with. You know those guys are not designed for monogamy. What if you got shot? All those factions there—the least scary one is probably the CIA. There's barely a government. And salmonella! Mina says there's no sanitation."

Mal raised her hand to protest. "Juan's described the many risks, Kleio, but this is a bigger thing. It's like my mum who stuck by my father when he fought the factions that wanted to hold on to empire. She disagreed with him, but she supported him because she loved him. We commit to those we love."

"But Nicaragua, Mal! It's not your country. Think about it: *not* your country, *not* your culture. Not your revolution, either. There are nationals, abler than you, who own the issues. They should go. Why you?"

"Because he asked me to. I love him. I'm doing it for love."

Kleio bowed her head with nothing to say to that.

—∾∾—

Managua, March 1, 1981

Mal stepped onto the movable staircase after Juan, stretched the kinks in her calves and inhaled the air of Central America for the first time, wood smoke and dank that resonated with the unforgotten illustrations in her beloved childhood book, an almost naked Pim-Wie, a fresh-killed spotted ocelot in his grip for grilling on a fire by a river bank, a scene framed by palm fronds and liana. She shivered. Here at last!

Her arrival was the perfect moment for beginning a memoir of the only Tame ever to join a socialist revolution. A tingle spread over her arms. Mr. Bromley in Fifth Form would faint to know where his earnest politics had propelled his star student. And Group? Those bittersweet goodbyes at the Departures gate earlier that morning, so long ago now—Mina, Gwen and Kleio—assurances they'd be there upon her return. But would she return? Her future was wide open from here on out.

The poor dears never caught on that Group had been for her an expanded version of her boarding school. By contrast, Nicaragua's revolution was *actual*—by which Juan meant current, real and in progress. Nicaragua was the perfect environment for self-transformation, more so than a Manhattan that smacked too much of home.

The staircase reverberated in the wake of Juan's clatter to the bottom. Its steps were filmy with dew. She steadied herself, feeling slightly lightheaded and possibly about to vomit. Elbows nudged her to move along. She turned and raised an eyebrow. Excuse me? Kindly do not rush me. Let me fix my first glimpse of Managua through its morning haze. There! A squiggly line, the contour of palmettos would do. She gripped the handrail and descended as her head spun.

He had rushed ahead without waiting or checking on her— as ever, Juan's afterthought, not much of a bother this time, because this was his moment, too. She could finally hear herself think, after a flight spent listening to him. His high state had been exhausting. Changing planes in Mexico City, he was full of advice about her nerves. Goodness! Are you never apprehensive, she had exclaimed, pacing the waiting lounge. Rarely, he'd answered. Overhead, the Mexican folk art, *papel picato* he'd called it, vibrated nervously, bright colors fluttering.

Her feet were firmly on the tarmac. She stood in Nicaragua. How gorgeous, how lush the hedge of brilliant red and yellow hibiscus! As she focused her vision, it resolved into the backdrop for six militia men and women in khakis and Che-style berets who shouldered long, black rifles and refused eye contact. Not the visages of the innocents Juan had summoned up with talk of his people, *el pueblo,* whose heroism had been posted on walls, *in memoriam.*

Good Heavens, how terrifying. She had never seen a rifle or a Sandinista soldier.

The militia waved their weapons at the new arrivals to herd them toward a concrete box of a building, newly renamed the Augusto C. Sandino International Airport, its cutout letters mounted across the top. Its control tower was so small she could likely scale it. *In there?*

Curiouser and curiouser: the weapons, the cold faces, and the Tinker-toy airport. A rivulet of sweat startled her, rolling between her breasts. Her cotton sleeves stuck to her wet armpits, but her princess heels marched her on, sinking into the fudgy blacktop, resisting, then snapping against the balls of her feet to pitch her forward. *Dr. Who*, she thought. Have I somehow landed in an episode?

She was herded inside the terminal portal where Juan had disappeared, into the small baggage claim area. A rickety conveyor belt beeped and jerked to a start. A fan on a folding chair in the corner circulated the reek of DDT, perspiration and mold. It grew stifling, the fan too small to accommodate the incoming passengers.

Juan was in a bear-hug with a fellow in a beret. That would be Jimmy, their official greeter, in a neatly ironed shirt, khaki shorts and sandals. She could hear their loud hail-fellow-well-met Spanish from the entrance, watched their ritualized hand clasp with a mutual pounding on the back.

Jimmy saw her and extended his hand. "*Bienvenidos,* Señorita Mallory. Jimmy Martínez, *a sus ordines!* It was a good trip? Wow! What fantastic hair!" He chuckled as they shook hands, then he reached to touch her long, white curls. She flinched. He drew back, grinning. "You're gonna be the easy one to spot in a crowd, Señorita! I'm calling you Blanca!"

"How original." She drew herself up to meet his eyes. This tosser would learn straightaway she was no *Nica-chica*, easily pawed and objectified. "Look here: you shall address me as Mallory, Mallory Tame. I would appreciate it."

"Whoa! You misunderstand me, Señorita! Here, everyone has a tag. Sorry, no offense! You are royalty or something, right? Juan tells me. So, you go ahead—you choose a tag you like. Let me know."

He had the effrontery to wink!

"Mallory Tame," she repeated. Who was this prat who spoke and acted American? Moon-faced and flat-cheeked, he was ugly. She stared at the grooved, broad teeth of his unflappable grin.

Sensing Juan about to intervene, Mal turned abruptly to the conveyer belt for the bags. What she already knew about Jimmy confirmed her instant dislike. Jimmy had befriended Juan on his last trip and made a big impression because he had shot and killed six Somosistas. A killer, then? Of course, Juan had agreed, her disdain lost on him.

She didn't trust this Jimmy one iota. Not only full of himself but a phony. A "false friend" like the Spanish cognates that tripped her up because they were not what they appeared to be but meant something entirely different in Spanish.

They followed her to the conveyer belt. Juan caught her eye, shook his head and rolled his eyes in reprimand.

"I'll take the passports and clear you through Security, ahead of everyone," Jimmy said. "We'll catch a taxi to the Casa Sandinista in Bello Horizonte—to register you there as your official residence in Nicaragua. Then we go to your apartment."

When he left, Mal grumbled. Jimmy acted like a minder, not an escort. He had been quite rude to her. Juan was an official guest of the government, no? He had been invited to return to Nicaragua, no? So why the folderol about registration?

"'Cause we have a civil war going on! That's how it goes. Don't be aggressive and read into things. Don't take everything so personal. Of course, Jimmy's no minder. He's a facilitator, courtesy of the Leadership."

Why did Jimmy Martínez speak American English?

"He's from Chicago. He is a member of the CDS—you know—Intelligence, and high in the ranks. He is a great guy, Mal! Be nice, will you? Show him your famous good breeding."

"From Chicago? He could be CIA. How do you know he isn't?"

"Be reasonable, *chica!* How can he be an American *federale* and in our country's Civil Defense without anyone catching on? You think our Intelligence people are mental deficients? Okay, so you don't like him. I do, so don't give him attitude. Re-la-a-ax! We just landed. Enjoy the moment. We are here together. Who can believe it?" Juan embraced her. Coming home with Mal by his side—it was all good. She'd see.

Perhaps. Despite petulance, lightheadedness and the incongruities of revolutions in progress, she would shush.

Jimmy and Juan were just like her father and his colleagues at the House of Lords, preoccupied with important men's work. Wasn't it? Just men conducting their men's business, missing forests for the trees, the clues and cues? Thus far, this *actual* revolution smacked of machismo and officiousness. She had expected better.

She gave Juan's arm a squeeze back and smiled brightly, aware of her sick stomach. "I'm fine. I'm happy as well, to be here at last. But my tum could use a fizzy drink."

Jimmy appeared outside Customs and waved them through to the crowded Arrivals Hall and returned their stamped passports. They were getting a great apartment, he said as they headed toward the main doors and the taxi line outside. Expropriated from rich Somosistas who had fled, so it had stuff like air-conditioning and a washing machine. After they rested there, he would return to take them to a late lunch, to spell out how it would all "go down."

Such an Al Capone, Mal thought. *Expropriated*—really? It was theft! So, did this revolution upend morality, to boot? Socialism was supposed to be based in fairness, was it not? "And if they return, would they get back their flat?"

"Never gonna happen, Blanca. It belongs to the people now."

So, it was eye-for-an-eye justice, revenge politics. What was revolutionary about that? She counseled herself to let it go, to listen and learn.

Juan put his arm around her, noted her skin was clammy. She couldn't already have salmonella. She hadn't eaten anything. Maybe Jimmy could find her a carbonated drink for her upset stomach, and he'd take her outside to the fresh air.

Out on the curb, the air was heavy with diesel oil and humidity that made her feel worse. A band of ragamuffins at the entrance noticed them and approached, clamoring, *"Chee-klay!"* Juan spoke sharply to them, but they carried on, *"Chee-klay, Chee-klay!"*

Gum.

"They need more than gum," Mal observed. "Look how underfed and thin they are." She shook her head and held out empty palms to them in sympathy. "No C*hee-klay*."

"*Lay-dee! Lay-dee!*" They turned their attention to her, pressed toward her in a group and began to yank at her skirt and touch her hair. Juan shouted sharply and moved quickly to shield her. She shrank behind him.

Just then, Jimmy appeared with a soda and argued with the children, shooed them away. They shouted back, unintimidated.

"It's your hair! They want to touch it," he chuckled, "because it's white. You are a *bruja*, a witch, they say."

The children retreated to their station at the entrance, except for two bold girls who crept back to stand close and stare at her. She turned her gaze away, sipped her drink, her heart beating. This was dreadful. Could they not see she was as human as they?

Jimmy and Juan loaded the bags into a taxi. The two girls inched closer to Mal and stretched their dirty fingers toward her hair. She backed up against the taxi, calling to Juan as she whipped her hair away. Jimmy appeared and shouted until the girls ran off laughing.

"Go to school! Learn to read!" she called after them.

"They are harmless. Get inside, Blanca. The revolution has a greater priority now—the adult literacy campaign. But one day, we will round up those *marginales* and teach them inclusion."

"I was not afraid of them," she shot back. "I gave them what I have, some good advice."

"Ah, but you spoke in English. They don't know what you said." He chuckled.

"Hey, Jimmy!" Juan joined in. "Don't remind her. Not speaking Spanish is Mal's sore point. But just give her a little time. *La chica es muy lista* and damn smart."

"Don't patronize me!" she snapped and settled into the back of the taxi.

Juan placed his hand on her knee to hush her. "What's the matter with you? *Cálmate.* Don't be mad."

"They understood my tone and heard my voice. I am a human, not a witch," she insisted to the rotter know-it-all in the front seat. She turned to face the window as the taxi departed for the highway.

On the ride into Managua, Juan in back with her and Jimmy in front conversed in Spanish diagonally, crowding her out. Good. It was far more interesting to collect first impressions for that future memoir. Clearly, she was a world away from Manhattan or London. Palm trees swayed everywhere in the morning wind. It could be Ibiza if not for the rest of it. Stuck in stop-and-go traffic, she watched people rush about, spilling onto the roads, hustle-bustle. She'd never seen so many Nicaraguans. Preoccupied with morning business like anyone in the world. Amazing. These were the people who had fought off American dominance. Their new goals were drawn up, Juan had explained, with advisors from East Berlin and Cuba. Fidel was right. The Third World was in flux, as the bustle she watched seemed to indicate. She felt a rush of excitement to realize she would join this flux as a teacher in the literacy campaign, based on what they termed the Cuban Example. In Cuba, it had gone great guns. At a house meeting, Kleio had read them an article full of comparative statistics. The high illiteracy rate among women in the countryside was truly shocking. Kleio had come round. Her détente with Juan had been a great relief. If going was Mal's decision, Kleio would support her working at the grassroots level.

She appreciated the boosterism. It was Kleio's suggestion to keep a journal for a future memoir. As a foreigner, hers would be a unique perspective on an authentic revolution. Mal softened to the women rushing outside her window. She would help them. She would commit to learn Spanish quickly, being, indeed, smart as a whip.

Her stomach troubles receded as she focused on engraving the details for Chapter One, Mal's First Morning: the blue smoke curls from burning firewood; the haze lifting to reveal the pell-mell activity against a backdrop of palms and dahlias blooming in flame-hot colors. It was March. They dressed in jeans and shorts, sleeveless tops, Rolling Stones and Coca-Cola logos on their tee-shirts, flip-flops, sandals, and suits without ties. The women were dark-haired and bleached blonde. Stature was small like her, and thin with that burnished skin tone that made her feel so white.

As they entered the thick of traffic—1950s autos, Caddies and lorries—diesel fumes blew into the open window. Crowded buses loomed over their VW Bug. In the gutters, mongrel dogs licked at wrappings. Passing a green expanse of forest, Jimmy identified it as a park renamed La Plaza de la Revolución.

"In July," he said, "there's where we're gonna celebrate the end of the Somoza dictatorship. Gonna have a gigantic parade. You guys'll march with the *brigadistas* in the literacy campaigns from all over the country and everyone who learned to read. It's gonna be a big national day. Fidel will come to speak, so you'll get to hear him in person."

So exciting to imagine the different person she would be by then, "accustomed" as they always said, a teacher of literacy, a speaker of Spanish, a proud contributor who had earned her right to celebrate the national day. She was a Tame for sure, and all that meant; yet she would achieve what was needed for Mallory. She smiled. Done and done, all in five more months. Beyond that? Too early to say.

They drove down wide avenues lined with stuccoed buildings, cinemas, shops, a hotel built like a Mayan temple. Their taxi, lacking an exhaust pipe, chugged alongside trucks laden with melons, hemp, hay, fruits, and mule-drawn wagons. Every corner had telephone booths, kiosks, and pushcarts selling *chicha* and soft drinks. Juan and Jimmy answered her questions about the street vendors, the food wrapped in dough envelopes, the women on curbsides hunched over hibachi grills.

The street noise was deafening. Radio ads and music blasted over honking horns and shouting, roars of motorcycles. Rush hour in the revolution. It was jubilant. She had expected to hear socialistic marching music, like her records of the Soviet Army Chorus. Mr. Bromley had made socialism seem dark and wintery, the Moscow of 1917, but in Managua 1981 the American Top Forty competed with marimbas, merengue and reggae over the traffic din. Mr. Bromley would be pleased to know that the music proved his theory that revolutions, though they followed a Marxist-Leninist script, expressed the specifics of the culture. But where was this revolution? she wondered. What were its signs?

A radio blasted a familiar ABBA song, "Chiquitita," that Mal loved, a song of sympathy sung by a mother to her daughter, a Spanish-sounding tune with English words. How ironic to hear the English here. She hummed along.

These people had socialism as their hope. They had died for it. In America, socialism was the arch-enemy of capitalism. In Britain, socialism was a predictable choice of ethnics and the Labour Party. Seeing the larger context reinforced her worldly feeling.

She would learn everything about Nicaragua. She would give herself to knowing without judgments and preconceptions. It was all so Wonderland-like, so *Dr. Who*. The "Chiquitita" melody repeated in her head, about the sun being in the sky, the sense that all was right with the world, and her eyes welled with tears. The words synchronized with a yearning for assurance, which she needed, that everything would go well. She leaned into Juan, felt his heart beating, his warm, damp skin.

The taxi stopped at the Casa Sandinista in Bello Horizonte, a white villa with Moorish architectural details and landscaped palmettos that could have been transplanted from Ibiza, surely another expropriation. Jimmy led them through to an elegant living-room and library with artfully placed Lladro figurines. In the center was a French provincial desk—authentic, she surmised from the proportions—where an older man in military uniform sat, the black beret on his head. Definitely expropriated.

The man growled, *pasaportes,* without looking up while handing them forms. She sat on the immaculate white sofa as Juan filled them in. The man photographed them one by one. Jimmy translated the man's instructions: register with Casa Sandinistas wherever they traveled. He returned their passports with identity cards. The man resumed his paperwork and they left without a goodbye, a protocol most surreal, Mal thought.

Their apartment building was on a street of large homes, coconut palms and blooming bushes. The air was thick with DDT, the amenity of a wealthy neighborhood still intact, Mal noted. Jimmy unlocked the door. The apartment was musty. The wood-paneled living room was dark, but sunlight from underneath drawn shades streaked the floor. It would do perfectly for a photograph to send her parents, proof of her civilized accommodations.

Mal had lied to them, and it made her sick to know it. It was not the first time she had manipulated or withheld information for their protection, but never had she spun an out-and-out untruth she would have to continue and embroider for the rest of her life. Juan had convinced her that as an adult, she was not obliged to divulge anything. And while Mal shot back that lying was hardly a sign of maturity, she agreed a lie would avoid needless worry.

Juan invented the details: she would spend her last semester in Nicaragua to research its evolving alternative economy, free from the filter of American propaganda. She would complete her degree upon her return. In fact, her advisor had approved her leave in exchange for producing a publishable paper on the Nicaraguan banking structure's transition to a socialist economy. You'll never write it, of course, Juan had said. *Brigadistas* had no time for research, and Juan doubted she would return, anyway. Instead, she would explain Juan to her parents as someone she'd fallen in love with, her reason to remain in Nicaragua. A perfect story, Juan assured her, flexible, open to variation as needed. Very good.

Her parents' gullibility—or was it their unquestioning trust—induced guilt. Perhaps it was the lie she carried and her uncertainty about the future—with Juan, in New York or London—that made her so out of sorts.

Examining their apartment, Juan discovered several business suits. The occupants fled quickly, he remarked.

She felt more guilt. She identified with their loss of country.

"Don't, *mi amor*. They are happier in Spain or Florida. You will be happier here." He poked around, whistling. Settling onto the bed, he told her that the Spanish word for a double bed was *matrimonio*.

"Ah, one more 'false friend,'" she called from the shower. The water ran adequately and hot. Everything would work out. It could be easy to get comfortable with expropriation.

"Just don't get too comfortable, *querida*." Juan came to her in the shower. "We'll leave for the mountains after our training. Living is simpler in the countryside. But this is where we return between gigs. That is the Sandinista arrangement. Now listen closely. If, for any reason, something does not work out, if there is any trouble we did not expect, I want you to remember 'Corn Island.' Corn Island is where I grew up, where my uncle is living. In an emergency, I will always go directly there to him. Never here where it is approved. Got that? No matter what you are told or what I may tell you. This apartment is state-owned. My uncle has private property. He and I, we made a secret plan to get us out if a problem arises. No one knows this, not the Sandinistas, not even Jimmy. Now you know. Do not be alarmed, *querida*. All will go well."

Mal put aside the apprehension his words elicited. They lay down together, and she—more exhausted than she realized, her body aching, her back sore—fell into a deep sleep. She awoke to Juan gently shaking her in the unfamiliar room. Jimmy had returned. Mal dressed, lightheaded still, and disoriented.

Jimmy sprawled on the Chesterfield as if he owned it. "Feeling better?"

"Yes, thanks. Must we watch the water? Can I brush my teeth?"

Jimmy grinned. "Sure, Blanca, here, but on the road, better to drink beer. Never buy water from kids selling it. They find old bottles, fill them up with whatever. Eat only cooked vegetables, no more salads, only fruit with rinds you peeled yourself. I got salmonella when I first came. Now I'm adjusted. And avoid anyone coughing. Tuberculosis is common and very contagious."

Half listening after she heard "Blanca," she wondered if he purposely imposed authority by ignoring her name. Wasn't that an interrogation tactic practiced by the secret police? Perhaps he was just dense. She was on guard with him again. It was significant that Juan had not divulged to Jimmy the secret escape plan. She did not have to love this guy.

They walked to a commercial street and found a large restaurant with tables under shade trees. At this time between lunch and dinner, it was empty. An elderly man in a proper waiter's jacket appeared with menus and presented them with formality. Did he think they were Somosistas? Did he resent them?

No, Jimmy answered. Usually, the older people were neutral, waiting to see what would happen next. They presented no danger to the revolution. Mal sympathized with the waiter, who had to live in a world turned upside down. Mal took a roll from his basket. She requested a Victoria beer in deference to Jimmy's advice. This is nice, she thought, until Jimmy resumed his teaching voice to explain that restaurants, formerly available only to the wealthy, now welcomed "the people" with artificially lowered prices meant to reorient the economy.

"Unwise economics, I'd say. However, I shall include it in my paper." She smirked at Juan who glanced away. The seafood they ordered arrived on wooden planks in veils of smoky aroma. "Delicious," she pronounced with her first bite.

"Finally," Juan approved. "You are relaxing."

Juan was happy, she saw, while Jimmy was inscrutable. During the meal, the men spoke in Spanish and translated intermittently, for her benefit. She protested. She needed to listen to them and infer meaning from the Italian cognates she recognized. They were similar enough languages. How difficult could Spanish be?

Jimmy said he would collect them the next afternoon and escort them to their two-week orientation. They would receive practical information about living in the rough. They would learn Sandinista protocols and how to spot and report Somosistas and CIA-backed troublemakers who moved about causing chaos—all in two weeks. Mal was dubious but game. "What about Spanish? How will I learn to teach in Spanish?"

Jimmy considered she might be paired with a bilingual teacher, as other foreigners had been. The literacy coordinator would decide when they met him.

That night under damp, cool sheets, Mal snuggled closer to Juan, assured he would not abandon her. This was their adventure.

———∞∞∞———

The next afternoon, Jimmy announced that plans had changed. Their orientation would be in Matagalpa, a town in the mountains. They must pack quickly to leave in an hour by public bus. They were to bring only clothes for living in the rough, medications and their identity papers. They would be stopped frequently to present them.

What a bother and a disappointment. Mal was already attached to their new flat. They had left it only to find breakfast that morning. This fortuitous apartment with its *matrimonio* was their test drive for matrimony, now gone before it began. Rubbish! Couldn't Jimmy have told them last night, she demanded, instead of springing it on them? Juan said it must have just come down from the Sandinistas. Don't escalate a fight, she thought, don't push his buttons. She needed him now, much more than he needed her.

Their 4:30 bus waiting in the station was a grimy yellow and green, round-nosed like a bullet, built before their births. It shot freezing air out of an overhead vent that barely reached their seats in the back. Finding seats together had been difficult, but Jimmy insisted on it—for protection or spying? They would reach Matagalpa by midnight with a two-hour stop somewhere for supper. The bus smell—diesel fuel, worn plastic seats, fried oil and chickens—revived her nausea. It was packed with families and crated colorfully spotted fowl Mal had never seen the likes of. There was even a pig in a basket under a seat, crying pitifully whenever they hit a rut. Where the bus stopped for cows to cross, to let passengers in or out or for unexplained reasons, children appeared at the windows holding up plastic bags of ice and cut papaya. Jimmy advised against it. Mal was thirsty, her throat was sore, and the children were insistent. How she disliked Nicaraguan children! "What about Coke?" she asked. "Can I buy that?" Jimmy unbuckled his backpack and offered her a warm can, warning that the next stop was in two hours, so she'd have to hold it, if she needed the facilities. He was so sanctimonious.

"So you drink imperialist soft drinks? *Chicha* not good enough for the leadership?" she snapped at the little bastard. Juan nudged her arm to stop. She sipped enough to wash over the soreness and gave the remainder to him. She already needed a loo. He smiled, wearily: *easy, querida.*

The bus chugged along a single-lane highway with little motor traffic. There were horse-drawn wagons loaded with goods. Alongside the road ambled *campesinos* on burros or ponies laden with firewood. On the horizon, mountain silhouettes slowly darkened against the dimming light. Mal was uncomfortably hot. Juan was dreamily quiet. When darkness fell, the driver turned on bright, interior lights. She would never nap.

Jimmy was animated. "Now is a good time to brief you, Blanca."

Mal raised an eyebrow. She was too uncomfortable to focus, queasy and headachy with the jiggling and swaying. The radio speakers screamed adverts in a fevered pitch, excited dialogs of male and female voices, then merengue. Passengers began unwrapping food. They laughed and chatted louder over the speakers. The motor droned, and every bump made something inside jingle or creak. Please wait, she willed him. Surely, they would pick up bits and bobs on their own, soon enough.

"Do you know Paulo Freire?" Jimmy began, "his method of teaching adult literacy in Cuba?"

She nodded. He was described in the paper Kleio had read to them.

"Your teacher in Matagalpa came from Harvard. He is a student of Freire. He will teach the *brigadistas*. The National Movement for Literacy that begins this month will continue through the summer. Then we will evaluate. In Bluefields, there is a special program for the Miskito and Sumo people to read their own languages. Juan might be sent there. Maybe you, too, since English is the language of the Atlantic Coast. So you see, your English is useful, Blanca."

This was new, the hint of separation. They would be far from that Bello Horizonte apartment she liked so much. She saw that Jimmy had received additional information since yesterday. "I see. Wake up, Juan." She jiggled him. "This is important to hear."

Juan's eyes fluttered. She could not rouse him. From the window where his head rested, a sliver of sun slipped behind a steel-colored lake. Darkness was complete. "Chiquitita" on the speaker entered the mix of noise in the bus. She watched Jimmy's moving lips as he spoke. She blocked him with the words of the song until her eyes closed, too. It was all too overwhelming.

—⁓—

The next morning, Mal scanned the school gymnasium, transformed into a classroom with folding chairs, as it filled with her fellow *brigadistas*. She had been transformed into a *brigadista* by the Registrar. Progress. The gym contained a hundred literate

Nicaraguans, women and men of all ages, including teens. Jimmy had collected Mal and Juan from a villa where he had deposited them upon their arrival, and where they would sleep every night for two weeks. Mal had fallen onto the new bed, too tired to react to Juan kicking a dead bat across the floor out to the balcony. The strangeness of everything was numbing. Sleep was the only way to reset oneself.

She was heavy with the need for more sleep when Jimmy arrived in the morning. They were to meet the Harvard volunteer, Fredo. Jimmy hinted again they might be transferred to Bluefields for training. Juan was excited. Mal was horrified.

Juan advised her: *sea tranquilla*. Wait for the Sandinista to weigh in.

Fredo. An American so trusted he was the main advisor to their Literacy Council. Fredo was Fred Hochburger from Sacramento, California, maybe thirty years old, and very cocky about literacy campaigns, letting them know he had been an organizer in Cuba as well. Well over six feet, he towered above them. He seemed sympathetic to Mal and to her situation, agreeing she should stay in Matagalpa, the best place to be, with him, an English speaker as the instructor. Mal was relieved. The Atlantic Coast campaign had "start-up problems"—he air quoted—attempting to juggle several indigenous languages, so it was not safe for her. He omitted what he thought about Juan, she noticed. The overall plan was for the literates to learn how to teach in one week, and in the second week, to pass it on to new recruits before going out to the field. In fact, the new batch was expected next week, bright middle-schoolers culled from the private schools. Repeating this two-week process throughout Nicaragua would yield thirty thousand *brigadistas*, who would fan out to teach more than half a million people to read. For an illiterate country in a hurry, pretty efficient, right?

None of this concerned her. He was omitting something screaming at her: what about Juan?

She interrupted to ask if they would be placed together.

He could not say for sure, but he would personally pair her with a bilingual woman to help her learn Spanish simultaneously.

Mal proposed she be paired with Juan. He was bilingual.

"Sorry about this," Fredo said. "In some cases I am separating couples to allow women to teach women. It is less intimidating for the *analfabetisadas*. We learned that women relate to each other better, so will learn faster. Sorry." Freddie smiled warmly and thanked her for her generous support of the revolution, then turned to others waiting for him.

Juan said nothing and hugged her. Maybe he had known this all along, tricked her into this: abandonment. Mal felt herself about to burst into tears. "Did you know about this?" she demanded. He shook his head. "Sorry," she said, "but I do not accept separation from you. That was never the plan. I shall go home. I shall call Kleio!"

"No, *querida*. Stay calm. You'll see it won't be bad. Give it a chance. Remember why we are here—to help and to work." He embraced her, kissed her and led her to a corner to console her.

Mal thought if she could call Kleio and sort it with her, not Juan, she would know whether to stay or leave, rather than be managed. Kleio knew how it enraged Mal not to be in charge, to follow others' dictates. And now, to be separated from Juan in a country with an unintelligible language! Mal allowed Juan to console her. She thought of Kleio and what she might say, set into focus her shining smile and lively eyes. Kleio would advise she do as she was told this time, because of what she had invested to be there.

"Go with the flow," as Juan gently hinted now. "It will be what it will be," he consoled.

"This was your choice, Mal." That is what Kleio would say. The only good reason to leave was if Mal obstructed the progress of the revolution, if she got in the way. Yes, that was Kleio. She need not call. She knew her best friend well and heard her voice. And Juan would help her, too. She trusted him. He had divulged a big secret for how to be together if anything went wrong. He protected her. He loved her. He would marry her, someday.

"I'll be fine," she assured him as he wiped her tears from her cheeks. "Change is never easy."

Mal regarded those still searching for empty chairs, chatting and happy in anticipation, not bothered by assignment issues. Only she.

Jimmy approached them. She felt certain Jimmy knew about the separation but had relied on Fredo to tell her. Truly, this was a new chapter in her life, learning to adapt. Silently, she took the hand Juan extended to her as he and Jimmy spoke. It meant he felt for her; he understood the fear it presented for her. He said *ciao* to Jimmy, who was not staying for Fredo's lecture, and they found seats together. "We shall discuss it later, *querida*," he whispered. "Don't worry too much. *Te amo*."

Fredo lectured in Spanish. There were long, unintelligible stretches, but by concentrating she was able to listen for cognates and write them down to ask Juan to be sure, later. Fredo explained the Freirean goals for teaching literacy: creating class cohesion and political awareness, fostering political participation and creative, analytical thought. Quite reasonable, thought Mal, not so different from her goals for Group. So, Group had prepared her. It had not been a wrong turn. None of her life so far had been a wrong turn, in fact; the decision to come to Nicaragua was on a continuum that made imminent sense.

Fredo passed out the workbooks they would use to teach with. She flipped through the first few pages and thought she might use it to teach herself Spanish. She realized then, and confirmed with Juan, that the *brigadistas* would not actually learn what to teach or how to teach, but rather to frame lessons around issues in the community. He called it a banking theory of education, quite logical to her, the economist. Though she'd never taught anyone anything, she found the prospect less daunting as Juan explained the political theory Fredo proposed during the lunch break.

During the afternoon lecture, her mind wandered and she felt sleepy. Who was the woman she would be paired with? She looked the women over. Where would they go, together? Would Juan be nearby? She hoped not the Atlantic Coast for him. Maybe they would be close enough to have weekends in Managua. She reminded herself that she was on the road to revolution, sitting in a Matagalpa gymnasium absorbing a language she barely understood to help strangers improve lives she had no inkling about, via the basic skill of reading.

The research that Group had engaged in and passed on to others had never been as challenging as this. It had, at best, provoked the authorities, but had not changed the status quo. Teaching literacy with the Freirean method made change happen with its multiple goals and long-term outcomes.

Dozing now and then, her head bobbing forward, she was at peace. At day's end, Juan said he was proud of her; she had not fled or fussed. She thought of Gwen at that first interview, appreciating the courage it took to choose the unpredictable and, possibly, the dangerous.

Luz Gonzalez y Sanchez turned out to be the woman Fredo assigned to her the following day. They shook hands. Luz was shorter and smaller-boned than Mal, with a face like Juan's that ended in a point. She wore her thick ebony hair cut extremely short. She seemed to be in her thirties. Her smile was warm, almost maternal, the few times she did smile—not very often. She seemed pleased to have Mal as a partner. She too, had spent time in the States. They agreed to lunch together to get to know each other. Mal ordered Juan to go make friends, confident to be on her own, and curious to know a woman unlike either the *hermanos'* girlfriends or Blair Beaufort. She was of *el pueblo*, the people, Mal thought. Authentic.

Juan was in his element here, she saw, watching him approach strangers. He was friendly and likable, quick with the funny remark, the warm sympathy. He had the makings of a national politician, she felt certain. He listened and joked so easily. She felt proud of him, too. This new context was good for them both, brought out the best in each.

Luz led her to the patio where others were eating and found empty seats at a school table. She lived in Matagalpa and had brought a homemade lunch for them. She unpacked a basket of bananas and pipian, avocado and tomatoes. In a round, covered tin warmed by a lower container of hot water was *gallo pinto*.

"We cook it all together—the red beans, fried rice, onions, sweet peppers—to make this simple dish. You will eat it a lot in the next few months, you can be certain."

Mal's stomach heaved at the list of ingredients and the pungent aroma that arose when Luz removed the lid. She was sure she wanted none.

"It's delicious. You must try it. You will like it."

Mal said her stomach was delicate still from travel, maybe from a bug. Watching Luz spoon out the mixture onto a plate was too much for her. She took some bread. She feared it was salmonella, maybe from the plane food. Luz offered to take her to a medical clinic after the class, later in the evening.

Luz asked about her hair. Was white really the true color? "*Muy bonita.* You are so young for white hair. How many years do you have, Mai-o-ree? May I call you Mai? Okay with you?"

Mal blushed, pleased to be asked permission to change her name; Mai was a terrific resolution. Why had no one ever thought of it? Premature white was a genetic mutation in her family, she explained. Except for Jimmy calling her Blanca, no one here had addressed her white tresses directly, though she was aware of people staring.

"Perhaps to really blend in during the campaign you would dye it?"

It took Mal aback, but the suggestion came from thoughtfulness, to help her fit in. Luz was sensitive to Mal's discomfort. She needed this Luz on her side, the new Kleio.

Luz had two little girls at home, seven and five, and a husband, Nando, who also was a *brigadista* and a Sandinista. She pointed him out, a burly fellow, taller than many, sitting with a group of men. Luz was not as devoted to the Sandinistas as Nando, she admitted. She didn't agree with everything they said or did, but Nando wanted her to do this for him, so she would leave her girls with her mother. And Luz was pregnant. Three months along. She had majored in English in college and had worked for a year in the State of Illinois, in Urbana, taking care of a professor's children. She had liked Urbana; the rural areas reminded her of Nicaragua. She did not resent America. It did, *effectivamente,* what every country did with opportunities. Power and politics were more interesting to men, Luz asserted.

She agreed to be a *brigadista* and please her husband because she wanted to help women. A woman must be able to make something of herself, she said, to take responsibility for her own life, to learn what she did not know and be proud of what she did know. Literacy sped that process. "I want this for my daughters, too," she asserted, "to be independent so not to have to accept whatever the husband says. The man is not God. He does not own the spouse. Nicaraguan women are strong, but they are kept down, not just from capitalism—I say this to Nando—but from our own culture, and what we inherited from the Spanish and the Church. This Paulo Freire—he is a good man. He understands this about the nature of woman and man. It is why I agree to be separated from my husband and children, temporarily. It is worthwhile, *vale le peina.*"

Mal smiled through her nausea. She liked these opinions. Luz's frankness reminded Mal of Kleio. She was pragmatic, not taken in by the lofty visions of a better future that seduced Juan, men. Luz reasoned and acted on her own terms. She had something strong within her, as did Mal, that motivated her: equanimity, a center. Luz was someone Mal would be pleased to know over the next few months. She would learn from Luz. Good choice, Fredo, she thought. Thank you.

"Ah, now I understand why I like that ABBA song, and why it is so popular here. It fits the situation. You know it, right? It's on the radio everywhere you turn. The little girl being comforted represents Woman, you know, disillusioned women. Even though everything is a disaster, your pain will end. You will sing again, even sing new songs. This is the woman's story. You see, we are strong. We keep going."

Luz laughed. "Those ABBA *majes* surely know a lot about disillusion hanging around with those men!" Then she added, soberly, *"Ai,* for sure, the woman is strong, but at what cost, *chica?* At what cost? *Ya.* And after each disillusion, the woman pays an even bigger price to hold her head high."

Mal was silent. She heard a reference to something personal to Luz, a disappointment not to be delved into. Perhaps it was her marriage, perhaps her children, or perhaps this Nicaraguan revolution itself.

That evening, Luz came to the villa with Nando to pick up Mal and take her to a clinic. They left the men in conversation and ambled slowly in the dusk down the street lined with white stucco houses and painted doors.

Mal felt at peace, a part of small town life. It was easy walking with a local woman whose home this was. There were no stares or suspicious looks from people on the street or on verandas, as happened when she walked with Juan. "I may wait on dyeing my hair," she mused. "Let's see how much it distracts when we start to teach."

At the clinic, they waited on a bench with the sick until it was Mal's turn. Luz stepped up to translate the symptoms to the intake nurse, nausea, vomit, aches and pains. Mal felt safe in her care; Luz was maternal. She heard the respectful tone Luz used with the nurse to talk about her.

Another nurse examined Mal. Mal gave both blood and urine. Luz stayed with her through it, at times taking her hand. They returned to the bench to wait for the diagnosis. They waited an hour. The nurse emerged and said to Mal, *"Voces están embarazada, Señora Mai."*

That was how Mal learned the Spanish word for pregnant.

Her watch read 3 AM when Mal woke for the second time with a start. Again, it had been a dream about the pregnancy. She was breathing hard and must have been holding her breath. Ironic, she thought, to spend the last two months denying it while awake and dreaming of the second heartbeat inside her in the dead of night.

At least it was what Luz claimed to hear when she put her ear to Mal's scant mound of tummy. It seemed to grow, which meant she could no longer avoid a decision. Enough time spent on her obsession with Juan's silence. Three AM was as good a time as any to decide about that baby in there. She shuddered and pulled up her sheet. She and Luz estimated it was around twenty weeks old. She must get herself back to New York for an abortion, if abortion was to be her final decision.

It would be easy to be a killer, a Jimmy. Kill the damn thing—except that the idea was too drastic for words. It is a life, as Luz reminded her at every opportunity, the original and unique creation of Mai and Juan. Time was molasses here on the mountain, hardly budged, but perhaps it was too late for an abortion. And anyway, she needed to stay in case Juan wrote.

She sat up on her cot and stared at the darkness, brushed sweat from her forehead. Luz breathed evenly, asleep across the room. Gladys and her three children made no sounds asleep in the adjoining room. She heard the incessant chirps of insects, the random cries of birds and animals, and the rhythmic heart beat within her: the baby. Their baby.

Two months on the mountain. Nights like this, replaying that abysmal goodbye kiss when Juan boarded the bus to Bluefields, replaying the scream in her head: *Tell him now that he will be a father! Say it. It's your last chance.* No words had come and off he went. With each replay of her silence, a spurt of gastric acid seared her gut, just deserts. By now she had accumulated a million justifications for her silence, and with his own silence it hardly mattered, did it? He'd abdicated his right to fatherhood. And to her. Where was he, damn it! Why had he not written?

After the bus took Juan away, she and Luz boarded another headed in the opposite direction. And Mal made her error in judgment about Luz. Settling themselves on the bus to Jinoteca toward their new assignment, having known Luz for only two weeks, she had confided that Juan did not know about the pregnancy, and that she intended to terminate it. She'd made Luz a surrogate Kleio and had expected Luz to respond like Kleio, like a sympathetic sounding board. Big mistake, that. Who would have guessed that Luz was both a revolutionary and a practicing Catholic? It flummoxed her, and what was worse, her revelation had ruined their budding friendship.

Mal argued that Juan's reaction, whatever it might be, would complicate a decision that was hers alone to make, that she just didn't want it, that pregnancy was inopportune. Her future with Juan was no foregone conclusion, not yet anyway. He had a history of unreliability. He might demand she keep it, then leave her or, worse, feel obliged to marry her. She would not be saddled with an unintended life to tie her down forever. She'd been rational not to tell him with the intention of aborting the fetus. Unaware the practice was illegal in Nicaragua, she would return to New York. Soon. And return afterward. He might never know. Years from now, if they were together, she and Juan could always have children. There were too many unknowns in the here and now.

"*Mira, Señora!*" She had raised her voice at Luz. "Do not go dogmatic on me! You carry your own to term—with your husband and family to support you. In effect, I have no one. Do you believe my parents would be delighted? They don't even know about Juan. He will never leave Nicaragua, but I may. I am not Nicaraguan. I don't want a child. I never did."

But if she kept it, as Luz insisted she must—and it seemed she was doing so, passively, through her inability to leave—could she carry to term here in these primitive conditions? Best return to the States with its world of options and friends. Such huge decisions to make on one's own: go or stay; with Juan or without; abort or give birth; become an unwed mother or put it up for adoption. Certainly, she'd been correct to exclude Juan, at least until she knew what she wanted for herself.

Two months, and no word. Living in a mountain enclave so inconsequential it even lacked a name, until Luz had dubbed it *Sin Nombre*, Without a Name, and had convinced the Sandinistas to mark it thus on their map, to make visible the needs of impoverished dwellers above the valley town of Jinoteca. Without a name they were non-existent, Luz had argued to the men. So, too, this fetus: let it be nameless.

No discussion, no decision, no action. So unlike the Mal she once was. Early on, she'd considered a call to Kleio. But she'd doubted such a call would result in discussion. No. Kleio would issue a firman, order her return. Mal did not call. She concluded that since Nature terminated pregnancies by miscarriage, so could she, by abortion. She had got no farther than that.

She would go to New York tomorrow, except for waiting for Juan to write. She had sent him many letters care of the Casa Sandinista in Bluefields. She had visualized his response arriving in a canvas bag from Bluefields, stamped by the Jinoteca Sandinistas, held until Luz appeared to pick up mail on her frequent runs for supplies. It had become an obsession. She believed he received her letters and that his silence was not necessarily indicative of a problem; he had been silent the last time he was in Nicaragua. It was so Juan. Still, maybe—maybe—it might come today with information that all was well, so freeing her to act.

She tossed on her cot, remembering being stunned by Luz hissing, "When was pregnancy ever convenient? Pregnancy is a gift from God! He alone created life and delegated His power to bring forth life to the woman. Not the man! We are unique because of that gift. And you have the audacity to reject His will? What woman does that?"

"More women than you might imagine," Mal had muttered. "There is nothing unique about carrying a fetus."

What an ugly argument on the bus! She had been so sure, seated next to Luz Gonzalez y Sanchez, that she was in the right. She felt no feminine pride to keep her "gift from God."

Would she even want children with Juan, who had yet to demonstrate the qualities of a husband, let alone those of a good father? Juan was a question mark. She knew nothing of his upbringing on Corn Island. He was simply Juan without the appendage of a past. She knew Mina better, and Mina barely knew her brother, having met him in New York, just two years ago, after a separated childhood

Mulling this over, scratching at her bites, her stomach gurgled. Diarrhea. She curled up tight in her cot and made an insect screen of her sheet, pulling it over her head, and hunching protectively over her tummy in hope of delaying going out of doors. The truth was, up here was hellacious. Not just from morning sickness, insect bites and digestive problems, but getting through the day's muddle of sounds.

Not comprehending Spanish was her daily challenge. They spoke a dialect here, to add to the confusion. At least insomnia allowed her to think without incessant day-time babble in her ears. There was comfort in the gentle night cries and the whistle of the wind, rain pit-pattering on leaves, insect hums ... lulling her into nightly acceptance of her prison.

If the window of opportunity for a legal abortion in the States had closed, then she might as well wait for Juan here and grow it into a baby, as Luz had argued. Luz insisted there was little risk in giving birth in Jinoteca. Look at all the successfully produced children! Luz was not worried about being pregnant while here. Spending one's pregnancy teaching women to read was worthwhile, worth boarding with Gladys and her children and getting to know the realities of rural life, Luz said.

Gladys, their landlord of sorts, was the poorest woman around, an itinerant peddler of vegetables one day, rags another.

Luz paid Gladys with Sandinista money to house them in her hut, larger and set apart from the other dwellings. The ladies they taught lived in scattered lean-tos, resembling the wikiups in her childhood picture book with a new, exotic child's story in each chapter. Mal would have given anything to meet them. She smiled because her big crush had been for "Pim-Wie of the Amazon," with bowl-cut hair and orangey skin—the book used only orange and brown inks—climbing a date palm in nothing but a loin-cloth. Juan had replaced Pim-Wie.

Mal drifted and began to doze. The images came with sounds, the clinking water pipes of home, Dad's voice reading the words, *wikiup* and *tepee, longhouse*. Her pink flannel pajamas in a scatter of cowgirls on horseback and roping steers from Dad's trip to America. Central American countries like puzzle pieces on a map, the pea-green triangle that was Nicaragua ... when she grew up, she would go there.

The reality was ugly. Luz had pronounced the well water of Sin Nombre polluted, fed by seepage from the unclean lake. Gladys's hut lacked every necessity; her companion was rarely around to help out. Her children worked. Doris, the teenager, cared for others' babies in exchange for handfuls of beans. Her body was underdeveloped, and a tumor sealed one eye. Small Lydia had a goiter bulge on her neck, and the toddler was covered in a rash even inside his ears. Could he hear? He never made a sound.

Reality had been missing from *The People of Other Lands*. Reality was cooking on a *tenamaste*, four syllables that gave importance to three stones around firewood for boiling beans or river fish spooned onto leaves. No plates, no forks. Reality was *afuera*, outside—for water, washing and loo. Reality was Luz rushing down to Jinoteca for endless alcohol wipes and iodized salt.

Abort she must, rather than bring a child into this squalor. Arriving full circle, she fell asleep.

In the morning, Mal reprimanded herself for getting stupid. She was an economist. In the ledger book of her future, she had been accumulating debits, not credits. Today would be pivotal. She would make an empirical study of reality, identifying and tallying it. If she disliked the totals, she would leave the next day and get that abortion. This could be her last day in Sin Nombre, and if he ever cared to know what had happened to her, her Pim-Wie would have to look beyond the land of the Indians.

Upon first arriving, Luz had used Gladys's help to assemble some fifteen women. Luz had explained to them that she and Señora Mai, an *Inglesa* who spoke no Spanish, had been sent by the FSLN to teach them to read. Ready or no, interested or no, those silent, dour women were now part of the great National Literacy Campaign. The Sandinistas had been victorious against the corrupt Somozas and the imperialist interests of the *Americanos del norte.* The first step in rebuilding their country (as per Fredo's strategy) was for the women to tell what they most wanted to change in their settlement. The Sandinistas would gift it to them.

The women knew immediately: new homes far from the water's edge, up on higher ground close to natural springs. Everyone agreed: yes, move us away from mosquito nests and flooding. Luz wrote it down and read back to them their collective voice. The Sandinistas would arrive to work with them to build new, better homes. The women murmured approvingly.

And their next wish?

Stop the men from drinking. A woman added: Stop them from forcing themselves on us when they are drunk!

Luz wrote it down and read it back as, "Have a group discussion with men about rape. Introduce family planning and contraceptives." An apparently amusing discussion ensued in which Luz described the contraceptives she would obtain for them. What more?

As the women discussed with greater interest, Mal observed their bowed heads lifting and saw light in their eyes. She had no idea what was said, unless Luz stopped to translate for her, but it was clear, their grim mood improved. For all the Jimmys and machismo, and the separation from Juan, it was obvious in that initial meeting that answering their needs was more important than the discomfort she and Luz experienced. *Vale la peina*, Luz had taught her to say: it's worth the hardship.

Luz followed through, and in the following weeks their respect and trust grew. Luz was kind. She actually taught them to read the words for home, for construction, for settlement, for mountain, for contraceptives, for mosquitos, for clean water, always reiterating that these were the changes they had themselves demanded, that the Sandinistas would fulfill. So elegant and brilliant was Fredo's method of forging allegiance in exchange for empowerment. Such were the gold bars in the Sandinista bank.

Mal did not deposit her allegiance into the Sandinista account. They were still men, suspect and macho, forever monitoring their success through Luz. What were "our ladies" (Luz named them) to do with their literacy after the campaign, Mal demanded, and Luz shrugged. Whatever the Sandinistas said would be next. So, there was no plan? They would be forgotten to bumble along in isolated poverty? What would change? Nothing, except for the better housing and improved drinking water.

"Is that not a big change?" Luz had snapped.

"For male thinking," Mal argued. "To help women keep a tidier house."

Luz slapped her forehead in disgust at the feminist ideology. *Aiye que sentimientos norte americanas!* Such North American sentiments!

"I shall come up with something better for them."

"You do that, *chica*."

But she hadn't, yet; and this morning, she hardly cared anymore. There was always the language barrier. At first she had assisted Luz where she could. She imitated Luz's teaching style, her pronunciation, even her gentleness with "our ladies." But Luz complained that Mal was interrupting too often for translations, adding to her burden. Luz seemed to have no real plan for how the two should work together, rather expected Mal to watch her teach. She admitted that Mal had been assigned to her; it was all Luz knew, increasing Mal's feeling of being warehoused.

She sat with the children, Doris and Lydia, to watch the mothers in Luz's class. She didn't like children. Kleio's children's museum in Bed-Stuy seemed to Mal of only theoretical value, but the saving grace of these girls was their use of the universal language of pointing. They managed to communicate a bit. She had innocently remarked to Luz that Gladys's girls seemed intelligent despite their physical ailments. Luz had quickly jumped: "See? The infant growing inside you encourages you to like children. When you first came, you cringed if they stepped too close to you."

This morning, Mal joined Doris and Lydia in "the children's circle," as she called it with a note of irony. She smiled to remember her kindergarten Circle Time, crossed knees to sit "Indian style." In that progressive, post-war kindergarten, at Circle Time the children had learned songs that repeated numbers in different languages. They learned how the people in other countries greeted one another: *Bonjour, Hallo, Buenos Dias, Guten Tag*—and how the countries counted to ten. The Spanish number song with the catchy melody had stayed with her, and she had once sung it to Juan to make him laugh and show the limits of her Spanish. *Uno dos tres—cuatro cinco seis!*

That was an idea. She took Doris and Lydia to sit apart under a tree. She sang them the Spanish number song and used her fingers to demonstrate the numbers. Singing it again, she wrote numbers in the dust with a stick. She encouraged them to sing it with her, and she worked their grimy fingers into the correct number as they sang. They smiled. They understood.

It tickled her to hear the girls' shy soft voices sing her old kindergarten song. She helped them to write the numbers in the dust. She could teach them maths, at least. At lunchtime, Luz heard her out, agreed it was doable. Yes, she should take it on. Luz jotted down a Spanish maths vocabulary for Mal to memorize and use.

Mal would need another day for this. That night in her insomnia, she felt content and smiled in the dark. She thought of games to teach addition and subtraction. I cannot leave just yet, she thought. I am finally useful. The debits and credits were equalizing.

The next morning, Doris and Lydia were waiting for Señorita Mai. They continued lessons for the rest of the week. Doris and Lydia were eager learners and hungry for Mal's attention. Mal forgot about Juan for hours at a time, nor did she worry about her pregnancy. The connection with the girls was satisfying. They accepted her and had from the beginning, never shying from her foreignness, her lack of language, her white hair. All of it was just Señorita Mai. She noticed Gladys watching them together, looking pleased. Gladys had always made clear that she liked Mal, and Gladys loved her girls. It was deep, this love, its tender expression that had surprised Mal, even in this hardscrabble setting. It was deeper than the despair at having little to give them. It allowed the children to survive.

Kleio would crow to see Mal teach children, of all God's untamed creatures.

At the end of the week, Luz attributed Mal's new interest in the girls to her pregnancy. You see? Her heart understood the purpose of motherhood, even if she did not. Mothers were capable of enormous depths of love for their children and felt great pain when they could not provide for them. "Our nature is to have these extremes of feeling. It goes with our female purpose."

Mal blanched. Those hack sentiments again, silly romanticism, a trap for fools. She would not be taken in. Why had Luz and her sophomoric pronouncements ever cowed her? Mal was clearly the more intelligent one.

"Luz," she asked, "do you think I can transform the ladies into businesswomen? With enough time? Perhaps, I shall stay on and have the baby here. Perhaps, marry Juan—or not." For herself. For them. And why not? The activist Nicaraguans had their babies and did their political work simultaneously, minus First World distractions of baby showers, prams and Lamaze classes. They carried on.

In her second week of teaching, some ladies brought her their children to teach them *los numeros.* And Mal, thinking of Fredo, made Doris and Lydia the teachers. She sat back in awe of what she was accomplishing at last, enjoying the shy voices teaching the numbers song of her childhood. Most amazing. Doris and Lydia emerged quickly from self-consciousness. Their physical problems were irrelevant.

Here was her purpose, discovered at last, she informed Luz at night. To teach the girls what she knew. Yes, she saw herself having the baby here, regardless of Juan. He would just have to cope when he found out. She chuckled at the prospect of becoming a mother, beating out Kleio and Mina with their fantasies of raising children communally. In Sin Nombre she had an authentic communal setting. She had no need of artificial urban communes. She, Mallory Tame, was as ever ahead of the crowd!

The runs continued. She ate less because digestion hurt her gut. She worried about her health.

Luz downplayed it, labeled it *gringoismo* to complain about Montezuma's Revenge, and advised her to stick to rice. Luz would buy more in Jinoteca. "Keep boiling that water, and it will pass. But you remind me that we must teach our ladies more about hygiene. And someone must bathe that boy for the first time in his life! His smell worsens."

"I shall volunteer," Mal felt bold, stepping up to the challenge to be the first, as she had in Group.

In the morning, she began by heating a kettle of water over the *tenamaste,* and had another idea. She sang to herself, in the tune of the counting song, thinking: *I am so creative. My mind is so unstuck! I am so much cleverer than Luz!*

"Luz, please, would you tell the ladies to watch me demonstrate a method for keeping their children healthy?"

The women were curious. They followed her to a hillside covered with aloe vera bushes. With a machete, she cut off several long, thick leaves, each side lined with a row of pointed barbs. Gingerly, she carried them back to the impromptu table of crates beneath a tree and slit the thick green skins. She squeezed out strips of gelatin from the insides into a bowl. She looked about for dead leaves and grasses for scrubbing, took the silent boy by the hand, spoke softly to him in English, and led him to the *tenamaste*. She put his fingers into the heated water and splashed with him.

Oskar was his name, which sounded when they said it, like O'ka. "Okay, little O'ka, honeybunch. *Mi amor*? Let us make bubbles!" She sang to him, "'Wash these fingers, wash these toes! Wash these shoulders! Wash that—nose!'"

O'ka, expressionless, stared at her fingers dabbing the slippery aloe gel on him. He batted the water with his fist and produced bubbles while she slathered his pimpled skin and his ears, rubbed him gently with a cloth and rinsed him, then daubed more on. She turned to the women to explain the healthful use of aloe.

They smiled at her stumbling attempt and shrugged. *Pobrecita*. The poor white one cannot speak.

It was no use. It was not just the vocabulary but their idiosyncratic dialect, so effortless for Luz. Mal was centuries away from knowing it. Face it: she had no real way to communicate. Her eyes filled with tears. Whatever did she think? How grandiose to have believed—that anyone believed—she could contribute anything. In one week, all she'd done was taught some numbers and bathed a dirty child.

She looked around for Luz, who was busy with a chalkboard in a one-on-one reading lesson under a tree, ignoring her. "Luz! Come here, please! Kindly explain to our ladies about this aloe plant growing all over the damned place. It is medicinal! Luz, tell them for me. It is *muy, muy importante!* Now! *Ahorita!*"

Startled, Luz joined her. The ladies murmured about the audible conflict between the women. Luz translated Mal's explanation. The women questioned it, but Luz kept at it, Mal could tell, pleased to have Luz on the same side. When the back and forth ended, Luz complimented Mal and patted her shoulder. *"Bien hecho, chica.* Well done. You have them interested. Suddenly, they call us their guardian angels. That is progress!"

That evening, Luz asked where she had learned about aloe, complimenting her again on the successful lesson, because, Luz admitted, she was running out of new ideas to teach.

"From Juan's sister, actually. In Cuba, she'd seen the whole procedure. She gave me a tube of aloe from a homeopathic shop in Manhattan as a going-away gift. I've been daubing it on my insect bites. From the picture on the box, I recognized it growing all about here. I had even intended to go directly to the plant after my expensive little tube was done.

"Why don't our ladies know about it? They can eat it, too, if they do not already. It can be mixed in food. It's healthy. Let's not forget that, Luz. And there is something more, too, our ladies could do with the aloe vera, as is done in Cuba. They could create an economically viable business by stripping it themselves. They'd only have to transport it to Jinoteca and truck it to a port. I would love to write them a business plan. The Sandinistas surely would provide a truck, even build them a factory. It could ship through the Panama Canal—"

"*If* the women even want to, Mai! And forget about shipping. *Oo*-SA threatens to embargo our exports. To you white people everything looks easy, but we see exploitation. Look what happened to our natural resources—tin and gold, coffee and cotton. They became American businesses because of the so-called American aid. No. The women should decide what is best for them after some history lessons. Anyway, the Sandinistas will never approve it, because they did not propose it."

The pot of cold water Luz tossed on Mal's idea did not deter her. She would try another way: "If the Sandinistas must own it first, perhaps you could present it to them?"

Luz softened. Yes, literacy should lead the women to a further stage of development, to participate in the country's economy. A self-sustaining business was reasonable to consider; it communicated that a world existed beyond Sin Nombre. It could empower them or, if not them, their children. She could raise it to the Sandinistas at the next meeting, but she knew that literacy, not sustainable development, was this year's goal.

Mal rolled her eyes. Her contempt for the Sandinista bureaucracy, to which Luz unceasingly kowtowed, was boundless. Undoubtedly, they would sit on it or, if accepted, would credit themselves with the idea. So she had an idea. She would begin describing it herself to the women, or to the girls. She could say *una fabrica por aloe vera para venderlo.* She knew those Spanish words: a factory for aloe vera, to sell it. It could work. She had just succeeded in getting Luz to think outside her little box, for a *momentito. Vale la peina.* Definitely, worth the effort to try.

That night, awake again, Mal was happy. She was useful to the children and to their ladies. She felt acceptance. She had gotten Luz to talk with her as an equal, not a subordinate. With time and with Luz as an ally, they could develop a strategy to make an aloe vera cooperative run by the ladies.

Mal was unafraid of the Sandinistas. It might be uncommon for a Nica, even a political one like Luz, to control her own destiny, independent of men and society's conventions, even in revolution, but not for her. Social change was ever so much slower than she had ever realized—molasses, getting all the ducks in a row to march in the right direction. She was a player, a small one, but free from the constraints of political theory and the authoritative male voice. She was too creative to be hampered by the usual conventions.

Thinking positively inspired a new idea, again from her kindergarten years, of how she and Luz might work more efficiently. She was certain Luz would like it. In the end, all it had taken for Lux to accept her was to give up on an abortion.

In the morning she proposed to Luz that they could join forces to work together. Mal would offer actual demonstrations like the aloe vera while Luz provided a running commentary that would result in vocabulary for a literacy lesson. Yes, agreed Luz, a good idea. It grew increasingly difficult to find new themes, and her pregnancy was tiring her. Mal could do it.

"We can call it *mostrar y explicar!*" Show and Tell, as in Mal's kindergarten. Mal would invent the new themes based on what she could demonstrate. Luz was satisfied. They were finally a team. They began to spend evenings planning lessons and sharing anecdotes about their ladies' progress.

This was how to change the world: little by little. *Poco a poco.*

Mal felt freer and happier. No reason now to keep her pregnancy from Juan; she would go to term, regardless of his reaction. She would frame the news to him about the new person-to-be as their personal contribution to the New Nicaragua. She hoped he would accept fatherhood. But if he could not, she would be a single mother. She wanted the life she nurtured to come into being. It was a liberating concept, she told Luz.

And Luz, for the first time, expressed disgust at Juan's silence. He must be a man and take care of Mai, she insisted, going on as to why she placed value on marriage and the two-parent family.

Mal nodded. She had heard these sentiments her entire life. Mal entertained other options. She knew Juan.

The morning sickness had passed. Mal began to have what she described to Luz as leaking.

Spotting. Nothing to worry about. "You must be in the second trimester, which means things are fine. No one ever miscarries this late. But visit the clinic in Jinoteca when you have a chance. Just to check."

Mal silently began to worry about her little fetus now that it mattered to her, the birdling hanging on, in need of protection. Surely, it lacked vitamins, poor little creature. She should eat fresh vegetables and apples. Oh, how she longed for an apple! Yes! A lesson for the ladies! Why not plant a vegetable garden with fruit trees with the ladies? An absolutely enormous amount of vocabulary to mine there. Surely the Sandinistas could round up saplings from somewhere? Another future product for the ladies to cultivate and ship around the country... There was a wealth of new vocabulary related to nutrition she could turn into lessons for the month of May. It was almost May: three months now and no word from Juan.

On May 1, International Workers' Day, Luz declared a holiday for everyone while she went down to the Casa Sandinista in Jinoteca. The Sandinista volunteers, seven men and women, had recently arrived in Sin Nombre with building equipment and materials and had begun the construction of sturdier structures further up the mountain, assisted by the ladies and their partners. It was indeed "Workers' Day," they joked. Their arrival and activity brought credibility and laughter to replace the depressing grimness. A brisk wind carried the racket of shouts, hammers and cement mixers churning. Sin Nombre was bursting with change.

Mal was content this particular May 1 morning, except for the gnawing silence from Juan. It felt almost homey at her table under the tree, the wind blowing gently, while she wrote down gardening words for Luz to translate. Luz seemed to enjoy the new ideas that sprang daily from Mal's imagination and reacted with less opposition. Mal enjoyed her small but active realm of creative superiority.

Mal was inspired this morning to design a garden for Gladys and thought hard to remember just how Mummy had organized hers, interspersing flowers and vegetables. She thought the girls might help with the planting as a lesson in maths. She doodled hoes and shovels, thinking how to fashion a digging implement for O'ka. He needed to learn how to play. She delighted at the prospect of describing it all to Juan in a letter and touting her successes. If he could only hear her progress in Spanish as well, he would be truly amazed. She knew many vegetables and *plantas* already, as the teamwork method proved educational to her as well. Today she would write him about her pregnancy. She was finally showing enough to wear an oversize man's shirt that she had purchased down in Jinoteca, reluctant to enter the maternity shops that abounded there.

A most glorious morning, it was: the air was still *fresco,* the "false friend" word that meant cool. The sun flickered through the wind-tossed branches and cast dancing spots of light in the dust. The mountains were dove-hued, and the aroma of wood smoke from the *tenamaste* wafted about, making her slightly hungry. Primitive as it was, it was also innocent here. She would be sure to write to Kleio that she was finally "accustomed." She would not divulge her pregnancy, inappropriate to tell friends before Juan. She smiled to imagine Kleio's shock when she met Mal at the airport, a tiny Juanito or Juanita in her arms, her very own. Having a baby was absolutely self-transformative. Which had been Luz's point.

Luz had left early and taken Doris and Lydia. Gladys's companion had shown up, so she was inside today. Mal babysat O'ka, who took care of himself anyway, wandering on his own or sitting at her feet like a pup. She'd come to like the little tyke now that he smelled less. Her goal was to get him to smile someday. As she unfolded and smoothed her writing-paper, looking for a rock to secure it against the breeze, her eye caught the movement of a panda-like form silhouetted by the sun, loping up the path. She froze. She knew that shape. Jimmy.

How could it be? She shaded her eyes and squinted, praying she was mistaken.

"*Holà! Blanca! Que tal?* What's up?" His voice on the wind was laugh-filled and warm, as if they were old friends. He waved both arms to her, and in one hand he held a paper. She noted he carried a backpack and was not dressed in his CDS uniform but a tee-shirt and jeans shorts.

Mallory ran to meet him. They embraced like good buddies, a big bear hug from which she could not extricate herself until he let her go. She laughed. In fact, she was pleased to see someone she'd known longer than the ladies and who was a connection to Juan. He stepped back, put his hands squarely on her shoulders and looked her over, stuck out his lips, the Nicaraguan way. "Man, do they feed you anything here, *flaca*? You've lost some serious poundage!"

"Oh shut up, *gordo*. It's the country life. And my name is Señorita Mai. So use it." She slapped his tummy none too gently. What a little brat. "What brings you to picturesque Sin Nombre?"

"It's what you call this place? Ha ha. Sin Nombre! *Sin Existencia* is more like it. I brought you this. From Juan." He handed her the envelope. "I came to deliver in person and to see Luz. You know, for *cuecho*. Gossip. 'Word.' She's around?"

Mal took the envelope, which she noticed lacked the customary huge black Sandinista stamp to indicate it had been opened, read and approved. It had only her first name in Juan's hand. She stuffed it into her breast pocket.

"No, she's not. Luz is down in Jinoteca now, at the Casa. She went this morning to hand over the latest list of what Sin Nombre demands from the revolution, including a better name. She's there all day with the leadership."

Jimmy looked around. "Too bad. How've you been making out, the two of you? With the women?"

"Excellent. Couldn't be better. Ladies reading, children squeaky clean. All good. Did Juan give you this? Where you in Bluefields? Did you see him? How is he?"

After a second of silence, Jimmy said, "Well, I was out there a couple of weeks ago. Yeah, he's there, but I never actually saw him. Funny thing. He was, um, working. He left it for me to pick up from a mutual friend. Does he tell you what he's doing? No? No letters? Really? That's a disgrace! So, since I'm here,

I'll just poke around—meet some of your 'students.' Get their 'evaluation' of your work. See if you earned an A. Ha-ha. Then I'm on my way. I wanted to see Luz, but I'm heading over to San Isidro."

Mal shrugged. She returned to her table, now aware that some time ago, Juan chose to avoid the normal communication conduit, the Sandinistas, by passing the letter along by hand. Did it mean something? She watched Jimmy enter Gladys's house, wishing he would leave so she could open it without questions. She touched the envelope, pressed it against her because Juan had touched it. She opened notebooks to appear busy.

Ten minutes later, Jimmy emerged and approached her, a quick glance at her pocket. "So, I'm off. Good to see you again. Sorry to miss Luz. I'll catch her on the way back. Tell her. *Ciao.*"

"Sure enough. *Ciao.*"

She watched him lope out of view. How perplexing, his brief visit. He had not been to the Casa Jinoteca but had skipped it, clearly, because he would have met Luz there. Why? The guy still made her skin crawl. She tore open the envelope.

Querida, mi vida—how I miss you. Things not like I expected. I will leave the coast as soon as it is safe. In the meantime, leave where you are and wait for me in Bello Horizonte. We should be together by end of May. Do not worry. I love you.

Mal examined the letter, dated ten days ago. He wanted her to leave Sin Nombre. How could she do that unobtrusively now that she had become committed? What did it mean—not as he expected? Why did he say "the coast," not Bluefields? He did not send it through the Sandinistas but passed it to someone trustworthy. Jimmy? But Jimmy hadn't actually seen him. The go-between then? Was Jimmy truly Juan's friend or his enemy, looking for him? Had Jimmy searched her things when he went inside? Had he already opened and read the letter? If so, he would believe Juan was heading to Managua. She studied the envelope she had just ripped. Had it been resealed? How could she tell?

She dashed inside to see what he might have moved or taken, but it was impossible to determine because she kept things a beastly mess. If Luz was partisan with the Sandinistas, but Jimmy had not stopped there, were Jimmy and Luz even on the same side? Why had he wanted to gossip with Luz? Or had he lied? Mal's stomach churned. If Juan was fleeing, why didn't Jimmy, his good friend, already know?

Or did he? Was this a trap? A puzzle, indeed. She put aside her lesson plan and considered how to leave without arousing suspicion from the Sandinistas or Luz. But not for Managua. She knew what he'd told her so seriously back in Bello Horizonte. The note meant he was at his uncle's, waiting for her. The letter was a ruse, sure to be read by any authority. There was no such thing as privacy in a revolution. Only secrecy.

Luz arrived late at night and sent the girls to bed. Mal noticed that her mood was off. She turned away to avoid looking at Mal. She was uncommunicative about her day with the Sandinistas, though normally she gossiped non-stop about who said what. She handed Mal a letter from Kleio, her only mail, she said. It bore the Casa stamp and had been opened, no bother to reseal. Luz was unfocused and left sentences unfinished; her face muscles were tight. It's an interior argument she's having, Mal deduced as she scrutinized and parsed every detail about the woman before her. Mal said nothing of Jimmy's visit, though Luz would surely hear about it from Gladys. She said nothing about Juan's letter. Something had happened down in Jinoteca that Luz wanted to keep from her.

Luz had brought back bread, and she was hungry. Though she'd fed those girls well in Jinoteca, she herself had been too upset to eat all day, she said. Then she was silent. She sat down on her cot across from Mal with the packaged bread in her lap. "Here, let's share it." She slowly untied the string, unfolded the paper for reuse, and removed the bread. She tore off an end and handed it to Mal, then tossed her a cola from her knapsack. She sighed.

Mal bit into the bread while studying Luz. It was taking Luz time to open up, but it would come. Mal sensed it.

"Okay. I will be honest with you, Mai, because we are good friends, over and above the demands of the Sandinistas. Men don't understand that women make bonds. And I know you pretty well now. I debated whether to say this, but I trust you, and I think you should know it. About Juan. You are an honest person, Mai. You've proven many times over your support for the revolution and your willingness to stick it out, even though it is obviously difficult for you. Now, they've asked me to report on you, in particular about what you hear from Juan. I told them so far you've heard nothing from him at all. Right? Ever since we left Matagalpa? They insist that is difficult to believe. They suggested someone brings you his mail in secret."

Mal's eyes widened. Jimmy! So! He was indeed at odds with the Sandinistas. He was on Juan's side, whatever that was. "What? That's crackers, Luz! Absolute rubbish! Bringing me mail? And who would that be, pray tell? I have not had one word from the bastard! You know that. You know my agony. Why do they say such complete nonsense? What is going on?"

"I don't know, Mai, except that apparently Juan is in big trouble. He has disappeared. Not in a bad way—not killed. But he left the program suddenly. They don't know where he is. They keep such close watch on all foreigners in the country— their movements—so they are baffled. Yes, it's true. They think of him as a foreigner, that he is CIA. They believe the CIA came into Bluefields to take their man home and maybe that is why they can't find him. They've long suspected him to be CIA, because he went to the States instead of staying to fight. And he has returned. Twice. They believe he is a destabilizer, that he reports to the CIA about our troubles on the coast. Right now we have very big trouble there, an eminent civil war. They suspect you, too, Mai. But I insisted they are dead wrong about you. I know you are not here to destroy our revolution! You just aren't!"

"Oh good lord, Luz, of course not. Such rubbish! You, of all people, know that. You told them, right? About the pregnancy? That Juan supports the revolution? He fantasizes about being the president someday, not by overthrowing the Sandinistas but by being one. I just want to be his wife—assuming he can handle the responsibility. He has not written to me. It is typical of him. I told you. I am here to help the ladies read and plant gardens, and to keep this fetus alive. And learn Spanish. And work with you. It upsets me—to hear what you say, to be mistrusted after everything I gave up to be here and remain here."

"Yes, but do you really know Juan?" Luz was agitated. "Who he is, really? What he does? He came here with an Argentine fellow they know is an agent of the CIA, a Paco something. Jimmy—the one who brought you to Matagalpa; he is a very powerful person in the CDS. Not the kid he play-acts, Nando says. Nando thinks Jimmy was assigned to watch Juan both times. Nando knows things I don't. In Matagalpa, the Sandinistas assigned you to me, to keep an eye on you. They separated you and Juan to make collaboration difficult. Your letters they open before they go on to Bluefields. They admitted you look clean. Here, for them, you are out of the way and isolated. It's fine with me being with you. I'm near my kids anyway, and my husband."

Mal was speechless. She stared at Luz. "I cannot believe this. You are my *minder*? So they never took me seriously as a teacher. After what I abandoned back home! And you too believe Juan is a spy? You're all cracked! So if he is such a danger, why did they invite him to take part in the campaign? Why did they send him to Bluefields, if there is trouble there? You people make no sense whatsoever."

"Well, you don't know much. How could you? You are an outsider." Luz was defensive and hesitated. "But you understand that the literacy campaign is different on the coast, right? It is not under Sandinista control at all. It is run by a coalition of Indian groups called Misurasata, to teach literacy in the native languages instead of Spanish. They are the ones who asked for Juan. The

Sandinistas said okay, his roots are there and his father—well, you know, was important, was going to be named ambassador before he died. Maybe assassinated, Nando says. The coast people are a mixed bag of antecedents: Dutch, English, Africans, the various Indian groups. Today they have competing interests, and they are without infrastructure. Still, they demand self-determination within the Sandinista-led government. Maybe someday they will have political autonomy. But today conflict festers among them and with the Sandinistas. The situation is unstable, so the CIA stirs it up to hinder and distract, to undermine the Sandinistas. Somoza allowed the CIA to operate freely around Bluefields, supposedly to penetrate the drug cartels. Nando thinks the Sandinistas put Juan there just to tail him and learn about other CIA connections. Jimmy in the CDS, he is the go-between, at least according to Nando. It is all so secret, we don't really know. I can't really say Jimmy's role in all of this. But he has one."

Mal was shaking. She ran Luz's information against what she knew and what she intuited. Such a relief not to have mentioned Jimmy's visit just four hours before and that he sought Luz. There were disconnects everywhere. And Nando as the major source of the inferences—was he reliable or a troublemaker? Was *he* in the CIA?

"I know this, though. I trust you, Mai. You are easy to read. You are naïve—like the Americans who volunteer for our coffee harvests. Juan is the complicated story. His allegiance cannot be trusted. And how well do you know him? You say you are used to him leaving you, disappearing, not communicating for months. I told this to the Sandinistas."

Super. Still, unreliability did not mean Juan was an agent or a traitor. It was in his personality, how he handled crisis. He ran. She explained to Luz that it was traumatizing to lose his family so young. "He idolized his father. He is hypersensitive. Stress and conflict he handles poorly—even intense emotions. He leaves to cool out, to change channels. To think he is CIA is paranoiac. Completely off base."

Still, Luz had a point: how well did Mal know her quixotic boyfriend, so poor at communication, so at ease with lies, so expedient? She was certain only of what he told her. Had she been naïve to believe him? Her thoughts jumped to Jimmy. No wonder she'd feared him! That Jimmy was a minder had been a correct assessment, but of Juan, not of her. Was he thus a danger to Juan? Had Juan entrusted him with the letter, or had he intercepted it from someone else? She hated this. Suspicion was the ultimate poison. Revolutions should be about higher values and noble goals. Good guys against bad guys. But she was learning that revolution was not clean. Even she had understood that the literacy campaign was a tool for political gain. Must good works be encased in bad stuff? The stuff of evil?

"Luz, if they should find Juan, or if he shows up here, what will they do to him? Would you report him?"

"*Claro*, I would. They? Jail him, I guess. Kill him. It's what they've done to others, not to take chances. I know they actively look for him. They don't mind killing, so don't go near him if he shows up here. Behind him will be someone with a gun."

Mal winced. Jimmy! He had come in search of information about Juan. If he had opened her letter and knew Juan was headed to Bello Horizonte, it would be reasonable for him to think Juan had already come by here. She must leave immediately. She needed a good lie.

"Luz, I am petrified now, really petrified. You are so right: I don't know him. What a ghastly mess I am in, and Juan is to blame! I am pregnant. I must get home for this baby. You have been a sister to me, and Juan has abandoned me. It's so obvious now. He has gone. He won't contact me if he was removed by the CIA, as the Sandinistas believe. It sickens me. I want to go home immediately, to make sure my baby is safe." She had stood up for this outburst, and she sat back down, hoping Luz was convinced of her disillusionment.

Juan had sent her the signal that he hid on Corn Island on his uncle's pineapple farm, an uncle who was ambivalent about the Sandinistas. Even if he were a CIA agent in trouble, he had not fled. He was waiting for her. She would go to Corn Island. He had given her a month. How many Davila farms could there be there? They would escape together via the Atlantic coast by sailing to a Caribbean island that had been on her childhood map. If Jimmy had read Juan's letter, he would head to their apartment in Managua, the other direction and 168 miles from Jinoteca.

"I shall go tomorrow," she announced. "I must get myself home."

"Tomorrow?" Luz was shocked. "What about the girls? The ladies? You do so well with everyone. I told that to the Sandinista boys. The women love the White Lady. We have a good thing going. I need you, too, Mai. Once you leave here for Managua, the CDS will follow you. Be safe. Stay here with me. Juan might yet come here for you."

"And you would turn him in. To be killed. Sorry, Luz. I am done with Juan, but he should not die on my account. The Sandinistas have it right: he's already left the country. It explains why I've had no word. Right this minute—formally, to you—I quit Juan, and I quit this revolution. Pregnancy ... it changes a woman's perspective, as you said. It was given to me as a gift. I see that now. I must leave for my unborn child. We need serious health care. I have the spotting and leaks." She lowered her voice. "You understand? I have been abandoned. I cannot help the revolution any longer. I owe it to my baby to get us out of here. To go home."

"But how, Mai? Wait a bit."

"I'll go to Managua and fly home. Let them follow me. I am guilty of nothing but bad luck. I have an open return ticket. I can leave whenever I choose. Carry on this bloody literacy campaign without me, Luz. I am done with it!"

A shooting pain gripped her insides and made her double over. It was real, no act. Spurts of something warm begin trickling down her leg. She winced and headed for her cot.

"You're just upset now, *chica*," Luz put an arm around her to help her. "I am so sorry that we end like this. We were doing so well. We became sisters. Get some rest now. No one ever miscarries in the second trimester. You *gringas* can be so *frágil!*"

—∿∿—

Mal was really leaving. Nothing to pack, truth be told. All she'd come with folded easily into the rucksack. She tossed in a large jute bag that Gladys used in her vegetable peddling. A memento, she explained.

Luz and the ladies accompanied her down to the highway to wait for the afternoon bus to Jinoteca. Mal hugged each of them in turn. She had not expected to weep. What an embarrassment. The worst was saying goodbye to Doris and Lydia and little O'ka. His skin seemed improved, and she kissed him. She regarded the two girls, their independence already in evidence. What was to become of them? Who would encourage them, if not her?

Luz. She hugged Luz, tightly. "At least my leaving ends your responsibility for me to the Sandinistas, the better to concentrate on our ladies, yes? And the girls. And the new life to come." She lightly patted the hefty bump that ballooned on Luz.

"I will send you pictures. We will write."

"I think not, Luz. I regret that this is our goodbye. Let us say that the demands of the revolution take us in different directions. But our time together was well-spent, was it not? We learned a great deal together. I treasure what we accomplished." She embraced Luz again and couldn't help but weep into her shoulder, loving and hating this woman. She looked up with a laugh at Luz's wet eyes. The conflicting emotions of loyalty and betrayal, love and hate were about to split her.

"Oh dear! We shan't meet again. Luz. I wish you such good *suerte*: good luck. I shall miss you all."

She stepped into the bus, and as she blew kisses to them from the window, it pulled away. Mal trembled in the awareness that within days Luz would know she had been lied to by a woman she had trusted, as soon as Gladys told of Jimmy's visit. Within days, they would denounce her as a fugitive and a CIA operative, an enemy of the revolution, or some such stupidity, as they had Juan. She would be in danger then, so she would move quickly. She stared at the passing farmland along the highway and shuddered. She was in a ghastly mess. If only her own warring emotions would settle, to stop the morass of goodbye sadness, guilt, finality, fear for her fetus, and dread for her future with Juan, hoping she had guessed right to head into the unknown. She was committed to him, not the revolution, not to saving the world. At least that much was finally settled.

She and Luz had invented a vaguely true story for the women and the Sandinistas about Mal's sudden departure for Managua. Señora Mai required immediate medical attention. The ladies concurred: she grew skinnier each day. *Mira!* Even her hair was too weak to hold its color! Mal imagined they would forget her in time; so many new people now penetrated their isolation. But for her the ladies and their children had been the most meaningful part of her time in Nicaragua. Like them, she had changed a great deal because of the association. Willingness to learn had been the common leveler. That, too, was settled in her mind. She fell asleep in the sun that beamed through the window.

The bus pulled into the Jinoteca station an hour later. She had promised Luz to visit both the medical clinic and the Casa to register her departure for Managua. Before leaving the bus station, she studied the timetables. She discovered there was none for Bluefields. It seemed one took a bus to El Rama, and from there traveled to Bluefields by *manga,* whatever that was. The Rama bus passed through Jinoteca every second day.

Mal held her breath. Yes, it was due at four-thirty that very morning, some twelve hours away. On a poster-sized map of Nicaragua with a black circle inked around Jinoteca, she located El Rama to the east, a dot on the Rio Escondido, upriver from Bluefields, itself a dot on the Atlantic Coast. She estimated the distance to Rama as 250 kilometers, an all-day trip. She searched for Corn Island and discovered it forty-five miles into the Atlantic Ocean. *Heavens!* How daunting this journey was to be! She was taking a huge risk, but Jimmy's Cheshire cat smile loomed in her mind, waiting in the pepper-red blooms of the flame tree outside the Managua apartment. She bought tickets for Managua and Rama, and for good measure, for León, to confuse anyone tracing her path.

She had no intention of wasting time at the clinic. What could they do for cramping and spotting? She would manage until she saw a proper doctor. She left the bus depot in search of a pharmacy and found one, nearby. Studying colors, she chose Lady Clairol Natural Dark Caramel. She purchased a scissors, several boxes of sanitary pads, and disposable adult diapers. Then she taxied to the Jinoteca Casa. It was after 7 PM. She was exhausted and severely cramping.

The Casa was blessedly empty save for a teenager. Presenting her passport and ID with the Managua ticket, she watched the girl laboriously record in old-fashioned cursive Mal's name, tomorrow's date and the bus information. Mal exhaled. Free as a bird now. At a kiosk, she bought snacks and water for her trip. No hope of a *Herald Tribune*. Her only news of the larger world for months had come from Group, and she hungered for it.

She handed the address of a cousin of Luz to a *taxista* and climbed into the seat with her packages, eager to rest. The cousin would put her up overnight so she could catch the earliest morning bus out. The exhausted-looking, unsmiling cousin who came to the door carried an infant on her hip. Mal paid her in advance. She would let herself out, she explained. No need to get her breakfast.

Claro. The woman offered her dinner and empanadas for her trip.

That night after the family was in bed, Mal locked herself in the bathroom. She showered, then took a scissors to her white locks, giving herself a curly pixie-cut as best she could. She dyed the close crop caramel. La Blanca was gone. She smiled at her new self and carefully cleaned up, stuffing her cut strands into a plastic bag that would go, together with her rucksack and extra clothes, into one of those bins that exhorted bilingually, "Keep Nicaragua Clean and Beautiful!" Everything else in her possession she wore or fit into Gladys's jute *bolsa*. With it slung on her shoulder, she looked less like a luggage-laden foreigner and more like a Nica, if no one noticed her lavender eyes.

She dressed to be ready for the early start and lay down, cradling her sensitive, crampy abdomen. She felt increasingly feverish. Nothing to be done for it: mere discomfort had never stopped her. She dozed but awoke to heavy bleeding. Panicked, she undressed and placed the clothes she had intended to discard underneath her to absorb leakage. She lay down again, worried about oversleeping. It was 2 AM. During a brief and intense dream, she watched the little fetus slide down the copper piping of her childhood home and into a plastic bin liner that Americans used for raked leaves. A sharp contraction and hemorrhaging startled her awake. Was she miscarrying? Was she dreaming? The pain was severe, making her hyperventilate and whimper into the pillow.

I'm going to die.

She stuck her knuckles in her mouth and bit down. Next came hot spurts of liquid with excruciating, intermittent contractions and unbearable pain. She stuck a jumper between her legs and hobbled into the bathroom in time for a volume of sticky blood to slide from her insides into the toilet. She moaned and cried with her lips clamped together, feeling she would burst. There was so much of it! Was it a placenta? She looked away and flushed. She clamped her mouth shut. She cleaned herself and the floor thoroughly, and stumbled back to her room in pain. She panted and longed to sleep, but the pain was nauseating her. She felt dizzy and heavy. She fainted.

No. She was fine, she told herself coming to. That had been nothing at all. Luz insisted no one ever miscarried in the second trimester. Never. She had not died, nor was there anything to fear. She was a neurotic *gringa*. English girls lack *cojones*, in Luz's words of superiority. What happened was probably normal; the body ridding itself of extra gunk. She did feel better, yet such a ghastly episode! She went back to wash again and looked into the toilet bowl. What had it been? She put a towel underneath herself and dozed, relieved that all trace of her ordeal was gone. At four, she arose, woozy and disoriented but without cramps. The towels and clothes were a disaster. She would dispose of everything, and would leave money to replace the towels ... clever to have purchased adult diapers. She put on two of them.

She slipped out of the house into the dark street and got her bearings. A dog began to bark and stirred up others, but she was very much alone. No echoing footsteps, no shadows but her own. The stars glittered faintly and the air smelled clean, *fresco.* Of course. She walked to the bus depot and found a trash bin into which she stuffed her bulging rucksack of refuse. She found the gate for the Rama bus and waited alone. It arrived late. Daylight had already broken when she boarded. Such a night! Whatever had that been? Luz's voice insisting miscarriages never occurred in the second trimester rang in her head.

As she tip-toed down the aisle of sleeping passengers, a wave of utter loneliness and grief overwhelmed her. She was completely on her own, and no one on earth knew where she was. She felt weak and leaden beneath her waist. There was no returning to Sin Nombre. Her plan was to get to Juan. She would do it.

She found an empty double seat in the back where she tucked herself up against the window and breathed deeply. In Luz's cousin's bathroom, all pink and gray tiles, she had experienced a nightmare, but about what? She focused on everything she could remember.

Until it hit her. No no! It could not be, but it was. Hot tears welled suddenly and dribbled down her cheeks. She sobbed, softly. Luz had been dead wrong. Luz, who acted on top of everything, who fancied herself more knowing than Mal, but who could not invent one good lesson without Mal's help—so self-assured the Sandinistas entrusted her with monitoring the foreigner: Luz. Dead wrong about miscarrying in the second trimester.

Mal had seen it, the placenta that contained the fetus. Mal's baby was gone, no more inside her. That was the void she felt, the empty aloneness. Her baby had fallen into the toilet, one piece with that bloody mess swirling in bright red streaks, suctioned away when she pulled the cord. She had dispatched it herself. And had stuffed whatever remained of it in the trash at a bus depot.

She retched. Her precious baby made from both her and Juan that had taken her so long to want—she had flushed away. She vomited spume into the aisle. She exhaled a loud keening howl she had never heard herself make and long hiccupping sobs. She could not control anything. Her shoulders shook. She covered her face and cried—unstopped—into her hands.

An old woman in the seat in front of her turned around in alarm. "*Qué pasó, querida? Estas enferma?*" Are you ill? She looked ancient, deeply creased around her eyes with white thinning hair. It was all Mal took in through her tears. The woman reached out to hold Mal's heaving shoulders.

The gesture made Mal cry even harder. How she wanted her mum!

"*Mi bebé,*" she whimpered to the woman. "*Yo perdí mi bebé anoche. Era embarazada, pero yo lo perdí.*" Her own voice came from outside herself in clear, correct Spanish words. How ridiculous that her mind could editorialize while she cried. Her first comprehensible Spanish sentence announced that she had lost her baby during the night. The Spanish words had been tucked away inside her and had emerged effortlessly.

The woman quickly rose from her seat and spread her newspaper over the vomit on the bus floor. She took the seat next to Mal. "*No importa. No te moleste.*" Do not worry yourself about it. She took Mal in her arms, and Mal let herself be rocked. The woman patted her back and made soft sounds as if saying, "There, there." She told Mal that she, too, had lost babies, three times, but three others had come to term. Her three children now were grown. It would happen for her, too. Mal was still very young. *Joven.* She and her husband would try again. *No lloras, no lloras, mi hija. Dios sabe lo que hace.* Do not cry. God knows what he is doing.

Mal disagreed vehemently. God knew nothing at all. She fought off wanting to be held. She wanted desperately to forget it had ever happened. She pulled herself away, saying she needed to sleep. The lady nodded and returned to her seat.

Mal could not sleep. She reviewed each pain, each leak, each attack of nausea. And an hour later, she pretended to sleep when the bus stopped and the lady looked back at her before departing, as if to say goodbye or good luck, or God be with you. Mal did not want to hear it. She felt the woman touch her shoulder and squirmed away. Maybe the baby had already died inside her, before she had flushed it away. If not, she was a killer. The horror of that possibility was too terrible to contemplate. It was something she would never know, at least. She would tell Juan everything the moment she found him. They would mourn together for their lost child, one more casualty of the revolution. They would make another. The old lady was right about that. She would not feel bad forever. Mum never tolerated feeling sorry for oneself. Death could not be undone. She heard her mother's voice.

Mum would certainly counsel, were she ever to know, that miscarrying had been for the best: most likely the fetus had been damaged by her poor nutrition on the mountain and caused her body to expel it. Perhaps God did know. *But Mummy! I so wanted that baby!* As if Mummy had denied her a sweet or a balloon. With all you have on your mind? Don't be silly, Mallory, she'd admonish. You cried enough tears to last you a lifetime in Nicaragua. More just will not do. Enough.

By noon, when the sun beat mercilessly through the window, Mal was calm, able to watch the countryside of palms and grazing cows breeze by. Someone cleaned up her mess during the two-hour stop for lunch. It was a lovely day for travel, clear and bright. She reflected on her arrival in Managua, a lifetime ago, when she had wondered what her life would be like by July. Never had she imagined this.

What did the lyrics of that ABBA song really mean? That women were strong? That another day would come to sing again? It was just a song, after all, written by a Swedish man to console a Spanish-speaking woman. How could he know what women suffered? And anyway, the song had nothing to do with her life.

Brushing away the occasional tear that seeped through her eyelids, Mal was able to nap for the rest of the trip to Rama.

—◦◦◦—

She was the last to step off the bus into the jungle town, Rama, onto its main street. She stretched her legs, certain she inhaled the most humid air she had ever encountered in her life, worse than that first intake in Managua, definitely worse than New York. She dripped with condensation and sweat. Or fever.

Black clouds sagged low over hills, and behind them were long streaks of orange and navy sky. The bus had emptied its passengers a block in from the Rio Escondido, which showed itself between buildings, glinting platinum and inert.

Her legs ached; her stomach was upset. The bus rumbles played on inside her ears. Diesel fumes were in her nostrils. Crowds of people were about, blacker and browner than those she'd known on the Pacific side. The babbling sounds were more foreign than Spanish. Donkey carts clogged the traffic of honking cars, bikes and wagons. As if civilization ended there, there was no station-master for inquiring about a next leg. But all to the good: she was here. She glanced about for anyone who might be studying her and saw a *chicha* stand. "Bluefields?" she inquired of the seller.

The man pursed his lips, à la Nica, and nodded them toward the river. "*La manga.*"

She asked a teenager, then another. *La manga* everyone answered, indicating the direction of the river. Yes, but what was that?

A small boy studied her confusion.

She placed a hand on her hip in the bold Nica stance she'd seen so often and demanded, "*Dígame: que es la manga?*" She must find out what a *manga* was.

He smiled and waved her to follow him down the street of hexagonal pavers to the muddy tract at the riverbank. The fishy odor of river mixed with diesel oil made her retch. She looked where he pointed.

"*La manga, Señora.*"

She gave him four cordobas and he ran. Was it too much, what a *gringa* might tip? She looked about again. No one had noticed. The *manga* was a wide double-decker ferryboat, its passengers emptying out onto a rectangular cement pier that jutted into the river. She approached a worker coiling a rope. "Bluefields?"

Mañana en la mañana. A las seis. Díez cordobas el boleto. She understood perfectly and smiled. She really did. She repeated it in her mind in English, very pleased with herself: in the morning at six. Ten cordobas for a ticket. She had somehow achieved comprehension. It felt like magic. It felt good.

Claro. But what to do until tomorrow morning? She approached a cabbie to ask if he could drive her to Bluefields. He laughed. There were no paved roads, *Señora.* She must take the *manga.*

Claro. Six in the morning it would be. She wished for a bath with hot water in a big tub. Back on the paver road, she noted it was lined with hotels and tried to identify the most upscale one. Hotel Paraíso it had to be, because of its actual screened door through which backpackers and dreadlocked hippies came and went. Mal had not seen a screen in ages. An amenity!

Hotel Paraíso, Class D, offered her a cage-like cement box, screened in on top and open to the heavens, tarped for rain, a cot and a light bulb in the wall that excited moths and insects. To bathe was to hose down with rain water collected in an oil drum at the end of the corridor. Disappointed, she paid the cordobas and went down to the lobby wondering how she would get around unnoticed until two English-speaking backpackers about her age entered from the street. She approached them and introduced herself as Sandra, the first name that came to mind, asking for their help in confirming her poor understanding of how to get to Bluefields due to her limited Spanish comprehension.

Mies, who was Dutch, and Pierre, who was Belgian, were happy to oblige. They had been traveling together since Honduras, and luckily they also happened to be experts on Bluefields, having just arrived from it on the *manga*. After they checked in, would she join them for supper at a restaurant that had been recommended by an Aussie traveler?

Brilliant. Mal was starving, and it would be clever to hide in the cover of tourists, lest anyone be searching for a single female traveler. When they returned to the lobby and got directions from the desk, the three stepped into the crowded street. How was it she was on her way to Bluefields, they asked. And traveling alone?

Mal had a quick answer, thought up while waiting. She'd come from Managua, she said, where she'd had a break-up with her American boyfriend. She'd decided to tour until her return ticket date, as far from him as possible. She'd heard Corn Island was beautiful, but had no idea how to get to it, except through Bluefields.

Oh it is, quite, they said, for they'd stayed on Corn Island for two weeks, coming down by boat from Honduras. From Corn Island they had flown to Bluefields. The entire Atlantic coast resembled the Caribbean, they assured her, easy ganja, easy to live under the radar. And the reggae music was fine.

Over dinner, Mies and Pierre related anecdotes of their travels, and Mal asked them questions about the Nicaraguan revolution and changes it had brought that they might have noticed. No, they'd come for a lark and were disinterested in the local issues. The two seemed foreign to Mal, interlopers. She felt in synch with Sin Nombre and the real struggle for life. How good to have been part of that world, involved as intensely as their ladies in change, in the extraordinary exercise of reciprocity.

She felt quite nonwhite, sitting with the two blond, blue-eyed fellows. She was conscious of the transformation she had undergone, both excruciating and exhilarating. She beamed sweetly at them. She owned something valuable from being here that they did not.

Easy to get to it, they continued, to Corn Island. In Bluefields there were fishing boats for hire, but flying was the better option, except flights were irregular and space was limited. She would possibly have to wait in Bluefields a few days. Just avoid those boats—nightmares on the rough sea. They knew.

Who lives there, she asked, on Corn Island?

Just simple natives and a lone Cuban doctor they'd come across. The doctor had taught the natives to boil their drinking water. But they wanted for nothing. Everything for the taking—coconuts, fish, hashish and the harder stuff: a regular Eden.

"So, no agriculture? No plantations?"

Nothing so complicated. An island lost in time. One felt like Robinson Crusoe, a cast-away. It was easy to go native there. A great life. No need to work.

Idle thinking engaged Mal as she stretched out on a surprisingly comfortable deck bench of the *manga*, her eyes shut to the overhead sun's brightness that entered red through her eyelids.

Calm at last. Funny things, lies. Her lies to the Europeans the previous night felt no more false than their idea of truth. To lie was simply to present a plausible alternative. Quite elastic, actually, was truth, she thought, quite dreamily, and counted up her lies on behalf of the revolution—the lie to her parents first among them. She was still Mallory Tame, who in the commune had valued a rigid definition of honesty, but now she was easy with lying. She smiled into the warmth the sun cast on her face. The *manga* engine droned. She hadn't relaxed like this in months.

She squinted open an eye to watch the banks of the wide Rio Escondido glide by: a gorgeous, under-inhabited country. The true tropics. The engine drone lowered an octave to power against increasingly stronger currents. The *manga* stayed mid-river, between banks thick with coconut palms, tangled fronds and vines, and occasional clusters of thatch-roofed houses set on bamboo stilts. Children were everywhere on the banks, all sizes and ages, playing and caring for little ones. Though a few waved, most people on the verandas and in the water ignored the ferry. What did they think of the boatloads of strangers drifting by each day?

Juan's mother had been one to venture from the Atlantic coast to marry his father, from virtually a different culture on the Pacific coast. As for Mal, it was the romance of wikiups and Pim-Wie that had lured her out of England and brought her here. She had always fantasized floating on a tropical river such as this. The blue of Bluefields was a mystery about to be revealed. But she felt a shiver of fear. In truth, she was ready for the safety of home, preferably England, extremely ready.

From Corn Island she would go home with Juan. She was certain that his foray into Nicaraguan politics had come to an end.

The large billboards of text installed at intervals on both banks, aimed at those on the water, reinforced her anxiety. Black capital letters repeated a threat in Spanish, English and Miskito:

"Counterrevolutionary! 200,000 Eyes Are Watching You!" Mal shuddered each time the ominous threat floated past her. She feared for herself and Juan. The deadly civil war had lost its romance and idealism.

On this boat, at least, she was invisible. No one knew her whereabouts, not the New York group, not Luz, not Juan, not CDS spies, not even the two hundred thousand eyes scanning for counterrevolutionaries. She shut her eyes and adjusted her face again to meet the heat of the sun.

She was almost dreaming when she felt the warmth replaced by a cool shadow. She opened her eyes, and her heart leaped. Of all people!

Jimmy.

"*Hola chica!* I thought it was you I saw! Your new hairdo threw me at first. But your eyes, Blanca, your eyes are forever violet. S'cuse me! You are no more Blanca!" He smiled and sat down next to her.

Startled, she began hyperventilating but stared straight ahead to avoid his gaze.

He pushed. "The last time we met was on the mountain. You were writing under a tree."

"Last time I saw *you*, you were going to San Isidro. How was your trip?" She was terse and ironic—nothing like feeling trapped to enrage one. She could not escape him until they got to Bluefields. And then how would she? Push him off the side of the boat before they got there?

"Okay, I won't lie to you, Mai, I never went. I was rerouted instead, to Bluefields to search for Juan. Though not for the reasons you might think. I am here to get him out of this area. We got word he is in danger from a Miskito faction out to disrupt our work. They intend to kill him, a revenge killing. I need to get him to Managua where he can be safe. Why are you going this way? Is he is expecting you?"

She refused to answer this creep. "I shan't lie to you, either, Jimmy: I disliked you from the beginning, immensely so, in fact.

I do not trust you. I think you are looking to arrest Juan, or kill him. I don't know where he is. I came to find him. So you have been following me all this time?" Her voice was acid.

Jimmy laughed. "What? No way, *chica!* Let me assure you of two facts: I am not out to hurt Juan, and I did not follow you! It is coincidence to meet here. Juan is one of us, in the CDS. He never told you, right? I am pretty sure, since the membership is on the Q.T. But he is in danger now, and you will be, too, if you find him. It is lucky to run into you. I can protect you. Man, Bluefields is one dangerous hellhole! I went up to the mountain just to give you his letter and to get any *cuecho* from Luz. You know, just like I said. She's tight with the Jinoteca group. You were supposed to stay there and be safe. Why did you leave it for this cesspool? Does Luz know you where you are?"

"Listen, you little bastard. I'm not telling you a thing. To be square with me, you must be totally up front. No lies." Involuntary tears of fear filled her eyes. "Tell me everything, because not much is making sense. What do you mean that Juan is in the CDS? Luz accused him of being CIA! And *I* thought he was a Sandinista."

She saw his eyes soften.

"Well, Luz is dead wrong. The Sandinistas keep her in the dark. Look, Mai. I'll tell you what is true. No lies. Juan is a good friend of mine. Did you know he used to come visit me in Chicago?"

His voice lowered. "I know for a fact Juan loves you and wants to be with you. He got that letter to me through safe sources to pass on to you. I didn't lie. I never saw him in Bluefields, like I said. He apparently went underground. I'm back to get him out, but I don't know where he is. No one does. He's in deep shit. Apparently you must know something since you are here. But no, I didn't tail you. Honest Injun. When I saw you on the mountain, I already had instructions to turn around, find Juan and get him safe, but first I wanted to give you the letter and see what Luz knew, if anything. Like I said. There are no exit points from Bluefields overland. Rama is it. Even planes have to refuel in Rama. But he's not in Rama, hasn't passed through it, according to our mutual connections. They think he is still around Bluefields, so I'm going there. I know he grew up on Corn Island. I could try there, too, but that's one hell of a trip unless I catch a plane. Look, we both want to find him. We'll stick together. I will get you both out of the country. Easy."

Mal was silent. Why trust him?

"So what is *your* big idea?" he continued. "That we search separately? That is both ridiculous and dangerous. I am charged with finding him, Mai. He is one of us. Trust me." He patted a bulge under his arm, indicating a pistol inside his shirt.

Trust him? If Luz was right, then Jimmy could be the very one sent to kill Juan and would use her to trap him. That made her a danger to Juan. She pushed. "Jimmy, you are still not specific enough for me. Tell me: who exactly is after him? And why did he go to the Atlantic coast?"

"Yeah. Okay. You're in the middle of the mess now. You should know everything. We needed the intel in Managua on who does the dirty work around here. Because of Juan's Miskito background, he got the assignment. And we stuck you on the mountain to keep you safe. Juan didn't know it was his assignment when you both arrived. He was fine with it, expecting it to be short-term. But we, the leadership, wanted you out of the way—for practical reasons, so as not to risk an international hostage incident. Some misinformation got spread about Juan to discredit him: that he spied on the Miskito using his mother's relatives as entrée. Could've been by some Costeños, the coast people—or possibly, it's CIA; we don't know which, and who cares for now? Someone is out to silence him. Kill him. We have real issues here on the Atlantic side. We cover up with nice stories about Sandinista successes. But I don't have to tell you, it is proven that no revolution succeeds without bloodshed."

Mal was silent. He spoke seriously, without his false, jovial irony. He sounded sincere. He was right, of course. Juan was no traitor. She knew that. And Juan was in danger; his note had been quite clear. But what about what Luz had said, that the Sandinistas believed Juan worked for the CIA, in direct contradiction to Jimmy? She felt abruptly frightened at just how life-or-death the truth was. At the heart of revolution was war to the death. All over the world, every single day: struggles for power. Who could hold the power, and for how long to keep it?

Luz, wrong about miscarriage, had to be equally wrong about Juan. Mal should work with Jimmy. She turned to face him while her innards, which had so briefly found stasis, churned again. "Okay, Jimmy. I agree. We search together."

They shook on it.

———

Each settlement mooring on the way to Bluefields appeared to be more primitive than the last; the people smaller, darker and poorer; the children more numerous—as if, Mal thought, the *manga* was sailing them back to sixteenth-century outposts. They arrived at Bluefields in a downpour—opaque, wet sheets slipping off every roof and overhang. Mud was thick, and Mal's sneakers squished with every step. The town center was sodden and disappointingly a dreary brown, not blue at all. She was hungry for vegetables. She longed for a green salad, but Jimmy advised they would find mostly shrimp and turtle stew. They trudged through the rain to a building with its face open to the street, protected by an awning, with a few tables deep inside on a cement floor. The owner offered them moldy-smelling towels and beer and a meal of fish steamed in banana leaves. It was delicious to Mal, though rather peppery. She guzzled her beer and felt better. "What's next?"

"Well, *chica,* I told you what I know and still you remain quiet about what you know..."

"Not yet," she cut him off. "First, tell me where you plan to look in Bluefields."

He had people to visit. For her safety, he insisted, she shouldn't know who, or where he would go. If he found Juan, he would reunite them, he promised. In any case, he would return for her. She would be safe waiting in this restaurant, a clandestine safe house. She should not try to disappear. Bluefields, true to its history and heritage of piracy, was a drug haven, trafficking shipments from Jamaica and moving them up the coast to Honduras for distribution to the States. Petty narcos and big cartels operated from here. As a foreign woman alone, she was an easy mark, a hostage for trade by the narcos. He doubted if President Carter or the Queen would rush to save a Sandinista supporter. She must stay with the restaurant people. They knew Juan. He often came here.

It sounded ominous, despite bringing her closer to Juan. The information that compounded her worry, besides the CIA, was that drug interests were players in the revolution. She understood in a flash Mies and Pierre's true interest in coastal travel: cheap, accessible drugs. She had missed the point entirely, fooled by their amiable backpacker stories. No doubt, the entire back-packing clientele of Hotel Paraíso, Class D, were drug tourists.

She considered telling Jimmy that she believed Juan to be at his uncle's farm on Corn Island, but no, she decided. First let him check out Bluefields, lest he go to Corn Island without her once he was out of the door.

Almost as if listening to her thoughts, he asked again what she knew.

"Nothing," she blurted. "I know nothing. The letter you brought me was indeed the first I'd ever received from him. In it he said to meet him in Managua, as things weren't going well here. As you see, I took the scenic route to the capital. I intended to find him in Bluefields before he left and to leave together via the Caribbean. I had no idea he was in the CDS, and I didn't know until his letter about any trouble." If Jimmy had indeed read it before her, her truthfulness now would reinforce her credibility.

After they ate, Yunely, the cook, took her upstairs to a small room where she could rest until Jimmy returned. Yes, she knew Juanito; she smiled in a motherly way. He often stayed in this room. *Muy guapo hombre*—handsome, and a good boy, she added, in a maternal tone.

Mal lay down on the cot, ignoring the dank smell of humidity and mice. She felt comforted that Juan had lain here too, and shut her eyes.

When she awoke, her watch said 1:30 AM. She heard Jimmy's voice below, speaking with a man, but it was not Juan. She got up. As she descended, he looked up and smiled at her. "*Bueno, chica*. You stayed. *Mira*. This is Nelson, Juan's local counterpart. Nelson, meet Mal, the *novia* Juan talks about endlessly."

Nelson looked astonishing. He could have been in the movies. Tall, muscled, of African origin, high-cheek-boned like Juan, with a commanding mane of golden-hued dreadlocks and a hint of mustache. He shook hands, heartily. Yes, he'd heard so much, he already knew her. He spoke lilting English, like Jamaican, but with its own Costeño drawl, not easily comprehended.

He guessed that Juan had skipped over to Corn Island. Generally, people didn't know about Juan's connection there, but Nelson knew it, and about Juan running scared. A Miskito had jumped Juan with a knife, and Juan had beaten him to a pulp. The guy threatened to return with a group and kill him. Juan could be stuck on Corn Island with no safe way off it. How he got there was anyone's guess, because most fishermen were not trustworthy.

Mal shuddered at the news. Then she wondered if this conversation was being staged for her benefit. Nelson sounded off, inauthentic. She didn't know why she thought that—a tone of insincerity? Over-familiarity? She could not pinpoint it. Juan beat someone to a pulp? Was Juan capable of that? She remembered what Mies and Pierre had counseled about planes. Perhaps his affluent uncle owned a plane that had flown Juan to the island. Was that how he intended to leave it? Were these guys safe? Her thoughts spun round.

"Corn Island? We can try it," she finally concurred, deciding that sticking with them was the best option. She met no argument. They would travel together. Was it a trap? Were these the ones who would take her hostage? She trembled. She wished that she too had a gun and knew how to use it.

Nelson had a family connection with a fisherman who would head out to sea in two hours. The storm had passed. The sea was choppy, but darkness was a good time to make the run, undetected by the drug boats.

Within an hour, the three were standing on a pier in the dark in a stiff wind. The waves swished wildly, and docked boats knocked one another, their bells clanking. Farther out, where it was even windier, she heard the erratic bongs of bells on buoys. It would have been exhilarating except for the mounting dread Mal felt, being with these two strangers bigger and stronger than she. She vacillated between seeing them as friends or as enemies. Her genius at reading people, what every tick and facial muscle meant, what they intended with their gestures and body language—where was that facility of hers now? Lost. She trusted none of her readings. She was on foreign territory, vulnerable and dependent.

Nelson led them to a small vessel, the *Eldorado*, and introduced them to its captain. They climbed into the tiny cabin, and the boat started out to sea. The trip would take up to four hours. It pitched and tossed as the engine revved harder. The dock quickly disappeared behind them. Mal felt nausea rising. She was going to be sick. She went out to the side and threw up. She breathed deeply and held onto the rail. Tears filled her eyes. There was more to come.

Jimmy came up behind her and put his arms around her waist to hold her. "So you don't fall into the sea," he shouted against the wind and engine thrum. "The tossing is very strong." He was right; she could not keep her balance and slipped with every step on the slick deck.

She felt powerless, gripping the cold slippery metal. He let her go suddenly and stretched out over the rail and vomited. Mal crouched down to sit on the sea-slick floor and leaned her head against the cold wet rail. The wind was swift and strong, and spray drummed her back as the boat heaved, chilling her. She was so light that her body slid around as they hit a swell or pitched deep. She gripped the rail as tightly as possible, but her arms were tiring and her hands were numb with cold.

"I may not make it!" she shouted up to Jimmy, who kneeled down on the deck floor, put one strong arm around her waist, and gripped the rail with the other hand. He had her lie flat on her stomach, to be able to vomit over the side without losing balance. He did the same, clutching her, to keep her on board. After what seemed like an hour, there was nothing else to upchuck, and Mal shivered with cold, soaked through with spray.

"I won't let go of you," he breathed, heavily. "Don't worry. Lean into me and sleep if you can."

Just let me go overboard. It can't be worse than this, she thought, and leaned into the warmth of Jimmy's body. She was out, instantly.

When she opened her eyes and looked around, the sun had risen, and the sea was calm. In the distance, she saw the shore line contoured with coconut palms.

"Corn Island? We must have gone to hell and back," she said to Jimmy, who held her in a tight embrace as they sat up together. She released herself and smiled at him. He had kept her from drowning.

He looked sheepish. "So, you didn't slide into the sea. It happens, you know."

"Yes," she smiled. "It's the proof that I can trust you. If you were going to kill Juan, you could have let go of me, and no one would be the wiser…"

He raised his eyebrows in agreement. For sure.

Nelson appeared from the cabin as the engine was cut, and they drifted slowly toward the dock. He claimed, like Jimmy, never to have been to Corn Island. He said his cousin told him the Davila plantation was inland. They would need bikes. He would borrow some at a tour company when they landed. He handed them each a lime to suck on.

He chuckled, "*Gringos,* both of you!"

On the pier they caught their breath, walked around on their wobbly legs, and tried to dry themselves out as they waited for Nelson. He returned on a bike with a boy walking behind him with two bicycles. Mal, still queasy, mounted and wobbled on it behind the men as they took off on a paved road. Who'd have guessed that today she'd be biking on Corn Island? Not she. She would see Juan very soon.

Nelson had directions from the tour company to the Davila plantation. They turned onto a washboard road, past palm trees and children. Shrill, squawking parrots flitted through the palm fronds, and monkeys called and leapt about overhead. There was something peaceful about it, Mal thought, rather timeless and untouched. The sun shot streams of heat, though it was not yet nine in the morning. It felt good to be in sunshine and on land after the relentless wet and cold of the night.

The few people they passed were of African stock. She remembered Mies's and Pierre's comments. This was not the Nicaragua she had come to know. At last: the tropical jungle of her Pim-Wie fantasies.

The road narrowed. They turned off onto a footpath. Her wheels slowed in deep sand, and she lacked the strength to push. Dismounting, she walked her bike and fell farther behind Nelson and Jimmy. The path ran along fenced-in private property.

"That must be it," she heard Nelson point, "The Davila plantation." He saw the villa first.

It came into view at the end of a wide driveway flanked by flame trees, a stuccoed villa in Spanish colonial style, the color of butter. She just knew Juan had to be there. Where else could he be? Her heart pounded with excitement. The paved driveway made movement easier. She mounted her bicycle and caught up to the men, who had stopped at an oval with chain across it. Leaving their bikes, the three climbed under the chain and headed toward the villa, perhaps a hundred feet ahead at the other side of the oval. Mal thought one might find such a home in Ibiza, porticoed and framed by decorative palmettos and many-hued bougainvillea. Planted close to the pavement were stands of pineapple and banana trees in a kind of garden. So this was where Juan, the revolutionary fighting for the disadvantaged, had grown up. There were no signs of habitation.

"You're sure of this? Will we be shot at if we approach?" Mal asked Jimmy. "What will you do when we find Juan?" Help him or kill him, she wondered. She had trusted the protection of Jimmy's arms around her but knew he had killed Somosistas and had his gun with him.

"We'll strategize how to get out of here," Jimmy answered, matter-of-factly. Nelson was silent and walked ahead. Really now, who were these men? She trembled. She—she and Juan—were in their hands, whatever they were up to, whoever they were. They stopped in front of the steps of the villa.

"I'll go knock at the door," Mal volunteered.

"No. Better to call out to him," Nelson said. "From here. Call out to him. He will know your voice. He will see you are with friends."

"No," said Mal in a fit of suspicion, fearing she could be used as a decoy. "*You* call him. He knows your voice, too."

Jimmy said nothing, as if waiting for Nelson and Mal to decide. If Juan mistrusted Nelson or Jimmy, he would not show himself. This back-and-forth hesitation seemed odd to her, out of sequence. Who was in charge? Her mind raised questions. She half-way trusted Jimmy, but Nelson? She didn't know.

"I will call him." Jimmy said and took a few steps forward. He shouted, "Hey! *Flaco*! You in there? *Venga por aquí!* Come on out! I brought you someone."

The front door opened a crack. Then wider.

"Jimmy?" It was Juan's voice. From where she stood, she could see Juan's beautiful Miskito eyes peering at them from the door.

"Juan!" Mal dashed ahead of Jimmy and Nelson toward the steps as Juan flung the door wide and laughed to see her, throwing up his arms. He ran out across the veranda to the steps and headed toward her to embrace her, laughing, crying.

"Mal! *Mi amor!* I can't believe you made it!"

Snap-snap-snap.

Mal stopped, startled by the strange sound. Before her eyes, the joy in Juan's eyes turned to shocked disbelief, to staring. His body crumpled.

What is happening?

She watched him collapse like a deflated balloon. He was a heap sprawled on the veranda.

It had been a gun.

She stood frozen until her mind unlocked and registered it: he was shot!

Acrid smoke filled her nostrils. She jerked around to the source. Nelson stood with blue puffs of smoke drifting around him. Nelson stood with a gun in his hand.

"No!" she howled. She turned toward Juan up on the veranda, and Jimmy ran up the stairs shouting, "No! Juan! Get up! *Figa te*! Run!"

Juan stayed sprawled across the top step. Inert. Blood pooled under him, dripped down onto the first step.

Oh my god! No! No! This could not be!

She caught up to Jimmy, who was screaming, "Juan!" Juan! Bro!" He pulled out his gun and turned around toward Nelson, but Nelson had disappeared. He had become the movement in the stand of pineapples and bananas. The fronds shook, then were still.

"Juan!" Jimmy screamed in shock. "Quick, we should move him flat," he ordered Mal. "We can stop the bleeding."

Mal had crouched down to touch him, sobbing. Juan! Juan!

They rolled Juan slowly from the step onto the veranda floor as the blood pooled on his chest. His lids were blue and closed. His skin was pale.

Was he breathing? No.

"He is gone," she heard Jimmy say.

She looked at Jimmy, who was crying too. She sat closer to Juan's body. She lifted his heavy head and set it into her lap.

"Stop it! Stop it, Juan! God damn you!" she shouted, "Come back to me. Right now!"

Jimmy knelt with her. Her thighs grew hot with Juan's blood seeping onto them. Bright red blood. She cradled his head. His dear face. His dear, high Miskito cheekbones.

Juan.

—◇◇◇—

Mal had not much memory of what happened next. In truth, she did remember, but she hated to relive it or dwell on it. Best not to.

She sat on the plane, waiting for takeoff next to an empty seat. Of course, she knew perfectly well what had happened. They had buried Juan there at the plantation where he had grown up. The uncle had appeared, having heard the shots. He was a kind man, she had thought at once, and so distraught to lose Juan. His son, he kept saying. *Mi hijo, mi hijo.* He was my son. I raised him from a boy. He was a wonderful boy. A good boy. This the uncle repeated like a mantra.

Yes, she'd thought, he must have been a kind parent to Juan. Juan had been loved, which was why he was able to love her so, if she had ever doubted it. But no, she could not stay on, she'd said. She had to leave. She had to get away. She had to put her life, broken and destroyed by this foolish revolution, back together.

After the burial everything became dreamlike. She knew that Jimmy returned with her in the uncle's private plane to

Managua. She remembered wondering, as they flew over dusky, densely forested mountains, if they were passing over Sin Nombre. She asked Jimmy. No, he smiled gently. That was in another direction.

She landed once again at the Managua Airport. She remembered her famous memoir, which she would be loath to write now. To say what? That her heart died, courtesy of the people's revolution in Nicaragua? That she hated revolution? That she hated do-gooders? That she had lived blindly in one political sham after another?

That she would go on in life to live as if this present disaster and the disaster of her dead baby had never happened to her?

Jimmy took her back to Bello Horizonte, to pack the clothes she had never worn. She hung the clothes Juan had left with hers next to those of the people who had fled earlier. "The Clothes of the Departed," she'd said to Jimmy.

They took a taxi to the airport. Jimmy saw her off. Of course, she knew that. She knew, too, that at the last minute, she must tell someone, even though she had sworn to herself never to tell anyone until Juan knew. She had to tell to put it to rest. So she could forget it and continue as if the worst had never happened to her.

She told Jimmy, because he had witnessed what she had suffered, and he had cared, and he had loved Juan, too, and especially because after this, they would never meet again. She told her secret, the horrible death of the unique life created by Juan and Mai. That she had not wanted it at first, but had taken care of it well enough, and then she had flushed it down a toilet. That she would never think of it again. It was her plan.

Sitting on the plane, waiting for takeoff, she went over the words she'd told Jimmy, words she would never forget because she knew it had really happened and believed those words with her whole heart.

I was pregnant, but I lost our baby. Juan's baby. The child might have grown up in Nicaragua, a child born of the revolution—in Sin

Nombre, perhaps. At least until Juan's political work was done. I liked it there. I was useful. The Sandinistas would have built me a house away from the lake, near the springs, near our ladies. I would have planted gardens. It might have been a boy. I never saw the fetus. I would have named him Juan. Juanito. Or, if a girl, Doris.

Know that you are the only one who will ever understand what it was like. You know the price of revolution. You said it: no revolution succeeds without bloodshed. So, Juan and I, we contributed a lot of ours. Now, good luck with it. Suerte.

And she had kissed him goodbye. And now it was over.

Fox and Crow, Inc.

Jasmina, 2001

"Fox flatters Crow's voice as it feeds in a rose-apple tree. Crow replies that it is noble to recognize another's virtue. As a reward, Crow shakes down a fruit for Fox."—Jambhu-Khadaka-Jataka

Massachusetts, June 15, 2001

CAR RIDES CALMED BABIES, SO IT SHOULD WORK FOR HER. MINA Wright started up her Lexus, her face still wet with tears. She had just stormed out on Dr. Ramos, where she'd sobbed hysterically. Tears of outrage, really. She did not need a psychiatric referral. How dare he even suggest it! Her state of mind was due to stress—to be expected with a husband at death's door. (She must stop using that expression. Richard would recover. Eventually.) She was fine. Except for that embarrassing outburst—screaming like a madwoman at one doctor she actually trusted. Her head throbbed.

Mina drove out of the town center, thick with afternoon traffic. Life got a little out of control sometimes; that's all it was. She needed some organizing. She should deep breathe on her way to Bette Palmer's to be calm when she arrived. She inhaled, counted to ten and released.

Dr. Ramos threatened to check up on her tomorrow. She didn't want that. She could head him off by calling him first, to apologize. Right now, she was late picking up Skye at Bette's. And they'd be late getting home to Richard. And she'd left her cellphone somewhere. Where? She could call Richard from Bette's. No need to panic. Or find the damned thing.

The sun was shining, but rumbles overhead meant a storm coming in, really bad news for her internal chaos. Electrified air, sudden drops in barometric pressure—what happened outside made what happened inside worse. Being the overly sensitive type, as everyone reminded her: Dr. Ramos. And Richard. Her colleagues. She needed calm before getting to Bette, *la loca* who exerted some weird, orbital force that destabilized whatever equilibrium Mina could muster—when she could—which was getting rarer. *La loca* had rattled her so many times, in fact, that Richard had ordered her to avoid Bette. She is poison for you, he'd shouted. You don't know how to handle her! That was back when he could blow his stack and breathe at the same time. His frustrations more recently deteriorated into teary despair. She missed his stern lectures, the schooling that she used to take with a smirk and a grain of salt, but which kept her on an even keel.

As she inhaled and exhaled with determination, the candy-colored clapboards and new-leafing sugar maples in Bette's neighborhood dissolved into two children frozen at the side of a dark highway, like a horror film. Mina! Stay here, she ordered herself and blinked hard to make them vanish. *Forget them. Forget Dr. Ramos. Next is Bette's street. Pick up Skye. Get home to Richard. He's waiting for you. Keep this fact straight: today is not June 15, 1969.*

Still, it was June 15, both her birthday and the anniversary of her parents' death. The image flickered but fought to stay: two children in the black of night, on the shoulder of the Garden State Parkway in a state of shock. *Leave them there. Someone will come along for them...*

The image faded in the sudden clarity of Bette Palmer's yard that popped into view a block ahead, with Bette herself standing high on a ladder underneath the branches of a pin oak, one in the row that created the property line. Mina watched Bette lurch into the lower branches with a long-handled implement to bat at suspended egg shapes blowing about in the stiff wind. Hundreds of them swung wildly like alien spawn. Like prehistoric insect pods. Like lollipops for giants. Like mop heads. Mina paused at a stop sign and counted to three. *Don't even ask her. Get Skye and leave. Stay out of her crazies.*

Closer up, she recognized it was long-handled garden clippers that Bette wielded to attack the dangling pods. Always something with that woman. Nothing better to do with her time. She had it easy compared to Mina. A roll of envy traveled through her. Mina eased into the driveway and turned off the ignition. Bette, high up on the ladder with her back to the driveway, apparently didn't hear. She kept at the attack.

Thunder growled lower; the sun blinked between passing clouds that created shafts of darkness and made Bette appear and disappear in the branches. Mina looked away, so much effort to make sense of the scene. *Neutral, mi niña,* her mother's whisper. Closing her eyes, breathing evenly, she brought the present moment into focus, noted the fragile stasis before the in-coming storm. Alas, stasis never lasted. Her eyes opened. She stared into the rearview mirror and saw bedlam staring back. Under her still watery eyes were half-mooned shadows; her black hair, short to spike up, lay flat; foundation pawed all day exposed her sallow coloring. *Be calm. Bette will climb down. Or fall down. Lunática!*

Breathing evenly at last, an unexpected well of gratitude surged inside her and overpowered the more usual envy she felt for lunatic Bette, who was generous to take Skye home with Polly at noontime. Was it an Alzheimer's symptom, she had asked Dr. Ramos, to forget early dismissal on Skye's last day of school? Her daughter had left in the morning excited about the end of first grade. Totally slipped her mind! What a mess she was. *Thank you for keeping Skye.*

The dashboard clock read five-thirty. She'd stayed politely, to hear out Dr. Ramos, all his suggestions and descriptions of the benefits of anti-depressants for times like these. His accent was a comfort. It reminded her of Juan, her brother who had never lost his Nicaraguan accent, as she had hers. Hearing those Nicaraguan intonations was a secret solace that her monolingual Richard would never comprehend. Had she made the appointment with Dr. Ramos just to hear his voice? How pathetic of her.

Busy-bee Bette, *la demente,* looked crazier up there on the ladder than Mina felt, if that was possible. Mina exhaled hard. Deep breathing was a bore. Well, TGIF—the work week was done, the school year was over. They would bumble through the summer. Richard's condition would improve. She would space out Skye's play-dates with Polly to cut down contact with Bette, to please Richard; she would get Skye into day camp even though the deadline had slipped right by her. Playing catch-up described her best these days. But she would get it all done. She had to.

Mina lowered her shoulders. At least she was no more her ten-year-old self, that little girl on the highway, Jasmina Davila. For seventeen years now (*seventeen!*) as Mrs. Richard Wright— wife, attorney and mom—she'd functioned quite appropriately, even as the orphaned Jasmina slumbered within her and awoke at the worst times. *Skye is seven. She will not be orphaned like Jasmina! Richard must make it, and so must I.*

So, what *was* it that Bette was cutting down? Socks? Were those actually *men's socks* hanging from the trees? Bette chopped one that thumped onto the ground, bounced and rolled into a large bed of dead tulips that formed a deep black apron under the pin oak. Bright white socks lay scattered here and there. She'd certainly been busy with those clippers. *Just don't ask her. She'll pull you in. Act like it's normal, like you see this every day. You still have dinner to make.*

Dinners: three different dinners still to prepare. Would Skye eat frozen pizza again? And what to make for Richard that he could keep down? Or for herself, because she wasn't hungry. Eighteen pounds lost this year, and a small universe depending on her, Dr. Ramos had reminded, as if she could forget it. He'd wagged his finger. She must keep up her health, physical and mental.

How she hated her immature behavior with him. He was a good man, but as an internist, what could he do for her? Still, he reminded her so much of Juan, his mannerisms, not just his accent. He had encouraged her to talk about her problems: her non-stop rambling, her distractedness, forgetting where she was, where she was going, who she was talking to, her impulsivity, her worries about falling apart, her frenzied, all-subjects-all-the-time chatter that irked Richard so terribly, especially her switching subjects midstream. She couldn't turn it off, did it right there—switched right on Dr. Ramos—babbling about the state of their finances morphed into her fear of insanity. So, early onset Alzheimer's?

Bette screamed. The clippers clattered downward and the ladder teetered.

Mina dashed from the car to the ladder and grabbed it with both hands before Bette lost her balance.

"My God! Bette! What *are* you doing up there?"

"Oopsie-daisy! I almost fell, didn't I? I reached out a tad too far." Bette giggled and gingerly descended.

Mina held the ladder and stood back as a dirt-creased heel just missed her face. Dr. Ramos had suppressed a chuckle. No, not Alzheimer's. Generalized anxiety because of Richard's illness; all that responsibility landing on her shoulders. Anti-depressants could even out her ups and downs.

Should she? *Dios mio, Jasmina! Wake up! Just snap out of it! Despierta! Animate!* Mina would snap out of it. Five thirty already. June 15 with its pile-ons of significance was almost over. With all her chatter, she'd totally forgotten to tell Dr. Ramos it was June 15!

"Thanks, Mina. Didn't hear you drive up. I'm cutting down these damned soaps. I cut down every one of them yesterday, but during the night, the witch hung up new ones. It's the third time this week I've done it. Just look what she does." Bette picked a sock off the ground and thrust it into Mina's face. "She sews Irish Spring soap bars into socks and ties them. With ribbon. A regular Martha Stewart. Look!" She turned the sock to show its artful packaging. "Then she strings them to the branches above my flowers. That's what's killed them. Just look at my beds! She wants me to look crazy to the neighborhood association to force us out. Would I ever put such stupid things in *my* trees? She claims the branches hang on *her* property, so she's allowed. Is that true? You're the lawyer."

Mina blanked, unable to make sense of the tirade. "I guess. What are they even for?"

"She says it protects her vegetables. She thinks deer hate the smell of Irish Spring so she makes an Irish Spring barrier to keep them out of her garden. She says I should be grateful to her for saving my garden, too. But all my flowers are deer-resistant! And she's killed them! Those socks leak soapsuds that burn the plants whenever it rains. The storm's coming, so I'm rushing. To prevent more soap dripping. I showed you my beautiful garden plans, right? Didn't I? Now everything's gone. Every beautiful tulip. Death by Irish Spring. I'm taking these damn things down!"

Bette started back up the ladder and on her way grabbed at a low-hanging sock that bobbed away like an apple in a tub of water. "Will you steady me, Mina? Just hand me my clippers."

Mina shook her head. "No time. Listen to the thunder. There will be lightning. You shouldn't be on a metal ladder. Can I use your phone to call Richard? Thanks so much for keeping Skye. Doctors are never on time ... he'd kept me there..." She heard herself rambling.

"Let's go in," Bette agreed, not budging from the ladder to study the dangling socks.

They surveyed the line of pin oaks, and Mina observed that the socks were suspended in all five trees like Christmas ornaments. They were meticulously positioned at measured distances and gradated lengths, to swing without touching. Now, the bright white shapes agitated maniacally, whipped by strong drafts as steel-colored clouds overtook the sky and flickered in the greenery—an art installation. The witch had an artist's eye.

"What will your neighbor say when she sees you've cut them again?" She barely heard her own voice in the wind. Richard's voice warned her: *"Mina! Stay out of this! Get home!"*

"Oh, who cares about her! She puts them up; I cut them down. It's been going on since February. It's what I want to talk to you about." Bette smiled down at her and began her descent.

"Richard. I must call him right away, Bette." *Just act like* la demente *is normal.*

When she'd first met Bette in the fall, when Skye had befriended Polly, the new girl in class from Texas, Bette had seemed like normalcy itself, a 1950s throwback with bouncy blond curls like Betty Crocker. But she was no Betty Crocker— far from it. Bette now reminded Mina of folks in Millville, where she'd lived with her mother's family, *Tia y Tio*, after her parents' deaths. Millville was several social rungs below Scotch Plains, where her family had lived when her father was transferred to the Nicaraguan Mission in Manhattan. Bette was just like the Millville kids with chips on their shoulders, with bad decisions spiraling into bad results, senseless and incomprehensible to her. *Tia* warned her to avoid them and emulate instead the parents she had lost. But those dead-end kids, Social Services wards, sunk in mires of unintended consequences had fascinated her. She should have told that fear to Dr. Ramos. Yes, Bette reminded her of them.

Bette took Mina's arm to walk her toward the house, saying she needed a favor. She wanted Mina to sue the witch for harassment. And trespassing. And property destruction. Those soaps killed everything. Couldn't she sue for at least one of those things? She'd let Mina decide.

"I can't get into this now, Bette. I'm late for Richard." *Such lunacy.*

"Come in. I'll get my phone." Bette kicked open the front door with a dirty toe that flashed the new summer tangerine color featured in the fashion mags in Dr. Ramos's waiting room. *Dreadful on old feet, Tia would have said.*

"Hey-ho, Jon-o!" Bette fluffed her toddler's hair as she passed him on the sofa where he watched the local news about a prostitute found strangled in a ditch. He stared on, not responding to his mother.

"Is Jon-o sick?" Mina asked. Once Mina had recommended a pre-school for Jon-o, but Bette wasn't having it. Pre-schools made kids sick. He'd bring home diseases. Mina remembered the rant. Ironically, Jon-o was usually in front of the TV looking ill. The woman was uninterested in bettering herself ... themselves ... the boy. He needed children to play with. He would be an outsider in kindergarten, without social skills. "He looks unwell to me."

Bette moved on, her mind evidently elsewhere, and Mina followed through a labyrinth of unpacked boxes, strewn clothes and toys, increasingly disoriented by the squalor. It was still a fixer-upper. The Palmers had started their renovations outdoors, tearing out the entire lawn and reseeding; planting beds and beds of flowers and tree saplings to remind them of Houston. *Such upside-down values, these people,*

"I really can't stay, Bette. Where are the girls?"

"Don't worry," Bette insisted. "I'll get the phone and the girls."

Bette had it easy as a stay-at-home mom. In that same time, Mina had been caring for Skye and Richard, dealt with insurance claims and finances, got the hospital bed installed and moved Richard downstairs. She'd interviewed several caregivers and hired an expensive day nurse so she could return to regular office hours and a restored income. Her partners had been impatient with her aborted office appearances and the lost business. She had no time for favors. She had serious problems. Bette could hire a lawyer.

She hesitated to step into the dirty kitchen where Bette had just grabbed a chicken thigh and swirled it around in a plate of raw egg. The puckered skin shiny with eggy albumen made Mina's stomach turn. Bette tried to catch the swinging U's that slipped to the floor as she tossed the chicken thigh into flour. She wiped both hands on her shirt. "My phone's upstairs. Wait here."

Mina retched at the afterimage of swinging mucus. Her eyes watered. She shifted her focus to the gutted kitchen, its surfaces covered in sheetrock dust. Nails lay scattered on the floor. Jon-o. She stooped to gather them and set them on the counter next to the chicken, the up and down movement dizzying her. This was not where she wanted to be, what she needed to do. Richard needed her. Last night he'd waved away her attempts to be helpful, rasping and heaving. He seemed weaker this month and would need physical therapy to walk again. Did insurance even cover home rehab? Another call to make, another cost to juggle till it got worked out. He needed her. Skye needed her. She had to get home. Now.

"I'll make us some coffee with cardamom." Bette was back, and handed her a sticky cell phone. She must stop this woman from assuming they were friends. Richard blamed Mina for encouraging her, sharing information about the neighborhood and the school. He didn't understand. It was how women functioned. Sharing was Gorilla Glue; sharing created the trust that came in handy later, when they needed to rely on one another without family around or nannies to help out. He didn't know all the responsibilities women shouldered.

He had rolled his eyes.

She began to dial, but stopped. *Animate, Jasmina, before she makes that goddam coffee!* The trap of cardamom. Damn! "Bette! No, don't. No time for coffee."

How stupid of her to describe the Indian coffee roasted with cardamom. Why had she ever divulged her year in an ashram? Bette was so uneducated that she thought India was in Africa. Politically, socially, culturally, Bette was so not Mina's kind of person. She was one of those others. Those coffee klatches had become a vortex of Bette's crazy complaints, toxic insanity she beamed into Mina's head, sucking her into a world of paranoia that Mina tried to fix with unheeded suggestions and recommendations.

A hot flash shot through her followed by chills. She was going to be sick. A migraine? Richard argued: moms don't have to be friends just because the girls play together. Stay away from her.

Bette dropped another chicken piece into the flour. The plop sound was riveting and a little cloud of flour floated up. Mina swallowed to suppress the retching; her eyes flowed tears.

The girls' laughter swelled from the basement that Patrick Palmer was simultaneously renovating along with the kitchen. She had been taken on the tour and shown the floor plans.

"I know you are the one to do this, Mina, to sue her. One sec. I'll be right down." She left again.

Before Mina's eyes, the girl and the boy appeared as they would appear to a passing driver in a backdrop of upturned, mangled car, nipping flames and acrid fumes. She heard Mami's screams. Moans fading under explosive hisses and pops. Papi silent. She saw the flash of the buck's head and its glassy eye staring right at her.

June 15. The anniversary had her off her game, she knew. Years later when they met again as adults in New York, Juan had given her the details he remembered, that the impact from the buck had flipped the car right over. He made her see the streak of red-brown viscosity dripping on the plate glass, its honking cries, his yanking her arm to drag her out, her cheeks scraping along the asphalt. Blood, her own; shouts, his, to get moving: "Wake up! *Animate, Jasmina! Despierta!*"

Her brother, Juan, had saved her life. She was grateful that they could piece together the accident that had redirected their lives and separated them until then. Juan had become a macho twenty-five-year-old, full of himself, but he had wept in front of her from the shame of not having saved their parents. She had comforted him: he had been but a boy. He had saved *her*. For what? she wondered now. What was good about this life she had ended up living? Only her daughter. The rest amounted to one failure after another.

She steadied herself against a post to stem the hyperventilating. She could not drive like this. She focused on Patrick Palmer's handiwork: the holes smashed through the old drywall, the beams behind it, and the silent black space. She saw stars spinning.

Bette stood before her with a sheaf of papers and a camera. "Come to the dining room. Coffee's ready."

"I really can't..."

Jon-o toddled to his mother and whined; his diaper sagged below his taut, round belly flecked with oatmeal and trails of snot. His red-rimmed eyes and damp skin looked bad. The child was not well. His nose dripped. A sour poopy odor was in his wake, the smell of illness. The sadhu smell. India. Mina's stomach churned. What to focus on?

"Go, Jon-o. Momma's busy." Bette gave him a little shove, turned and smiled at Mina. "Let's see. How are you anyway, dear? Now, first grade's done. The girls, they play so nice together. Where were we?"

Images fused of the girls playing tag, Jon-o's sagging diaper, and the brown Deccan Plateau littered with split-open sparkling geodes. Her nose wrinkled with repulsion that fought with sympathy for the child.

Bette tugged Mina's arm and led her to the dining room. Jon-o followed, whimpering.

The toddler wanted his mother, but he was disgusting. Not only smelly, but snot caked his nostrils just like the naked holy man in Udaipur with hashish-addled eyes, encircled with blue chalk, that fixated on her, the outsider. The sadhu wanted money. She had intended to help him, but she did nothing, stood stupefied as he twisted, snail-slow, into a contortion, shrinking into the size of a basketball, his privates jiggling below his balled-up body, his blank smile, his piercing eyes staring at her. She ran to a taxi stand without leaving him even a rupee. Jon-o's griminess, his bully smell of old poop and stale urine, that sadhu smell, repelled her. Her compulsion to help ran impotent every time. She failed at saving the little things. "Too sensitive," *Tia* had said, tossing in the trash her rescued fledglings and wounded strays that died. Even the bigger saves—volunteering in the workers' revolution in Cuba, joining anti-nuclear activists in New York—amounted to nothing. Even at the ashram, itself a sham of imperfect people trying to correct an even more imperfect world—she had bombed on all fronts. She'd failed to stop Juan from his impulsive romanticism. She'd argued with him to quit the Sandinistas in Nicaragua, then reversed herself to support his commitment to the grand historical moment that killed him. Her urge to protect was sentimental and self-serving, Richard claimed. He warned her to stop tampering with the impossible, and he was right. "You, Mina, are hardly the one God designated to bring justice to his failed world." The world was too complicated for a big-time fix. "Work at your level. That is enough."

She barely managed that. She had nothing inside herself anymore for puppies or sadhus, less for her immigration cases at the firm, and zilch for Bette Palmer. Richard's survival took everything she had, and she was failing at that, too. *He is not getting better!* She just had to face it. She had to steady herself.

"I must sit a minute, Bette. My head is spinning. It's the storm, the drop in air pressure. As soon as I'm okay, we'll go."

Bette sat Mina at the dining room table and placed the phone she'd requested beside her. Jon-o's whimpers turned to angry cries. He yanked at his mother's shorts, blew bubbles from his nose. Bette's eyes stayed on Mina.

"Please, let's not do this now, Bette. Your son wants you, and my husband's waiting for me. Is he really okay? Jon-o, I mean." She looked at the phone. *What are you doing? You can't call him from here.* After their last row about Bette, it would send him over the edge.

"Oh, he always wants me. He's not been very well, I guess. Nothing serious—a spring cold with a low-grade temp dragging on. Well, months. This New England climate is so changeable, colder than Texas. He'll be okay. We're all busy, Mina. And this is important to me. I need you!"

Jon-o shrieked, but Bette talked over him describing her neighbor's maliciousness.

"He needs you, Bette!" The boy and girl on the highway waiting to be saved, and no one coming. The relatives had divided responsibility for them. Juan returned to Nicaragua with their father's brother. She became an American.

The girls' laughter in the basement broke through to her.

"But you see what I mean?" Bette beamed anger at the camera she held.

Mina hadn't been listening. "Please, can you get Skye up here?" Her heart raced. She counted down its thrumming—the only useful holdover from the ashram—and pushed her hair behind her ears. Her forehead was damp. Torture, trying to leave.

Bette disappeared. When she returned she held a coffee pot, a whole cardamom nut and a grater. "I called the girls. Mina, you are so kind. You understand. Not like them around here who want us out. Jon-o! Go watch TV!"

He retreated in full wail.

Mina flinched. He needed his mother. "I'd like to help you, Bette, but I can't. Be patient. A new place takes time. Give yourself a couple of years to adjust. I moved around a lot. I know what it's like. I know India better than the States, maybe except for Ladakh, which I'll visit someday. My firm could send me..."

God help her! Rambling! Richard's voice filled her ears: *they'll fire you sooner than send you to Ladakh!* She hated how effortlessly his club of pragmatism smashed her fantasies. How well she'd internalized his reactions; hated that, too.

Bette nudged the camera closer to Mina's face. "This is what I want you to see. Look! Listen!"

Mina turned her head and half stood, but Bette pulled her by the arm back into the chair.

"Please, Mina, I know you're in a rush, but hear me out."

Bette's insistence was unbelievably irritating, but the sooner she complied, the sooner she'd be free. "What am I looking at?"

"*Evidence,* Mina. This is the *evidence* to use when you take my case."

Take her case? She was crazy. Why had everyone figured out Bette Palmer but her? Mina made her normal. Normalized everything to keep things going smoothly. It was her way. Except at work, where the immigration problems with the INS paralyzed her. She knew that her partners had modified her work to keep her from meeting clients, had her work by phone arranging visas for businesses moving abroad. They recognized her failure as a lawyer.

"My neighbor, the witch! See her with the Irish Spring? It's the evidence!" Bette stood to remove mugs from the breakfront behind them and set them on the table. She poured the coffee.

"No coffee, Bette, really. I can't do this now. Skye?"

"It's especially for you, Mina. You liked how they grind cardamom with the coffee beans in India. I do it like this." Bette grated brown flakes over Mina's coffee.

Mina sipped. The smoky, minty cardamom evoked a memory of harmony. She took another sip. The flavor on her tongue was lovely and made the present moment tremble like a mirage and dissolve into a crow, an image from an Indian children's book. The crow perched high in a rose-apple tree and considered the words of a crafty, sienna-colored fox below. The book was Mina's tattered treasure, discovered in a Calcutta bookstall, kept all these years. She had wanted to show her treasure to Dr. Katkar, Richard's specialist, who would appreciate it, but Richard had shut her down in horror. Dr. Katkar should concentrate on curing him, not on fairy tales. What was Mina thinking?

Truth was, she had loved India and its unpredictable chaos, smelly sadhus and all. There the past co-existed so smoothly with the present; the people—complex like Dr. Katkar, reasoning, teaching her endlessly, even tiresomely—had enchanted her. India had distracted her from Juan's death. But retrospection had refashioned it as another well-intentioned mistake in judgment. Since Juan's death, she felt unbearably out of place. Tasting the coffee brought India back. She imagined herself as the crow. Trust the fox? Listen to his wily story? Bette and she were both displaced people. She cradled her cup and inhaled the rising steam. Her eyes filled with tears.

Out of nowhere, Skye and Polly dashed through the dining room in chase, shouting and laughing. For seven-year-olds, friendship was so easy, motivated by a mutual need to expend energy and not much more. Up the stairs they thundered, before Mina could call out. She stood up, but Bette pulled her back.

"They'll be back. Drink up. Tell me you'll do it. I filmed it with you in mind. And I kept records, too. I go out in the rain to measure how deep the soap suds are. I photograph my plants as they die. And I save the dead ones. Look here. This part. You see?" Bette pointed at the screen. "I filmed the witch in action!"

The shot was from below, perhaps from a basement window, aimed at a long view of the trees and soaps dangling down the property line, then a zoom across Bette's dead flower beds. Yes, it was odd that her tulips had died ahead of the tulips blooming all over town, but tulips had a notoriously short life, gone before you knew it. Bette may have planted her bulbs too early, thinking spring in Massachusetts arrived on Houston time.

A woman's legs walked into the frame. The camera moved up to her arms that cradled a box and a colander filled with bars of soap. She set the colander down under a spigot and drenched the soaps with water. Then she opened the box and judiciously poured white powder over the bars. Mina noticed writing on the box. The woman inserted each sticky, coated bar of soap into a sock from a hamper by the spigot. The film ended.

"See? Proof! She's out to kill my flowers. When I told her to stop, she called me a crazy Hoosier. I don't even know what that is! My film is evidence." Bette's eyes shone. "I want to take her to court. Did you hear her? 'Stupid lady,' she says."

"Not really, Bette. It's unclear. Anyway, you can't prove it's *you* she is talking about."

"It *is* me! This is my evidence. I need a lawyer. You! What do you say?"

"I say you don't need a lawyer. Just go talk to her. Explain that you both got off on the wrong foot. Work out a plan to your mutual satisfaction. Don't discuss who first did what. You're going to live side by side for the foreseeable future. You don't want the hard feelings to continue that a lawsuit would bring. Anyway, how would you ever prove damages? Your flowers died. That's what flowers do. No one was hurt."

Bette's eyes flashed. "They didn't just die! They got a black burn on the leaves after the rain—from the suds—and *then* they died. It's too late for talk. She went too far. Now she's telling the neighbors to stay away from me. Now *all of them* stare at me, and they avoid Polly at the bus stop by waiting across the street with their children and cross only when it comes. They harass us, and they have no right! I see the neighbors the whole day long behind their curtains peeking at us. Their kids tell Polly on the bus that her mom is a crazy Hoosier. That damages my Polly, if it's damages you want, Mina. You know the law. Please, help me?"

Mina sank. "Bette, mine is immigration law. And Polly is not emotionally scarred. She's not on anxiety medication. They are within their rights. It's a free country with free speech. People can look out their windows whenever, say what they want, stand where they choose. Harassment on the bus—that's a school issue. Get the school to address it. Anyway, you wouldn't want to drag Polly into court; you'd have to, by bringing Polly into it. No one wants that for their kids. You have good reasons to talk it out. You filmed her preparing her soap, but that doesn't show intent to kill your plants. I see no case here, Bette. Just go over and make nice. End the fighting."

"But the witch put them up to name calling. Where did they learn that word, Hoosiers? Who will help me if not you?"

"Not me. The police?"

"Oh, I've already been! Went and emptied a big old trash-bag full of my poor, dead tulips—the whole mess—right onto the officer's desk. That got their attention. But they said I needed more evidence than dead tulips. I should go to some judicial court. But I can't. I'm no good with words. I don't have a fancy education. So I filmed her. For you."

Mina knew the town's detectives. She imagined their reaction to a mound of putrid tulips at their front desk, Bette's outrage, her arms akimbo. The police clearly saw no case. They had deflected. They probably even knew the town word on Bette Palmer. Mina had heard it.

People made fun of her bare feet and lax child-rearing.

Mina had stood up for Bette a few times because she was a new arrival. Mina knew about moving to a new school, a new community. She knew the gossip mills that spewed outlandish speculations about the kid who looked and spoke funny. Little orphaned Jasmina had gone to live with an ancient aunt and uncle who never cared about assimilation. She sympathized. Would neighbors really try to drive out the Palmers? More likely this was Bette burning bridges.

Polly and Skye thundered down the stairs, breathless, and stood before their mothers in high hysterics.

"Let's go, Skye! Polly, so nice of you to invite Skye. Skye, say thank-you to Mrs. Palmer. Off we go! Dad's waiting."

"My shoes!" The girls scrambled back up the stairs together in giggles.

Bette touched Mina's arm. "I am so lucky to know you. You are educated. Please. I trust you. You are a true friend."

A true friend? Mina smiled weakly, hoping her smile communicated nothing of her ambivalence.

"We had fun, Mom!"

Mina backed out of Bette's driveway into the storm in full roar. Thunder cracked in rolls, one after another. Lightning spotlighted the road with ashen light. The wind was up; sheets of water pounded the windshield. Mina had difficulty seeing the curb, flooded with storm drain choke. The yellow street lines had disappeared under a lake of water. She would get them home, safely. She hated driving. She worried about accidents.

"Polly is nice. Her mom ... she is so weird! All the kids say it. She gave us chocolate bars for lunch. I'm hungry. Do we have to go home? Can't we eat out, you know, to celebrate the last day of school?"

Mina squelched an impulse to lecture Skye about meanness and gossip and considered instead her proposal. Why not? Both had cause for celebration and she would avoid preparing three dinners, birthday gift enough—and have time with her daughter who got so little of her attention these days. Skye's seven-year-old perspective, all friendship bracelets and boy bands, was good medicine. "Let's check on Daddy first."

They chatted all the way home. Mina felt better. The storm began to drift away. She let Skye out by the mailbox. Getting rained on was fun to Skye. Mina drove into the garage and in the rearview mirror she watched Skye's blurred image, her mouth uplifted to catch raindrops. A faint strike of lightning zigzagged overhead, but the boom that followed a minute later sounded regretful. She sighed. The storm was fitful, a tantrum. It had exhausted her. She entered the house through the garage and went directly to Richard's darkened room. She closed the blinds against the tapping on the panes. The storm was heading toward the coast. She thought of Bette's garden. Was she out there at this moment measuring the suds level?

Richard slept deeply. Good she hadn't called and wakened him. She sat on the edge of his bed and studied his sweat-beaded face. He had aged so. His hair had thinned. His breathing was erratic. He exhaled in rasps. Oh Richard! She loved him and wanted him well again, back in their marriage that so often was their mutual chore. She blamed herself for the conflicts, fearing she had married him under false pretenses, pretending to be a rational sort, a woman with a plan, a woman like Juan's girlfriend, Mallory. Seventeen years of marriage had worn them to the bedrock of who they were. She was exposed as hypersensitive and impulsive. He was cautious, short on imagination. They loved each other anyway.

She took his cool hand in hers. How many more years would they have together? Seventeen years already, since she'd walked past that Boston coffeehouse and caught sight of him through the window as he strummed his guitar under a spotlight that burnished his shoulder-length hair blue. She'd gone inside. He was beautiful and earnest, singing an original folksong. He looked so *together*—the word they used then to describe the self-directed. He had an aura of certainty. She saw him, wanted him, suspected even in that moment it was a terrible mismatch.

By their second married year, his intolerance for her boomerang emotions made for constant friction. So many secrets she was forced to withhold from Richard's intolerance, dreading loss of his respect, even abandonment if she'd shocked him enough. He would never know that she had earned airfare to India by exotic dancing in the harbor area and posing nude for a photographer—or about the threesome she'd once been involved in. She had lacked a center until she met him, lacked an internal compass. Under the hand of *Tia y Tío*'s punishments, her parents' wisdom had faded. The foster parents lacked imagination about her bad behaviors. Their influence had given way to the allure of Group, the commune's realpolitik, which evaporated completely in the ashram blur of hashish and sex for world peace. She returned to America with belief in nothing. Finding Richard, she had put her faith in him. Once he had his law degree, he pushed her into LSATs, aiming for logic and a fallback should something happen to him. How prescient.

If dead flowers were Bette's greatest worry, then Bette surely lived the good life.

"Who are the Palmers connected to?" Richard had demanded after she told him that she had ranted in frustration to Bette about Richard's epidemiologist, Dr. Katkar, called him a "total stupid-head" using a phrase of Skye's.

"For God's sake, Mina! This town is a fishbowl. Bad-mouthing gets around."

Lucky for her then that Bette was the town pariah, she'd shot back. Bette had no friends. Her rants were safe.

Today she'd treated poor Dr. Ramos to her Dr. Katkar tirade about his damned non-diagnosis. Dr. Ramos patted her shoulder and advised a second opinion. She screamed, Stop patronizing! Too late for second opinions! It is obviously an extreme case of Lyme. Dr. Katkar fears a lawsuit from Richard, because he is an attorney.

Richard barely responded to antibiotics now, had worsened and weakened. He breathed with a ventilator, half paralyzed. Just get him better, you stupid-head!

Such an embarrassment in front of Dr. Ramos. One more in a lifetime of embarrassments, outbursts and poor judgments kept from Richard. Everyone made mistakes best forgotten, but she could not help mulling over her worst ones. It was a terrible habit. If not early onset Alzheimer's, Dr. Ramos, what about Obsessive Compulsive Disorder?

Last night Richard had broken down and openly sobbed, "What will happen to my family? I'm dying, and I worry about your security when I'm gone. It scares me that you can't manage it!"

His gasps for air as he voiced their mutual fear had terrified her. Some words should never be uttered. No one returned from crossing the Rubicon of words. She didn't trust words.

She grazed his cheek lightly with the back of her hand and said his name. If he awoke, she wanted to tell him today's date, June 15, her hardest day of the year. He would understand.

Richard's eyelids fluttered; they opened and he focused. He smiled at her. "Hey, sweetness. I felt you were here with me," he rasped. "I'm glad you're home." He closed his eyes and drifted away.

She'd leave him a note and take her daughter out for a quick supper at the chain restaurant in the mall. No need to talk. That would do fine for her birthday and Skye's last-day-of-school celebrations.

———

"Earth to Mommy!" Skye's frustrated tone jolted her. Waiting for their dinners to arrive, Skye had gobbled both complimentary biscuits and was coloring the kids' placemat and filling in the puzzles. "You have that scary look in your eyes." Her daughter was blunt, like her father. "You aren't looking at anything. You just stare. You're like a zombie, Mom! You creep me out."

Mina apologized and scrambled to remember Skye's question. "Ask me again," she said, not really willing to give up her thoughts. She had been mulling over the image of the children on the road that haunted her, and her question to Dr. Ramos: how could she see them head on, as if through the driver's eyes, when she was one, and Juan was the other? What was wrong with her? she'd asked. Nothing, he'd said. She had probably constructed the image based on Juan's description, imagined them, not seen them, to make sense of the tragedy. It would have been Juan who had noticed the white Oldsmobile with the tail-fins, a 1957 model. Such details a boy would notice. She had no memory of being in the back seat as the car flipped and fell, or the conversation in the car before it happened. Trauma had wiped it out, he said. Maybe that's a good thing.

She knew it wasn't. And trauma? Or pure rage, monumental rage, directed at the driver who had abandoned them at the side of the road with the smoldering mess behind them. Eventually, the police came.

Dr. Ramos had sympathized. "So many abandonments for you, Jasmina, but perhaps, that driver sped away quickly to get help?" Who would ever know? Let it go, he had said.

It's impossible, she had whispered. Juan had become another abandonment, another loss with no farewell. His death occurred years later, in Nicaragua fighting for the revolution with Mallory. If their father had been alive, he would have flown down and dragged him back by the ear. Her life was a checkerboard of black and white holes, she had told Dr. Ramos, with another black hole, edgeless, bottomless, looming: Richard. Was he the next one to leave her?

It was still June 15, the thirty-two years since her parents' deaths heightened by Skye's last school day and her own forty-second birthday. Skye's unplanned summer yawning ahead, still to arrange, her needs always on the back burner. No plan for Skye was a terrible plan. Chaos reigned omnipotent, with neither a spare minute for Skye nor a spare penny. Next summer had to be better. Next summer, Richard would be well. They'd have two incomes again. That damned Katkar! Not even a diagnosis. "*El tonto!*" Her mother's shrillness pierced her brain. She hadn't dared tell Dr. Ramos about her aural hallucinations. Did he have medications for that, too?

She concentrated on Skye's puzzle, pretending to be stymied when in fact she hadn't listened. Skye, not fooled, was accustomed to her mental absence, Mina knew.

Fifteen. What a number! Fifteen was another word for sorrow.

The next morning, pleased with her success at enrolling Skye in the day camp after the deadline, Mina relaxed at her desk at Herron, Lockheed and Davila Immigration Attorneys and reviewed the events of the preceding day. The Girls' Night Out with Skye had been fun once she focused. She had just left her message of chirpy well-being with Dr. Ramos's service. She wondered about Bette: was there anything to it, a due process for her? If Bette knew of Mina's failings as a lawyer, she never would have asked for her help. For Mina, there were a million sides to a conflict, making application of the law constrictive and suffocating.

Her partners were arriving. She would check with them, and if they saw nothing she would coach Bette to represent herself at the town council that mediated neighborly disputes, a fair exchange for taking Skye so often. The crow and the fox: an attempt at understanding the other. Finding rules to live by. Wasn't that the law, too?

She flipped the pages of a legal pad and her unfinished work notes without interest. How better suited she would be to her fantasy job, collecting children's books, owning a children's bookstore. Library science and business courses were all it would take to get a background. The town community college, a BU extension, offered them. She had looked into it once, but Richard had shot it down just by asking if she had analyzed the financials of changing careers. No she had not, and had not a clue what that even meant. He banished her idea to Fantasyland.

Even so, she kept the hope in the form of Skye's picture books stored in moisture-proof boxes in the basement, unwilling to give up. She had a gift for understanding the unique communication in children's books. Stories, yes, but illustrated with pictures that embellished the words with secret meanings. She empathized with the stories, interpreted the universal messages—Uncle Elephant, for example. Dr. Ramos was for her an Uncle Elephant who told stories to an elephant child whose elephant parents had drowned at sea. At the end, the parents miraculously returned. Or Alexander. She could be Alexander, a small mouse in a big world with a wind-up mouse friend named Willie. Her Richard.

She loved the physicality of those books she had bought for Skye, some too tall for the shelves, others miniature jewels she kept in Skye's little shoeboxes. There were colors and textures that embellished the pages that she wished she had invented, random shapes discovered in marbleized paper turned into creatures, enhanced with penned curlicues.

In contrast the law was hard, precise words: talking, persuading, convincing so as to prevent deportations, and doing what seemed so obvious to her, keeping families together. Her only argument before the local immigration court over the years was that people found themselves in the wrong place and needed to be elsewhere to be together, an argument she had exhausted. Relocating families to India for businesses was monotonous. Bette's situation was different, and what if taking it on could bring additional income to her family? It would infuriate Richard if she should even consider it, but he need never know; one more secret wouldn't hurt. She picked up the phone and dialed Bette's number. Could she stop by during lunch to discuss her request?

"I knew you would help me, Mina! Don't worry. I can pay you very well," Bette said as she opened the door without a hello. "I have my own little stash that Patrick doesn't know about. It's from when I worked at a gardening center. Do I pay you now?"

"No, no," Mina assured her and made her way to the dining room table where she cleared a space of dirty, breakfast dishes for her notepad. "It would be on a contingency. If we won a settlement, my firm would collect one third. You'd get the rest." That was fine. Bette was not in it for the money, but for justice.

Jon-o lay listlessly on the sofa in front of the TV.

"He looks worse than yesterday. In fact, he looks terrible. Don't you see it?"

"Just a fever," Bette said. "And this morning, Polly has the fever again, too, and the same runny nose and the cough. She's upstairs in bed. A spring cold. That's all. It's the New England climate."

Mina heard Polly hacking upstairs, sounding more serious than a spring cold.

She explained that before she agreed, she needed to know more. Then she could determine what the charge was, and against whom; what was their evidence and how she would obtain it. "Let's see that film again."

Bette handed her the camera from the breakfront. She left to make the coffee with cardamom.

Mina scrutinized the frames, found and zoomed the one with the box under the woman's arm. She could read the black, block letters. Ammonium Benzoate. Pleased to note the iconic skull and crossbones, she guessed that the writing block below it contained precautionary statements. Mina wanted some soaps to take back with her, to find out what they had been covered with. "Because it's not just Irish Spring soap, Bette. She sprinkled them with ammonium benzoate. I need to find out what that is."

"I'll ask her," Bette said.

No! Bette was to do nothing and leave everything to Mina.

Mina wondered if this could be a toxicity case. She knew from her anti-nuclear days in the commune about radioactive gases settling on farmland and the disputes about emissions from nuclear power plants. Arguments about Strontium-90 and Cesium-137; the Three Mile Island spill and government studies. There were so many emissions back then—and few protections and safeguards, everything whitewashed—they had argued and demonstrated about. It had been exciting and shocking when her group secretly and illegally measured the gas components that daily exceeded what was claimed to be safe. They had been outraged that a whole nation could be hoodwinked so smoothly. Toxicity was serious. She knew about cancer rates and genes damaged by radioactivity. And what about the commune's measuring activities? In retrospect, she wondered if they had endangered themselves, being young and believing in their immunity to danger. But one of them, Kleio, she had heard, had gotten cancer. Did anyone ever make a connection to exposure from their research activities? Mina shivered and looked at Jon-o lying in a listless daze. Connections were difficult to prove. A million things made people sick. It was not easy to prove. She knew all the defenses.

"Bette, you must do one thing for me. Take the kids to your pediatrician and get a diagnosis for their ailments. You must insist on a blood analysis to rule out or in what is in their blood. Tell about the renovation going on and your concern about the dust in the kitchen. Have them tested for allergies, too. I will want the report."

"Oh my Lord, no!" Was Mina saying Patrick had caused their spring colds?

"I have no idea, but let's learn all we can and get them well. Months are too long for a fever, and he looks worse to me. Maybe Richard's situation influences me, but let's know for sure about your kids."

She left with Bette's promise not to talk to the neighbors, to take her kids to the doctor, get them tested, and obtain a written diagnosis. Get them well.

Driving back, she began to expand her strategy. A suit was her goal. The soaps Bette had extracted from the trash could be tested at the college. She would research the chemical company for previous settlements. She shouldn't forget Bette's homeowner's insurance. She would get the drinking water tested and a soil test, too. She needed experts for backup. There was Patrick's renovation. She had to know what was in their house dust.

She would involve her partners, and hoped they wouldn't laugh at her. She knew other lawyers to consult. If her findings implied a connection between the children's illness and the chemical compound in deer repellent or even sheet rock dust, she would communicate it to the manufacturers. Laws could change. Settlement was good. At the least, Bette's house would get a good cleaning, its water would be certified potable, and she would have made the children safe. Only good could come from an exploration.

With her share of proceeds, she could cover a stay at the Mayo Clinic for Richard and invest in Skye's future tuition. And for herself, a children's bookstore could become a reality someday in Boston, maybe on Newbury Street. *Fox and Crow, Inc. Jasmina Davila, Bookseller.* She felt energized; maybe she could save her family, save Bette's family and countless others if that stuff was toxic. She would save herself.

At day's end Mina picked up Skye from the Y. Skye had found friends there, and the next week was a trip to a water park. Cool, right? Mina hugged her. Their happiness matched exactly.

At the driveway Mina let Skye out for the mail and watched her in the rearview mirror. How quickly children adapted to catastrophe. If Skye thought ahead or feared her daddy's death, she did not voice it: she was her mother's daughter. Normalizing...

Inside, Richard was awake. His temperature was normal for the first time in weeks. He was hungry. She proposed a family picnic at his bedside to cheer him. Cheer them. But he preferred the quiet, eating alone with his breathing apparatus.

Mina studied the refrigerator contents, stifling rejection because Richard preferred to be alone, hoping anyway that she had witnessed signs of improvement. One step at a time. What mattered now was that he felt hungry.

Skye wanted to help make supper for her father. Mina agreed. Dinner. "Great idea to help, Skye. Daddy will like that. Let's heat him a little soup now, and you can bring it to him." She microwaved a frozen organic soup and helped Skye prepare a tray.

"I used to cook with my mom, too. It was fun. Remember those Nicaraguan recipes I had? Let's make our own dinner together, too, like we used to. It won't be hard." Mina set a footstool at the sink so that Skye could wash lettuce leaves and carrots for a salad. She pulled another package from the freezer to microwave. She saw Bette in her mind, cheerfully flinging chicken into flour for frying in her dirty kitchen, surrounded by dust and nails, happily anticipating the return of Patrick and the family being together. She sighed. At her core, Bette could handle things; she could juggle. She was generous at heart, taking Skye home so often throughout the spring. "Work late if you need to, Mina. I'll feed her and keep her till you're ready." There was grace in that. She had been too hard on Bette, not really *loca*, just in need of company. She looked over to Skye, who was happy splattering water on the lettuce and on herself. "Like this, Mom?" Skye seemed content. It had been a long time since they had collaborated. That was Gorilla Glue, too.

Even though Mina just microwaved frozen lasagna, having Skye help her make dinner felt good. She stopped to demonstrate how to shred the lettuce and hold the grater for the carrots. She had loved cooking side by side with Mami, never doubting then that someday, she would become her mother: efficient, knowledgeable and very Nicaraguan. Shredding cabbage, chopping yucca and herbs, handing her the utensils she requested, washing out a bowl, fetching from the refrigerator, gestures reinforcing their connectedness. They'd made *vigarón* with *chicharrone*s, and for special occasions, the rum cake topped with custard. *Pio Quinto* it was called. She wanted to teach these to Skye in the same way, to help her know her heritage. Would there ever be two hours free to cook together like that? Who had that kind of time anymore, and wasn't Skye exclusively American like Daddy, caught up in electronic games and movies?

It had been a time of closeness, when her mother talked only to her, telling tales of Nicaragua and stories of Mina's own childhood in Bluefields and Corn Island. Mami had described her *Quince,* the party for girls at fifteen, the guests, their party dresses, and what they'd done. She'd said, "The time will come, my Jasmina, *mi niña,* when I will make for you a *Quince!* You will look so beautiful! You will be so happy!" Of course, it never happened, but she felt again her mother's delight to launch her daughter into adulthood and into her future. It was what a mother did, because in the daughter the mother saw a second future. And with that thought, holding the grater for Skye to push on the carrot while the microwave buzzed that the lasagna was ready, another picture came to Mina's mind: inside the car before the crash.

She stood still and let it form. She listened.

Skye shredded lettuce into the bowl, dropping leaves and water on the floor.

Mina heard her Papi's voice from the front seat telling Juan, who sat in the back with her, that he wanted to send Juan to a military academy, to make him better disciplined. He worried about Juan's impulsiveness. Yes. That had been the subject. And Juan got angry. Papi's voice grew stern at being crossed. It was dark. Few vehicles approached from the opposite direction with headlights that flashed light across the back seat. It had been raining earlier, leaving veils of fog. There were pauses and silences, breathing and fidgeting. Juan next to her mumbled, afraid to say too loud his rebellious words, but Mina heard him clearly. Mina was used to their arguing, as it occurred predictably now, Juan's automatic opposition to Papi's pronouncements. Mami spoke up, her voice high-pitched and anxious. Mina watched the contours of her parents' heads in front of her conversing in Spanish. Papi kept watch not to miss the overhead exit sign, Mami agitated. Mami did not like this new conflict between husband and son. She said so. She wanted Juan to understand that the boarding school was what the other parents at the Mission were doing, sending their kids to schools in the countryside where they could mature in a good way. Even Mina needed an extra polish, she laughed. Maybe Mina would go to boarding school too, in a few years. It proved their trust in their children and was meant as a gift of independence. Mina bounced up and down in the back seat, straining at her seatbelt. "I will go now! When do I leave?" At ten, what an adventure! Juan sat in stony silence.

There it was: the last conversation. It had been about the children's future, and had come to her intact. A wave of euphoria warmed Mina. She gave Skye a spontaneous hug and a kiss. She removed the lasagna. Richard would know how important this was to her, to remember. They had discussed their daughter's need to know more than their homogeneous neighborhood, even sending her to Nicaragua, but the politics were still too problematic. An opportunity had arisen to send Skye to England to stay for a few weeks with Mallory and attend an international art program. It would have been this summer but for Richard's situation.

Mina told Skye to set the table while she went to Daddy. She was excited that she could actually *see* them in the car, could *hear* the conversation; a memory tucked away all these years had found a way out, without explanation.

Richard was asleep. The soup Skye had brought to him was untouched and gelatinous. He appeared more translucent than yesterday, a setback. Wellness did not march in a straight line, she told herself. His blue veins pulsed in struggle; his breath was labored. His brow and hair were damp again. Fever. He appeared to have shrunk since earlier. She collected his dishes, adjusted his covers. He needed medication. Forget the past and accept the truth: the man she loved was dying before her eyes. She depended on him, and he was leaving her. She longed to kiss him, hold him and be held. She really needed holding. Did he, she wondered? Or was he past caring? She left him.

As she and Skye ate lasagna and salad, she clung to her new memory through the half-heard conversations with Skye, so that in her mind she could repeat Mami's words, Papi's, Juan's, her own. She tried to re-live the mood, to recapture every second, wished she could entrust it to someone in case it vanished again.

After dinner, Skye went upstairs for a bath and Mina sorted through the mail still lying on the floor by the front door. The only envelope not bill-shaped was birthday-card shaped. The English stamps said "Mallory." Mina ripped it open to read the long hand-written note about Mal's latest activities, the bank, spring skiing in Cortona, an old joke about her growing cache of estate diamonds—such cavernous difference in their lives. And she would be in Boston in two weeks. She hoped they might meet on the weekend. They had last seen each other when Mina was newly married and Skye was yet to be born. Mal hoped to meet her almost-niece, at last. Mina always had appreciated Mal's assumption that she was the almost-aunt and that Skye was the almost-niece, annually reinforced with presents, cards and photographs for Skye—Mallory's way of holding onto Juan's memory. Skye looked forward to the arrival of overseas gifts from the aunt whom only Mom knew and likened to a fairy godmother who sparkled with lots of diamonds.

Mina took the note up to the bathroom and sat on the side of the tub. Skye had several plastic dogs in the tub with her and was pretending they lived in a kennel on an island, her knee. They had persistent accidents and fell into the lake of bubbles, but Skye saved them with all the high-pitched, attendant noises of distress and relief to be saved. "Oh no! Here I am, you poor doggie! Don't worry. I'll save you..." One after another they fell in, some sinking to the bottom, all saved to fall in again.

"Listen to this, Skye, from your Aunt Mallory. You remember, you almost went to the art camp in England this summer and Aunt Mallory was going to take care of you there? Well, she's coming to visit us instead. She especially wants to meet you."

Skye's dogs continued their plops into the sea silently as Skye listened with interest.

Mina went on to describe the apartment in Manhattan where she lived with Aunt Mallory when she was in college and what the roommates did together. She said they had various projects, learning about revolutions in Latin America, studying women's rights. They shared everything, even researching nuclear power plants to let people know about the dangers to their health. Of course, she omitted the dubious networking among the many fringe groups operating in Manhattan and their illegal activities, cutting holes in fences to sneak onto government properties to take air samples at various nuclear power plants. Skye was too young to make sense of it. They were helping people, she said, trying to make it sound like Skye's volunteer work on Martin Luther King Day, because some power plants were poisoning the air, the water and the farmlands with chemicals and people had to know.

"Great, Mom. Let me know when she's here." A favorite program was about to start. She had to get out of the tub now.

Rambling again: the urge to talk, to tell about something that mattered to her, Mina. About herself and who she was. Even Skye noticed. Mina went downstairs to clean up, reflecting on people and events she hadn't remembered in years. What had become of everyone? Paco, her old crush—where was he now? Were the radicals still radical, or had their left-wing politics modified? Had hers? There was that deer repellent. Lying to the public was still illegal and had to be called out.

After she loaded the dishes, Mina checked again on Richard, hoping he was awake. She found him sleeping still, as labored as before. She needed him; her friend, her audience, her mentor. He was her everything. She was lonely for him. And she was scared for him. How their lives had changed. They used to talk. He knew about her communal life-style in Group, the sleeping around, Paco, the pot smoking, her Cuban *brigadista* stint, and her idolizing of Fidel Castro and Che. He knew of that year when she had rediscovered her brother and had the camaraderie of politically sympathetic friends. She had belonged somewhere. He knew that after Juan's death she had traveled around India with the Hari Krishnas, lived in an ashram. He admired her courage and fearlessness, but there was more he had disapproved, communicated through condescension. Richard blamed her misjudgments on Juan, who had introduced Mina to the Maoist-inspired group in the first place. He pronounced their pro-Sandinista, anti-government politics inherently dangerous and extreme. He claimed she had an unnatural attraction to danger that ultimately made her complicit in Juan's death. Danger attracted them both—a family flaw, moths to flame. He was glad she had given it all up—for this, she thought. Now she was tied to a small New England town with a needy daughter, a dying husband, shaky finances and her usual dithering anxieties. An imperfect life, built on the ashes of her mistakes and her grief. She longed to see Mal again. She so needed a friend these days.

~~~

"You brought the sun with you!" Mina exclaimed, delighting in the warmth on her face. It was a sun-burst day, and they were at the neighborhood pool to avoid the hospital ward ambiance of her home. Mina and Mal sat in lounge chairs. Skye was swimming with her friends. When Mal had arrived, Mina let her pop in for only a minute to greet Richard. She knew that his withered state shocked visitors, and she feared it would cast a pall on the visit, as she noted the sober change in Mal's mood. She had introduced Skye, and Mal enveloped her with a big hug and asked her lots of questions, suitably on Skye's level, and had put the child at ease. She had come with gifts for Skye: boxes of English candies, a Wedgwood blue bowl just for Skye's treasures, a small metal Christmas tree with ceramic miniatures of toys and decorations attached to the branches—objects she claimed Skye would still enjoy as she grew older—a soft blue cardigan with Scotties knitted into it, and a large fluffy stuffed cat with a blue collar and a bell. Everything blue, she'd exclaimed, to match her name. Skye was entranced. Someday, she said, Skye would come to England to visit her, and they would go round to see where the queen lived and travel about to the many beautiful places. This was Mal's old way, using words and deeds and enthusiasm to seduce you into her world and her ideas. She hadn't changed, Mina noted. Skye was sold. Can I? Can I, Mom? She hopped up and down.

As they sat by the pool, Mina still absorbed her astonishment at Mal's changed appearance, trying to reconcile the trim dowager-type who had appeared at the door with the spitfire beauty Mal had been and had remained in Mina's mind. Mal's wild mane of hair, which had been a billow of tangles and curls and a shock of premature white, was today carefully coiffed, and at last its color was consonant with the lines in her face. Still, much was the same: her House of Lords English, crisp as Mina remembered, her curiosity, her birdlike intensity, her verve were intact.

Sitting together again had an awkwardness to it that made Mina squirm. Listening to Mal chat about the satisfaction of renewing the friendships that meant so much to her back when they lived together in New York, she thought: this is Mal making bridges, finding commonalities among disparate people. It must be why she was so successful at her work for the British government. She *tried*. Mal reminded her about Gwen—whom she saw regularly, because Gwen went often to Europe—and told her about Kleio, who had suffered a bout with cancer but with whom, unfortunately, Mal had lost touch. She lived now somewhere in Greece. How wonderful it was to see Mina again and, finally, to meet her darling Skye.

They watched Skye and her friends splashing about. The boys leapt in like penguins, Mal remarked, one behind the other, imperfect fancy jumps intended to impress the girls, she was certain.

Mina said that Skye was coping admirably with her daddy's illness. Her main activity was playing for the summer, easily facilitated by her outgoing personality and her popularity. She was a lot like Juan, Mina noted. People were automatically attracted to her daughter, as they had been to her charismatic brother.

"I see," Mal said. "But my word, Mina, Skye is also stunning. Those red locks come from Richard's side, I suppose, and the ringlets, too? But those Miskito cheekbones are pure you—from the Davila side. I recognize Juan's features in her. I'd love for you to send her over to me some day. I would fancy having her. I would play auntie of the fairy godmother variety. She seems so bright and friendly. If it would provide some relief for a few weeks, during this difficult time with Richard, to have her come to me, I would willingly have her. Enroll her in that summer program, as we had discussed. She is artistic. She might enjoy the change. Tell me more about this little person, our Skye Consuelo Wright. What are her interests? How do you see her future?"

Mina started. She had not thought about her daughter's future past the weekend. To get through each day required planning enough. She knew she would never send Skye to England at seven years of age with her father on the brink! "Such a lovely idea, Mal, but now is not the time. As for her interests, well, she's so young still. Nothing stands out—the usual interests for her age. And her future? The conventional steps, I would imagine—not how we had operated back in the day, by casting aside the traditional roles. Skye will become quite a conventional young woman, I hope."

Such a question! Plans for Skye's future? How little Mal understood about parenting. Plotting a child's future was pointless, because nothing ever emerged as anyone wanted. Parents were ever adjusting, ever revising the present moment. The question irritated her beyond measure. Mal had no idea about children. She was a woman without responsibility: a void—husbandless and childless. How could a single life in middle age be otherwise? She would not lend her daughter as a surrogate! Pure Mal, assuming everyone wanted what she wanted. Everything from her own perspective, unable to put herself in the other's shoes.

"Skye has a regular American life. It's all I want," she added, somewhat sharply, then embarrassed, said: "You realize, Mal, the anxiety you've just raised by mentioning the future?"

Mal apologized.

Mina said no need. With Richard's illness, she did think about their futures, but in terms of what would happen if they lost him. It was so difficult, so many unknowns. "Richard. He's just not improving, Mal." They would test to confirm it as late-stage Lyme disease. His symptoms mimicked other illnesses. "It's taken a long time to be sure. Meanwhile, his immune system is shot to hell, so we've been waiting for his T-cells to increase to do more. I'm worried. Lyme can be fatal. Time is our enemy. I realize I might lose him, that our home is actually a long, slow hospice. I should be strong, but you know me. It's not like me to be strong."

"Really? Mina, you were our strongest one! You were so determined, so obstinate. So much like your brother." Mal said she hadn't realized the seriousness of Richard's situation until she saw him, pale and weak. Should she stay on? She was willing to, if Mina wanted her. They needed to do things for one another. Their friendship went way back, like family. "How difficult for you, on your own with this, and with a young child, too."

A kind offer, but there was no need to stay, Mina assured her. "I'm ready for what comes, as much as one ever is."

Yes, Mal agreed. "Death is a given, isn't it? It should be seen like that, as part of life. How I've tried to accept it myself. You and I, we went through a lot, and we emerged bruised, but alive. Chance played a large part in our survival, and here we are."

Mina disliked Mal putting them on a par. "But Mallory! You've not been through anything like what I have! Losing my parents, my brother! Now my husband is at death's door—to use an unfortunate phrase."

"I do not diminish your situation, Mina. No, I did not suffer exactly as you. But there were catastrophic events which bear no discussion now, but which were devastating, shattering to me. Let us say that endings equalize everyone. Endings bring us loss and grief, fairly unavoidable. It makes everyone more the same than different. In that sense, we are all one of a piece, are we not?"

Mina apologized. Yes of course, she said. She was hardly unique. She reached over and took Mal's hand. "I'm sorry to be so self-centered, overly preoccupied with my problems."

They knew one another in such a very old way, as temperamentally different siblings knew and accepted each other and felt a bond. There was no ill will between them; there was the glue. "You know, I do love you, Mallory. I do regret we weren't ever in-laws to keep us more connected over these years."

Mallory smiled, said how she too regretted it.

"It's Richard really needing the support. He sees death coming. *There* is anger! *There* is grief, to be helpless in the face of it. My heart breaks for him. I can't fix it. I make plans for living both without and with him. I have Skye." She described the worries and vacillations she had articulated that anniversary day to Dr. Ramos, followed by her decision to help Bette, reminding her of their old anti-nuclear days, a scheme she had hidden from Richard.

"But I should say, Mina, you came out of those sad events strengthened. You married Richard. You have Skye. Your legal practice. A good life. Your ups and down are understandable, and look, you have a plan to go ahead. Remember how angry you were when I was here last, complaining that Richard bullied you into law school? What a kindness it turned out to be, getting you educated as a solicitor, handing you a script for now. And wouldn't you agree that how a person lives far exceeds in impact the shock of how or when he dies? I think that about Juan. Did Juan's death matter in the larger politics of Nicaragua? I doubt it. But to him, he died for what he believed. He died in action. If it comes to that, Richard will have a good end knowing he provided for his family and its future. And Skye is his future. He mustn't die angry."

Mal insisted it would help Richard to be assured that his family would be safe without him. He was a part of them and would live on through them. She should tell him about her scheme. "Tell me about this case you've got on, that you say could change your life."

"Ah! Who better to appreciate this plan than you, Mal!" Mina happily described her progress to date. The soap used to ward off deer had been covered in a substance that was indeed considered toxic to humans; the children were sick all the time, ever since the soap hanging began. She had to show the cause and effect. So far, a blood test revealed that their blood contained toxic amounts of the chemical. Of course, it would be argued that it could not be stated with certainty that this chemical had caused their specific illnesses. There was more testing to do. Her firm was behind her. Colleagues were advising her. Everyone thought she would get somewhere.

"If I'm right, we can hope for a good settlement. And if I'm wrong, I know I tried my darnedest, and I prevented her kids from getting sicker. The husband is already installing a water purification system, and we want to determine that his home renovations did not cause their illness. We're having the air tested for particulates, inside the house and out. Similar to what we would do at the power plants. We will keep retesting the kids."

Mal raised an eyebrow. "Chemical companies do know all the twists. What if, in the end, the manufacturer wins?"

Mina, feeling fired up, assured there was more she could do in the court of public opinion. Publicity pushed settlements, and she'd discovered the company had settled in two similar cases a decade ago. There were other avenues to pursue. She'd just keep at it. It could be big.

"And this 'bookstore fantasy' as you called it, Mina. Why that? It seems a risky business in the computer age to start a children's bookstore. I would never have thought that for you."

"It's for later, Mal. My plan is to get a few degrees first, on the side, nights. It won't come to fruition quickly—a long-range goal. But I'm excited."

She had suggested to Richard that a business degree was useful for law, and he, too addled to analyze or argue her down, had not fussed. If she won her case, and he recovered, she would go to school full-time. She would get her new degrees before Skye needed tuition. If the worst happened, that was another story, but she would work it out. She had already begun to move on.

Telling Mallory made the children's bookstore concrete. She saw the words in bold Renaissance script fluttering in the wind on a long red banner trimmed in black and yellow: *Fox and Crow, Inc. Jasmina Davila, Bookseller*. The name was from a Buddhist folktale about empathy, that one's own humanity was found in all living things; thus all lives were worthy of compassion. Nice sentiment, right? She would fill her store with gorgeous picture books she selected herself; authors would come on Saturdays to read to children who could cuddle with their parents in beanbag chairs touched by sunlight streaming in from big picture windows. It would be a warm and wonderful place, a safe place.

She knew that such a place, her own place, would put the little girl and the boy on the highway beyond survival, cared for and safe, not orphaned after all, but having family, something like the little elephant whose parents had miraculously returned.

"Well, definitely worth trying, isn't it?" Mal said. "Bravo, Mina!"

Mina blushed. "So, crackerjack negotiator that you are, do you see my case as winnable?"

"Who can say? But do enjoy the fight, Mina. I always do. And take it on especially for Skye, who should see her mother fight for what is right."

They returned to Skye's future, which Mina admitted had not been discussed with Richard. She saw now they might never have that conversation, but she would try with him, if he were able.

"I want Skye to be a fighter, too, like you, Mal, and like Juan. And like me, to be observant. I hope she will exercise good judgment, choose the right man to love and good friends to care about her."

Mal laughed. "Mina, do you actually believe there is such a thing as the 'right' man? I cannot. Not really. Isn't there so much chance in who we meet and why we fall in love? Maybe, it's more useful if people—Skye—smartly follow through on the consequences of whatever choices are made, especially the mistakes. Not to get discouraged by mistakes in judgment. I would like her not to be overpowered by consequences."

"Sure, Mal, but isn't that just the hardest thing to do?" Mina said, thinking this was Mal again, speaking from theory, not from the concrete experience of life with a child and a husband. "We learn from experience; good advice will take you only so far. She may soon have loss, the loss of her father whom she loves. Richard's illness, my parents' death, Juan—how not to be defeated by the events out of our control? How to keep going? I struggle with that myself. I hope Skye will not be thrown off course by loss. I think I was."

They watched the children splashing and laughing in the pool.

Mina said, "See how children live in the present? More easily than we do. They don't obsess about the future. Or act like me, preoccupied with the past, how things could have been."

"At least it's what we like to think about them," Mal said. "Really, who knows? Why should children be so different from adults?"

Mina thought: there she goes again. She doesn't know. Except Mal was right about one thing: to talk to Richard and tell him her plan. He should not worry about them, so if he needed to go, it could be in peace. He was entitled to that. *Ease his fears ... be brave. Tell him about Bette ... the court case. Even about the bookstore.*

—⁓—

Bette greeted Mina at the door. She had asked Mina to come by, even though there was no news back from the tests. It was too early. Bette had neatened the area around the sofa, Mina noted. She had set a bench as a table and stacked it with what she claimed was new evidence: papers with lists and chronologies of name calling and slights by neighbors; photographs of burned, withering plants labeled "Before" and "After"; and a draft screed for the witch about all hell about to break loose.

Mina panicked. Her stomach knotted, and she felt cold. This woman really loved to fight. She sat uneasily on the leather sofa, felt herself slip around on it.

"Here!" Bette said. "This one! And this, too! This one is about yesterday."

It was zaps of anxiety coursing through her back and forth. She felt besieged by Bette flipping through papers, identifying them all, glancing back and forth expectantly for Mina's approval before she could even read what was there. Mina had to get control and remembered how Mallory used to do it. She interrupted Bette with a question. "First, tell me this: how are the kids doing?"

"Oh, better. It's good we went to the doctor. She has them on antibiotics. I have the report for you."

Mina took the report and skipped to the conclusion. Next, she lowered her voice as Richard had taught her, to sound firmer than she felt. She announced that as her lawyer, she would teach Bette how to fight—using strategies. But there were rules. One: Bette would take direction from her, and nevermore go off on her own. Two: no communication with neighbors unless Mina directed her—which she would do. Three: Bette would cease immediately the gathering of evidence, so-called. Four: their case was actually about something very serious, toxicity.

As if listening in from another room, Mina heard her own commanding voice. She envisioned her roommates sitting at their round Victorian table where Mal would address them just like that, with authority, willing everyone to pay attention to her. That was all it took.

Bette had to understand this: their case was about the toxic chemical that could be adversely affecting the health of her children, why her children suffered these "colds" that were not colds but blood poisoning.

Bette cringed and hugged herself.

Bette must not discuss the findings with anyone except Patrick. She had to get her children well. With the neighbors, Bette was to be cordial. Politeness counted.

"Bette, just think: it could have ended right away, without your kids getting sick. Instead of fighting, you could have asked your neighbor to hang her soaps inside Styrofoam cups to contain the suds when it rained. Your kids might not be sick now. She's such a craftsperson, she probably would have, willingly, even decorated them—"

"Nope. Never! I never want her hanging stuff in *my* trees! I want our property to be beautiful. The whole reason she's doing this is to drive us out of here."

"Except you don't know that for certain, do you? You don't know how she feels about anything except that she wants deer out of her garden. But it seems she used a product that is dangerous if it gets in your body. You must promise me to stop the fight now. In fact, I want you to write her a little note, leave it in her mailbox—an invitation for coffee to discuss how to accommodate your different needs for your respective gardens. At the coffee, you will make the suggestion about the Styrofoam cups. I shall write that note for you, if you'd like, because we need to prevent the soap and the powder from hitting the ground. We need to retest the children when she has done that. Our strategy is to show good faith. Do not accuse her of anything. You just want to contain the soap suds. Get it? Repeat to me now, what I just told you to do, so I know you understand me and will comply."

Bette repeated as Skye would have, adding a barb or two.

Mina frowned as she might have at Skye. Overall, she was satisfied that she could defuse Bette's attack mode. They studied the latest photos of the dying plants. Mina explained that they had to prove it was the chemical that killed them, that so much had been used over time that it leached into the drinking water. It seemed that even though ammonium benzoate was commonly used as repellent, it should be banned. Bette would do the entire country a service. She might become famous. She wanted to show that Bette's plants did not have blight or a fungus, nor had they suffered from weather conditions. They had to think like the other side, too.

Mina was assertive. Next, to locate the best plant and soil experts, she thought, gathering her things.

"Do you have receipts for the plants you purchased? See if you can pull that together. Also what you re-sodded with. Did you use fertilizer? Weed killer? We need to know the composition of everything you used to rule out that your own chemicals weren't what tainted your water. All the changes you yourselves made to your yard—I need specifics."

Bette took notes and could hardly wait to start, she said. It was a new campaign. She seemed focused.

—⁓—

"You're doing *what* for that woman?" Richard was incredulous, but he could not prevent her, she knew. Anticipating his response, she had waited until he rallied a little, showed interest enough to ask how work was going. He had been so out of touch, he said, but he wanted to know. He was weak. He raised his head from his pillow to emphasize his outrage about Bette.

"But you need to know this, Richard, that I have a plan, a good financial one. So you can stop fretting about us. We're going to be fine. You can feel good about it too, because you are the one who put this good plan into motion in the first place, by encouraging a law career for me. Here I'll be using it to full advantage." She saw the muscles in his face soften as he took in her words.

Mostly, she believed her plan would break the hex on her helplessness, the string of dead birds and puppies and family most of all, who had died and left her to fumble along in isolation, she told him. She described the details of Bette's case, more certain as she told him that she was building it solidly, with a plan, a strategy, and the players falling into place. She was unafraid. She was excited and energized. She explained to Richard that she'd taken the case to stabilize their finances, formerly his provenance, and that she intended to win it because it was the right thing to do. It was also socially useful, she continued, a case that could protect the health of others. She was committed to it, she said, firmly, echoing her resolve long ago to go to Cuba as a *brigadista* and help out with the sugar harvest, just because it was needed. It was a more consequential commitment than anything she'd ever done in her student protest days.

"Richard, I can use your help, if you feel up to it. You're so good at these things." She brightened at the smile on his wan face. Let me help him know—she thought of Mal—how a person lives is far more impactful than when a person dies.

Richard grew teary. He reached out for her hand and she took both of his, ice to the touch, the blue veins pulsing urgently. He squeezed her fingers with the strength he had. She reached down to embrace him, tightly. They were a team. They were friends. They'd never not been.

That night, Mina offered to read a story to Skye before bed. "It's been months since we read together." Her daughter brightened at the idea and ran to fetch her special blanket for the occasion. It used to be their special time, before Richard's illness took over, to cuddle, lights off except for the reading light illuminating a big picture book propped against Mina's knees. Skye scrambled into her bed and settled her blanket around her. She waited for her mother to choose.

"What do you feel like?" Mina asked her.

"Remember that old book of yours? That you used to read and then explain the story because it was really for grown-ups? But it had pretty pictures?"

Mina knew. Her beautiful, tattered *Tales from the Jhambu-Khadaka,* super-sized and copiously illustrated, not at all a children's book, "My treasure," she smiled, "that came all the way from India. Yes. Let's read from that one."

Mina flipped through the soft, vellum pages, yellowed and fading, aware of the satisfying weight of her daughter's head pressed into her shoulder, her long body stretched against her own under the special blanket. The reading light illuminated Skye's head and cast a marmalade aura from her ginger hair onto the page.

"*Fox and Crow.* Let's read this one."

Arcadia
Gwen, 2005–2006

"If the future and the past do exist, I want to know where they are. I may not yet be capable of such knowledge, but at least I know that wherever they are, they are not there as future and past, but as present."—St. Augustine

ET IN ARCADIA EGO: I, DEATH, AM EVEN IN ARCADIA. NOTHING lasts forever. Everything ends in death. So variously did Professor Nathaniel Smith paraphrase the words of the Roman poet, Virgil, in his lectures over the years, a favorite game. Gwen should have used the quote in her eulogy at his funeral. But it seemed so nihilistic. She did not.

—⁓⁓—

It was Gwen, not Horatio, who prepared the house in Philly for sale after Nathaniel died. Gwen agreed she'd be better at tackling the detritus of a fifty-year teaching career. She had the time too, since college classes ended earlier than in Roanoke, where her brother, Horatio, was up to his ears with work and family. At the time she still burned with embarrassment from the scathing *New York Times* review of the performance piece she had written for her acting group, *Lost Paradise*, mounted at the trendy avant-garde Unsung Arts Workshop on the Lower East Side. Very important people from the Manhattan theater world had been induced to attend and were witness to the disaster. It wasn't her piece so much as her dreadful part in it, forgetting an entire act and throwing everyone else off, so that no one knew how to get it back on track, and in fact, it never got back on track. Her mind stayed a complete, ignoble blank till the end. The performance had been the weekend after his funeral. She quit *Lost Paradise* altogether, even though she'd been its founder. Let them continue without her. She'd lost her heart for creative cleverness. She wanted the distraction of going to Philly. It would be the last time she'd ever visit the family home.

She had allowed herself only a week as there was so little to do. Daddy had arranged for his library of two thousand books to be donated after Mom died. An unbearable sadness continued to paralyze her. Her father, the constant foil to her life and her successes, was gone. She could have brought some company along, but her feelings were too inchoate and private to expose to her New York friends. She dreaded life without her father— in fact, never really believed he would actually die someday. No one occupied the void he left. For his eulogy, Gwen, being an important scholar of John Milton, had chosen lines from Milton's great mourning elegy, *Lycidas*, because they hinted at hope, lines she had quoted often enough to her graduate students. "And now the sun had stretch'd out all the hills ... tomorrow to fresh woods, and pastures new." Tears had streamed down her cheeks as in her mind light streaked across the landscape in fast-forward motion and became the day.

She'd left his study for last, and the last of that was his desk, a warren of cubby holes stuffed with neatly notated index cards, receipts, yellowed newspaper clippings, rolls of outdated stamps and more interesting ones torn from envelopes, also magnifying glasses—four of different powers—several scissors of various sizes and functions, timetables, CDs, pens and pencil stubs, a miniature pizza souvenir from Italy, a pair of tiny Delft boots tied with red ribbon from Holland, ca. 1975. The entire lot should be chucked, but it was all so *him*.

Daddy's hoarding was nothing new, but the big surprise was the 1974 wedding invitation of Taylor Bryce and Sigrid Christensen tucked into a drawer like a message for her to find, atop a bundle of crumpled maps that had been red-inked with routes to their old summer cottage on Lake Champlain. Daddy had sold that cottage in 1978 and, surely, had not seen the Bryce family since. Why keep that invitation? She put it aside with some of her belongings to take back to Manhattan.

She met with an auctioneer to price the house contents and sighed when it was done. This was Virgil's point, which Daddy harped on: nothing lasts forever.

Back at home on the Upper West Side, she propped up the wedding invitation in a corner of her own desk and glanced at it throughout the summer. Probably still married, Taylor and Sigrid, whom Taylor's mother, Marlene, had once called The Cold Fish. Gwen's parents had flown out to Minnesota to attend their wedding as acknowledgment of the friendship between the two families. They'd been summer neighbors on the lake for decades, and Daddy had always admired Taylor—felt "akin," he would say time and again: two scholars of rarified subjects. Did she dare to call him?

This morning is the last Sunday in October before she flies out to Minnesota, where Taylor still lives, so she should decide today. Just the kind of frigid sunny morning she used to like—that had one rummaging for the quilt in the middle of the night before the building turned on the heat. She awoke wrapped in her quilt and sad, as if she'd been weeping in her dreams.

Gwen ties the sash of her persimmon-colored kimono over her red silk pajamas. Only 7 AM and missing Daddy, the Sunday morning phone call to him. She feels half-dead herself, but couldn't stay in bed. Will this deadness ever lift and let her be? She has writer's block for her literary monographs and refuses calls from *Lost Paradise* actors, who want to entice her into collaborations. No, it's over. No thanks. Half-dead is the word. Tears well up. She lets them roll and drop.

She pads barefoot to her study, not ready for breakfast. Taylor's wedding invitation is on the desk, the mystery of why Daddy saved it never intuited. It had been a snap to find Taylor's home number when she'd returned to New York. And a snap again to contact her old student, the organizer of an English Ren-Lit conference in St. Paul scheduled for early November, to offer a presentation of her soon-to-be-published monograph on the pastoral elegy. She could use some informal feedback, she'd explained, not admitting she'd lost interest in it.

Wonderful to add you, Gwen; last minute's not a problem. It's because she is considered an academic coup. Her fame precedes her in any arena here and in Europe that includes seventeenth-century England and *Paradise Lost,* her specialty niche, just as Virgil was her father's.

Gwen picks up the wedding invitation and taps the faded orchid stock. Daddy had his sentimental streak, to put it mildly. Corny at times, larger than life, the blustery explicator of The Big Picture with XXL, Double-Extra-Large-size opinions inhaling all the oxygen in a room: Dr. Nathaniel Smith. He had, and she had inherited from him, she knew, the doggedness to get to the bottom of what could be known, no holds barred.

He'd genuinely liked Taylor Bryce, recognized his younger self in that youthful scholar of comparative religions who had eschewed the family fruit business for academics. Daddy had pronounced Taylor "more like *us* than his own family."

Daddy may have harbored the fantasy embraced by both families that Taylor would marry Gwen someday. Their mothers had said over the years they could see the little bookworms Gwen and Taylor as a future item. Mature emotions could develop between them some day. Daddy loved the story of Gwen's precociousness: that at four years old, our Gwennie grabbed a science book from ten-year-old Taylor's hands and read him a sentence. "She's rather a competitive little thing," Taylor's mother, Marlene, had observed, half in awe. The choice of the chilly Sigrid had been a big surprise to everyone.

"*Come and share in our exchange of vows as we begin a new life together,*" their invitation reads, penned by hand (hers?). Gwen smirks. They'd had a traditional wedding, in the same era that their peers went free-form, free love, free LSD. How had he managed college instead of Viet Nam?

She brings the invitation to the kitchen. Taylor was no radical in those days, when all the craziness was going on. Not like Gwen, who was—and is—a bold nonconformist. They were really so different at heart. The parents never saw that.

While he was a newlywed in Minnesota, teaching at the college where he still teaches, she had been earning her leftie *bona fides* in New York through anti-nuclear research and anti-government protests, living in the feminist commune Group housed in this very apartment. Mallory had added her name on the lease to give her right of first refusal when the building went co-op, which it did. She'd bought it with her parents' help, and today it's worth a small fortune, she is pleased to bear in mind. In counterculture fashion, Gwen had even dropped out of graduate school temporarily, abandoned corrupt "Amerika" for the island of Patmos to live a pastoral idyll with Ari, her sculptor boyfriend. Whatever became of him? Quite a self-absorbed bore, he turned out to be.

That youthful dissatisfaction with the status quo, she later understood, was the manifestation of an inner drive, honed over time to focus on her life interests. Politics turned out not to be her "thing," but dissidents and nonconformists are always in style. She had developed a feel—an eye—for the congruency between John Milton's themes and contemporary forms of artistic expression. With her drama friends, she cowrote interdisciplinary performance pieces, donning surreal costumes and eerie masks, building symbolic sets rife with Miltonian meaning. Marriage to Taylor or anyone, really, would have distracted her from creativity. Her life has been good, lived well—"a journey" in hackneyed parlance. Nothing wrong with journeys. It's just that her life, her spirit, her ideation, have crashed to a halt. She is half-dead, now her father's wholly dead.

To revive that journeying spirit, her experimental side, she will telephone Taylor and announce she'll be in his neighborhood and would love to visit him after thirty years. She reaches for her phone, ready with his number jotted on the invitation, and glances at the time. The problem is it's too early, only 5:10 AM in Minnesota.

He will surely remember her, given the intensity of what passed between them when she was fifteen. So what if at forty-seven her lips sag in tiny commas, her sheet of blonde hair fades at the crown; so what if she is shaken by opposing moods, one minute mourning her parents and a missed childhood, the next demanding adventures. Being single, creating a world exquisitely tuned to her singular interests, has kept her spirit young and innocent. She knows herself. She knows the three traits that drive her: courage, a romantic spirit, and a futuristic outlook. That third is the particular trait that has faded since their deaths. Her future looms elusively, lacking structure or intent. Clouded. Uninteresting.

Back in the study, waiting for water to boil—she'll decide on coffee or tea at the last minute—she glances at the golden treetops in an early morning shimmer above Riverside Park, reminding her of a flying carpet she'd like to ride somewhere.

Does she have the courage to call him? Is she ready for the consequences? That's what Mal asked her when Gwen talked about her idea of contacting him.

Consequences are the surprise of an unexpected action, she answered. The saved wedding invitation casts Taylor in a new light: he had mattered a great deal to her father. Who was he? Is he?

One time she'd found him quoted in a *New York Times* op-ed about youth and religion. "In Minnesota, Comparative Religions Professor Dr. Taylor Bryce says of the entering class." She clipped it for Daddy, commenting that apparently Taylor had not advanced to a top-tier college. You are a snob, Daddy had said. Taylor had tenure. He had contentment.

And she was a Milton expert, thanks to Taylor, she'd explained to Mal. Nothing wrong with looking him up to talk about the past. Seeing him—them, of course—will add a narrative to her life. Milton would approve. Her father would approve.

Her friend Shadrach definitely would not approve, would dismiss the idea as "self-referential performance art," or some such silliness. Shadrach is the master of the quippy label for whatever he doesn't understand.

Anyone else to warn her it's an iffy idea? Mallory, of course. "Are you quite sure, Gwennie? It sounds like stirring up the past is a cheap trip to the psychiatrist's couch. You will disrupt him by entering his life uninvited. Why should he want to see you? Has he ever reached out to you?" Mal, as one-time leader of the commune radicals, continues her role as a buoy in murky waters, now offering the same conventional advice Mother would have.

Gwen could reject the idea herself—if her call to him tells her that a dose of Taylor Bryce will not lift the gathering clouds of depression she dreads.

Horatio claims that Daddy's bluster was neurotic. *He was depressed, Gwen! You never saw it, because you lapped up all that self-indulgent bunk about the glories of the Roman past in exchange for his approval of that pretentious theater claptrap.* Is hers an artistic version of depression? She returns to the kitchen to make tea, her mind a jumble—Taylor, Daddy, Horatio, Shadrach, history, art. Life.

Taylor can't sleep late on weekends. Decades of early classes have trained him to wake up at 5:30, regardless. He stares out the bedroom window into rainy gray dawn. Wait for light. Sigrid, behind him, snores gently. She is serene. She rarely ruffles. They have lived in peaceful co-existence for decades, which people say is a blessing for low blood pressure and longevity.

So, what the hell is wrong with him? Taylor stares down at his bare feet, absorbing cold from the hardwood. The paperboy doesn't deliver for another hour. TV's got nothing. He can't make sense of the irritation he has been waking with. Annoyance at routine. The very routine they have become, that cocoons him.

He will make brunch later. Get out to the organic food market as soon as it opens. Avoid the crowds. Choose an interesting flour—buckwheat, flaxseed. Use most of it to make his own bread for lunch tomorrow, when he's alone. Monday is her private students in St. Paul. A useful Sunday routine, to make bread for his week's sandwiches.

Why this disquiet? Whoa! An image of smashing something. Release the tension. He is too peaceable a person ever to smash. Raises his arm. Bats the air. Just for the heck of it. Just to check. Nope. No will in that gesture. Awkward arm waving is all. If Sigrid opened her eyes and saw his arm flailing about? You've lost it, honey, she'd say. Exercise his imaginary dialog with her to absorb any need to ever articulate troubles.

He: *Sigrid, I am consumed by an itchy, unsettled feeling. I want to jump out of my skin. Smash something for relief. Destroy. Can't explain it. Why, Sigrid?*

Sigrid: *Don't take yourself so seriously, honey. Get back to your gym routine and hit things. Isn't that what they make you do there? Basically? Or run! It's just excess energy. You need an outlet. Too much comparative religion isn't good for a person.*

—◦◦◦—

Crossing from the kitchen to the living room, Gwen pauses in the foyer to wonder what Mallory meant by "eerie" when she came in from London for Daddy's funeral and stayed on to keep Gwen company. Flipping the overhead light switch, she admires the elegance of her apartment completely transformed since they all lived there in the 1980s.

People admire her engravings of *Paradise Lost,* from an eighteenth-century edition, which glow like cultured pearls on the cherry-red wallpaper. They often greet the second-century marble bust of an unknown Roman on an onyx pedestal, Daddy's gift for her Ph.D., and say something silly to break the ice. He's a Rorschach Test, she quips, with his eyes lacking irises. And there's the dramatically backlit vitrine that spotlights her beloved terracotta figurine of Pan, also second-century, from Syracusa in Sicily.

Her apartment is filled with what matters to her life. A bit of defensiveness rising, Gwen pointed out to Mal the enlarged spaces and improvements since they lived there as Group.

Mal said: Doesn't matter. She felt spirits hovering, old friends, alive and dead.

Mal likes to imagine ghosts, but she was a love to stay on those extra weeks. Gwen had needed a friend there with her. They sat at the old pedestal table and finished a bottle of wine, expressly calling up those old ghosts, laughed over who said what at those silly house meetings. Hilarious, their earnest political diatribes—they knew so little, in fact.

At one soul-baring session meant to emulate Maoist self–criticism, they each described a relationship that came to a bad end to analyze together what they might have done differently to preserve it.

Gwen disclosed her luckless relationship with Taylor. How she created it from thin air in ninth grade, the year her family moved to Philadelphia, where she had just begun yet another new school. There had been many moves to different states because of her father's short-term contracts teaching Classics, not in high demand at the time. It took nimble thinking to intuit what constituted acceptance at each school. At Pennrose, it was a prestigious boyfriend, so she borrowed Taylor from summers on the lake and created a persona. Taylor never had a clue, of course. He hardly ever spoke to her, the Bryce brothers being older than the Smith children.

She confessed to her commune-mates, whose mantra was honesty, her blatant lie to the new girls. She'd wanted to create a boyfriend more impressive than anyone else's, but with her limited experience, Taylor was all she had to work with.

Everyone in Group laughed at her cleverness. Everyone but Mal admitted to similar embroidery, so she wasn't embarrassed to explain.

It was a plus that Taylor lived in Florida, so far away. She made him worldly and sophisticated, conscious she was defining herself through him, which a feminist ought not to do, of course.

Mal pronounced it sad, using a boy to fit in with girls.

The point was *not* to fit in—but to be above them, cooler.

"Equally sad." Mal never would have done it.

"Because you never had to! Were you ever the no-name, invisible kid in school, having to establish yourself? No matter what, you were always Lady Mallory Tame. And everyone knew it. I bet there were rumors of your arrival before you even stepped foot in Lausanne."

The choices Gwen continues to make—to recede or to stand out or fit in, whether at school, in the commune, in academics or creative circles, or in her social life—define her.

To see Taylor again would be to feel compassion for her young self, her fears and her innocence, to trace the evolution to the successful, whole woman she has become, to recover the drive that pushes her forward. Yes, it makes sense. She has reason to call him at 9 AM and step into his life.

—⁓—

Taylor knows one thing about Sigrid. She never breaks concentration. An underground river of music constantly flows through her despite demands he makes on her. He admires that. He has seen her fingers move along an imaginary bow while she dictates the shopping list to him, focusing through pork chops, bathroom cleaner, you name it. She lives music in mind and body. Taylor has never dedicated himself to anything as intensely as she is dedicated to music, except maybe to his students. But that is different, isn't it, because students leave you. Your intense focus comes to an end when they leave.

He has never resented it; his dedication is to her. Perhaps this is his personal failing, his Achilles' Heel, but to her, it is his strength. He occasionally provokes her—he admits it, an assurance to both that when the friction subsides, their bond is the stronger.

He wishes the coffee to be ready, so he can leave the house.

—⁓—

Gwen catches her reflection, teacup in hand, on the glass panes of the bookcase in her study. She still looks pretty, enveloped in the silk Furisode kimono, a gift from Shadrach's trip to Japan. Shadrach said the sun colors that were worn only by young girls were "Gwen." He is right about that. She swooshes to the kitchen feeling like a full-size portrait of a *grande dame* by John Singer Sargent hanging in the Met.

This call to Taylor: intuition guides her. The point is to propel forward metaphorically, though she is unsure exactly how that works in reality. Being older now, the past will read differently to each. They will look older now, too.

She smiles, remembering what she told those Main Line girls—an ear cocked to her own coolness—his blue eyes and his retro black-rimmed glasses just like Buddy Holly's, inspired by "American Pie," the Don MacLean song. She omitted Taylor's knowledge of world religions so esteemed by her father, and for the same reason—too dorky—she did not mention that he played classical piano.

She jots down "Milton" next to his number, to thank him for that. She scribbles piano, then "Fun Nights," the evenings when the parents went out to dinner together in Burlington and left him in charge of his brother Hunter, and Horatio and Gwen. The icy Sigrid, if they're still married, should be curious about Taylor's childhood summers at the lake. Yes, plenty to talk about.

Gwen glances at the clock, close to 9 AM here, but only 7 AM there. What the heck. She pours her tea into the sink and takes the Chivas Regal and a juice glass into the living room. She sits down on the kilim as if in a garden of *gul*s, her back against the sofa. She studies the stormy, Turner-esque painting, rescued from a jumble sale in London, that dominates the mantelpiece wall and wonders if she really has the *cojones* to call him. She pours herself a shot.

Today, all day, Taylor knows Sigrid will be preoccupied with the custom-made viola bow arriving from Vienna tomorrow. He will accept the expedited delivery for her and will call her when it arrives, interrupting a lesson, because she is worried, even today, that it will be lost. He will assure her it is with him, feeling useful with this assurance, which will free her to imagine rushing home to let it rest in her palm, incrementally moving up to feel its weight and distance along the neck, lightly bowing imaginary strings. Testing. Face aglow from the sound she hears in her mind, her eyes closed. Ardor.

He's always loved her ardor. When he first knew her, he had never experienced anything like it. She glowed with an inner light; she was pristinely beautiful in performance, at one with the music. Her fervor was the fervor of power and sex. He loves how his own sexuality distracts her from her music. With that, he holds the upper hand. Yet he has lost interest, one might say, in power.

He will drink his coffee in the living room, leaf through yesterday's paper, and she will sleep a little longer.

Gwen has finished two more shots of scotch, showered, dressed and reread her monograph for the conference, waiting for 11 AM. She feels worry-free, has a fleeting vision of her parents drinking a little too much, playing rowdy Charades at the lake while she read on the porch, alone. No one could ever guess her father's Latin quotations—the more alcohol, the more obscure. ("*Non omnis moriar:* not all of me shall die! You didn't recognize it? It's *Horace*, everyone!")

"Gwennie doesn't like to play," Daddy explained. "She prefers her books."

Was he kidding? Was he blind to her solitary confinement without a friend to talk to? She pours a fourth shot, anticipating that memory of Taylor she's been skirting, when her loneliness evaporated during that one afternoon encounter.

It remains vivid, an intimate memory, her first time alone with a boy—reading on the porch, everyone else gone to town, Taylor at the screen door asking if she felt like hanging out. He was experimenting with something that was very probably stupid out back at the stream. He could use help.

Playing God, he'd described it, to alter the course of the stream and return to Nature the land that Civilization had stolen. He was inspired by reading John Milton. Did she know Milton? The forest around the lake was being sacrificed to new homes construction. To reroute the stream was his token gesture of defiance, a tiny, subversive act. His usually evasive blue eyes looked squarely into hers and smiled, sheepishly.

Gwen remembers she thought it was a dorky thing to do, at first. In fact, he utterly annoyed her, because as her fantasy boyfriend he had failed her miserably. The boys considered her "taken" with all her Taylor talk, and she'd not been invited to the tenth-grade dance. She'd felt increasingly invisible in that school. Eventually claimed they'd broken up, but the boys never took her seriously.

She was so bored that summer at the lake. She left the *Compendium* and James Joyce's *Ulysses* on the swing and followed Taylor to the back. It was something to do.

She agreed to help dislodge rocks and logs and drag them from the forest to the stream's edge to create a substantial barrier on its far bank so it would flood onto their properties. As they worked, Taylor described the conflict in Milton's *Paradise Lost* between Civilization and Nature. It made her think of Daddy's monologues on Latin grammar, except that Taylor asked her questions and spoke as if it mattered that Gwen understood. She recognized that passion to know as her passion too. He spoke to her like an equal.

She said she was plowing through the entire lot of eighteenth-century English writers to be able to put it on her college applications.

Then he should lend her his *Paradise Lost*. She could probably handle the seventeenth century, too.

Sure. She was flattered.

After three hours the bank on the forest side was draining and turning to muck where there had been water while the opposite bank along their properties was flooded over some two feet past the original bank. Taylor said when the muck dried it would become the reclaimed forest, and the lost property footage would never be missed. He drove some pine cones into the muck. Maybe they would grow into trees.

They declared it a job well done and shook hands.

Was she interested in seeing where the stream began in the woods about five miles away?

They cleaned up and met at his car. Here was another First for Gwen, a ride in a car with an older boy, sort of like a fantasy date with her fantasy boyfriend. She loved the irony of it, reality replacing fiction.

Bumping along the dirt road arched over with hemlocks and white birches, they spoke of reincarnation, the real possibility that each had been secretly adopted, the worship of tree spirits and springs being more logical than the worship of Jesus. He described his father's orange groves and his fights with his mother. Gwen hoped her comments sounded appropriately sophisticated.

Was she ready for a hike? He stopped the engine and, taking her hand, led her into the woods. He enjoyed talking to her, he said, adding that becoming a teenager hadn't rendered her stupid.

He brought her to a broad pool of water under the hemlocks. He pointed to the source, a spring that emerged from a rock crevice.

It's amazing, she whispered. They could be standing inside an Impressionist painting. Sunlight stippled the slow-moving water making its way around large granite boulders to cascade down over rocks and stones to become a stream that flowed out of sight. It was the same stream, he said, that they had just rerouted by their properties. Eventually, it would reach Lake Champlain. Probably thousands of springs like this, he figured, fed the lake.

The land should belong to nature. The streams should feed the lake. This was how it was meant to be. Milton was the first environmentalist.

It was elemental, he continued, for a spring to shoot up from the earth, like the Shiva Hindu image of the lingam, a rod-shaped statue. In Tantric Yoga, it symbolized power, the masculine principle, complement to the female principle.

Gwen drew a blank. Unknown territory as this was, his words evoked an image of private parts that made her blush. "So, you're saying a spring is a sexual symbol? A *religious* sexual symbol?"

He chuckled. "*Like* one. I guess sex is on my mind."

Intense connection was so demanding, she realized. Plus it was disconcerting, his more advanced sensitivity that seemed too private for her. She hoped he didn't notice her fluster. Still, it was exciting to be in his strange and mysterious world. She felt him grow pensive as he stood beside her.

He leaned toward her. His movement caused his glasses to flash a shaft of sunlight into her eyes, and she blinked. He was about to kiss her!

But he did not. He pulled away. "We should go back."

Right. What just happened? Did I do something wrong?

The ride back was awkward and silent. She could think of nothing to talk about. She was an awkward teenager, after all.

That evening he brought over his copy of *Paradise Lost* for her. And because many years later she organized her studies and then her academic career around John Milton, she believed her life's arc began with Taylor Bryce, brought to life by that almost mystical, confusing flash of light in the Vermont woods. The name John Milton ever after held the promise of something exciting and important about to happen; indeed, her life happened.

———

Taylor, starting the jeep to get to the organic market, is overcome by a second wave of anger that shakes him to his core. He has papers to grade this afternoon and thinks how he will miss that. His anger flares because he is now a lame-duck professor through no fault of his own. He will take retirement in June, well before he ever intended. Sigrid insisted because, although she will keep her own students, she plans to retire from her quartet at Christmas, after the Houston concert. She is feeling her age, which is sixty, and she teases him about being younger and spryer. They can afford early retirement to do things together. His father is a millionaire.

He dreads what lies ahead. He cannot see it. It's not like he will write a book about comparative religion in his retirement. Nothing interests him more than his students, his teaching, even the cycle of college activities. Sigrid is after him all the time now to define something (but not about religion, Taylor!) to enjoy in his retirement. You are so young, you can have a second life, she says brightly, as if he wants one. And travel. She glows. What about travel? Let's take the honeymoon we never could. Wouldn't that be fun? She is still waiting for it. Remember their plan to trace the path of Franz Liszt everywhere he went? It was to be their honeymoon, but they had no money. For him, the idea has lost its allure after three decades. Anyway, he hates travel. He hates hotels and not knowing your way around a place, bored by her quartet members—nice guys, yes, but what to talk about besides music gossip and food? What do professors do when they retire? Consult? Guest lecture? He swerves to avoid a stray dog ambling across the road in front of him in the pouring rain without a care. A mad dog. What else must he avoid at this hour on a Sunday? An Englishman?

—␣␣␣—

Gwen feels quite drunk—scotch on an empty stomach, but so what? This memory she is mulling, of who she was at fifteen and what she did with Taylor that summer, feels increasingly significant. She sees Marlene Bryce's smile as they grab food from the fridge for their excursions. On rainy days they stayed in at Gwen's house and he played his études. What feelings he elicited from their tinny old piano! She was transfixed.

Nothing physical ever passed between them, except for him occasionally holding her hand.

On their last afternoon together, he entrusted her with a secret. They sat on the dock eating cherries, dangling their feet over the water, trying to make weird shadows. He was in love with a music student from Minnesota, seven years older than he. Sigrid. She played the viola da gamba. She was a genius at it. They lived together on campus. Sigrid had gone to Europe for the summer and had written that she was choosing between him and someone she'd met there. It killed him that he might lose her. Sex between them was incredible, he added.

Gwen's stomach flipped in grown-up jealousy. She tossed her handful of pits into the lake. Minnows in a swarm surfaced, suddenly. Her feelings were tangled with admiration for this free-spirited woman with power over Taylor and anger that all along he had been pining for Sigrid, was never interested in Gwen, who, let's be honest, was a convenience, a summer-neighbor kid. He was used to an experienced, older woman. Obviously, they had sex. Wasn't that why they lived together, to do it whenever? Tantrically. Gwen had looked up Shiva lingams in her father's OED and the sketches of peculiar Tantric sex positions.

That was the last time she saw him. Over the years, with her own experiences, the intensity of that summer faded, except for the memory of that not-quite-first kiss. That remained first in her store of Firsts.

Also, that he had treated her as an equal, entrusted her with what was in his heart, and he had introduced her to Milton, not to be demeaned. Beyond those things, he, Taylor, the person, became irrelevant.

That last evening Taylor came over, interrupted their supper and announced he had to leave in the morning, shook hands all around and left. No personal goodbye for her. That hurt, but why did she expect more?

They learned the following year that Taylor had moved to Minnesota, was completing his Master's thesis and had got a teaching position in comparative religions for the fall. He would get his doctorate in St. Paul, and he was about to marry The Cold Fish, Sigrid Christensen.

"Bravo!" Nathaniel clapped vigorously, winked at Taylor's parents. "On all counts. Do you know that in Norse mythology Sigrid is the Goddess of Victory?"

Marlene was upset. Taylor was besotted and too young for marriage; there was no reasoning with him. Her best hope was for what she'd read about in *McCall's Magazine*, a "starter marriage," what kids did nowadays—married young, divorced after a few years, then found a more suitable spouse. No surprise to Gwen that Taylor married the frosty Sigrid who kindled fire in him, made him sweat. Maybe Daddy kept the invitation, waiting for the divorce?

Sigrid is wakened by the rumble of the garage door closing. He's back from the store, his mood so mopey recently. Not good. It's the retirement coming up, this semester half-done, then his last one. She snuggles into the quilt. She'll help him through the transition. He gets so stubborn about change. Her husband relies on her to deal with life's vicissitudes, which invariably blindside him. He dwells too much inside himself. Not up on the real world, like she is. And for one dedicated to the abstract nature of those large religious themes and their complexities, he has a tin ear for the emotional life and its need for creative expression. She kids: he is her cross to bear. Her own world bursts with emotion. The viola is the source of constant counter-play in music, expressing the tension of constrained feeling pressing for release to be shared. The relief of sound. The resolution of emotion, the life force, pushes out to be known and experienced. Taylor is so concrete. But I love you for that, she tells him. Reliable, dependable and of this earth is her man, which he complains is not too complimentary an image. She yawns, thinks about getting up.

Gwen is lost in thought; better stop the Chivas so as not to be incoherent and slur her words. The gleam on those Turkish copper plates flanking her painting on the mantel slips out of focus. She should make some toast, but this trip down memory lane is too engrossing to stand up.

And Ari in Patmos: not much to be said about the sculptor who distracted her for a year from her graduate work. Tending to his ego exhausted her. She awoke one morning completely out of love. She packed quickly, found a flight to Paris, where Mal was working at one of her many banks, and after a short visit returned to New York via a week's stopover in Oxford.

Advised by Mal where in Heathrow Airport one found the public showers meant for business travelers, she scrubbed off

Patmos and took a train directly to Oxford, to the Bodleian Library. She asked to see original Milton texts. She read his arguments for the morality of divorce, agreeing heartily that loyalty without love was pointless. No need for remorse about leaving Ari. She studied Milton's anti-monarchical activities in favor of the people and felt a thrill to read his original texts. Fortified with an array of ideas about overthrowing systems, she returned to Manhattan and reclaimed her sublet apartment.

Gwen wrote her dissertation on the poem "Hymn on the Morning of Christ's Nativity," which Milton had written in 1629 as a student, thirty years before he wrote *Paradise Lost.* It was a radical work for its day in its form, its ideas and the integration of pagan gods and Christianity. It fascinated her that Milton transformed the god Pan, a figure of chaos and cataclysm in antiquity, into a vehicle for humane ideas. With great enthusiasm she taught a course on Milton's support of regicide. The next time around, enrollment reached capacity, and she had a waiting list. Supporting controversial theories with scholarship and a flair for dramatic presentation made her popular with students. At international symposia, she claimed John Milton chose Pan because he was the only deity in the Greek pantheon with both human and animal features, the only god who ever died, the only one who oscillated between opposing natures. She described the goats in Patmos foraging on their hind legs in the mulberry trees—backlit in the Mediterranean sun, easily mistaken for harvesters—and arrived at edgy hypotheses that crossed disciplines, co-wrote papers and put into motion the theatrical productions born of late nights and cognac—fun, fun, fun; busy, busy, busy.

By the 1990s, with two hurtful love affairs behind her, her mother worried: you need love, Gwen. Everyone is entitled to love. Later on you will regret not having a partner, she warned. Just find someone, how difficult can it be? Mom's disappointment in Gwen was visceral. Horatio had made Mom a grandmother several times over.

Now Gwen neared middle age, and they were both gone. She had not imagined life without her parents in it. Maybe because of that, or because the politics of her students had changed beyond recognition—each new crop more conservative than she'd ever been—she felt like an ossified relic, one of those bits in a jewel-studded reliquary up at The Cloisters that no one saw the point to now. And the pairings of students, colleagues and friends—Shadrach, for that matter, with that fellow in Japan—produced wedding invitations she now declined, to avoid feeling odd and single.

Her mother's heart gave out in April, when Gwen was in England collaborating with Shadrach's partner on his art piece for the Tokyo Biennial. Her father followed a month later. The pastor cited his death, so soon upon his wife's, as evidence of the strength of their love. At least Gwen was with him at the end and held his papery hands in hers.

She so misses his voice, his love that was her comfort. "I'll rest in greater peace, Gwennie"—he'd taken up her mother's cause—"if you settle down with someone."

She dials the ten Minnesotan numbers.

———————

A ring. A click. "Yuh?"

"Taylor?" Is this Taylor Bryce?"

"Yup. Who's this?"

"This is—it's Gwen Smith. Hi. It's been a very long time, I know."

Silence. Breathing. "Gwen Smith? No ... I ... Gwen Smith? Is this a former student calling?"

"The Smiths next door at Lake Champlain?" *Think, Taylor! The skinny kid in the pines! You leaned to kiss her and stopped yourself. Think!*

"Okay, I've got it. Wow, what a surprise." His voice, laced with confusion, is proof he's not thought of her once all these years. Damn! Really embarrassing!

"So, Gwen. Gwen Smith. Sure, the Professors Smith next door. What's it been? Twenty-five years? Thirty-five?"

Gwen chirps that she'll be in St. Paul to deliver a paper at a Ren-Lit conference on Milton. "I became somewhat of an authority on him—since we last saw each other." Her voice falls into a pit of silence.

"It occurred to me you were nearby, so I checked with Information, and voila!" More silence on his end.

"And Sigrid? How is she?"

"Well, she's ... still asleep. You see, it's pretty early here. I'm making pancakes, actually. Covered with kamut flour. You say you're coming to St. Paul? From where? Why, again?"

Repeating, she adds that it might be nice to reconnect.

"Um, sure, Gwen, but how come? I barely remember you. Wasn't there a big age gap? Do you have something in mind, specifically?"

Be honest. It usually works. "Not specifically. My parents passed away last spring. Horatio lives in Virginia with his family. I am sort of at a crossroads here in Manhattan—reflecting on life, I guess. We knew each other at the lake. I'd love to reminisce; our lake house was a constant in my peripatetic childhood, always a familiar place to go. Yes, I was younger, but you introduced me to John Milton. I imagined I would thank you some day, since John is now the heart of my academic work. I credit you with that. I still have your *Paradise Lost*."

"You do? I did? Good to know. Thanks. Makes sense. I often mentor my students—the 'go-to' professor around here, you know, when students are confused? And Sigrid, she's great at helping out. She's got a knack for knowing what they're really after. But I probably can't help you, Gwen. I don't have many memories of summers at the lake, less of you. Not very important ones, anyway. Is this something we can take care of over the phone instead?"

"I hadn't thought of that, but sure. No need to actually ... I know you're busy, and meeting up seems a bit problematic..."

Gwen is dying. Never had she imagined rejection, or his stupid association to ditzy undergraduates and their majors. He totally misunderstands. This is a dead end. Cut it, Gwen! Now!

"No, no. Let me try to remember. I want to help. Off the top of my head, what do I remember about Vermont summers? And you?"

"Well, it's not meant to be a pop quiz, Taylor. It was just an idea of mine." Unbearable, the embarrassment.

"I got it: the erudite Professors Smith who lived next to the Farmers Bryce. To your folks, we were hayseeds from Florida, but everyone made a show of neighborliness. My Dad advanced into the millionaire tax bracket—orange groves—but probably, not yours—Virgil, right? College teaching. Publishing? I guess we both know about that."

She winces. "Oh, nice for your dad, good to know he did so well."

"Yup. So, let's see, now ... *your* cottage had the piano I used to play. Always a sight neater than ours, too. They're still down in St. Petersburg, my parents. I guess you'd want to know that. Sorry to hear about your folks. Horatio in Virginia, you say? Well, I do remember *him*. Hunter's age. right? A real pair, those two. I think that about sums it up."

Nothing! How can a person have no memory of his own life? The piano memory is something he has, and a prompt often helps her students get going.

"The piano, Taylor. You used to play so beautifully. Do you still? You always brought your music up from Florida. Once you presented our old piano—we called it Taylor's Piano—with a gift—its own high-tech metronome. We liked it when you played that out-of-tune old thing. You made my father hire a tuner every summer."

"Hey, you remember that? About *me*?"

"Well, sure. Many things I remember." A bit ridiculous telling him what she expected to hear from him. Pointless to go further. End this now. "So, Taylor. Sorry, to bother you so early. I wasn't thinking. It was a whim. People are all so different about what's important to them. The lake seems more important to me than you. Sorry I interrupted this way. Um, good luck with those pancakes. It was nice hearing your voice again, anyway. Bye-bye."

Gwen hangs up, exhales, unbelieving. What a car crash! She stares at the phone as if it is covered with plague. Don't you ever pull that again! Lesson learned.

The phone rings.

"Gwen? Taylor here. Listen. I would like to see you. I guess the shock, out of the blue like that, blew my mind. Why don't you come over when you get to St. Paul? Catch a taxi out to us. We can talk in a more relaxed manner. In the meantime, I'll give it a better think."

"Taylor? Who was that on the phone?" Sigrid, still under the covers, shouts down to him. No rush to get up. It's cold. It's Sunday. Glad to go to Texas in December. Hope Taylor is off that almond flour waffles kick.

Her mind is floaty after a good night's sleep. She first awoke at dawn and eyed Taylor, silhouetted at the bedroom window watching for the delivery boy. She thought: my puppy doesn't fetch. Just waits for the world to come to him. She drifted off again till the phone rang. She heard him, muffled. Then he hung up. A glance at another dotted line on the phone by the bed showed he'd made a brief call. Must be some colleague of his.

The sound of her husband puttering in the kitchen raises a well of contentment. How they fit together, just right. She yawns.

"No one," he calls from the foot of the stairs. "An old student. Needs an extra recommendation letter to cinch an application. I don't remember her. Can't write up a person if you don't recollect them. We made an appointment. End of the week she'll be here. What day do you leave, again?"

Red flag. Sigrid sits up and calls down. "Well, careful, sweetheart. Watch out for those students from the past, grown up, wanting more from you. It has happened before."

Many's the time she's rescued him from aggressive little sexpots throwing themselves at him. Her Taylor is so gullible. It is the girls these days. They've turned macho over the years. So aggressive! He'd never get entangled voluntarily. Taylor is Loyalty Incarnate, and anyway, an affair would require too much energy from him. She's saved him from scandal more times than he'd care to acknowledge. He needs her, and he knows it.

"Make sure she's not looking for a glorified father figure," she calls out for good measure. What is it with these fathers today, anyway—and their daughters? "I'm telling you: don't go intimating extra 'availability.' You know exactly what I mean, Taylor? You know what it's come to in the past."

"Yup. Sure will do!" He climbs the stairs with the Sunday paper in hand. "Read this review, Sigrid, on early choral music."

Sigrid knows when her husband is changing the subject. It raises the question, who *did* call him that he tries to deflect? And he'd made a call. A date he'd checked out and called back to change? Must've been a call from Hunter, his loser brother with no respect for the hour, the only one calling on a Sunday morning whom Taylor would call back. Hunter annoys her no end. Did Taylor fib to avoid another anti-Hunter tirade? Try it out. "What did *Hunter* want?"

"Huh? Hunter? Nothing special. Said to say hello to you. He's back from Hong Kong. He called up yesterday. How'd you know that?"

"Woman's intuition, Taylor. Antenna always on the alert..."

"Hm. Woman's *snooping*, I'd call it." He makes a big rustling show of turning the page.

Sigrid is sure it was Hunter, makes a face at him and grabs him.

—ⵑⵑⵑ—

On Friday Gwen perches uncomfortably on a pine IKEA chair in Taylor and Sigrid's living room in a subdivision of identical houses, ca. 1968. She feels for the spine of his *Paradise Lost* through her purse. He asked her to come on his day free of classes, so he intends to give her time. She is curious, she must admit, even hopeful about conversation. Sigrid is on tour; too bad to miss meeting The Cold Fish.

Gwen is surprised at how handsome he is—his hair salt and pepper. Still slender, no middle-aged paunch; the same large-framed glasses protect the blue eyes, the same sideways glances at her. He wears a red plaid work shirt for the occasion, with cords, country casual or flaunting that farmer persona? All in all, a good-looking man, grown into his features as men do at his age.

"You certainly grew up," he begins. "You've become very beautiful." He looks directly through those thick lenses. "I checked you out with my English Department colleagues. They *all* know who you are. Every one of them, and they're impressed that you're coming to see me. You really *did* make a name for yourself, didn't you?"

She withdraws his book from her purse and hands it over with a smile. "It's because of you, though. You started it."

He studies the cover, opens it and reads his name aloud, closes it and puts it on a side table. "Yup. It's mine, all right. Who'd've guessed?"

"So, thank you, Taylor, for my career." He could ask her *something* about her field, or refer to their Milton conversations about life and the universe, the obvious thing to do.

"I don't remember giving it to you. But there's my name in it."

He avoids making connections. Leave soon. He's never going to come up with what she's looking for. "Um, so how long have you lived here? Reminds me of your lake cottage."

But it's uninspired, really. His mother exhibited more style, copied from *McCall's Magazine*. Books. Cookbooks in free-standing bookcases across one wall, with stacks of CDs in vertical holders opposite. The furniture is ordinary, the beige walls unadorned, Venetian blinds, no drapes. In a corner, on a carpet of the type loomed by Indian children, perch two stands for a stringed instrument and sheet music; opposite, a baby grand piano atop a similar carpet. All Sigrid. Where is Taylor?

"The lake house," he repeats and taps his old book as if thinking, offers to make them tea. And escape their mutual discomfort? Then she will politely leave.

When he returns, he says, as if continuing a thought, "So, I liked you back then but can't remember much about you. What do you remember?"

She stays general. How about hikes in the woods?

"I did that on my own a lot."

"Taylor, I'm sure you've got lots to do today. I know how it is, your free day—"

He raises his hand. "You were cute, but not beautiful like now. You are very sophisticated. The black suit, the jewelry, that red scarf ... I remember your father and wondering how his students ever tolerated all those Latin quotes; your brother, Horatio; the cottage; the lake; your out-of-tune piano. This one here is Sigrid's. I don't play, what with Sigrid being the family musician. Let's see, my old 'Vette that we stored up there year round." He is quiet, as if bringing images into focus.

She senses nothing *felt* about his list. Most significantly, she is erased, invisible. Just plain ridiculous making so much of him. He did not merit it.

"You became a beautiful woman," he repeats. "Who'd've guessed the skinny girl at the lake would be a renowned Milton scholar? You followed in your dad's footsteps, I guess."

"I didn't follow in anyone's footsteps. I follow what I love."

She feels demeaned by the assumption that she imitated her father. Is he resentful because he did not distinguish himself? In fact, how responsible was he for her connection to Milton? Milton was a passing fancy to him, perhaps required reading. She owes him nothing. She made her own success, her own name, from what she loves. They are unequal. If she had researched him in New York, she would have recognized the huge discrepancy in their careers and the competition it would generate—and never would have called him.

"Luckily, I got early tenure and escaped your publish-or-perish game. I focus on teaching, my students. Suits me better. I'm a 'people' person more than an academic."

Gwen argues internally. A people person? Dream on, Taylor. One doesn't choose between scholarship and one's students. He draws lines to separate them. Let him. Don't start something. Be silent; leave quickly. This is silly.

"And Sigrid is a big help. She's real good with the girls, my freshmen, their first time away from home. She sees what I miss."

He turns to his old book again, picks it up and weighs its heft. He rubs fingers over the worn linen cover. He peers at her. "I think maybe you should tell me more, Gwen, of what *you* remember about the lake. Maybe that will help jog my memory."

At least he shows a willingness to try. Gwen says, "Okay, how about our last Fun Night? That was spectacular. Do you remember it?"

He smiles broadly and sits back in his chair. "Sure I do! I had to babysit you guys that night, but what a disaster! Never did like babysitting." He chuckles. "That last one! Man! It beat all."

"But it was the best one, you know, out of how many? Maybe two or three Fun Nights a summer? You took us out to Abednego Island, the little outcrop of rock and birches in the lake. To build a bonfire and teach us about beer."

"Wasn't that illegal?" He chuckles, his eyes crinkling behind his glasses. "Plying minors with liquor? It didn't register that it was the driest summer Vermont ever had, and bonfires were banned all around the lake."

Oh yes, a complete disaster on his part, but she had adored it. She should recreate it for him in its full glory, like a piece for Unsung Arts Warehouse, with Milton's biblical language permeating the narration. "Listen," she says, "to what it was for me."

She starts with the flashlight clipping the tops of the waves, and the guys rowing against a high wind. Adds the sounds—wind, waves, owl hoots, and laughter from the cabins on the shore. This Fun Night has potential—she's never been to Abednego Island, and she and Horatio are forbidden to take boats out after sunset. It's risky, but she feels safe—they are in it together, and Taylor is in charge. She describes wind gusts coming off the island, buffeting the canoe away from the beach, the drop into the biting cold water to pull it ashore. Soaked and shivering, they want a fire. She and Taylor go for kindling that he lays down carefully into a depression the boys dug beneath the birches. He pitches a triangle of logs and ignites his work of art; the flames crackle up strong and golden and meet the wind in a war of the elements.

"I shouted out that Abednego's spirit had come to life. The fire was like a person."

Taylor smiles. "Book of Daniel; a faith tested by fire—pretty smart association for a kid to make then."

"Well, you know—Dad's influence, plus the beer. That beer was a First for me. I always kept a record of my first experiences. The fire crackled and the burning sap snapped. 'Abednego speaks!' I shouted, seeing in the flames a fiery shape waving its arms. And there were so many sparks! Huge sprays of sparkling light flew like halos over the fire, every which way, blurring with the constellations in the sky. Like Christmas lights. I felt woozy too, like I was floating up above our fire, unhinged. I became the ghost of Abednego. Jeepers! I am really out there, I said to myself. I thought of throwing up. I heard the *ff-t ff-t* sounds overhead—" She sees in his face that he is rapt. "You remember?"

He nods, happy. "I can just see it."

"We watched a million sparks spiral into the dry branches over our heads, before we realized the leaves were igniting. Flames were blossoming in the dry trees and exploding like fireworks—pouf! You jumped up in a panic and started ordering us around. You told me to fill beer bottles with water."

"Yeah. I did. I smashed off the necks to make them into cups. It was all we had. We got a relay going, hurled that water way up in the flames. And you kept shouting your head off down by the water. Gwen—drunker'n a skunk—whooping it up. Got me so mad! I was sure we would perish. We had to extinguish the fire."

"I kept screaming how beautiful it all looked." Gwen is amazed at the vividness they revive, and shocked by her youthful impulsivity.

"We doused it for a long time," she goes on, "coughing away, our eyes stinging. You made us jump in the water to stay wet and keep going till the flames died down, so we were freezing, too. You went round checking for flames. Then we got the canoe into the water and pushed off. We were shivering and scared. I think Horatio even cried. But I! I felt victorious, euphoric. I don't know why. Abednego Island did not burn down. You saved it, you know. I thought of Virgil, *et in Arcadia ego*—that we had defied my father's words. Everything doesn't die. Abednego survives the fire test. Survival happens."

Taylor exhales. "Trust me, I did *not* think of Virgil! I was so scared and relieved—we'd gotten out alive without burning down Vermont. Amazing, your memory—so many details you have!"

She nods. It's because she treasures her past acts of defiance, beauty and passion, records them in her art. Sees them as life. Taken together, they give her a kind of strength.

"And you, Taylor, you showed foresight. You ordered us out of our reeking clothes, took them over to the all-night laundry before the parents returned. They never found out. And you put the kibosh on Fun Nights after that. It was okay by me, 'cause you would never top that one. You know, actually, it was pretty irresponsible."

"God, it was! Not like me now, really. This is good, very good—remembering my wayward youth, taking those crazy chances. What do you say to lunch?"

Gwen agrees without hesitation. A barrier is broken; a sense of the old equality, working together, the bond that once united them. And she is hungry.

In his car, seated next to him, she can see them back in that hollow in time. It pleases her. "So you do remember our dangerous adventure. And me."

He smiles. It had been tucked away. He appreciates her restoring the memory to him.

Oh well. An easy-going man, she would say, stuck in time and place, could use some unsticking. But nice for this Sigrid, married to a man of few demands with a generous streak to him—to try remembering because she asked him to.

"Why?" he repeats over lunch. "Why did you remember *me*? I'm flattered, but I still don't really understand."

She says, who knows? Historians value the past and its narratives. Since he was there with her, she presumed he would have access to her time at Lake Champlain, her haven. "Taylor, you were a friend when I felt pretty lonely, even if you don't remember. Maybe I overreacted to your attentiveness. You had your own pressing issues—love, sex, marriage, Sigrid. Abednego is a great example of *Rashomon*, how we remember each in our own way. For me it was freeing, for you terrifying. But I'm glad you didn't forget it."

"Anyway," he says, "a person probably owns several memories of an event, not all available at once. We remember the version that fits best what we're looking for at the time. We call it a fact, or the truth. Except it's limited by what we know, or who we are."

Or what we want, Gwen thinks.

"So theoretically, memory's subject to change as we change. I tell that to my students who take things literally—the Bible, for example. Happens a lot up here. I say there are no such things as facts. They freak. I guess I'd be a terrible historian."

"Or," she smiles, "a very good one, willing to revise your thinking according to what you want to know."

It turned into a good day, better than she imagined. She feels elated, in fact, and once she reaches New York, she calls Mallory to tell her about it. It was a sound impulse to find Taylor, brave, romantic and futuristic of her. She is back to normal now, hopeful, maybe. It is quite a voyage to take, to meet up with someone from your past.

"Not something I'd ever do," Mal says. "Look up someone from the past. Count me out. It's often wiser to let bygones be bygones." But speaking of someone from the past, Mal says, she's coming to New York. Would Gwen make reservations for Tuesday at seven at their usual place? And invite Shadrach to join them, too.

Gwen does not tell Mal about their parting, when Taylor leaned into the cab to kiss her goodbye and said, "I remember something, now. Didn't I almost kiss you once? I was tempted, but dire consequences flashed through my mind real fast, so I didn't—you know, complicating life with our folks, with Sigrid. You were too young, and I was too hot-blooded. I would have kissed you but wouldn't have stopped at that. I was mad at Sigrid for cheating with some jerk over in Europe. I was completely wild and mixed up that summer."

His admission elated her. Her memory was real. His explanation of why he never kissed her was honest. She reminded him it was on the day they rerouted the stream. She *was* young, and their parents *would* have gotten involved. A kiss *would* have traumatized her.

She was glad he hadn't. If they had kissed, what else might have changed that day besides the stream? How different today would have to be! In fact, she likes today, exactly how it went. "It's been perfect. Thank you."

She pulled shut the taxi door. Then she sat back and giggled. What a disaster it would have been had they really gotten together. Such an ill-suited couple: Gwen and Taylor. So glad that life is what it is. She has been released from the tyranny of teenage memories of Taylor, the imaginary boyfriend and mentor. Let them float away.

She watched the man from the rearview mirror, growing smaller as she drove away, looking lost in his own driveway. She had what she came for and was content.

She thought, as she delivered her paper the next day, that she was released from the overblown indebtedness about her Milton scholarship. She made a sterling presentation and felt a surge of pride from the applause. It was for her.

Off the phone with Mal, her eyes meet the Pan figurine in the vitrine. *Time to see you in a new light, little fellow.*

It is precious to her, the figurine that has survived two thousand years intact, but she feels humbled knowing she can only guess, never know truly, what it once signified in its own era, before the Renaissance and the present time assigned it meanings. Everything she believes so certainly is available for reexamination and reinterpretation.

The visit was cathartic. She has work to do.

—⁓—

A week later, dining at Quatorze with Mal and Shadrach, Gwen describes the Taylor Chase-Down, the search for a teenage fantasy that led to a rather ordinary, but nice enough, honest fellow.

"Well," Mal concludes, cracking the surface of the crème brulée delivered with three spoons, "it is impressive that you found him, and you get credit for your honesty. Isn't it the sort of thing we would do back in the day? You know, take a chance. Take a risk. See what happens. Accept the consequences. That was the deal, as we used to say."

Shadrach says, "Sorry he turned out to be a zero, sweetheart. You deserve better. But that escapade! You are the only person I know calculating enough to pull off finagling a reason to see him! Brava." His spoon enters the dessert.

Gwen rests her spoon, abstaining. "Calculating? I don't agree. Mal has it right. I pursued the truth, and I am happy to admit how 'off' I was. The difference between me and 'calculating' is motivation. Mine was pure—for knowledge." What does she even like about Shadrach, his superficial understandings and cynical quips?

The next day, she receives a packet by DHL, a photocopied essay by a nineteenth-century German theologian about his trip through Arcadia in Greece and the myths of Pan he discovered there. On the cover, Taylor scrawled the date of their meeting, October 31, 2005. "Gwen, thank you for a jewel of a day. On a necklace of dreary days, it hangs like a pearl. Sorry I didn't kiss you way back then. Life today might truly have been different. Taylor."

Nov. 7, 2005

Taylor, thanks so much. The essay is a godsend. His notes about Arcadia and the Pan imagery gave me an idea, something I've been looking for. I could follow the same route—he provided a map. Today there are excavations dotting his route. I might discover something for myself. See where it takes me—a monograph for my trouble. How thoughtful to have sent it. I am excited. Looking into a trip to Greece for June.

Cheers, Gwen

Nov. 8, 2005

I knew you'd make something of it. Will you allow me to be a kind of midwife to your project? Taylor

Nov. 8, 2005

Do I need a midwife? Doubtful. What is that, anyway? Thanks for the offer, though. Cheers, Gwen

Nov. 9, 2005

Oh, come on, think about it. I really do enjoy your mind (razor sharp, etc.), and it's a way to stay connected. I would hate to lose you again. T

Endearing that he wants to stay in touch, a new colleague in a related field. Why not keep him posted? It's only e-mail.

She receives from Taylor several arcane eighteenth-century sermons with references to the evils of Pan and of Satan in a goat form. New texts arrive every few days. He jokes: I am a man transformed by a mission.

E-mails with attachments and responses, compliments and appreciations zip back and forth once, soon twice daily. It is material she never would have found, sources from comparative religions, historical sermons and the like, unrelated to what she knows. She is grateful.

She writes, "I am excited about pursuing this. Never had a 'midwife' before," she teases. "You turn my Pan research into a newborn baby."

Quite fun to have a reliable colleague outside her field in on the ground level to whom she feels free to make any ridiculous statement or ponder aimlessly without censure; they've known each other for years. The camaraderie from the past is intact. He follows what he calls her "hunches to nowhere" without judgment. She makes mistakes, and who cares? She amends and goes on.

Up-tempo e-mails, short and long, continue through November. Gwen looks forward to each arrival, returning to her desk throughout the day to check New Messages.

In early December, he astonishes her by writing he is free to come to New York for a weekend so they can work together.

Gwen calls Mal immediately to report this peculiar turn in their distant but amicable friendship. "Weird, right? I guess it's okay with his wife. What do you make of that?"

"Be careful," Mal advises. "Probe the 'it's fine with the wife' line. I suspect he plots something extramarital, Gwen. You've got a middle-aged man nearing retirement with too much time on his hands. Careful, girl. You don't want a mess on yours. You know, fingers can get burnt playing with fire. Be careful."

Good advice. She presses Taylor for details. He describes a trade-off he's made, which she phones in to Mal. Sigrid will fly up from Houston to meet him at the end of his New York weekend. Together they will fly down to St. Petersburg to visit his folks, disposing of the annual Christmas visit earlier this year. Sigrid looks forward to meeting Gwen and invites her to join them for a drink at the airport before they take off.

Mal is horrified. "You see that? The wife travels *way* out of her way to meet you, fully cognizant that you are no academic ingénue in need of Taylor's assistance. She sees right through him. Her husband intends to stray, so she's coming with her leash. The whole idea is crazy. Do not allow any of it!"

Gwen agrees wholeheartedly. Anyway, who wants to meet Sigrid? Sorry, she writes Taylor. Having him there for the weekend, trekking back and forth to the airport, will eat into grading papers time. It is her last weekend before winter break. Please convey regrets to Sigrid who probably hadn't factored in the extra hours of travel time for Gwen to and from the airport.

A day passes with no response. She phones Mal. "It seems canceled. Too bad, in a way. It turned out well the last time we saw each other."

Then Taylor answers: make room in your schedule. He will come. He needs a vacation.

Gwen shrugs. Even if suspect, the situation is not as crude as Mal suggests. Via e-mail, they enjoy a relationship of the mind. What's the harm in person?

"Because, Gwen! Open your eyes. Alone together for a weekend? Don't play naïve with me!" Mal calls nightly for details of what she calls her Reality TV program. She must. It's what friends do, look out for each other.

"Mal. I am in total, *total* control. No interest in him *that* way. It amounts to two half-days of research. *Some* flirting is allowed to hold my attention, but not more..."

"You are taking a big risk. I hope you can accept the consequences," Mal says before saying goodbye.

As the weekend approaches, the physical desire in his e-mails is glaring. It's in the longer length, added-on paragraphs of reminiscences of her visit, references to childhood events at the lake, ending with his surprise at her beauty, as if he cannot say goodbye. When does he find the time to teach, to be a husband? Certainly, not her business. But what *is* in it for her? Collaboration? Friendship? Not really wanting a reason pinned down, preferring to discover it with him in person, she stays up till two and three in the morning, inventing witty e-mails for him to discover when he wakes up. Simple fun. A novelty from teaching. Can't lead to anything. They are middle-aged adults; it's a version of Fun Night, not Reality TV. He is bound to Sigrid, hook, line and sinker. They both know that.

Sigrid slides into the marble bathtub, filled with bubbles up to her chin, at the Hotel Cavour, Houston. She will miss this grand hotel with its Italianate façade. Her quartet always stays here. A disconcerting find in the land of the cowboys, with a Riviera-like pool in the atrium. Such a pastiche! She will order up tea, nap before the concert. Rehearsal went well. It will go beautifully tonight. Afterwards are dinner plans at a restaurant they've gone to before, famous for steaks and a four-page wine list.

Poor Taylor, freezing in Minnesota! Remind him to pay those bills stacked by the phone. Assure him her plane took off on time; she caught a taxi from Hobby, no problem. She does enjoy the university venues in Texas. People are so friendly. It's his loss because he hates to budge and won't ever join her. Too late now, because this is the last time; she sighs. Never, he insists. Not his world. You could skip the concerts, sightsee on your own. Not enjoyable alone, he barks back. He will travel plenty on their European trip, the honeymoon they never took. An itinerary of their choice, he says, not imposed by her agent's venues.

Remind him about the holiday traffic, to allow enough time for his flight tomorrow, to see this famous Gwen from his childhood who cannot manage her own work. Why would she want to see Taylor in person if they collaborate by e-mail so well? She winces. It had been bitchy of her to throw that at him. "Because she is working in *my* area—*my* expertise! She doesn't know a pig in a poke about ancient religion. She was kind to invite me, and I haven't been to Manhattan in a dog's age. I want to get out, Sigrid, for something that interests *me!* Do I grill you before you gad about? And don't you worry. She got to where she is by being the 'all work and no play' type. Relentless. Trust me."

It *was* small-minded of her. She hurt his feelings. He accepts her absences without complaint. Let him visit the professor in the flowered hat and tennis shoes, scour the library stacks for … Milton, is it? Not that the fuddy-duddy cliché she's dreamed up as "Gwen" fits a famous New York University professor; but English Renaissance does bring a bore to mind.

Taylor's unlikely to need rescue. The curse of a handsome husband! He has a point: it's been years since he stepped foot out of Minnesota voluntarily—and for a scholar, no less. He won't even budge for his own professional symposia. Hates crowds, he says. It's fair: one trip during his retirement year. Maybe the professor will take him to tea at the Palm Court. She'd go there herself if she were in New York City; dinner at Café des Artistes, or better yet, that Latin American restaurant in the airplane magazine, or even Japanese, which she has never tried. Their dates coincide to meet at La Guardia. The professor's too busy to meet his wife? Well, Sigrid's not really keen to meet her, either. His parents are handful enough, she tells him.

"Boundaries, Sigrid. Do not overstep." He doesn't sound as irritated as usual.

—~~~—

Gwen opens her office door on Saturday at noon and smiles up at Taylor, who beams down at her. His desire for her is palpable; she knows immediately. The e-mailed desire, now live, fills her small office with static electricity. His eyes behind those outmoded glasses devour her, communicating that he flew a thousand miles to see her again. He kisses her on the lips and hugs her seconds too long.

"Your office." He looks around as if to replace an imagined one, removes scarf and coat, checks behind her door for a hook, visibly nervous.

Nervous is sweet.

He settles opposite her in the chair for students with the grin of the cat that swallowed the canary. "So. Here we are. At last."

"So." She echoes his pace. "I'm so pleased that you actually did come. Here you are. In the flesh. Who'd have guessed?" Gwen, while expecting his last-minute cancellation, got her hair done, had a manicure and bought a turquoise baby soft cashmere sweater that set off her eyes to wear with jeans. Her figure looked perky in the mirror, she thought, pleased. She wears her Harry Winston earrings, gift of an ex-lover. No other jewelry. Exchanged her Rolex for the less intimidating plastic Swatch. Perhaps not intimidating, perhaps his entire millionaire family sports armloads of Rolexes. She restacks the papers on her desk in the awkward silence, as if waiting for a shy student to start.

"I'd never cancel," he says, "I *am* the midwife!"

Gwen abhors that word, effeminate and passive, that puts her in the driver's seat. She must change the language that has developed between them. A private language of jokes and terms, acceptable via e-mail, is horrific spoken out loud, hinting at intimacy. She should stop it face to face.

She takes charge, anyway. "Let's start with lunch. We'll talk. I'll catch you up on things."

As they move through the rest of the day, he signifies with gestures, glances and excuses to touch her, that for him, this is more than a meeting of minds. She will not encourage him; they will work hard until he leaves to meet The Dogcatcher with her net and leash tomorrow night.

The afternoon passes as it would with any colleague except for being more fun. By early evening she relaxes her guard, fully enjoying the repartee and the ideas, the laughter and silliness in it—*the magnetism*. She allows him to put his arm around her and accepts his hugs, but she keeps them in public—restaurants, Bopp Library. In the dusk that falls before five o'clock, walking from Washington Square, pre-Christmas Greenwich Village has never sparkled so brilliantly. He takes her elbow to steady her in the stops and starts of crowds and traffic, over layers of ice. He is gallant. When did anyone last care whether she slipped or got separated on the crowded street? She could offer him a home-cooked meal. She knows an impressive dish she and Mal learned on a weeklong Cordon Bleu class in Paris. Warning herself about blurring lines, she proposes an early restaurant dinner, then to drop him off at his midtown hotel. So he can rest. She is relieved not to have gotten them tickets for Lincoln Center. He unexpectedly kisses her goodnight—really kisses her—communicating his regret at the end of the evening, but he says nothing. There is information in the slow release of lips.

Riding uptown, it dawns on her that she has spent the day with a man in love. She reads this not only in the physical signs but in his observations and comments—the synergy from the city, the neighborhoods of Manhattan, the cost of rents and coops, the shops and entertainments, the cultural possibilities, above all, the contrast to home. Does he have the courage to admit it to himself? To her? Does love force a complacent man to be rash, to speak up? And if he said he loved her, what would she say in return?

In fact, after one day how *does* she feel about him? Flattered, *so* flattered—his attentiveness keeps her in a heightened state, a high. She *wants* to love someone. To be loved back. Is Taylor the one? She shrugs. She does not doubt her own need, and he wants her, imperiling the status quo of his marriage. It cannot happen, and she will not encourage him.

Having an affair is like leaping off a cliff with no parachute. A huge chance for disaster, but does she want that chance? Could she fall in love with him? Has she already? The questions make her squirm. Love affairs are time-consuming and life-altering. There is no future with him, so do not try to test it. Remember Mal's words, her buoy in murky waters.

At home she wakes Mal in London to say it was wonderful, actually, the day with him. She has so missed intensity, companionship, connection. He is an intellectual equal, it turns out, at home with texts and concepts. He has good opinions, smart ideas and intellectual acuity. Actually, he is helping her. And he is enjoying it himself; all in all, an exhilarating day. *And he wants her.* She is certain. It is the meta-communication of the visit. Mal says, "Well, of course it is. And?"

"*And* it's a high to feel wanted." In fact, he is totally gaga while saying nothing. He's touched her, watched her, acted moony, and kept her in stitches. And if she totaled the hours he already devoted to writing her in the last month, why, she is an altar and he is the priest. "These are the behaviors of a man infatuated— *with me.*"

"What do you feel for him?" Mal asks.

"Do I know? Adulation is a powerful drug. It's tempting to find out if there is more than feeling flattered on my side."

Mal groans. "Do not go there."

"So, listen." Gwen has an idea. "Here's what I *can* do. Perfectly safe. In my mind, I give him a deadline—say, by when he leaves tomorrow, for him to own up to his feelings. If I hear the word 'love' or an equivalent, I can *consider* taking him on, seriously. I don't have to, but we could, at least, have a rational discussion. An affair *would* be a mess, of course, but it's the only way to know for sure if there could be more with him. How else can I find out?"

A mental deadline is actually self-protective, to cope with what is definitely in the air. He may say nothing by then, so she'll drop it, know he is a tease—a maddening tease.

"I'm pretty sure that after he goes home, the infatuation will die. Don't you see? A controlled experiment. Science! Because there *is* chemistry to explore. It feels good to be together, even if I don't *know* him. Could I fall for him with more time? Who knows? Still, I cannot discount that his silence is because he wrestles with what he feels. But, Mal, don't you at least agree that by coming here and acting so moony, he is already cheating on her? And he *would have to cheat* temporarily at least, if he is going to know for sure what he wants. It's logical."

"Doesn't matter," says Mal. "Let him sort out his own life. You stay out of it."

"But maybe it's a nowhere marriage, Mal. Dead. She doesn't question the time he spends on me. Maybe, *she* wants out... No, I *don't* know what he tells her. But if she doesn't stop him, that means something, right? Yes, not for us singles to judge a marriage, but what do *you* make of it? He perplexes me."

Mal says: "I see. Gwen, dear, you know nothing about them. You don't even know what held your parents together. I mean about the glue, not economics or comforting fights or emotions, but the intimacy. No outsider ever knows what passes between people, developed over a lifetime. No one knows what binds or ravels or gets a bit sclerotic with age. People hardly know themselves. But those ties are there. I should call you a bit presumptuous, but I will not. I'll say instead that you cannot know what transpires between two people to keep them together in life or even afterwards, in death."

Gwen does not allow that abstract thought in because her mind is racing miles ahead. "Okay, let's say we had an affair. I could quickly be bored. He could go right back to her. I wouldn't care—I'd feel better for having checked it out. And if an affair developed into more, it could be good. I'd have love, a friend, a partner. Aren't we all entitled to love, Mal? It allows for a future, and I need that, especially now."

It seems so plausible that Mal's reaction surprises her. "Gwen, put me on record for strongly disagreeing with you. No matter how hot the love he might profess, we both know he is unlikely to leave his wife. They rarely do. We do not know why these fellows entangle themselves in such situations. But you will have heartache, darling, by going along with him. We don't want heartache for you. Heartache is bad. You just lost your parents, enough loss for one year. I advise you, do nothing. Even if he offers to die for you, *do absolutely nothing*. Protect your heart, dear."

Gwen ends it there with a shudder at the concept of "heart," which is particularly Victorian-sounding, separating emotion from thought. She believes in action after full consideration of the pros and cons: in other words, the modern way. Her plan is good. She gives him till tomorrow night.

It was just one day, but it's not like he is a stranger, Gwen thinks, preparing for bed. They've known each other since toddlerhood, but love is more than familiarity. One should love the present person, not a fantasy person. Because in love you give up your wholeness, the space that surrounds you that is in your control, your ideals and private dreams. Love is the trade-off for having to cast aside parts of yourself. To love requires negotiating with a separate, other individual. To love Taylor she would have to die a little, for that is what it feels like to give up total independence, to take another into consideration. All the time. Yet it is what people do. She quit on Ari and those who followed from impatience with their otherness. She never liked their impinging on her independence, having to give in, to compromise—to die, in effect. Love means an amputation of some part of herself, which she has been unwilling to suffer. She could have stayed with any of them, but she did not love enough to suffer the small deaths. She understands now that one's lover, partner, spouse must forever be disappointing in some way. To love Taylor *in the future* would be all she could agree to explore now, in the present—should he raise it. Such an edgy proposition, but she is ready for it—if it is to be.

The phone rings: Taylor saying goodnight. Who had she been talking to all this time? He couldn't get through. His tone is proprietary.

She bristles as she answers him, already an infringement on her independence. A friend in London. She doubts that he spoke with his wife in the interim to tell her his feelings for Gwen, admit that he was in Manhattan to check her out. If he had, he wouldn't sound so chipper. Gwen feels exhausted. Sleep is in order. Good night, Taylor.

—w—

The prospect of Sunday together is colored differently with Gwen's new ultimatum alive in her mind. They meet at the Metropolitan Museum of Art so he can see two different Pans in the Greek and Roman Collection. They begin the long stroll to the Public Library in the cold. He asks for more memories of him, and she likes that he listens intently. She tells him he played the piano with heart, Chopin's études. She describes his secret places in the woods, the lichen he showed her that bring down forests over millennia and the spring that was a source for Lake Champlain. She describes how they rerouted the stream in honor of Milton. He claims she delivers to him a life that has been lost. He senses how different he was then, how much younger, more open. How does Gwen do it? He asks her, why do you remember?

She shrugs. It is who she is. Her memories keep her together and whole, provide coherence as she goes here and there. Everyone is different.

He puts his arm around her shoulder, hugs her, growing silent as they walk.

"Sad? Are you thinking about something?" She asks him twice.

"No."

She realizes that it was ridiculous to believe he would think like her, or talk or act like her. It is quite possible that she misread him. Unless she asks him—and she will not—she will not know if he loves her. At a red light, feeling chastened by her error, she leans into the crux of his arm, against the bitter wind. A wan sun brightens the avenue, hits her cheeks. Nearing the library, she wishes he would talk. The walking was intimate, even in the silence. What happened to change yesterday's flirtatious mood?

Indoors, he grows aloof. He speaks of prehistoric religions, goat worship in Central Asia and Northern Europe to be looked into, Neolithic animal worship to be researched, if she's interested. In Hindu mythological imagery, the Vedic god of fire rides atop a goat; goats pull the chariots of gods. In Norse mythology, goats pull Thor's cart. The most important biblical reference goes to John the Baptist, who calls Christ The Scape*goat*.

She concludes, "So, full circle to Milton," and feels sated with the topic. Their time is coming to an end, and she has lost his attention. Though they sit shoulder to shoulder, thigh to thigh, he does not speak. Perhaps in the night he saw the folly of his being there with her. Perhaps he called his wife. Nothing will change, she knows now, frustration building. Not much time left in her experiment gone bust. Irritation at his silence rising, she fidgets.

In his hotel lobby, she waits impatiently while he collects his overnight bag, pays his bill.

"Do we have time for coffee, before I leave for LaGuardia?"

It is bitterly cold now, graying into dark and beginning to spit rain, the worst of Manhattan weather. She knows a place, a side-street café with a cozy hearth fire and Irish coffee—a last chance to name the magnetism that passed between them or to explain his withdrawal. In an hour, he leaves to meet Sigrid. And it's done.

He reaches across the table for her hand and holds it, a look of agony in his eyes. He covers her fingers with the heat of his palms.

She blushes at how her urge at middle age barely differs from the urge at fifteen. It embarrasses her, sullies her, not more than a sappy love song. She looks at him directly, says it has been a most unusual weekend and thanks him for coming to New York on her behalf.

"My pleasure," he whispers, leaning across the table to kiss her gently on the lips.

She lets him, and waits for more.

He draws back into silence, in which he seems to bid her to speak. He requests the check and helps her with her coat. With both hands he tucks her scarf around her neck, a motherly gesture that annoys her. He is motherly.

On the curb, he kisses her again and holds her tightly, silently, then lets her rigid body go.

She hails him a cab. He nods and steps in. The taxi pulls off. No word of goodbye.

She walks uptown for a while, not sure why she feels teary, but is careful not to slip, focuses on the valleys of black slush made by tire tracks. Such a lot of nothing.

On the phone that night, Mal offers a middle road. "How about settling for academic camaraderie? Let that part continue? It's what he is comfortable with."

Gwen says no. He withdrew his interest. He wanted to return to his wife. Best to end the academic "camaraderie." He is a man who doesn't know what he wants. He is a cliché, pandering to a midlife crisis. "Stupid of me—I see it now."

"So he got himself out of Minnesota, but he marched right back. Let's face it, dear heart, men his age do not reinvent themselves."

"Et in Arcadia, et cetera, et cetera." They laugh at Virgil's inescapable point—nothing lasts.

"Made Christmas plans yet, Gwen? It's time."

The beginning of January, back from visiting Horatio and his family, Gwen is ready for a fresh start, but Taylor's e-mails begin anew. He reveals that he has a lifeless marriage, describes a long, deadly shutdown of his intellectual, emotional, spiritual shop, realizing it only because of having been with her. He hated leaving her. He felt so alive with her. He apologizes for his glumness when they parted. It was all he could do to keep from crying.

Gwen calls Mal. "My experiment worked, in the end. He came through, albeit on his own time frame. What do you think of that! I can continue the experiment, take the next step, see how far it can go."

Mal is silent, and Gwen waits. Mal says, "You know, Gwen, yours is not a youthful social experiment like Group, like 'let's make a revolution, analyze the impact on the different sectors and note the various consequences.' This is your life, Gwen. His words tell you only what he understands as his reality. If you take him on as your own reality, you take a leap of faith. By now, haven't we all trusted many men—colleagues, lovers, fathers, uncles, teachers, mentors? We trust their words, and we go along with them. We trust them to the point of allowing them to change the course of our lives. We trust because there is something we want ourselves, something separate and apart from them, something we wanted way before we ever met them or knew them and their great plan in which they now include us. We had a void, and we believed they were the ones to fill it. So yes, go ahead if you want, but keep your own void in mind. He will fill it, or he will fail you, but that void is yours to fill."

Gwen tells him she will not have it—hearing about his marriage issues. It's not her business. It's between him and his wife. Instead she tells him about her new headway with Pan.

He writes that he told Sigrid his feelings about their marriage.

Gwen asks him to check a reference for her.

He writes that he told Sigrid that if she should die before him, he will go to Gwen.

Whoa! Now, you have my attention, Taylor. What did she say to that?

She said you are a reasonable choice.

Yikes! What is she? A saint?

Taylor's honesty is shocking. He has chosen her. It had been her timing that was off. Different personal clocks was all. He needed to go back and compare, something she hadn't considered. The same condition applies, in her mind. Her experiment: he must reveal his feelings for her, not just allude to them. Did he say he would wait for Sigrid to die first? What was that?

She describes her progress for June travel to Greece. She tells him when she finds an apartment rental on the Internet in Agios Andreas and books a jeep from the Athens airport. She lists sites she will visit and an itinerary, converting kilometers to calculate distances for him. She tells him she began a search for a travel companion for part or all of her trip from among European friends, colleagues and ex-students, keeping him abreast of the rejections she receives. In the places where she will go, archaeologists have found evidence of ancient Pan worship, even ancient cannibalism. Interesting, right? The archaeologists want to meet her to discuss her research project.

In February Taylor purchases her guidebooks to follow her itinerary more easily. That's the spirit, Taylor, she thinks. Keep me company.

In March she informs him that a London colleague will travel with her. Three weeks later, the colleague drops out. She hears Taylor's relief. No matter. Freer to be on my own, she assures him.

Taylor, studying the guidebooks, worries that she will be alone in uninhabited areas, about thieves, attacks on foreign women, lonely roads, being taken advantage of.

Worries about her well-being, she wonders, or worries about losing communication? It's okay, Taylor. The Internet is everywhere. I'll let you know I'm safe.

On April 1, he makes a demand of her. He wants to know her feelings about him.

Gwen, sticking to her rule that he must speak first, deflects:

For me, this is a grown-up Fun Night, an academic lark.

He responds:

Don't joke around, Gwen. Be honest, as I am trying to be. I am in psychic pain—not a joke. Am trying to figure this out. Do me the kindness of the same. You know we're on the same wavelength. Clear to me that in writing daily to you for nearly a year I've wandered into dangerous territory, but I can't stop. You keep me going in an emotional desert. I need to be with you to feel alive, like I did in New York. I beg you to say where you stand with me. Please make it easier for me to dare to say I love you. This is killing me. I am begging you to say what you feel for me.

There it is. It took him so much longer than she ever imagined, a weightier decision than she had realized, but he did it. He moves at his own rhythm. Perhaps, as Mal said, he had to know what bound him to Sigrid and why it no longer did. She likes the counterbalance to herself; she can slow herself down to be in step with him. Slowing down to his ponderous pace is the first of her little deaths, she realizes.

She trembles at her computer. What to say? Memories of old lovers stir nothing like this intensity. She feels the danger of this embarkation, but it is a mutual danger. She has been so back and forth about him but now feels giddy with possibility.

April 2, 2006

OK, Taylor, here comes honesty. You have entered my daily life, my work, my distraction. I begin each day waiting for you, thinking about you. I love our jokes and our compatibility, our mutualism. So, yes, it is quite possible, that I could love you, with enough time to know you more. We've barely seen each other, but I am willing to find out. This is emotionally risky for me without a fallback person, as you have in Sigrid. We cannot meet again unless you leave Sigrid and Minnesota.

Such a decision for you, based on so little knowledge of me, is risky and dangerous, too. What if it isn't love, but distraction? What if it goes nowhere? We need a plan with a goal. Any ideas?
   Cheers, Gwen

Reading it once before she hits *Send*, she understands how she pushes the future in the specific direction she wants. He answers in minutes.

Can't believe what I read. Haven't a clue what you mean by a plan or a goal. Am grading thirty damned papers, but will think about it. Writing just to acknowledge receipt. Gotta grade papers. More later. Love, Taylor. I love you, love you, LOVE YOU!

—~~—

Gwen cannot wait for Taylor to dream up ideas for getting from A to B. Time is short. To her, the momentum thus begun must be followed through quickly. Otherwise, she dangles. She types furiously to keep up with the thoughts that come.

Idea: Let us travel in Arcadia together for one month as a test period, after which we both assess if we have a future together—explore the question away from our daily lives, and in private. It would be clarifying for us both. No permanent damage done if we decide this is a terrible mistake. No one need know what happens between us. We can both move on, even drop out of the other's life permanently, if it is a terrible mistake.

She pauses. She feels so smart: an efficient, self-contained trip to learn quickly, given his proclivity for moving slowly. A great plan.

If by the end of the month-long trip we decide to continue, we will figure out the next step, then. Together. Of course, Sigrid must know of this unusual proposal from the beginning. She is part of it, too—as soon as possible—and she must agree that you try it. Tell her the trip to Arcadia is a test. You believe you are in love with me and it is a way to explore it. If it fails, she must take you back. But if you want to continue the test, Sigrid should graciously bow out. (Because why would she want you, in that case?)

Gwen thinks generously about Sigrid, puts herself in Sigrid's position: why would she *not* agree? She has no choice, really. This test suits Sigrid, too, allows her to exit a loveless marriage, or else it will be the validation of their marriage. Gwen sees the logic of it, fully satisfied. This is a modern version of the *McCall's Magazine* "starter marriage," in fact. The same idea really, a test period to check things out.

She ends with a description based on her Patmos year of an Arcadia filled with music and dance, temple ruins in the moonlight, flowery fields overflowing with fruit and nut trees. She can handle the driving, money, the language. She's used to managing in foreign realms.

Yes! I will go with you.

Yes? For real? She is joyous. Who would ever have thought that Taylor—so seemingly stuck, scared, deadened—would agree so quickly? He must be serious about her. Love *is* transformative. Right again, Johnny Milton! She advises him to expect difficulty from Sigrid but to be firm. It is only with Sigrid's agreement that it can work. He is braver than she thought. She is so happy. Who would have believed this could happen?

While she waits to hear about Sigrid's reaction, they fine-tune their month-long itinerary.

He sends an e-mail fantasizing about making love to her, which takes her by surprise.

Mal, who follows their progress nightly, is incredulous. Hadn't she thought about sex? Did she think he intended to be chaste? Tell him no!

Of course, she thought of it! But he can't have that, Gwen tells Mal. Sex without their ducks already in a row complicates the test, invites pain and heartache if the test fails.

She writes:

Taylor, you needn't be unfaithful to Sigrid. "This is only a test." Intimacy complicates the test. I want my own room and space. I need to know my own feelings, too. Right now, I'd like to know that Sigrid agrees—the most important point.

It flatters her that he wants her right away. If it goes smoothly while they are there, then ... she must decide if she can give up her independent way of life—preciousness itself—for a life with him. She must be very sure that she trades what she has created for someone worthy. Yes, that is the word: worthy. The trade-off.

Hey, Taylor, what does Sigrid say so far? It's very important that she agrees to take you back. If you decide for me, I hope she can be happy for you. If she really loves you, she will let you go.

Gwen sends the e-mail. Why the long silence regarding Sigrid? Surely Sigrid is following this, possibly reading over his shoulder, staying informed on the woman who features in his fantasy of her death? Is Sigrid alarmed? Resentful? Relieved? Doesn't care? Unless. It's the most plausible explanation—Sigrid wants out of a loveless marriage. Let him do the work. Why won't he say?

Taylor responds curtly:

Sigrid is my problem, not yours. Let me handle my wife. I know what to say. Leave my wife to me.

I get it, Taylor, and if you choose Sigrid, I shall accept your decision. I can take it. Pain, rejection, hurt. It hasn't killed me yet. I can handle it.

Et in Arcadia ego. Even in Arcadia am I. In the Renaissance, Arcadia is a verdant glen where partygoers celebrate life. Death crouches in a corner, in wait for them. But Gwen thinks of Death outwitted by four kids on Abednego Island. She sees the sparks rise and blow away. Life is victory. If she is not the chosen one, she will move on. It may not kill her, but she dreads it, if it goes that way. Virgil said Death was the great leveler, destroying all; whereas Milton, centuries later, was an optimist, even in his era of pessimism. The radical crux of his personal religion was "the second chance," the repair, the "do-over," as she writes in her work. Doesn't everyone need a second chance from time to time? The trip is a second chance for the three of them—Taylor, Sigrid and her. She hopes he believes that. Again she writes:

Taylor, tell her you need a second chance at living. Remember Milton.

Time's up. May is here. Classes end for them both. He has not written for a week. She must purchase the tickets, confirm her rentals. She and Taylor will begin a trip of discovery soon. Her third trait, her futuristic sense, is resurrected, alive and well.

During these months, they have had but one disagreement that eats at her during his silence. Is it a harbinger? She teased that if she been in charge of Fun Nights, she would have assumed greater risks than he had. He agreed, adding that her need for sensation was extreme. He believed she could rip out her own guts just for the experience. Gwen winced at the violence he saw in her. "Hey," she wrote, "that's not me! I'm gutsy, yes, but pathological? Never! Self-destructive, irresponsible, death-oriented? Wrong, Taylor." His simplistic understanding upset her. For her, the purpose of risk is to learn, to grow, to become more of the whole Gwen. For him, risk is fearful. That night she writes again:

Love makes heroes out of ordinary men, Taylor. It is time to tell her. Say: if she loves you, she will want your happiness and send you off with her blessing. If you are wrong about me, she wins. I will drop out of the picture. I promise. But if you love me more, and I love you, she must let you go. That is the deal you want with her. She must agree, or we cannot go together.

She hits *Send*.
Another day of silence passes.
At night Gwen writes:

Talk to me! What is going on?

Taylor's answer is waiting in the morning.

I'll cut to the chase. It is over between us, Gwen. I will not leave Sigrid. How stupid was I—to fall for your schemes and manipulation that began the minute you arrived in Minnesota. You faked a need of me and led me on all these months. You are ruthless. You offer to endure pain *as an experiment?* Do not ask me to participate in such heartlessness toward yourself and toward Sigrid. You are a masochist. *"To love is to die a little"*? If I've learned anything, it is that I am nothing like you, Gwen Smith. You mow down anyone in your way for what you want. I am loyal to my wife. You do not understand loyalty. I owe Sigrid everything good in my life, and I owe it to her to stay with her.

Reading it twice, she is numb. She knows she knew. She types.

Call me.

At midnight her phone finally rings. Taylor's voice is gentle, contrite, almost a whisper. She thinks Sigrid does not know he is calling her. He fears his wife. Gwen hates him for his cowardice.

"Gwen, are you okay? How are you doing?"

Now she knows it, for sure. Those were Sigrid's dictated words, the smug paean to herself. Sigrid rejects the truth that he doesn't love her. She twists his perceptions, makes *him* twist his own perceptions to see Gwen as evil. Well, guess what? It is Taylor, not Gwen, who is ruthless, willing to inflict pain with indecision and waffling, with teases and half-declarations.

Gwen screams into the phone. It feels so liberating she cannot stop. "You are such a coward, Taylor Bryce! That makes you the ruthless one! You are a brutal liar. To me. To Sigrid. You initiated this relationship! You *played* me, teased me, strung *me* along. Your weakness violates us all. Loyalty. Pooh! What are you, a Boy Scout? Is Sigrid the flag? I will heal from your violence, Taylor. I have a life, a good life. You never will. It is too late for you. You are too dead to know what you want! You died years ago." She slams down the receiver.

Taylor's gaze, Sigrid notes, is through—not at—her. He's been hooded eyes and monosyllables since leaving the harpsichord concert in the basilica; indifferent to being in the piazza to watch the sun set from a picturesque café overlooking the *vapori* parked at the water's edge. Sunset in Venice. What could be lovelier? More romantic? The only time she visited Venice was with Trevor, when she was poor and free. And so young. She had just enough money for a last weekend with Trevor in Venice. She wonders now where they stayed, a *penzione* with hardly a lira between them. Her visa was about to expire and she had to leave. Trevor refused to follow her to America. So Venice was goodbye. Trevor, the London *bon vivant* who didn't want marriage. Death in Venice, they laughed, chosen for their last weekend together because Paris had student riots at the time, and the two were "drop out" types, not "issues" types. Had Taylor known that about Venice? Is that why he insisted on coming here? One of his small provocations? She is here today with means and her second choice of husband on their European honeymoon, three decades late. "Better late than never for a honeymoon. Right, Tay?"

He won't respond.

"So sullen you are!" She gives him a playful jostle.

Europe has changed, as has she, as has Taylor. They have aged and they are tired—he of her, it seems, more than she of him. She should be furious at him. He wanted to stay home, but she would have her honeymoon, damn it. He owes her after his Gwen-scapade. Now he acts as if his indiscretion was her fault. He takes out his anger on her.

Her fellow musicians, *all' unisono,* would have made a run for this table, before the *turisti* noticed it had the best view of the sunset on the water. Their years together as musicians molded them into one mind, made their performances so good, so empathic. They knew how to enjoy themselves—savor the food, the wine, the sights. She misses them already, her quartet. Retirement will be an adjustment, she knows, not feeling as ready for it as she'd hoped. Of course, Taylor doesn't make it easy ... still, nothing lasts forever. This is their time to enjoy life together. Taylor. Look at him! He surely is thinking about that mad woman. Sigrid refers to her as Gwen Myth to taunt him. And why not taunt him a little? Her dig feels both clever and sad. She knows her husband better than he does. He needs her to keep him from falling overboard; still, each time she saves him, he overwhelms her with bitter fury just because she saved him, dragged him back on board, waited for him to dry out. He never saves himself. There is anger beneath his façade of all-is-well contentment.

This last episode is behind them. There will never be another, especially with her able to keep better watch. She will not mention his indiscretion here on their honeymoon trip. But does she ever really forget?

She should try. She loves him. Middle-aged men do this sort of thing. Six months from now he will forget, but it will grate on her that he did it again. Better wives than she would demand a divorce. But not now. What would they do without each other? He can't help it. Think of it as his little social disease.

"Jetlag, you think? Rather go back and lie down, Tay?" It is beyond her, why he insisted on adding Venice to the trip, stealing time from Vienna. Liszt didn't *go* to Venice, she had argued, exasperated, principally because they were in that arguing phase, bred of pre-trip anxiety and post-"other woman" resentment. Well, Nietzsche wrote about Venice, he snapped at her. And now they are here, has he found anything to enjoy? No. He is a walking phantom. She organizes their days. She bites her tongue rather than complain about the added expense of this pointless side trip and risk arguing, since he's just itching for something to explode about.

Still, Venice is marvelous, even with the sad memories of Trevor—so much here that she missed the first time. The food is wonderful. The waiter brought their Campari with a bowl of blue-black olives, picturesque on the citron tablecloth. So nice to even have a tablecloth! A limpid breeze skims her shoulders.

She's bought a beautiful shawl in a color she has never worn, persimmon, fine Italian wool, summer weight for the evening breeze. He owes her that, a four-hundred-dollar shawl. They had planned to eat after the concert, but neither is hungry. It is too early, anyway. It was a short concert.

"No, not yet." As if reading her thoughts he adds, "In fact, can we skip dinner tonight? I am tired. That concert in the heat knocked me out."

She agrees, but with regret. It would be fun to choose an interesting-looking restaurant at random—her quartet always did that—and avoid an evening of passive scrapping in the hotel. He seems not to want to be with her anywhere. He changes their plans daily, almost tyrannically.

She knows what he's doing. He is destroying their honeymoon, out of revenge. It wasn't supposed to feel grim, and it wasn't supposed to come on the heels of his attempt to end their marriage.

First he refused to attend the concert, then he tagged along, sulking. Just for her, he said. She knows why: as reproach for ending the Gwen Myth. She allowed it go on a tad too long, in the hope he would end it himself, but no. No guts, had to have it done for him. She is furious, too, if truth be told.

While he sits stony-faced across from her, she tracks the condensation down the Campari goblet with one finger, like wiping pablum off her sobbing brother's cheeks with a spoon, so hungry he couldn't gulp it down fast enough; their momma at some honky-tonk bar, avoiding her responsibilities. All whiskey and good times was Momma, who thought she was the new Patsy Cline. Her George Jones ran out on her and his kids. So Gwen Myth is who Taylor would go to if she died? What an insult! Unintended, surely. A weekend in New York was one thing, but Europe for a month? Give Taylor an inch, and he takes a mile. What husband travels with a single woman for a month? It is common sense, Taylor; society has boundaries. The crazy lady manipulated him. Honest, Taylor, how dense you can be!

You love her? On the basis of what? E-mails about goats? It's so absurd no one would believe it. Were you born under a haystack?

Another "save" from mid-life angst. What does *he* have to be anxious about? He has had an easy life with subsidies from his inheritance. She had better *not* be the first one to die; he wouldn't know how to function alone. He does need something engaging for his retirement. Something on this trip better grab his interest.

"Were you watching the harpsichordist's fingers, Taylor? Now there is an instrument to take up, what with your piano background. We could play that Bach *Adagio* together..."

Taylor acts as if he cannot hear her. He is adrift.

"Those aren't tears on you, are they, honey? Squinting directly into the sun will make your eyes water. Taylor? Blink, at least! I'm talking to you!"

A large, bearded, black and white billy in the yard lifts his head to chew and stares unblinkingly at Gwen, who waves at him from the kitchen window. Well, isn't it too ironic that her landlord keeps a goat! The clank of his bell called her to the window, just in time to see him climb onto the tailgate of a pickup truck in the yard to get at the straw bales. Gwen smiles. Her own private Pan! It is Greek siesta time, but Gwen's internal clock is thrown off by jetlag and the triumph of arrival. Siesta time is hushed, except for birds chirping on telephone wires, and the random clanking of the goat's bell.

Gwen opens the window wide, enchanted. Beyond is the spine of Mt. Lykaion rising upward; on the other side of it the Ionian Sea, Virgil's ancient Italia and Syracusa. She is exactly where she wants to be. She hears chortling chickens that poke about in the truck's shadow and cicada drones from the olive trees. Around the chickens, red poppies flop about in a low breeze, and smoke rises from a pile of smoldering grass, infusing the hot air with a smoky scent. She is at peace. Past and future exist here in the present.

All these years, her father's interpretation was incorrect. Virgil meant something else, entirely—*et in Arcadia ego* is not Death's voice warning the living of his presence. *Ego*: I am. It is present tense. Virgil meant that life and death exist simultaneously, in the present. She speaks to her father's memory: Virgil understood that as we live we are always dying—little by little, bit by bit. Just that simple and not a radical thought—it is a motif in the minor key of a happy song, a sigh of cool breeze in the sunny afternoon that signals evening. Nothing in the *Fifth Eclogue* speaks of finality and gloom. She must write down this new idea. See what others have thought.

Taylor must be in Minnesota, an arm around a fetid corpse. Inertia, fear, cowardice are Taylor's choice over Arcadia, where it is glorious and filled with life and promise. He is out of love with Sigrid. He knows it. Did Milton understand that some people reject their precious second chance, even when handed it on a plate? Not everyone is brave enough to take it. It requires great courage, and Gwen owns courage. It is her intrinsic trait. She's always known that. She took the chance. And it paid off. And in Arcadia am I, at last. *Et in Arcadia ego.* Like her father, she paraphrases it as she wishes.

She and Taylor: two sparks arcing up from the bonfire on the island. The two are proof of Mal's observation before Gwen left for Greece, that one must be the agent of one's own change. Evolution is not foisted by one upon another, nor does it sprout from social experiments. That's where we went wrong, Mal said about Group, in retrospect. It was an artificial construct. You can't force change. You can nurture it along, is all, and then there is the role of chance. Taylor's spark was extinguished. Her spark floats high, igniting what it needs to stay alive.

She has come to believe that what is intrinsic, what makes her Gwen, also makes her creative ideas, which she thinks of as her children, come into being—the ideas born and nurtured in her mind that may contribute to human understanding once they are out there. And yes, she will say in honesty that she loved Taylor for the kindness and generosity he had to give her. He taught her this fact about change. That counts as something good. She accepts the truth of who he is. His life is his own to live and with whom, his choice. Her life goes on in the exploration of ideas and in the expression of her intrinsic self, which she believes will live past her in metaphors of art and written thoughts. She made no bargain, no trade-off for her passions, which were hers before she ever knew him.

Reunions
Skye, 2011

"We know what we are, but not what we may be."
—William Shakespeare

Arcadia, 2011

IT'S ONE DISASTER AFTER ANOTHER WITH YOU! MINA-THE-BITCH
always ends up screaming, no matter what. Skye never catches a
break with that woman.

Lady, you ain't gonna like this one, either, Skye's thinking.
Skye Consuelo Wright, your Life's Disappointment about to die
on a Greek mountain. Look up: it's a rock cliff twenty stories high.
Look down: it's a twenty-story drop into the Mediterranean. No
way out. She's a goner. Ironic, maybe even funny, if she wasn't so
freaked. Her little kid whine, way down deep wants her mommy.
Not her actual Mina-the-bitch mother, but a nice one, an Aunt
Mal to save her from disaster. All her disasters, actually.

About to die at only seventeen, flattened like an ef'n pancake
the minute some semi races down at a bazillion miles an hour
two days after landing in Wacko-World, aka Greece. Always
sideswiped by something or other. It's killing her.

"Wouldn't you want to lower your stress level, Skye? Put some
distance between you and your mother until the trial?" Aunt
Mal had offered. "I promise, you'll adore the Peloponnese, dear
heart. You'll feel at home in the mountains. Like the Berkshires
but more rustic."

Yeah, right. Mal forgot to mention that in Wacko-World no
one speaks English or gives a hoot about you. And the food!
They expected her to eat a rabbit!

"Sure, I like mountains," Skye had answered, polite-like, to
the old geezer Mr. Theo that morning, to be translated by The

Twerp, Sophia. Sure, mountains sounded doable. She could take pictures, maybe of eagles ripping their prey to shreds, talons dripping blood. Or pumas. What a joke! She's standing in the middle of a road with no shoulders, waiting for Death to arrive. On their so-called National Highway—duh. It's just a mountain road. Get real, people!

The old geezer Mr. Theo lumbers on crutches up ahead, thinking he's gonna catch a tortoise that's lumbering a lot faster. Really? He had to stop for some dumb-ass turtle? She left her camera in the jeep just to send him a message.

Okay, so no semi. Yet. Not even another car. It's a zoo up here—vultures screeching *Peter! Peter! Peter!* up in the sky, waiting for their road-kill lunch: her when she's dead meat. Hawks! The Twerp corrects her, sounding pretty fed up. It's crazy: the eerie wind-howl, wham-banging the scrub every which way, gnarled branches creaking away, whispery leaves scraping rock—everything clinging to the cliff for dear life. She can't even.

And this twerpie kid, Sophia. Really? *Must* she stand in Skye's *personal bubble? In her face?* Explaining everything while the old geezer chases a turtle? Skye hates chatter-boxes after her *residency* in the Commonwealth's primo warehouse for Jay-Dees—oopsy—'scuse *her*—youthful offenders—the Essex County Youth Center holding pen for perps.

Skye kicks a stone all the way to the edge of the cliff and watches it tumble over the side while Twerpie's giving her the play-by-play, like Skye's some kind of retard.

"See? Uncle Theo moves his crutches very gently, not to frighten the tortoise. Uncle Theo is our friend, our *family* friend. I may say *Uncle* Theo, but you must say *Mister* Theo to show your respect."

Really? She squints down at this blondie with eyes the blue of Mina's willow-ware china, ever ready with her Hot Tips for Survival. "*Respect?* Are you kidding me?" Skye has shown enough respect to dazzle the whole *world* by now.

Now what? The Twerp leaves her and heads toward the bajillion-story drop to the sea at the edge of the road.

"Hey, Sophia! Get away from there! Now!" The Twerp can't hear her against nature's racket. How's Skye ever gonna be the *au pair*? Suckish to be the boss of an eleven-year-old that acts smarter than her. *Is* smarter than her. The Twerp's some Genius of the Universe, apparently. Shows off her Greek and English and French. Who knows what they're even saying in this wacko place? And who said she even wants to know?

To top it all off, in the jeep the old geezer announced, via Miss International Translation Service, that Skye should be called *Ourania,* the Greek word for sky. He says it like he's revealing the Secret of Life: Ourania was the muse of astronomy.

Why? What for? This geezer's gonna totally wipe me out? My name's all I got here!

She's still pissed about that one. She touches the skin in the part of frizzy magenta hair which, apparently, is on fire. No one said to sunblock it. Now, she's gonna catch skin cancer. Instead of ankle monitor torture, in Greece you get a hot frying pan on your head all day. What's gonna happen to the magenta? And her tats? Bleach out is what. First her name, and now her whole self is gonna disappear. Her shoulders are so peppered with little blisters—redheads have delicate skin.

The Twerp's leaning over the edge! *What the hell?* Well, Skye's sure as hell not gonna stop anyone from jumping, if that's what Twerpie's thinking about. She knows plenty about suicide watch from Jay-Dee School. So go! *Jump already!* Then she can go back to Aunt Mal in London, where she was very happy for five whole minutes. Sure as jack-shit, she's not going back to Mina-the-bitch until September for her trial. And it's only July! She's so stuck here.

"Sophia! Get away from that damn Brink of Death!"

Twerpie stares daggers at her, turns and looks out at the sea. Ocean-staring is not for Skye. Those traveling whitecaps so far below them make her want to throw chunks. And anyway, even looking at the ocean she feels it dragging her down with a weight of some sadness she can't even name.

Skye, hoping she'll be visible to any oncoming semis, imagines a yellow center line and paces up and down on it for a bit. She has no leverage with that kid, what you need in these power situations. In Juvenile Detention School group sessions they said: *before you run your mouth, check your leverage—it's a social skill that might keep you outta the fights you're never gonna win.* Gotta remember that—to check her leverage. Which she doesn't have any of.

And the other tons of advice for getting through the summer she's gotta remember, too. It's already enough for her brain to handle Kim, the only probation officer she ever half-listened to. *Lose your Loser Act—A-sap. Be a role model for the little kid. Can the cursing. Act like a winner, and you'll be one, Skye.*

Sure. Winner? Loser? Who even cares in Greece? No one knows what she's saying, let alone what she's friggin' thinking. It's downright scary so all alone.

Meanwhile there's "Mister" Theo about to close in on that tortoise. Skye's taller and stronger than him. She could shove him over the cliff after The Twerp falls in, steal his jeep and head back to the airport. Down, down, down, *plop!* Into the sea he'd fall, cartwheeling legs flailing, crutches flying after him ... *plop ... plop.* Legs like in that painting about some Greek myth from Art Appreciation Unit in middle school. Right? Now she's living in a Greek myth herself: it's the actual sea the dude fell into! She had exclaimed: Teacher, that farmer plowing is ignoring the guy drowning right in front of him! Teach said that wasn't the artist's message. It was "don't be conceited," 'cause the dude flew higher than he should've, and got so close to the sun that his wax wings melted. Then he fell into the sea and drowned. He wasn't humble enough. Teach, you are so dead wrong! 'Cause Skye knew pretty much everything then about being ignored while you're drowning. Back when her dad died and Mina was so caught up in her stupid "emotions."

The vultures start big-time squawking and flapping and circling like crazy, a ton of them out of nowhere. She makes a brim with her hand over her eyes and sees them suddenly having a nervous breakdown, super-hyped about what they know from way above all the switchbacks twenty stories below. *Told-ja!* A semi's coming and she's gonna get *creamed!*

"Hey, Sophia! Mr. Theo! We gotta get outta here!"

No one can hear with the wind. But The Twerp suddenly jumps up. She saw it too, from the rock she sat on.

She dashes uphill, yammering a mile a minute. "Skye! Do you want to see something quite typical? A farmer on his donkey is coming with a big bundle of mulberry branches. For his goats. Mulberry leaves are their favorite food, but the trees can't grow this high up, so he brings them to his goats. He must live even higher up. He is what the tourists come to photograph. He wears the old-style pants. A *vrakhi*, it's called. Get your camera! You can take a nice photograph!"

Skye can't even. She's supposed to *want* to see a man with *a bunch of branches*? With his *pants* on? What the? She shakes her head. Absolutely *do not need* to see one more old geezer.

She squints: a black pea against the sun, it's a donkey all right, plodding toward them, a man's shape lurching on top of the pea. A huge bundle of sticks rounds out the view. His pants are baggy. So what's the big deal?

Sophia waves to him, and the man tips his cap to her. Donkey keeps on truckin' toward her. So let's get this straight, people: *a man sitting on a donkey* is about to cross paths with *a man chasing a tortoise*. She's gotta tell Aunt Mal this bizarro-ness, because just two days ago Aunt Mal and her were in *normal* Trafalgar Square watching *normal* people wearing regular, *American*-type clothes dodging traffic and *pigeons. Basic* compared to this.

The donkey passes her so close that Skye hears the jingly colored beads on its bridle. A gold cross dangles on its forelock. It has eyelashes. It reeks of sweaty hide. Sorrow strikes her for that poor donkey in the heat, saddled with a grown man and a bunch of sticks, a fellow beast of burden. It *ka-klop-ka-klops* past her without a howdy-do from the man who scans her purple hair, her clothing, her tattoo-covered arms, averts his eyes. Onward, to the other geezer. The donkey stops while the two old guys yammer and guffaw. Mr. Theo leans on his crutches like a gnome, the wind lifting his long white beard on his chest like a sheet. Meanwhile, the tortoise waddles an inch further while it's got the chance. Go for it, Tortie! Two beats later and the donkey, like a pitiful old Eeyore, disappears around the next switchback.

"*Ellate koritsia!* Ourania! Sophia!" Mr. Theo yells in his weirdo language.

She and Sophia start toward him. Skye shouts to Sophia through the wind, "How does a person not speak English? It's like a world language."

"He never learned it," Sophia shouts back, "so he doesn't have to talk to Americans."

Figures. The world hates us.

Sophia runs ahead. Skye dares not do whatever The Twerp does. He's the boss of them on this road trip he concocted so she can photograph wild animals that supposedly live on the mountain. So what does she get? A tortoise. Big yucks.

He hands his two aluminum crutches to Skye—instead of to his best buddy The Twerp. *What the hell!* She's never touched a crutch before. So light. Nervy to assume she'd hold them for him.

He bends down behind the still tortoise that's pretending it's all by its lonesome, just taking in the view. The Twerp Translation Service is on standby.

"He says the tortoise froze, but it feels his presence. So it is still dangerous. Where's your camera, he says."

"I don't need a picture of this shit. What's he gonna do?"

"Carry it to the side so it won't get hit by a car."

Rich: they get smashed by a semi, but the tortoise gets saved. Hey, it would leave a disgusting blood and guts pie: tortoise splat. She wouldn't mind photographing *that*.

He lifts the creature by the rim of its shell with both hands and stands slowly. A heavy guy, apparently. Its barbed feet kick like crazy at leaving the ground, its horned tail twitching like a harpoon wielded by a maniac. Its goofy head vanishes. Up close, it's an oversized, lethal football, decorated with rows of black and sand-colored rectangles—each one etched with its own fine gray spiral, sort of artistic. All of a sudden its flailing weapons disappear inside it. It's gone, dead. Cool.

Mr. Theo wings an elbow out to create a space under his arm and nods at her. Skye sets a crutch into the crook of his armpit, surprised she understood what he wanted. "*Bravo,*" he says.

Oh, so he does speak English, or maybe she's catching on to Greek.

He leans into the crutch and takes a step with the opposite leg. He hops himself and the tortoise toward the cliff wall.

Skye, following behind with his other crutch, notices a narrow depression between the side of the road and the cliff wall where she could have waited if she'd looked. He drops his crutch to the ground and bends, knees splayed out, to set the rock of a tortoise into it.

"It's too stupid to know it's back on the ground," Skye says.

He reaches for the crutch in her hand and nods at the one on the ground near the tortoise. She crouches where she is and reaches out to draw an end toward her.

"*Efcharisto.*" He smiles at her. "Then-kee-oo."

Gentle smile, actually, for an old geezer, bushy brows, crinkly eyes. Kind-looking smile, like he's pleased at their successful collaboration.

Sophia says, "Come. We're done."

Skye's shaky all of a sudden. She stomps back down to the switchback, scattering stones and pebbles, raising dust, to where the jeep is parked. She plunks herself in the oven of the back seat. Did he have to endanger her life?

Mr. Theo and The Twerp get in front. He hands Skye both crutches to keep in back like suddenly she's their custodian. A flash image of the old gimpy dude at Jay-Dee School, the actual custodian. At least she's not there.

Out of nowhere, a red and chrome convertible thingy comes up from behind them and just misses the jeep with a quick swerve toward the precipice and back onto the road. Zoom— gone. What the!! What if they'd still been in the road? She shivers. She's missed Death by minutes.

Calm like it never happened, Mr. Theo pulls the jeep to the center to continue the drive up to the top. The dumb tortoise just sits where he put it, then vanishes from the side-view mirror as they near the next switchback.

"See?" The Twerp says, all happy. "We just saved it."

"Ya *think*? That gonzo's gonna toddle back and get creamed anyway."

Her words hang there. Usually she's quite the conversation starter. Everyone, the warden, Mina-the-bitch, sometimes even Kim, will come right back at her smart-ass remarks with their own lame ones.

Mr. Theo says—Twerp translating—when he held the tortoise, he was struck by the traits people and animals share.

Oh, must we? Dance this duet between the two of them? The three-way, crisscrossing talk hurts her head.

The Twerp says: "He believes God invented a small number of intimidation behaviors that are used by all living things. God expects the humans—us—since we are blessed with reason, speech and empathy—to know when they hold us back and when they are useful for survival. He asks you: has Ourania ever noticed this? That we share the traits of animals for our protection?"

"Nuh-uh. Ask him how does *he* know what *God* expects."

Sophia shrugs and does not pass along the question. "He says lions, for example, roar ferociously and glare as a warning to back off. He says that for the ten years he's known my mother, she roars and glares to scare others away." Sophia giggles. "It's true! My mother does exactly that. When she's mad, everyone must run!"

"I guess," Skye says, but really she can see it. That lady—Twerpie's mother, Kleio—could be a lion: wild mane of salt-and-pepper curls, a King of the Beasts attitude. Definitely possible. Not so for Mina-the-bitch. Mina would be a minnow—darting every which way to get away—especially when you want her. Skye suppresses a smile. Mister Theo doesn't need the satisfaction of knowing she gets his funny idea. All this time she sees his crinkly eyes under the bushy brows observe her in the rear-view mirror.

"He tells you that I have a protective behavior, too. I change my colors like the chameleon so as not to stand out from the stranger. He says, 'Sophia does not enjoy feeling different.' He says to witness Sophia's facility with languages to fit in with so many people. And German is coming next?"

Skye's watching The Twerp's perfect profile nodding at him. Funny, she's actually pleased to be a *chameleon*. Honest. It's a love-fest between those two. Moi? Being different is my M.O.

"And Skye, you are like the tortoise we just saw."

News to her. Skye leans forward from the back of her seat. "What's that supposed to mean?"

"Ourania has a carapace of embellished skin and purple hair. She retreats into herself to be a stone to the outside world."

Oh yeah? He's so smart? He'd croak if he knew the universe going on under the magenta hair. "So okay. I act like a tortoise. It's novel, anyway."

"He is telling you that the tortoise lacks God's gifts of reason and empathy and trusts no one. It intimidates the creatures it perceives as dangerous with a show of barbs. When it feels completely helpless, it becomes a stone. But if a *person* chooses barbs and stoniness as a way of life, and refuses God's gifts to distinguish between friend and enemy, that person is soon avoided and ignored. It is a tactic that results in loneliness and despair. For the person, not the tortoise."

"So?"

"Uncle Theo says he believes God wants people, the species to which he gave reason and heart, to live happy, purposeful lives."

Skye interrupts. "Tell him he sounds nuts."

Sophia shrugs. "He says: if I may continue, Ourania—'"

"Yeah, sure. I'm all ears, dot dot dot."

"I see that trauma made a home in you. Your beautiful green eyes see danger everywhere, even though you are perfectly safe. Your wide-eyed stare was created by trauma—your eyes are always wary. I have observed this same stare in clients I have visited in jail."

Skye covers her eyes with her hand. No one's gonna read her irises.

"Sophia tells me you were in a jail for juveniles?"

"Yeah, for a year. A 'court-adjudicated juvenile detention center.' Jay-Dee School to us inmates. 'Cause my mom couldn't handle a felon. Sucks for her."

"I am sorry for what it did to you, Ourania. Sorry for your suffering. Sorry that your freedom was revoked, because in freedom one can learn from one's mistakes. Tell me, Ourania, would you say you were helped in this detention center? It seems to me it dulled your young spirit. Now you play the tortoise for all you do not trust."

Skye's eyes flash in silent protest, in silent agreement. What is he saying? Unexpected tears of confusion creep in. She searches for a tissue and turns toward the window, concentrates on the scrub flitting past. They've climbed so high her ears ache, and below them the sea is a glittery bowl of blue soup with steam rising from its surface. She can almost see cartwheeled legs from the middle-school painting kicking madly in the tiny eyebrows of whitecaps heading toward the horizon.

In the iciest tone she can muster, she says, "Great *hot tip*, Mr. Theo. Ask him what animal is *his* protective behavior. Ask him *that,* Sophia."

He chuckles to hear The Twerp's translation. "Mine? I am like you, Ourania. I always recognize a fellow tortoise." He strokes his wayward beard, flashes that warm, unjudging smile in the rear-view mirror.

———ᴠᴠᴠ———

When he drops them off at Sophia's small farmhouse, whitewashed, with curved terra-cotta roof tiles like all the others she's seen, nestled among tall poplars and squat fruit trees, they find Kleio on the balcony leafing through a photo album in her lap. Kleio asks if they found animals to photograph, and Skye, in a sudden urge to speak, cuts Sophia off.

"A stupid tortoise, a dumb donkey and a bunch of lizards. Literal epic fail." She watches Kleio's face. Not a twitch. Not even eye contact.

Kleio turns to Sophia. They speak quietly in Greek. Probably about her.

Kleio says, "Well, look, girls, I found my album of old photos. Skye, would you like to see what your mom looked like in 1979? And Mal? Before she went to Nicaragua? Your Uncle Juan took the picture. Your mom was about your age—her first year at Barnard. We four were political activists then. We lived in this apartment building." She points to the gray façade looming behind the four women.

"The year after this, 1980—Ronald Reagan was president—was a terrible year. John Lennon got shot. Then your Uncle Juan was murdered in 1981. We dissolved our commune and all went our own ways."

"Where is this, Mama?" The Twerp asks.

Skye already knows about them. Group.

"In New York City. The Upper West Side. It had a lot of collectives then—urban communes, alternative lifestyles, they'd say. Some were focused on war protests and politics, some were about drugs, some were actually cults. Us, we were feminists against nuclear power. These big apartment buildings—'prewar' they were called—had been built big for families with servants, early in the century. They were perfect for the group living experiments. It was quite an era for experimenting."

Skye leans down to peer at the cracked color glossy, a 5x7 stuck to the faded green page. She knows all about Aunt Mal going to Nicaragua with her Uncle Juan, who was shot by the anti-Sandinistas. After that Mal went home to England, and Mina left Barnard and went to India for a year. After India, she married Dad. She's heard those stories, but she's never seen pictures of her mother in the commune. It's so weird. What were they thinking? Her mom and Aunt Mal have stayed friends ever since. They still talk about Uncle Juan. Skye likes the sound of him. So cool. The women agree Skye takes after him.

The building of turrets and windows looks like a wedding cake. The laughing girls stand together and wave at the camera. Skye shivers to realize they were waving at Uncle Juan, who was dead by the next year. This picture was what he saw, looking at them. Her uncle who she never knew chose this particular moment to photograph. From the angle she can guess he was crouching down on the sidewalk to get that halo over them of the masses of hair blown up by wind—dark, blonde and silver-white. Over the turrets is an iridescent sky. That is her Aunt Mal, hair already prematurely white, a cloud around her young features and open smile, like she's an alien visitor from another planet, not just another country. Her features are the most in focus, telling Skye he was looking at Mal, not the others. Well, he loved her. Skye doubts she loves anyone, but at least she trusts Aunt Mal. Who may actually be an alien from another planet, because Mal never judges her.

Mal pushes back strands of hair from her face, smiling. She's thin, her diminutive height accentuated by a red polka-dotted mini dress. Everyone's thin, in fact. And young. Her mother, Mina-pre-bitch-era, looks more Latina than she does today. Juan, who she knows from photographs Mal has shown her, did not resemble his sister. He had more of the Miskito Indian in him, the high cheek bones and straight, coarse hair. Mal said he wore a bandana across his forehead and a fringed shirt when she first met him that made him look like a movies Indian. Skye smiles at that image. A sudden taste memory hits her of her Miskito grandmother's dishes that she and Mina would prepare together with pimentos, limes and guavas. She feels lonely for the child she once was, the one who cooked with her mom and had friends and saw truth in the paintings in Art Appreciation. She has lost a lot since her dad's death.

Kleio gets in her face. "This is Mina. See her pointing at the camera? She was yelling at Juan when he snapped it—she was always yelling at him like he was a bad child, even though he was her older brother. There's our perky Gwen. Just needs a guitar and someone to harmonize with her on 'Hotel California,' her favorite song. And me, the throw-back hippie, right?" Kleio lingers over the names that hold the memories. She's smiling.

"Why do you have this out, Mama?"

"Jesus H. Christ!" Skye is compelled to cut in again. "Take a gander at those *god-awful shoes*! Who even wears that *crap*? Look at my mom's skirt, all flouncy and girly-girl and a ton of necklaces *like a gypsy*. That one supposed to be *you*, Kleio? You look like a *man*! Are you Jimi Hendrix or something, with a bandana and an Afro? The one with the long *Snoopy-ears hair*—Gwen? She's supposed to be a flower child? Weren't you guys *embarrassed* to look like that?"

Skye sits down next to Kleio and grabs the album to leaf through the pages on her own, a glance at Kleio who does not resist but disapproves, Skye's pretty sure. Well, no biggie. She gets that from people. She turns the pages faster, glancing at the photographs, each one a greater affront than the last. They irritate her, testaments of a happy time she's been locked out of. She feels inconsequential, and now she is losing control. She could land a punch on the ones of Kleio and Mal together. Best friends. Hah! She happens to know different. Mal told her. They had a big fight.

"Look at you guys! Such *dorks!*" Just hates how they act together, laughing in a kitchen, toasting each other with coffee mugs, sprawling over each other on a park bench—so hilarious. Yeah, right? Arms draped over the other's shoulders, giving the finger to a *Danger! Keep Out!* sign. "I shoulda been in *that* one." She jabs it with her finger.

The commune girls lying on beach towels in bikinis, making V-signs at demonstrations—lots of those—speakers lined up on a dais. Children with drawing pads sprawled all over a museum floor, Mal's face aglow, cheeks puffed to blow candles on a cake surrounded by the others in silly hats. And more silly hats: a New Year's party welcoming 1978. Mal turning to wave to the camera in an airport terminal under a Departures sign. Mal mugging the camera. Kleio, serious, reading to Mal from a book and Mal laughing. Mal kissing Juan in a close embrace.

"That's him, my only blood relation, except for Mina-the-bitch." Nice. She's just made Kleio flinch. "You took this?"

She studies the close-up of their profiles. Mal's arms encircle Juan's neck. He is taller. Her eyes are closed; a flowered, green kerchief controls her hair. His long eyelashes, his full lips—Skye sees that he smiles beneath their kiss, another twinge in her chest. Her uncle looks sweet, and he was quite the hottie. She can see him smiling at her in her mind.

This record of friendships make her uneasy. She says, "So my relatives used to have a different life, my mother and my dead uncle, back when my mother used to be Nicaraguan."

Kleio looks at her, as if encouraging Skye to go on.

"Yeah, the bitch. She used to be Jasmina Davila, right?" Skye thinks: when she spoke Spanish and wasn't a bitch, when she used to be her mom. When she told Skye funny stories about her grandparents adjusting to America, and growing up in a place called Corn Island, when she cooked food that tasted good. When Skye had a dad. Well, that's all gone, isn't it? The bitch is moving on: to her new incarnation, or whatever, in Boston, giving up lawyering to own an ef'n bookstore. Her lawyer husband's dead. Time to switch gears, start over. That was her line when he died. Sort of. Make lemonade, or something. Skye knows

Mina is closing the book on what is left of her own childhood life, and she hates it. Getting rid of the problem daughter is her next move. Why does she hate me? Skye wants to shout, but says: "So—everyone's been friends for years. Isn't that 'special'? You, Mina and Mal."

Kleio's silent, just watching her. Skye's pretty sure she's got the woman terrified by now. Figures. Some lion she turned out to be. She's just a mouse.

Anyway, none of this means anything to her. Kim always says get a life—your own life, Skye. Bugs Skye to discuss "friends." Says Skye's gotta have some "peers" to get over her loner image and have something more interesting to talk about besides how rotten The Bitch is. Skye's only friend is Mal, but being in jail and all, and Mal living in England, kept a damper on things. Now Mal's packed her off here. Gotten rid of a problem kid?

Mal is not hers is what this album screams. Mal belongs to these other people, this Kleio lady and Mina-the-bitch. Skye arrived on the scene as an afterthought, after this other life had happened, after Uncle Juan was dead. Well, that's history for you; doesn't pay to invest heavily in it. People are temporary. They go away. They die. They pack you off. She's gonna tell Kim that. Her nose starts running cause she's trying not to cry.

"*Ee*-oow! *Lesbos!* Ugly A-F! Put some clothes on, Lady—would-ja? You're ugly as *shit*. Who is that? Hitler? That hair is seriously bad! Do you mind? Gross! I can't even! That's just so basic."

Kleio stands up, pretty rigid looking. "Dinner's downstairs, in the kitchen." Her tone is flat. She goes inside. The Twerp follows. Guess she's got them both scared A-F—the lion and the chameleon shivering in their boots. Skye shuts the album and follows them. She is hungry.

Kleio has a fish dinner waiting for them. She gives them the menu: tomato salad and some kind of tomato-y rice. Dessert is fruit.

"I don't eat flesh! It's disgusting. And I don't do fruit."

"Well, Skye, nice to see you're finally opening up. Suit yourself. There's peanut butter and bread. Make a sandwich." Kleio scrapes Skye's portion of *barbouni* onto Sophia's plate, leaves her own plate untouched and goes back upstairs.

Skye has a choice as she sees it. She could starve herself to death or cave and find the peanut butter. She chooses starvation. She sits rock still, no more talk to entertain these people. Let's see what anyone's gonna do about her Silent Treatment.

Sophia squirts lemon on the fish. "Mm-m-m ... I love to eat fish *flesh*! And fish *skin!* It's so-o-o *crispy* and *crunchy!* Yum!"

—◈—

Sophia clears the dishes from the table when she's done and goes to her room, leaving the American brat sitting silent and motionless at the table. What is wrong with that strange girl anyway? Either she sneers incomprehensible words or doesn't speak. She has no manners. Sophia puts on her nightshirt and gets into bed.

Many troubles whirl in her head tonight, including the prospect of having this horror around for the summer. She's been studying the brat's freckled, green-eyed American face these last two days. How disturbing it is to realize she has similar non-Greek features as the brat: the small nose, the deep-set, light eyes, the angular high cheeks, and a round head shape. And height. At eleven, she's almost up to Skye, and she passed Mama a month ago. She stands out in a crowd of Greeks. Sophia takes the hand mirror she uses for studying her face and whispers to her reflection in Greek.

Maybe I look more like Skye than Mama, but at least my skin isn't scribbled all over with animals growing out of each other. And what she wears! Black net stockings on the mountain? Ripped shorts with holes that show her underpants to the neighborhood? Is that American dress? She is blind not to see the ring in her nose is ugly. To be pulled around like a bull? And that gold ball in her tongue! I thought she had a tooth growing there. No wonder she's afraid to eat. She could swallow it and choke. I bet her purple hair never met a comb. Such a rodent nest! She was mean to say I am normal-looking. Just look at my face! It's like hers! How is that normal?

—◦◦◦—

Kleio, that same hour, feels worn out, has had it with this obnoxious child whose rotten mood taints her home. She returns to the kitchen to put dishes in the washer, and mop the kitchen floor with vinegar to stave off a night invasion from ants. The girl is still at the table, sitting like a statue. Kleio approaches the table, mop in hand. She is damned abusive. She won't budge, won't even pick up her feet.

Just ignore her, Kleio decides. Do not acknowledge behavior befitting a three-year-old. She mops around Skye's feet, around the chair legs. To suggest the girl lend a hand would not end well. Pain in the neck, you slab of concrete! You hope to provoke, but concrete never bothered me.

Kleio pulls out the chairs, pushes them back as she goes. Just as she finishes mopping under the table, Skye stands up and goes upstairs without a word.

Good riddance. From the direction of footsteps overhead, Kleio knows Skye heads to the back balcony overlooking the bay. Such a beautiful view, even at night; it is the best feature of the house. And that says a lot, because Kleio loves its rafters made of rushes and its two cone-shaped fireplaces, her nineteenth-century farmhouse. It will be breezier as the air cools. When she's done, she will bring the girl a shawl, a sign of détente, and have a talk.

Twenty minutes later, Kleio stands at the balcony door with her cashmere shawl purchased in New York when she left the hospital. It's dark. The light of a candle flickers in rhythm with the breeze. She knows Skye sits in the chair against the wall facing the view.

"I brought you this in case you feel chilled, Skye."

Nothing.

Kleio sets the shawl down next to Skye's chair. Such a toughie. Kleio leans against the doorjamb a moment more, breathing slowly, calmed by the vista of an obsidian sea, shimmery under the full moon. Truth is, she is too tired for confrontations or fathoming teenage moods. Does the girl appreciate where she is? Is she not moved by the swooshing ancient waters, the crickets calling? Does she appreciate the velvet night? Maybe not. She's too toxic to notice anything outside herself. Kleio does not want a problem child here. Mal wildly misrepresented the girl. Not Skye's fault; she just doesn't belong here, probably dying to leave. Kleio will make it easy for her.

Kleio peers where town lights twinkle below them. She loves this spot of ancient mountainside facing the sea she's made her home. She will miss it. It will be even harder for Sophia to leave, but Kleio's no fool to think that she can beat cancer a third time. They must move to the States to be prepared. This prospect of beating death—no one ever does—troubles her most right now.

Theo, a compassionate friend from the beginning—more than a friend, a mentor, a guardian angel, a lamp—made it possible for her to live here with Sophia. One couldn't ask for better, to have met a stranger late in life with unyielding kindness toward her. They love each other. It gnaws at her that she has not told him about her intention to leave. She should. But the thought of it hurts too much.

Random headlights flicker behind switchbacks going up the coast. The lamps on the night-fishing boats out in the bay hold constant, reflect like spilled glitter. The full moon shines cold and bright. She sighs. How like that night in March this one is, before she left for medical treatment in New York. Four months ago, under just such a moon, she and Sophia had planted a sapling, a living talisman for her return, healed and well. That tree grows strong, and she does well, her second chance to live, thanks to the wonder pills that shrank the tumor by the time she was flying back to Greece. Her tiredness is the slow unclutching of fear. She can forget she was ever afflicted, until that fear returns and decimates her. She doesn't need a troubled teen distracting from her recovery.

She fears that Skye's anger is so destructive that she will eventually goad Kleio's world to the same pitch of fury. Toxic, she is. It seems Skye has already managed this with poor Mina, her mother. Well, kiddo, who doesn't have crosses to bear? Stop putting them down for others to trip on!

"Skye, I wondered if you feel homesick. I know it's your first time so far from home."

"Not my first time. I was just in London with Aunt Mal. I was fine. And anyway, I'm not going back to Mina-the-bitch. I wish you didn't show me her goddamn picture."

Kleio chuckles. "So-ooo—the cat's not got your tongue: you don't want to go home. But that is exactly where you will go tomorrow. In the morning, I personally will drive you to the door of the next plane to Boston, if you don't stop the bullying and get rid of your abusive language. We don't want it here, and you don't need to do it. Stop it tonight, Skye, or it is *adios amigos* in the morning. Easy-peasy to arrange, as your Aunt Mal would say."

Skye turns abruptly, glares at her and grabs the shawl off the empty chair, opens her mouth to speak.

But Kleio is first. "*Hey!* You don't want to say it! And I don't want to hear it. That's the deal. Take it or leave it. Good night, Skye."

Kleio leaves the balcony for the kitchen, smiling. That went well. Next is Mallory, whose e-mail arrived the previous night and prompted her to get out her old photo album. She sets her laptop on the kitchen table.

It still disconcerts her, writing back and forth with Mal these last months after years of silence, having been written off without explanation. Mal has said it was envy, the reason she abruptly ended their close friendship that had started back in Manhattan in the 1970s, and she wants to explain it. In person.

Still, it's been a trip to have Mal back in her life, if only via correspondence, to hear her familiar voice on paper, to recognize her comfortable ways of thought, while noting that Mal is different. Difficult to pin down how. She's at a turning point, Mal's said, about to retire from the Financial Services Authority created by Parliament in 2000. Mal's dad would have been really proud of her.

They both abandoned their activism at the same time. Who could forget the house drama of Mal going to Nicaragua during its civil war? The earl, Mal's father who always voted Conservative, would have stopped her had he even known she planned to go. Kleio had threatened to tell him and still wishes she'd had, since it ended in disaster, and Mal came back a mess. Instead she'd supported Mal, because Mal would do anything to stay with Juan. But Juan was killed, and she returned demoralized. They dissolved the commune and went their several ways. You can't control outcomes, Kleio thinks, so you indulge in magical thinking that outcomes will be good. We treated the cancer again. We will leave our home in Greece and move to the States. We believe everything will work out fine. Outcomes will be good.

She scrolls back through Mal's e-mails, scanning for hints she may have missed about why Mal is back in her life.

...it was at the Popover Café. Do you recall our being at daggers drawn in a cloud of pink and yellow chintz, the sunlight making lacy blue shadows through the curtains? Your decision gobsmacked me, Kleio: to adopt an infant *at your age*, in your post-cancer state, and move to Greece. Because some man you barely knew was determined to sell you property. I thought you'd gone mad. I predicted a tragic end. I'm so glad that it worked out beautifully. Do tell me about the baby. How old is she? What is she like? You'll find this difficult to believe, but I do enjoy children, while quite content they belong to others, of course. How wonderful if your and Mina's daughters knew one another ... so Group could continue for another generation...

Of course, my grief over Juan is different now, after three decades. But it is never absent. My life would have taken quite a different course.

He was so determined to become the president of Nicaragua … very possibly, he might have … perhaps he is my reason to keep contact with Mina and her family, to remember him … perhaps because Mina and I both endured deaths that happened too soon. Richard should have been diagnosed earlier…

… constant touch with Gwen. We laugh because we thought ourselves frightfully courageous in those days, but we were crackers, really. Regrets about things we did? Perhaps a few. But all of it, the good and bad, contributes to my current understanding. I live with an unassuaged sorrow that I have shared with only one other soul, wherever he may be, or if he may be still … I want to tell you and the others, but not via correspondence. It is so painful to me … I believe now it was grief that sparked my envy … I should like to share…

I know you can help Skye … troubled, hurt … smart, loving, innocent … her brash exterior … misdemeanors not committed … unusually protracted probation egged on by immature decisions on her part … highly punitive system created by their President Clinton. I hope you will help them, Kleio … when Mina's husband died the impact on Skye was devastating. I've known her since her infancy. She has tons of charm … a beautiful girl, many-talented … an artist's soul … a gift for photography.

Kleio wonders what she might have said besides "yes, of course, she would help Skye" for Mina, their commune mate, their old friend, as much to show Mal that bygones were bygones as to forgive her own teenage errors. Everyone can use a second chance. Mal too. Friendship is a rare and fragile thing. It takes a lot of compassion to understand another, and life is shorter than one expects. She too needs friends.

Still, a huge mistake, this Skye. She'd like to write Mal that she was dead wrong. But she can't. Mal sees only what she chooses. Always did. She's never had children—and how to help them seems obvious to the uninitiated. Mal imposes her yin/yang Confucian rigmarole over what cannot be controlled: endings. Death. See how she does not forget Juan? Not accepting endings underlies Mal's wish to unite Skye and Sophia as the future Group generation. Mal is unrealistic and idealistic. Kleio knows her well, a decade of silence notwithstanding … do people really change? She thinks not.

Kleio's choice, adoption and moving to Greece, had nothing to do with Mal. If Mal had been worried about her decisions, why then drop her? No logic there. And the rejection had hurt. Kleio saw it as a pentimento, a ghost-image that must have reappeared in the life of the Honorable Lady Mallory Tame. Her tradition-ridden heritage extending back to Richard III must have surfaced to obliterate the newer Mallory, the radical feminist.

And what is worst, Mal wants a return to the past: a Group reunion.

We'd love to come to Greece—Mina, Gwen and I, to cheer you in your recuperation, generally catch up and enjoy a good time, together once more. I will gladly organize it if you agree, locate a spa for us, like the one we visited right after your first bout, where we can again mull over transitions.

Two distressing developments Kleio must address, no matter how tired. It's 10:15 PM, 17 July 2011. She types:

First item of business: Skye. A seductive idea you had, to hold the ranks for a new generation by getting the children together. But Mal, Skye is no charmer. She is closed and hard: a dead weight, gratuitously rude. And you've given her to us for six weeks! I cannot be a halfway house for troubled youth. I've given her an ultimatum to show respect by sun-up tomorrow, or back she goes to you. I'll keep you posted, but I doubt there is hope. She's too in love with her anger.

Second item: a Group reunion. I am thrilled to have you back again, Mal dear. In cancer's second appearance, our friendship matters more than ever. But Group? When it comes to reviving the past, I find Heraclitus remains a reliable voice: we cannot step foot into the same river twice. A different river flows now. Group was a temporary construct that fit a particular historical moment, uniting disparate women who have since moved on. I see no value in a meet-up beyond nostalgia, for which I lack the patience, so no thanks. No reunion for me.

Kleio writes a bit more, hits *Send*, shuts her computer, goes to Sophia's door and knocks. She wants to ask how Sophia has managed with Skye. The chit was supposed to help her out with her daughter. That was the deal.

"Hey, Soph. We didn't get a chance to talk today. Can I come in?"

"You can, but no talking. I'm avoiding you." Sophia stirs in bed and sits up. She squints in the sudden light. "I am mad at you." She yawns.

"Because of Skye?"

"Uh-uh. Not Skye. She's okay. She's just bratty and scared, so she acts like a tortoise. Uncle Theo said. No, I'm mad at you because we have to move to the States. I'm mad because you made this my home when you adopted me, and you made me grow up to be Greek. But I am not! Everyone sees I'm different. No one even imagines Sophia Platon is really *Albanian*, because she is blonde like the Albanians. They accept the Albanians. I even put my arm across Besjana's to compare us—and, guess what. I'm even blonder than her! The *yia-yias* say, oh, darling Besjana, such a pretty child. Her golden halo is like an angel. Bah! Besjana's hair looks like old straw a goat sat on. Her eyes aren't even true-blue like an angel, like mine are. But me? They still ask me *what I am!* I say I am Greek, and they shake their heads. They say I am foreign. I get jealous of Besjana because Albanian isn't foreign. And now I must go to another country where I won't fit in still! My English will sound wrong to them. Everyone will ask me where I am *really* from, even with my American citizenship, because I'll sound different. I won't understand anything they say. I hardly understand Skye."

Kleio, tired, won't say that Sophia's origin is no one's business. Still, it is surprising that the old gossips continue to speculate, won't let it go. They have always gossiped about her, too. They still ask from where the unmarried *Kyria* Kleio got her baby. Is Sophia illegitimate? Why no husband? In America, her baby will fit in just fine. She'll see she looks American, and that no one speaks great English there. Appearance and language will be her easiest adjustments.

"And when you stayed in Geneva with Aunt Anthi and Uncle Georges? How did you feel with so many blonde and blue-eyed people?" She reaches to touch her daughter's hair, but Sophia pulls back. She sits down on the side of Sophia's bed, picks up Sophia's blonde doll that she sleeps with. "Hm. Rositsa told me she had a pretty good time in Switzerland. It never mattered where she came from, or what she was."

Sophia takes the doll from her mother and snuggles it close. "But Rositsa *felt* different. She doesn't like that feeling. People asked where I was from, because I didn't match my Greek aunt and uncle. My French was not so good, either. Skye is rather dumb. She can't remember one Greek word I teach her. Mama, please let's not move where she lives! Please!"

"Oh dear. You will discover, Sophie." She strokes Sophia's head, feeling the fine textured hair between her fingers. "That everyone feels out of place from time to time, dislocated. What matters more is how you make *others* feel. I'll rub your back to help you sleep."

Once she's left her daughter's bedroom, Kleio's eyes fill with tears for having unsettled her child, but there is nothing to be done about it. They shall move to the States next spring. It is the right thing to do. She understood it after her surgery and discussed it with her sister who'd been with her. Change is wrenching, but moving sooner will give Sophaki time to adapt, perhaps spare her a more severe dislocation someday, if she had to go alone. Kleio draws the mosquito netting around her bed.

The candle flickers out on the balcony. The girl sitting out there—she feels dislocated, too.

—–w—

The next afternoon at siesta time, Skye is not only relieved that her morning apology was accepted but that she was given the keys to Kleio's lime green Nissan Micra to drive herself down to the town's Internet café. She doesn't have her license yet, but Kleio said no problem outside of Athens. A student driving permit is fine.

Skye's gotta unload to someone. That talk was so awkward. Better no one knows about it. Still, she's gotta yammer on to someone to calm the mess of weird emotions inside. She may explode from it. She can't reach Kim, who only has a cell phone and no land line, from here. Definitely nothing about it to Aunt Mal, who would get disappointed in her, decide that sending her to Greece was a literal epic fail. Mina-the-bitch. She should yammer to Mina. Isn't that what mothers are supposed to be for? Mina will just spout platitudes anyway. Skye can handle that. That's what she'll do, so no worries...

Reaching the townlet, one street stretched in a long arc across from the beach, Skye finds a shady side street and lodges the car in a too tight spot between a rusty truck and a shiny motorcycle. So she scrapes the Micra a little. Everything's a crate around here anyway.

She climbs the outside stairs to the Internet café on the floor above a bakery and nudges open the door, wary. Never know what's gonna happen when you open a door. It is pleasantly dark and cool, surprisingly modern in shiny chrome and gleaming white subway tiles. A girl her age dries glasses behind the counter.

The only customer is an Adonis-type, suntanned to a shade of Golden Glow with shaggy blond hair, in a faded shirt with cut-off sleeves and bulgy triceps. He writes in a notebook and sips from a glass of something frothy. A definite hottie. He looks up at Skye and smiles as if he's just seen a goddess, making her stomach zip in self-consciousness, followed by the lonely pit of not having a boyfriend. Who's got the time, what with fighting the law and jail and the rest, all her options being those sneering, leering Jay-Dees? So it's been maybe never that a hottie smiled at her so open and warm.

And damn if the counter girl doesn't speak English! Always a plus for looking less like a dumb-ass when you try to make yourself understood. She could like this little den of serenity that's in her age group.

The girl brings Skye to a bank of computers, demonstrates how it all works and asks if she would like a frappé.

Sure. Whatever that is.

"How much sugar?" the girl asks.

"Probably a lot."

The girl smiles. Gentle smile.

Skye shoves one of Kleio's shiny Euros into the slot. She can't change her own money at the bank without Sophia to translate, since the hours are nuts-o, closed when it should be open.

The girl returns with the same frothy drink as the guy's. It's an iced latte. Skye creates *wackoworld3* as her password and types Mina's address.

It's so primitive here I can't text anyone. Mountains run interference. I'm at like a public computer place that costs a Euro to use. Don't know how much it's in real money. Write back here and I'll get it next time I come in, like tomorrow. I'm okay. The kid is easy, Sophia. The "helpful" type. We're at the beach or hang in town. Haha you should see this "town" just one street. Forget shopping. Staying at Aunt Mal's was more "uptown" know what I'm sayin? London is cool. Maybe I'll move there. They have guys with Mohawks, so I'd fit right in haha. Get a "flat" like Aunt Mal's. She was like really nervous if it was the right thing for Kleio to have me here. Forget me! I can't call Kim from here to check in. Confusing time difference. Expensive. You have to do it for me, say I'm jim-dandy we talk daily. Say since they approved helping a cancer patient as my community service, just ef'n trust me to do it. I won't bale. How far would I get anyway, since no one speaks English? I already checked it out, JK. Really, escape is impossible since you didn't give me enough money. Everyone's a weirdo and wicked loud—always shouting, waving their arms. By noontime they take a nap to rest up from yakking all morning. PLEASE! Send American food! It's all yuck-o crap. You wouldn't believe it. I will never eat animal. They dig weeds and flower bulbs out of the ground and boil them. To eat! I need taco chips and salsa. Oregano is on everything. Geez—even potato chips! The only edible food is fries. Their tomatoes remind me of dad's garden. That's all I'm eating—fries and tomatoes. I cried last night. How are you? This'll be over in 47½ more days. Hope your bookstore is coming along. PS: some old geezer friend of theirs changed my name. I guess Skye is just too hard to say. Really?? Now I'm Ourania or something.

She rereads, making sure there's no hint of Kleio's ultimatum. She'll be damned if she'll go home. Can't be anywhere *near* Mina this summer while the bitch *transitions* to Boston—or ever. Aunt Mal said, Skye, make it work. Do whatever it takes. Show maturity and goodwill. Rise to the occasion. So she will.

Skye returns the empty frappé glass to the counter. The girl's gone. The guy's gone, too. Making out together in the back maybe? She burns with a pang of jealousy. She's always been jealous of girls with a perfect life and a perfect guy, the popular girls. They show "maturity and goodwill" without even trying.

She leaves a Euro coin on the counter.

And now, two whole hours of actual freedom, no ankle monitor, no one watching her. She's got her camera. Time to check out what's happening at the end of this famous National Highway. Kleio said the last town is Leonidio, then the road turns into the mountains. She can't miss it.

She's got this.

Turns out that the National Highway keeps swerving and winding up and down, a two-lane road blasted out between mountains and sea. Up on the cliffs are bits of hanging hamlets with English names too long to read on the signs beneath the Greek letters. On the coast side dropping to the sea, blankets of olive groves and scrub. Overhead, a bluebird sky. The wind rushes against her face and hair from the window she's opened instead of air conditioning. Sort of glorious, this freedom. This nature.

Forty-five minutes on, a steep decline all the way to flat sea level, it looks like the traffic, and Skye as well, sank to the bottom of the National Highway at Leonidio. She can only inch along, but no prob. Plenty to see when you're inching along a narrow street lined with stores, mechanics shops, butcher shops, the electric company, telephone company and other stuff in capital Greek letters. Who knows? Honking trucks and cars, pedestrians spilling off the packed sidewalks into her path, kids everywhere. It's a zoo. It's fun.

Skye sees a chance to pull onto a side street and figures out how to parallel park the Micra on a steep decline between a motorbike and a Smartcar. Quite the accomplishment. She really is on her own, taking care of business. She really is free. She really can do it.

She is brave.

She finds a café in the small town square and orders a frappé, now that she knows what it is, nods to what must be the question about the sugar amount. Feels quite fluent. She nurses it at a painted metal table and watches the Greeks walk briskly, men with clipboards and satchels, women with shopping bags and children, understanding that they head to lunch and naps. Some trick it must be to make the whole country take a nap, but it is definitely over a hundred degrees. The sun is burning.

Is it weird or what, to sit here invisibly, peacefully, in a foreign country at the end of the National Highway, just watching people living their lives? They don't know her, where she's come from, what she's been through. And what a relief is that. Next time, she'll bring Twerpie, who'll want to show her the sights 'cause every place around here has its sights to see, according to her. Kinda okay town, really.

So what's next on her agenda?

The Micra's been cooking on the street. Inside, it's an oven. On the drive back, she will really study everything more carefully. Like the photography teacher said to do. Look at the details: those bilingual town signs, the red graffiti on the cliffs, the posters for politicians, olive tree trunks, house roof tiles, unmanned roadside stands selling what could be wine or olive oil in plastic water bottles. Olives packed in reused jars. Scrawled on cardboard are numbers with a lot of zeros and big Euro signs.

She pulls over to the shoulder several times for views that interest her, a slice of glistening sea as backdrop for a boulder or an oddly shaped bush, and once stopped she sees even more. The sea is always changing its blues; the monumental cliffs glitter with mica or are dark in shadow; the fast-sailing clouds on their way to somewhere, slipping behind the cliffs or out to the horizon.

She's intrigued by scrub. She "sees" spindly needled evergreens, gnarled and twisted trunks bashed by the wind, scraggly branches grabbing at the clouds. She shoots them large in the foreground, connecting the copper-colored soil and the streaky hues of sky and sea. Everything bolted to the ground is reaching up for the sky. She shoots a pile of boulders so that their contours make a wall from which she imagines leaping out into open sky. Ah! She's got the dude's name: Icarus!

Her mind loosens as she works. Thoughts tumble: replays of Kleio calling her bluff, the hottie smiling at her. The last time she had a boyfriend was in sixth grade. Ryan, was it? What an ef'n relief that there's other things in life besides fights with the world. Kim had it right: give up the juvenile delinquent routine already. It's exhausting.

Too bad she's already come to the turnoff that takes her up to Kleio's mountain village. She recognizes the pattern of Greek letters, plus there is a bus stop and the Arco gas station. Total freedom's on pause for now. But it was good.

The turnoff is a widened goat path that's been paved, according to Sophia. She'll take its hairpin switchbacks as fast as she dares. Maybe a car will descend so she can try out Kleio's advice. If a car comes at you, pull onto a shoulder if there is one. If not, you work out with the other driver which of you reverses to find someplace to edge into. There's logic to it, Kleio said: minds communicate through car metal. If you drive in Greece without dying, you can drive anywhere.

Damn straight she wants to stay here. She has become quite the apologizer. Sorry, very sorry, she said first thing in the morning, being a bitch just comes natural since her ordeals. Looked Kleio in the eye to show her sincerity—another Jay-Dee School hack. Kleio was chill. Didn't yell or anything, said cut out the crap and you're welcome to stay. Asked about the upcoming court appearance, her probation, and what started it all.

Gave Kleio the short-form version. But when you do that, you hope the person reads between the lines to know she's actually innocent, that she'd been framed by how the detective wrote the report. But never ever say he used the system to screw her. Act contrite because you're toast if you're honest. Give the minimum; hope you don't sound too unsalvageable. It's a concept she's played around with a lot, The Unsalvageable Concept, when she was back living with Mina and was cutting herself.

Wouldn't it just be grand to forget all this shit and be a photographer? Kleio had said. Her sentiments exactly. Kinda shy, actually, to tell Kleio, photography's on fleek—you learn about your inner self when you take pictures. The photograph is really a picture of *you*. She'd learned that from a photography workshop in Detention. Snap the picture. Study it. It's a picture of you. She's really into it, she'd told Kleio. During the Save-The-Tortoise trip, Sophia told her that the tourists photograph the scenery, and the locals photograph one another, so Skye should photograph animals. No one else was doing it. She and Kleio laughed. Your kid's a card, she'd told Kleio. Kleio asked, Well, do you like her? Do you want to spend your days with her?

Sure. The kid's chill, a walking encyclopedia.

"Well then, go for it. Stay on. Be Sophia's *au pair*, take a ton of pictures. Put in hours photographing, day and night. You'll get really good that way. You can have a day off each week just for your photography. Use my car. Explore. End the abuse. You know what I mean, Skye? Deal?"

Deal. She was contrite, for real.

Then Kleio did the weirdest thing anyone ever did. She stood up, came over to Skye and hugged her, long and tight. What Kleio doesn't know is Skye does not permit anyone to touch her. Ever since her dad died. Even her mother was not allowed to hold her when she was breaking in two at losing him from her life. Skye gets apoplectic if anyone tries to. But so as not to hurt Kleio's feelings and get sent home, she accepted the hug.

It's nuts. She can still feel the warmth like an after-image, sealing you off from the space around you. A safe feeling.

Don't tell anyone, but actually, she wants to stay in this freaking country. This mountain they're on, Mount Parnon— won't ever make *Cosmo*'s "Top Ten Secret Getaways for The Best Ever Vay-cay." But it's cool.

It's growing on her, even the sun, your basic persimmon set on fire. Like how the mountains go from gun-metal to black. And flower colors—a regular heart attack—hot pink, piercing yellow, blowing their heads off on the highway meridian like maniacs.

Daphne bushes, said Twerpie, then she has to fill her in on Daphne and Maenads.

Skye says, Really? What about those meek little pink and orange ones in people's yards?

Lantana. Geesh. Twerpie makes it her job to know the name of everything on the planet.

Kleio said, Here we take you for who you say you are. If you change who you are, that's chill. They don't embarrass you about it. And she can take pictures.

She asked Kleio why's everything here either falling apart or not finished being built.

Sorta like people, actually, Kleio said, and laughed. And they had a little chuckle about Twerpie.

She told Kleio that she had been bitching about the smells to Sophia. Incessant smells, wherever they go. Okay, she's hypersensitive, she admits, but sometimes, it really stinks. Other times, it's just weird and unidentifiable. So now Twerpie has to call out exactly what *she* smells. Geesh. Herbs! Dust! Goats! Wood smoke! Diesel oil! The sea! Dog fur even. On and on. TMI, Sophia. Too Much Info.

It's a game to play, Sophia said, real happy. To the Twerp everything's a game or an educational toy. She's a regular public television station. Her excitement reminds Skye of back when she used to be into stuff.

She's smiling when she steps out of the car, and The Twerp herself dashes out wearing a bathing suit, wanting to go to the beach. Her mother is pestering her.

"So, let's beat it, kiddo." Skye gets back behind the wheel again, pleased to cruise right back down without having to see an adult. Sophia gets in front with her.

"Hey! Kids sit in the back!"

"They do not!"

"Yeah? Then, at least wear the goddamn seat belt!"

"Why should I? We're just going to the beach."

Don't argue with The Twerp, 'cause there's no way to make her do it anyway.

She'll put *au pair* power into action by buying the gas—*venzini,* it's called—on her own, even if she hasn't a clue about liters and Euros.

Back down at the Arco on the National Highway, she hands Kleio's *venzini* card to the little guy who pumps the gas for her. So what if he said *yiasou* to Sophia but stared quizzically at her? She's not about to say that strange word, *yiasou.*

"Haha. *Highway*? Gimme an ef'n break!" She pulls onto it.

Sophia says her mother is mean.

"You think so? Come on, she's not so bad. Not like mine. Mine's a witch. Her favorite saying? 'Skye, your father would be *so disappointed* if he were here.' You think that's nice? If he was alive, I wouldn't be such a mess. Stupid-ass bitch! Oopsie! Look, Sophia. I'm really gonna watch my language, okay? So just pretend you didn't hear that."

Driving to the beach, they are quiet. No such thing as a radio station with the mountains interfering.

Anyway, it's weird music. Snaky, crying sounds. And it's not in English.

Sophia blurts, "Why did you say I look normal when you first came? I am not. I'm pretty strange-looking here."

"Well, if you're strange-looking, kiddo, what does that make me?"

Time for her second apology of the day: "Chill, Sophia. I didn't know *normal* was an insult. I meant it compared to me. By comparison. I'm your standard problem child. I lived in a place where they handcuff and strip search you for nothing. Where you're not allowed to speak for days at a time. My mother has no idea about that. She thinks it was some finishing school to get improved or something. I'm a miscreant with a record. The only *actual* person with an *actual* idea of what it was *actually* like is your friend there, Mr. Theo. He really blew me away."

"Oh, I see. I thought you didn't like him. You didn't thank him. You just ran out of his jeep. That was rude. And you didn't appreciate what he said to you. What he said about me is true. I'm a chameleon. Even with you. I am studying your very unusual vocabulary, looking your words up. You talk nothing like my Mama, and nothing like what they teach in English class. And, by the way, you take the curves too fast. Slow down!"

"So shoot me." Skye brakes into the next curve. What do kilometers even measure? "Okay, but I don't recommend talking like me. Your mama's not gonna like it. I was a little mad that day. Mad is my M.O. I'm usually a 'little' mad. I'll apologize to him—which I'm really a pro at doing."

"Well, what makes you so mad?"

"Hmm-m. I gotta think. I used to not be mad, back when I was your age. Eleven was a good year as they go, before my dad died. Bummer. He was just sick then. I had to avoid Mina—my hysterical mother—by hanging out in my closet, which I turned into a secret forest by hiding my stuffed animals in it. By eleven, you should be into boys and rock stars. I didn't care. I just needed a place. I stole the idea from Winnie the Pooh: made my own Hundred-Acre Wood. Christopher Robin made that whole place up because his parents didn't care about him. At least I had more animals than him, nine. A cat, a hedgehog, a rat, two dogs, an elephant, two monkeys and a peacock—each one had a personality and special thing it did. Except the cat, Addie—she couldn't do nothing. Addie was a rescue cat."

"Wait! Rescue cat?"

"I *rescued* her from hiding under a car."

"Wait! A *real* cat? I thought you said they were toys! I'm so confused!"

"They *are* toys! Geesh! I *pretended* that I rescued Addie. She's about yay long, all black. Why am I even telling you this? Because you can't blab it to anyone back home. I never even told the therapist about them—"

"Wait! Therapist?"

"It's a doctor you talk to that's supposed to help you. Mina made me see one since I was depressed from my dad dying and my trouble with the law happened. *Awk*-ward! Don't you ever wish you had a dad? At my age, you're supposed to be *yearning for independence*, not dwelling on if you have a dad. The therapists all said that. I had four different ones. But Mina stopped them since I got jack-shit from it. No skin off my back. I was supposed to blabber my thoughts, such as I thought I killed my dad. *I didn't*. Don't worry! I just *felt* like I did. Shit. I'm no homicidal maniac, you know, just a felon. Ha ha. Therapists think they help you to understand yourself and crap while they gun you down with questions. It starts innocent, but it ends like a drive-by."

"Okay. Stop! I don't understand anything of what you say. Hey, Skye—Ourania, or whatever—is that why your tattoos are of animals? From your hidden collection?"

"My tats? I never noticed. Observant little kiddo. Is there another beach we can go to? I'm already bored with yesterday's."

Sophia gives directions to drive farther up the National Highway, the most ridiculous name for a road. "In Massachusetts, this would be a lane. Greece is so *miniature*!"

Sophia shrugs. She advises where to park on the shoulder. Taking their gear, they walk back along a chicken-wire fence to an opening cut into it.

"Pretty strange beach entrance."

A sandy path leads them to a sun-bleached pinkish building topped with a cross.

"This is St. Christopher Beach, because this is St. Christopher Chapel," Sophia explains.

"Who puts a chapel at the beach?" Its squat bell tower is a pyramid of iron poles like a search tower, with a bell hanging inside it. "I'd call this Tinker Town Beach."

Through the rods Skye catches the dazzle of sparkling turquoise sea, so bright it hurts her eyes. There is a beach with tables like an open-air restaurant. People sit in sun chairs, and children shout and play in the waves. The juxtaposition of chapel, restaurant and people in bathing suits is just wrong. "'Toto, I've a feeling we're not in Kansas anymore,'" she says to Sophia.

Sophia shrugs and opens a blue door. "It's okay to go in."

What the hell. Skye follows behind Sophia and is immediately blinded. Black as sin inside. She stops short. As her eyes adjust, staring faces emerge from the walls, chipped and peeling, grouped as if encircling her within a small closet-like space. Above is a dome with a large bearded face staring downward. Its eyes are attentive but do not see.

As her eyes adjust to the dark, a thin light appears from a single candle in a free-standing stand. It sags, about to be extinguished in a tray of watery sand. Sophia pulls out a thin yellow candle from a slot, brushes its wick against the flame and stakes it into the sand. Now there are two lights. They watch as its wick sputters, then elongates into a steady flame. Sophia makes the sign of a cross on her body and moves to a picture on an easel and kisses it. It's a picture of man with a miniature person perched on his shoulders. "Do you know about St. Christopher? He was a really strong fellow with big muscles, so he earned money by carrying people across very dangerous rapids and slippery rocks. One day he carried a little boy who got so heavy that Christopher got scared he would fall and drown them both. But his tremendous strength and will got them safely across.

Then the king had him killed because that is what kings did to good-hearted people in those days. But today everyone asks for him to help with their heavy burdens. Because they know he can do it."

"Okay."

It's all shivery and weird, getting killed and heavy burdens, this picture-kissing and cross-making activity in a miniature dark space like a cave.

More light is good. She reaches into the slot for a candle, ignites it with Sophia's, and steadies it in the sand. What the hell. Very otherworldly this scene. She should come back and photograph it sometime. See if she can capture the safety she feels here.

Sophia taps her arm and leads her back into the dazzling sunlight toward the beach.

They pass the people chatting and the children calling out and laughing in the water. It is noisy as all get-out, what with the whooshing of wind and waves and the clanking of ropes against a flagpole. Every sense gets assailed here, Skye notices.

Sophia finds a spot, sets down her gear, opens a raffia mat and pins it with rocks against the wind. She runs to the water.

Skye prepares her towel the same way and strips to her suit beneath her shorts. She lies down and turns onto her stomach, immediately feels the heat on her back and the cold tickle of wind coming off the water. She closes her eyes, letting her mind roil with images of a dark cave with unseeing faces, a man with a child on his shoulders, her own dad, how he'd hoist her up and she'd squeal and grab his hair, all the burdens that were on his shoulders...

Icy droplets suddenly prick her hot back. Startled, Skye looks around and up. It's the blond guy dripping over her, grinning.

"Weren't you in the café this morning?" He tips back from his forehead a frayed, straw Stetson.

Wow. That great smile. That funny English. Still, it's her very own language. Smile back or keep a poker face? She meets his eyes, ice-blue with deeply tanned smile lines. She sits up on her towel and cocks her head. She has leverage, so confront, she decides. "What were you writing there?"

He kneels down to meet her face and whispers, "Poetry."

"I e-mailed my mother." Shoot me. Was that stupid to say, or what!

Where is her mother? (Boston). And where she is from? (The States).

She asks where is *his* mother? (Sweden). And where is *he* from? (Stockholm and Athens, both).

He laughs. "Okay, now the fathers."

Hers is in Massachusetts. Dead. His is here. Alive. Names: he is Abbo. She is Skye, but also Ourania or Rania while she is in Greece.

"*Ja*, they know it better," he agrees. "Rania. It is very good."

A Greek man gave her that name.

Abbo pauses, smiles the killer smile. And so, too, with him. His father is a Greek man and gave him also the name Aleksander. He uses both.

She laughs. "This is a funny game."

"Why laugh?"

Because what he says is, like, so unexpected.

Oh. What about her tattoos?

So, what about them?

Why so many?

Why not?

Silence.

Sophia appears, dripping a trail of water spots in the sand. "*Yiasou, Aleko.* This is Skye. Visits us for the summer. Aleko and I, we know each other—but from a distance."

Yes, he agrees, and from a distance, he knows Sophia's mother, the Greek-American. Because the Platons are close with his father's lawyer, Mr. Theo. Greece is a small world, *ja*?

"For sure. Mr. Theo is who named me Ourania. Full circle."

Silence.

"That your camera?"

"Yes. That one is yours?"

"Of course. Who else's?"

Continued attention from a guy so impossibly cute gets her nerves going. And the way he talks, pushing her to say more, is unprecedented.

He says he can fit them both on his Moto and take them about a kilometer down the road to get gelato.

"Okay by me," says Skye in the most off-hand way she can muster, totally panicking. Every other minute some stranger is taking over your life, suggesting something you can't even. A Moto is some teensy Micra-type car? A Smartcar maybe? There are a gazillion of them here.

"Okay by me!" echoes Sophia. "I am totally psyched. Just don't tell my mother!"

Abbo laughs.

Skye knows that Sophia, the walking Language Sponge, heard "totally psyched" from her. Gotta watch her step with that kid.

They leave the beach, stash their gear in the Micra, and head toward a gigundo thing on the side of road, the Moto, slightly smaller than a Harley Davidson. Wait a minute! Three of them on that thing? On the road? She's really gonna die this time. And what if Sophia falls off and cracks her head open? She is the *au pair*. If Sophia dies, does she go back on probation?

"I dunno, guys..." she says. No one listens. Abbo is busy pointing to where she should straddle the seat as he sets Sophia, who is laughing hilariously, on the handlebars.

Skye clambers onto the seat waiting for it all to tip over, but it doesn't. Abbo climbs into his seat right in front of her. He leans back, way too close to her. She's gonna have to touch him.

"Lean into me!" He shouts to her against the wind. He sounds miles away. "Put your arms around me!"

OMG, does she have to really touch him? She leans into his sun-warmed naked backside that smells of sea and sweat. Puts her arms around his waist. She has to, or stay behind. She feels his response, a push back of his body, a kind of snuggle that creates an electric shock in her. She lets it run through her every limb, shuts her eyes. Yup, she's gonna die, one way or the other.

Sophia's voice floats back, calling out in Greek and laughing those anxiety squeals Skye knows all about, half excitement, half terror. The kid's a hellava lot braver than Skye.

He hunches them forward, bears down on the handlebars, turns the ignition key and stamps hard on the left gear in his flip-flops. Varoom! They shove off with a jolt. How slow they really go Skye measures by a green car that zooms past at the usual million miles an hour and sweeps a wake of hot sand in her face. She scrunches her eyes, presses her ear against his back and feels the vibrations of his voice shouting back and forth to Sophia in Greek.

Her damp skin on his warm back is heaven. She holds onto him, her eyes closed, her cheek sliding slightly on the sweat of his back. If they crash or die, she's ready for it. Please God, just don't let me see it happen. Then the motor stops. The bike lurches. "Okay! Everybody off!"

She opens her eyes. They're parked in front of a gelato stand set back on a widened shoulder of the road. Sophia glows and hyperventilates, jumps off. Runs and skips in a circle, so excited. Comes back to Skye who is dismounting, trying not to wobble. A beautiful, happy child, that girl. Gotta say: a blonde angel who shines happiness. Downright dizzying, all this.

"Promise you won't tell my mother, okay, Skye?" She is breathless, hyped up. "That was so fun!" She jumps up and down, shrieking, "I can't believe I did that! Rode on the handlebars!"

Skye is upright. She might be sick. Rolls her eyes. "Thanks a bunch, Abbo. I'm about to throw chunks."

She sips a bottle of water while Sophia and Abbo dig into their pistachio and raisin gelatos, all three seated knee to knee at one of two red metal tables. The look of gelatos melting—milky, floating raisins, drowning nuts—keeps her stomach gurgling.

Abbo takes a swig from her water bottle. Hey! Boundaries, buddy! A little too familiar, wouldn't you say? But she doesn't say because a boundary got broken when she had to lean against him. All her normal boundaries are getting ridden over.

When she feels stable—he keeps asking her if she's feeling better, so she's gotta say yes sometime—they ride back to the beach, back to flirtations on the sand, Skye saying she's pleased as punch that she survived that whole Moto ordeal, but she's meaning pleased that they touched, too.

Eventually he says he must leave. Yeah, they should go, too.

"Here." He hands Skye his notebook. "Until we meet again."

"*Yia-sas!* Bye!"

"See you around."

Hope so.

Driving back up the mountain to home, they get giddy. "Such an adventure! My mother doesn't permit me on a Moto! Do you have them in America? Tell me about where you live there."

And Skye, feeling free as a bird, riffs on, natural-like, no filler crap, about the Bay State. The green mountains that turn orange and yellow and purple in the fall, softer-shaped than these big granite guys. Yes, very different, but come to think of it, a lot of Greeks live there, too. Yes, they are Americans, but they have their churches and festivals and things. It's just like having a friend, talking back and forth about where you're from, then the Moto ride, and about Abbo—he's hot—friendship with this little twerp who's got more guts than she has.

Today being July 20 makes it one week since Skye arrived and her first full day to photograph. Super. She's earned it by keeping her trap shut. *Hey there, Kim? Kleio? Mal? Are ya watching this? I can do it. Yep. Adjust.* Kills her to think it. Hey, a person can change, right?

Enjoy the day, Skye! Kleio and Twerpie call out together, sincere, as she leaves the house on her own, to the Micra. So bitchin!

First stop, the Internet café. Check that mail. Maybe the Wicked Witch of the East wrote back.

She could write lots back, about the Moto, Abbo, the driving, the beaches, and the chapel, the Kid, the Geezer and the Lion Lady. The photography.

Skye climbs the stairs, opens the door, walks to the bank of computers full of expectation, you might say. But nope. Still nothing. She looks around, sees the girl. But nope, no Abbo either.

Best drive around, find stuff to photograph. Sophia and her animal kick: gotta get more observant 'cause it's been mostly geckos. Mr. Theo will pick up Sophia after siesta time, to give Kleio a longer break. He is nice that way, protective of her. Skye thinks: And of me, too.

——*∿∿*——

Sophia has been waiting on the balcony since she awoke to listen for the particular chug of Uncle Theo's jeep as it plods up the mountain. Her mother is still asleep. She finally hears it, knows he'll arrive in two minutes. There are two topics she is eager to discuss. Skye is one. It's her opinion that Skye is becoming less tortoise-like. She improves. Skye is funny, and she teaches her many American swear words. But the second subject she may only mention *if* her mother already told him that they will leave. Who else can she talk to? No one. Her mother cautioned about hanging underwear on the line for the gossips to study, or some such.

"Eh? Sophia?"

He's at the gate. Her mother prohibits "Eh" as a greeting. It's a country way. Uncle Theo likes to act more country than Athens—that is her mother: super-critical. She runs out to the gate and hugs him.

"Where to, today, my love? If you have no preference, I have a client at the women's monastery to see, the abbess herself. I can use your help with the abbess, who is more partial to children than to lawyers. We'll drop in unannounced to take her off-guard. And they make some very good pastries at her monastery, which they will surely offer us. Shall we go, you and I, to learn what bee buzzes beneath the bonnet of the abbess?"

In the car, Sophia begins her progress report. "Skye is much better than Marie-France, who Mama sent back to Geneva after a week. Even you said it was no great loss, since Marie-France banned candy, *'qui pourrit les dentes, m'petite!'* Skye buys candy every day, even my most favorite, with the center hole that whistles when you blow through it. For herself, too. We whistle together! Skye's other good points are: she likes the beach and now ice cream, and always gives a good report about me to Mama. She has a nice camera that I want, too. Mama says I may get one at the end of the summer, if I'm good. Not a problem, because I am always good. Would you buy me the whistle candy, please? *Vielen dank, Herr Theo!* See? I *am* like a chameleon, ready to try any language." She stops there to assess whether he knows or not. He is smiling, just driving.

He can't know. It is a subject so earth-shattering he would ask her about the catastrophe.

She must not raise it then. It may only be discussed with Mama, who has but one unfair position: they will go to live in America. She must cover her frustration. She hopes Uncle Theo is not the mind reader he claims to be, or the Knower of What Makes All Children Tick, his other claim, to know how upset she is. She *wishes to hell*—what Skye says—that he had the power to stop her mother's terrible plan. Another thing they share: she and Skye are both furious at their mothers.

―⁓―

The eleven-year-old, neither adult nor child, according to the abbess's dry assessment, must sit at the far end of the table, so as not to hear them speak. "She is old enough to comprehend and repeat monastery business on the outside."

The mean old abbess announced this when they arrived, and she sat Sophia at the end of a table so long it fills the entire length of a narrow library. She and Uncle Theo hunch together at the other end. Sophia asks the abbess if they built the room around the table. The abbess harrumphs, of course not. The walls up to the cracked, cobwebbed ceiling are crammed with books in dusty bindings, a claustrophobic space. Sophia will listen as hard as she can to show the abbess she will not win. *Nyah-nyah-nyah.* So there.

They study a map in a large antique book and dispute in whispers.

The abbess has provided paper and a pencil to keep Sophia's idle hands busy, told her to do sums. Instead Sophia sketches the fat mean abbess with oversized eyeglasses and a black mole above her lip but quickly sees that realism is rude. She blacks it out and looks about for a neutral subject. On the far wall, the curtain-less window opens to a flowering tree. To draw it keeps her oriented in their direction, the better to read their lips as she deciphers the whispers. It seems to be about a disputed property demarcation, which they keep pointing to on the map. The abbess must search for the posts outside and let him know when she finds them.

Yes, he insists, they will be there. She must look. He can do nothing until they are found.

Bo-ring! Skye would say. Sophia hopes the pastries are worth this tedium, or she'll never return. She squints at titles on the book spines across from her, some inscribed with the old script used on icons, others with modern letters. The books are boring, too—lives of the saints, individual and collected, collected sermons of bishops, collected funeral orations, and patriotic poetry—these are the worst. She's memorized such poems that glorify the Greek past with flowery words no one uses today, with sing-song-y rhymes about its old greatness. It sounds so phony she never believes it. Is it Sophia's heritage just because she grew up here? She is in doubt.

She knows there could have been another heritage, completely unknown to her, that involves her birth parents. Why did they give her up? What if they hadn't and she never came to Greece? What would she be then? Is that first past her real identity? And will she ever meet them? She wants to, and not.

She squirms. To wait is insufferable. When will they finish their whispers? When is the pastry coming? In case the abbess wants to inspect her artwork, she quickly sketches the row of library books, but she adds her own titles in minuscule English—My Birth Country, America My New Home, Poetry is Boring. Greek Poetry is Phony. Worried the abbess may read English through those thick glasses, she scribbles lines through them. When can they leave? This is terrible!

Finally, the abbess stands and shuts the big book. Uncle Theo winks at her. The abbess wants to inspect her drawings and harrumphs.

"The pastries weren't so good," she tells Uncle Theo on the way back. "They looked okay, but since they were made with goat milk, they smelled."

Down the mountain road they pass the spot where they found the tortoise. Sophia rolls down the window and shouts in two languages, "*Yiasou Kyrie Khelona!* Have a happy life wherever you may be now!"

In town they stop for the whistle candy for her and Skye. Uncle Theo takes her home without stopping to greet Kleio, because he must return to Lithoi before dark, as the abbess, the strict taskmistress, assigned him too much homework.

Sophia wonders if they avoid each other. They have had rifts before. Maybe he, too, is mad at Mama for leaving, so mad he can't even say it.

—∿∿—

In the evening Theo settles at his father's oversized roll-top desk, in which he keeps a diary, to write about events and about those closest to him without having to speak. Keeping thoughts in a diary avoids all manner of arguments. He voices opinions and prejudices without betraying confidences and without the risk of gossip. If nations kept diaries, he believes, there would never be wars. Equally, he is a proponent of voicing what is right. Voices make for cohesive communities and, through dissent, arrive at a common good. Thus he considers himself a very private, and, as much, a very public person as the situation requires, and as energy permits.

He turns to the next blank page. Sophaki and her unstoppable energy, the abbess and her unstoppable suspicions, women and their inscrutability—why must they think and behave so differently from men? How many years has he sat at this desk to write the astonishing ways women complicate his life?

Men are uncomplicated. They abide by patterns of behavior, both good and bad. With predictable consequences. At least those he has known.

On humid nights like this, a faint fragrance rises from the desk of almond wood, reinforcing his appreciation of his inheritance. The desk was constructed as barter when drachmas were scarce, when Theo was a child, its grain ink-streaked from the days of straight pens and inkwells. Respectful men seated round it on folding chairs, watching his father and the documents he notarized. He remembers the long talks, the meditations, then the ceremonious reach into the drawer for the inkpad and the selection of a stamp from the many kept within, and the final actualization of the contract. His father was an uncomplicated man who did what was right.

Theo hopes he has emulated him.

This home is one of his inheritances. He was just a toddler when the ground floor where he sits now went from a *kamari* sheltering goats to become his father's office. A man with foresight, he had renovated the old house at great cost to accommodate his growing business, his growing family and the future aging that would make stairs difficult.

Custom dictated that Theo should have himself constructed a home for his Austrian bride when they married. Instead he proved he was a man of reclamation and conservation. To respect the planet, he intended to leave behind the smallest evidence of his existence by bringing his modern wife to live in his father's home. He smiles at the irony that their modern marriage ended in a modern divorce. He chuckles: the old ways had value after all, to intertwine property with marriage to one's own kind to insure both would endure.

On the day he and the girls conserved the life of the tortoise, he continued the drive up to an older homestead, another inheritance. The girls explored the nearby caves for animals as he took stock of the farmstead of his forebears. From it they had rained guerrilla attacks on the Ottomans and left for him a legacy of country and beliefs. This is his greatest inheritance.

The girl, Ourania, was shocked that he picked almonds from the ground and offered them to her, collected cherries from the trees in a well-used grocery bag. Isn't he stealing? She demanded of Sophia, lacking understanding of inheritance. He shook his head, mystified by her black and white logic, her absent curiosity.

It strikes him as strange the ease with which foreigners come to Greece, his first wife included, Kleio included. They arrive unencumbered by connective bonds, and they search for what they want. This girl came too, looking for something.

He would never live elsewhere. Every room of his home is history. The bedroom on this ground floor contains the *ikonostasion* that displays his family's eighteenth-century icons tucked round with grasses twisted into crosses. The icons glow over a flame that was walked from the church, lit from the single midnight candle at Easter. At this tableau, his parents made their prayers together, in the ancient tradition. Later, in that room, he installed a blackboard for his wife to give German lessons and removed it when she left. In it, he recuperated from the removal of the tumor in his spine and practiced the use of crutches after the surgery until he was able to take the stairs.

There he put Kleio to sleep when she came to see the house he'd found for her, now a decade ago. He tucked her in like a child that night, felt her vulnerability. He knew in that moment that he loved her. He had never met a woman like her. It was not the time to say or act on his feelings. Bruised from her own illness, she sought something other than romance, a future she imagined with some urgency. Her determination continues to educate him; they are close friends. The time for consummation has long passed.

He thinks tenderly of the emotions that have filled that room. Sometimes he will leave his desk to make a prayer as well, to ask for wisdom, though he holds no opinion on the existence of God, faith being beyond opinion.

By drawing two vertical lines on the blank page, he makes three columns. He titles them The Spouse, Kleio, Rina. Under The Spouse, he writes *placid lake*. Under Kleio, he writes *deep ocean*. Under Rina, he writes *river*. He reads his words.

It is all he has to say. He may add more contrasts in time, if they come to him. He could write more about Rina, but what? She came from Athens as a client wanting property on Mount Parnon, and he found her a spot that enchanted her. She has the same quality as Kleio, wanting, yearning. But Rina is different. She is of this place. She is gentle, joyful and full of hope; she is capable of finding what she wants. It is a relief to him that she lacks the intensity that drives Kleio and sometimes makes him nervous. How can he better describe Rina? A river with an undercurrent of anticipation?

He flips through earlier entries, it being instructional to read old ruminations in the light of time passed. His last entry, 15 July, was the day he met Ourania, her first day with the Platons.

Sophia begged me to intervene. Disinterested in their arguments, I offered them a sight-seeing drive, believing that the heat had unsettled the new one, unaccustomed to our climate. Sophia was plainly furious, and the new one, decorated with pictures, muttered uncivil American under her breath and never acknowledged me. Kleio greeted me with tears in her eyes. I dared not ask what had occurred but drove them to a higher altitude, hoping a destination would reveal itself. Passing the new home constructions, the old farmsteads, the monastery turnoff, I realized I was heading to the top, to Rina's, an excuse to see her again. Kleio and I chatted. She remains tense since her return, now two months to the day. There is something sad in her. Skye and Sophia spoke more civilly, but of their Anglika I understand nothing. Three such different women in one house for two months! It will not hold.

Kleio asked me about changes during her absence. I described the abbess's plans, with which I disagree. Few others, I answered, as God wills, not divulging the change for me—Rina.

She said she had undergone many while in America; she had been re-Americanized. Do not fear, I assured, regression does not happen so fast.

The fig and olive trees by then gave way to the tall pines of the upper altitudes. We drove in pleasant breezes and arrived at the forest clearing of Rina's handsome new restaurant of timber and stucco. Rina was warmly welcoming, as is her nature. She was happy to see me, which gives me hope that between us it is not ended. She has growing success with the restaurant. Buses from the sermon tours have discovered her and begin to stop on their return from the monastery. She would like a hostel constructed for hikers. Private conversation was not possible. We discussed the adjacent property that she would like me to negotiate. I believe Kleio, who is intuitive, did not believe property dealings were our only transaction. I will tell her about Rina when I think she can hear it well.

The highly embellished Americana with the Druidic wild hair, garbed to flaunt tattoos of a ferocity I've only seen on German skinheads, announced to all that she ate no meat, then pushed away Rina's offering of beets and skordalia. I requested for her a large tomato, sliced and plain because she is hyper-sensitive to smells,

Sophia informs me. Kleio was irritated that I call the girl Ourania. Why confuse her? she snapped.

Because she needs dislocation from everything she brings with her, I explained. The girl suffers. Look at her. She is off-center. Let her be Ourania in Greece. Sophaki chimed in, saying Ourania was a bad choice, claimed it resembles in sound gourouni, "pig." Thus I learn another English word, "pig." But I am like the never-advancing Sisyphus: for every newly learned word, one is forgotten.

Sophaki translating, I told Ourania she would see the wisdom of her new name. The Muse, Ourania, guided men's knowledge of the stars so they could navigate on the open sea at night. Understanding the skies loosened their dependence on the shoreline, made them brave enough to cross the water and encounter new people with new ideas. The metaphor was lost on her. She stared at me, dumbly. She knows nothing of Plato and precious little of anything else.

Theo knows he reads her correctly. Their next encounter involved the tortoise, about which the girl named for the muse most closely associated with curiosity seemed most incurious. Yet he had noted a spark. There is no key to understanding women. Best leave ruling the world to us men. We are not inscrutable. We are obvious. He is tired. He reaches for his crutches to head up to bed.

—⁓—

Mal needs a strategy to get this reunion on board, but what? On her divan, a snifter warming in her palms, she is bathed in the rosy rake of sun setting in a sky that was flattened gray with rain for most of the day. She does not draw the velvet curtains nor light a lamp—feeling discomforted by Kleio's downer e-mail of yesterday. It appears Mal's plan for Skye might fail. So be it. But, she must save the reunion at all costs. She always did need strategies with Kleio. It had been genius to send Skye to Kleio in Greece, as it is equally genius to send Group there next. Each of them needs a holiday; each has her own turmoil. They would thrive to be united again. She knows it by intuition. Besides, she wants a neutral place to come clean with them. To tell them, and especially Kleio, about her ordeal in Nicaragua that she's kept under wraps for thirty years now. It's because even though she made herself ignore it—and who would want to dwell on it?—she is ready now, without shame to tell them what she would not say back then. What else could she have done then but seal it off? She had been raised not to wallow. But the memories return and return the stronger the more she feels for Skye and what Skye needs. Funny that. It is reasonable, and she can even think of it as such, why she abandoned Kleio so abruptly. She remembers it more easily now, flushing the embryo that would have been her own child down the toilet, running to Juan with his killer by her side, caressing his dear lifeless head that had been so full of ideas and future, her thighs beneath her skirt warm with his blood. Who willfully would remember those horrors? Who wouldn't say such were the casualties of war? Move on. Still, the experience of those deaths sat like a time bomb within her and exploded in the moment of hearing Kleio's words of hope. A baby. She will make that reunion happen. She will explain it to them. To Kleio. She will repair the damage she has caused them both.

And Skye. She will stay true to Skye, who needed distance from Mina. Poor Mina! Who unfailingly does a spotty job helping Skye cope. And deflating that Kleio has no comprehension of the child's needs, now she's met Skye. Kleio was always one to understand young people. She has the temperament for it, and Mal lacks it, generally speaking. Kleio must give Skye another go. Where is that maternal instinct? She adopted that baby. She ran that place for children in Brooklyn. Mal herself felt Kleio's empathy when they were out of the gate in Manhattan, rather depended on it. Kleio has the patience to do for Skye what Mal and Mina cannot. Kleio can tolerate someone being lost and angry, while Mal gets upset and Mina gets frightened. Kleio dear, fix it! You can.

Mal's inexperience with children is not from lack of heart, she knows, though she refuses her friends' invitations to volunteer with them as baby-holders in the hospital. She tells them she is infant-adverse. No one in her current life need know of the miscarriage—the death of what would have been her only child followed just days later by Juan's murder. Few people bear such losses without scars. Her life got twisted up by going off with him so innocently—no—so naïvely, to help a nation build itself. She'd returned from Nicaragua and kept mum about what had befallen her. She'd left behind an infant's remains and Juan's grave and locked up all memory of loss till now. Now it aches, wanting to be told. Group, her closest friends, must know. She owes it to them. She disbanded Group upon her return, sent them packing and left.

She's always felt affection for Skye. God knows, if she had been the one to raise an imaginative but impulsive girl who enjoyed provoking authorities—just like her Uncle Juan—Mal would never give up on her as Mina did. Kleio always had insight about these kinds of impulsive children. She'd had such insights about Juan. She wants Kleio and Group in her life on an honest footing. She practically tastes the need to close this old chapter by telling them, then to open herself up to a new span of life.

Her floor-to-ceiling windows make a frame for the silhouettes of cargo ships gliding on the horizon to the North Sea. The sun sinks, puts Mal in the dark. She doesn't mind.

Two weeks ago, Skye sat right here with her. It was good fun playing together, doing whatever was of interest, shopping, a rock concert in the park, a Punjabi restaurant and the trendiest in vegetarian, just as it once had been fun with Kleio in those New York years. Kleio and Skye are explorers, so similar, though one would hardly know to hear Kleio whinge on about Skye. To be fair to Kleio, Mal's not only never raised a child, she's never had two bouts of cancer, either. She draws a blank trying to imagine what it would be like and sips from her snifter.

She hadn't expected to feel so empty when Skye left, such a complete surprise. The emptiness begs the question of what to do as replacement for her professional identity of the last thirty years. Like Skye, she must make a plan for herself, except that the young have time on their side, and Mal feels old. Well, older. Kleio is the one old, a decade more than she, but as the mother of a pre-adolescent, is bound to be occupied for years to come. Mal never imagined arriving at the end of things. Funnily, to her, living in the present was proof of nothing changing. But it had. What needn't end is friendship.

She returns more easily these days to memories of Juan and fantasies of their bi-cultural children taken annually to London to know their English heritage. The fetus with no chance would be a young man today. (Stop! There is no son.) She must not allow Kleio to nix a reunion, because gathering them all together, they would be burst out with hilarious ideas for her future, and she wants to hear them, poo-poo them, laugh. Follow them up. And she wants Kleio to be part of them again. They were creative as a group. Should she demand? Insist? Craftier instead to mount a sales campaign. Mal tips the snifter of brandy between her palms and sips again. She flips a light switch and goes to her computer for the first foray.

18 July 2011

From: Mallory Tame
To: Kleio Platon

Your hesitation about a reunion is completely understandable, because without contact for so long, you can't know who we are today. I assure you that Gwen and Mina are better friends to me now than when I was an arrogant know-it-all. In fact, we all have mellowed. Living has the effect of making one malleable. One's ego tires and deflates some with age; expectations soften around the edges, and one's thinking broadens out. One discovers the multiple facets to everything. One sees consequences previously unconsidered. I agree with you about the uselessness of grudges, all this being the better side of age. I believe you would enjoy knowing us today, Kleio; being together would brighten your life. We have become ever so much more clever! Come on, Kleio. Where is your curiosity? Do reconsider. I shall arrange that the others write, so you may reconnect.

As for Skye, I would advise you that patience is the key. Beneath the prickly exterior is a tender, fearful child. Think of a rosebud, on a stem of thorns, about to bloom. Do be quite clear with your expectations. She knows how to cooperate. You will soon discover how truly alike you both are. I love you both. At a minimum, you both enjoy laughter. I miss that about you, Kleio. I'd love to hear you laugh. We all are so eager to see you, I more than anyone. Much love, Mal

—◆—

Mina has her hands full as usual, doing far too much. She's just come in from buying staples and picking up take-out for dinner, entitling her to take a breath and relax. She tucks in her legs on the sofa that the movers plunked in front of her elegant Georgian-style fireplace, probably original to the brownstone. Does it work? She forgot to ask. For the last fifteen minutes she's actually begun her life on Bay Street in Boston. This is to be her first night. So exciting! And she's free of worry about Skye, who is happy for once, she hopes, with Kleio. Kleio used to be such fun. She hasn't felt so carefree since, since when? Since she lived with Group on West End Avenue, so many lifetimes ago...

She should have bought herself a bottle of wine to celebrate, wonders where the nearest liquor store is in her new neighborhood. She'll go exploring tomorrow. Her take-out is Indian, *tikka masala*, onion *pakoras*. Wine wouldn't go with, anyway. Skye makes such a nasty fuss about Indian food, and now a Bombay Delight is virtually across the street! Her dream is really happening. Ten long years preparing for it.

She burrows into the sofa, notices the worn patches for the first time. Probably it's been like that for ages. She has brought just a few pieces of the old furniture, excited to buy new, wonders how she'll arrange it all to fit into her new home. Reupholster the sofa. It has good lines.

The window is open to the roar of five o' clock traffic, music to her ears after quiet subdivision life in the 'burbs. Well, they had a good life there, raised their daughter there. Practiced their careers there, and Richard had his garden. She winces, because he had late-diagnosed Lyme disease, so his garden was literally the death of him. She should have sued the hospital for the late diagnosis. She misses him. It's been so long. Watching her from above, he would not approve, though—would he?—the radical change she's made at fifty-two. Perhaps her worried upheaval is also what Kleio felt when she up and left the country, and adopted a baby to boot.

Mina feels more than ready to let her own baby go: Skye, in need of independence. Look at what Mina had accomplished by Skye's age and against all odds—full scholarship to Barnard, early admissions. Skye will surely straighten out by the time she's eighteen. Mina will no longer be responsible. A weight off her shoulders, although you never stop feeling responsible...

So who does that: adopts a baby in her fifties? She wouldn't have foreseen it as a choice for Kleio.

Her own plan for a second life is much saner, to open her bookstore filled with the most wonderful children's books anyone can imagine. Carpet it, bring in soft light, place beanbags in corners, create a nook for authors to give readings. It will be lovely. *Fox and Crow, Inc. Jasmina Davila, Bookseller.* She's sticking with that name. It will become the premier children's bookstore of Boston. She will do it. She has it in her. She's signed the lease for the space.

It would have been so nice if Skye had wanted to join her in this venture, to be her assistant, but better she goes her own way. Dr. Ramos said the same: Mina, you can handle it on your own. You handled so much these last eight years, Richard's death, Skye's situation. Dr. Ramos, the only doctor she'll ever trust. She would have sued Dr. Katkar, Richard's doctor, if Dr. Ramos hadn't advised against it. A case of doctors circling the wagons to protect their own? One never knows ... water under the bridge now. Eyes forward.

Life transits at such dizzying speed. She'd love to squeeze in a little trip to Greece at summer's end, if Kleio allows it. Mal urged her to write Kleio, to push the reunion and to explain more fully Skye's situation, because apparently her daughter has been overwhelming her hostess. Writing feels like pressure with so much to think of, and she so hates being told what to do. But Mal insists. She's helped enormously with Skye. Mal is the one person Skye does not demean or scoff at. Doesn't she also owe Skye a note? Oh, and there is Kim to call, mustn't forget. Kim's been phoning to know what is going on, and really, what can she tell her? Skye is always so cryptic, talks in opposites. Maybe heat up the Indian food? Mina goes into her railroad kitchen, newly renovated, convenient and adorable, loving that black and white harlequin floor.

How does one convince Kleio to welcome them, the old Group? Group was good for her, for them all, despite its zaniness. It was of the times. And wouldn't it be nice to see where Kleio lives? Skye has squandered so many opportunities; hopefully, not this, too. That child!

She'll use her new fuchsia stationery, embossed JD, Jasmina Davila, a statement of her new self. Omits her married name, Richard's name; that part of her life is over. She will write to Kleio with whatever is in her heart. On fuchsia. She'll get a start while the food heats up.

Boston, July 27

Dear Kleio,

It's been long, hasn't it? Mal has strongly suggested—as only Mal can—that I provide some details about Skye for you, and asks me to urge you to join up for a Group reunion in Greece. We are so curious to know about you since we were last together. West End Quartet: I wanted it to be our name, much more elegant than utilitarian Group. Do you remember our arguments about it? But you and Mal were adamant about not changing it.

I understand you went through reverse immigration by moving to Greece—as the immigration lawyer in me notes. And you adopted at the age that women are more likely to become grandmothers. That is the Kleio I remember, true to her own path.

I married an attorney and became an attorney myself—now widowed. I'm about to embark on a second career. Skye must have told you. Unfortunately, in the distraction of my husband's situation I neglected her, with the upshot of her running into emotional and legal troubles. Traumatic, always, to lose a parent, but as an adolescent she was devastated. You may remember that I, too, lost my parents young, perhaps why I handled it poorly. You've probably heard that Skye broke the law. We dispute if she actually did, but we took a plea bargain five years ago. Her long stint on probation ever since is due both to legal mires and to her provocations, too numerous to mention. Do not be intimidated by those tattoos. They are her body armor, which I hope she'll remove when she has come to terms with her father's death, someday. I can't see her being any trouble to you. Mal says you're in the country, rather isolated, which I prefer for her. You must know by now that Skye is a picky eater and lactose-intolerant, so do avoid dairy. Soy milk is the better choice. Also, do buy gluten-free products. Skye may have mentioned her current "no meat" policy that complicated my life and dinner preparations. I hope her idiosyncrasies won't be an inconvenience. As you have a daughter, you can appreciate what I suffer.

Kleio, isn't this the perfect time for us to reconnect? I understand you've just had cancer surgery for a second time. It must have been tough, but Mal says you are on the mend. Such a dissonant quartet we were, but as much in harmony. All my love and many thanks again for your generosity.

Jasmina (Mina)

P.S. Do expect a big box of American food shortly. Your daughter will enjoy it, too.

———

Dear Diary: Mama will kill me when she learns I broke her confidence today. I just couldn't hold it in any longer. This is my home and I want *to stay here. Florian says I am an International like him. But he has a Greek mother and Austrian father, and I have only a Greek-American mother. I belong here. It doesn't matter to have American citizenship, because I never lived there. Florian says I am more Greek than my mother. And I am, too!*

Whenever we visit our American relatives, Mama fits in, talks differently. She laughs at jokes I don't follow. Florian said the same happens when they go to Innsbruck, except Florian doesn't care. Besjana says I am so lucky to go live there. She wishes she could be me. Florian says Besjana is also an International, even though Albania is just across the border. She could walk to it.

The worst is that I also told Uncle Theo. His eyebrows went up like two lambdas. He said it is childish to think only of my own feelings. I should ask Mama more about it. That her need is greater than mine now, and to put myself in her place and imagine what she went through. He says Ourania is in even greater need than me. I have an adult job to do around all these mending, broken people. Be easy with them. Don't judge. Help them be peaceful. Nice for him to say! He's already a grownup. I can't help it. When I get mad, I get mad! What the hell! Shit! Mama will be furious that I told. Uncle Theo promises to pretend he doesn't know when she does tell him.

———∿∿∿———

In the morning, when Sophia comes down to the kitchen, Skye has poured Sophia granola and is reading from a notebook at the table. Mama is asleep.

"What's that you've got?"

"Abbo's poetry book, from when we saw him at the beach. I'll return it when we see him again. Some Swedish words, some Greek—you can translate and say what this stuff is about. He's got some words here from Arctic Monkeys: *Don't sit down 'cause I've moved your chair.* Really? What's that supposed to mean?" She passes the notebook across the table.

Sophia is not in the mood for this boy-girl stuff about monkeys. She is worried about Mama finding out, and thinks she'd better admit it before that happens. Maybe she won't have to. Maybe Mama will tell Uncle Theo today, and that will be that. She closes Abbo's notebook.

"Will you have granola, too? Try it. Mama got a letter from your mother. She asked me again why you don't like the food. I understand if you hate our food, because I hated Swiss food when I stayed with my godparents. Their worst is slithery mushrooms in cream. I told Mama you said everything here has a smell. Did you know that Switzerland smells like spoiled milk? Even the outside air. And their breath is like rotten cheese. I had to turn my head. I held my face tight not to flinch. Like this, see?" She can make Skye laugh by pulling her cheeks taut and crossing her eyes.

Skye laughs. "You crack me up. You're a card, kiddo!"

She says it *cahd*. Sophia has noticed the different ways Americans say the same words. She will have to learn them all when they move there.

"In Geneva, I spoke in French. I learned in school. It was fun to try in a real French place. You must learn Greek. It's handy. If you learn Greek, you can talk to Uncle Theo."

"Don't need to. I have a translator."

Skye pours a teaspoon of granola into her hand and touches it with her tongue. Sophia is disbelieving. Mama would say: grain, a new food group for Skye.

"But how do you know if I'm translating correctly? Maybe I make up stories, or speak behind your back. Do you know that I told him not to call you *Ourania*? Because it sounds like *gou-rou-ni*. Pig. And like *ou-ra*. Tail. *Ou-ra-ni-a* makes a funny picture in my head. He said a new name will inspire you. He says that's why you came here, to be inspired. Is that true? He says stuff I do not understand, but he says, don't worry. Someday his words will return to me in big capital letters and will light up my mind like a billboard on the superhighway. Anyway, he's very kind, isn't he? When you asked if I felt bad not having a dad, I thought of him. I wish my mother would marry him so we could be a family."

And they wouldn't have to leave, she adds silently. She takes a big spoonful and chomps, in awe that Skye nibbles the granola, grain by grain. Sophia is unsure if she engages Skye or not, because Skye's eyes say she is elsewhere.

"Here is a word Abbo might use: *volta*. A walk. 'Let's go for a walk.' *Mia volta*. You can say that, right? *Volta*? See? You have the *gourouni* with its curly *oura*. And now another word. Everyone's always going for a *volta* around here. '*Pa-me yia volta?*' You'll hear that. If you just recognize *volta*, you'll know you're invited to go for a walk. You just smile and start walking."

Skye actually repeats *VOL-ta*. Then she says *gou-ROU-ni* and giggles. "Hey, Sophie! I'm taking my curly-tailed *gou-ROU-ni* for a *VOL-ta!*"

She play-acts being dragged by a large animal on a leash all around the kitchen, trying to roll the R. "Hey! Wait up, you dumb *gou-ROU-ni!*"

Sophia laughs, repeats the syllables. Skye imitates her again. Pretending she is being dragged out the kitchen door, she circles the patio and comes back inside.

"Just think, if you learned Greek, you could live here and never go back. What happened to you there, anyway?"

Skye drops her imaginary leash and looks down.

Sophia understands she caused pain, which Uncle Theo said she must not do, so she says quickly, "Abbo is really cute, isn't he? Do you like him? Flirt with him! Ask him if he'll go on a *volta* with you and your *gourouni*."

"Come on, kiddo, eat up. We can go to the St. Christopher Beach. You're cuckoo, you know? I bet no one taught you *that* word, right? Cuckoo?"

———~~~———

Late in the afternoon, they sit on the balcony sampling the snacks from the box that arrived at the post office from Skye's mother. Skye demonstrates how to scoop salsa with a tortilla chip so it won't break. A true *aht,* she says.

Sophia, tasting and making faces, says she is not sure she likes true *aht*.

Down in the valley shouting erupts and reverberates between the arms of the bay, funneling cheers upward to the balcony. A football game at the high school. Sophia listens for the name of the visiting team coming from the megaphone. "It's Megalopolis. That means, 'Large City.'"

They burst into laughter together. It's so silly! Where around here is a large city?

Sophia says they can take the public path below their house to a paved path all the way down to the high school and watch the game. Maybe Abbo is there. They haven't seen him for a while.

"No," says Skye. "It's not like he's been exactly looking for us, is it? If he's with a girl, that would be suckish."

Sophia shakes her head and leaves for the kitchen. She returns with big chunks of watermelon for them both. Greek watermelon is better than Mexican food. Skye has begun to eat watermelon, even while she complains it is too sweet. Sophia has noticed.

"Let's just stay here. I'll tell you what happened to me at home, and about Polly, my last real friend. We were besties when I was your age. Sit down for this one, kiddo. It's gonna sound really weird."

Sophia loves these stories of Skye's filled with strange, often bad words and surprising images. She sits next to her.

"So you know that my dad died, right? So Polly, my bestie, got this strange attitude about his death, like, oh well, no prob. It hurt me that she didn't care. He was my dad, already! I loved him. Then she started doing something crazy—competing with me! Like *her* dad might die, only from something much worse than mine. She'd riff on and on, all the time.

"It got me so mad that she wouldn't shut up, and one time, I shoved her off a bleacher at a school ballgame. I pushed so hard she actually fell a few risers down to the ground. Hit her head and broke her arm. Then her nutso mother tried to get me expelled from school for being a bully, even though I said I was sorry. I didn't plan to hurt her, just to shut her up. Her mom lied to the principal about me being a very dangerous kid. She said she had photographs to prove I was hitting kids. So crazy because what bozo just stands there, photographing kids fighting, and doesn't break them up? Anyway, it wasn't true. But I started playing hooky from school because other girls started ganging up on me, siding with Polly. Her mom filed a charge against me of harassment. What a lie. It was Polly and her gang doing the harassing! My dad had just died and my mom was schizo from it. Still, I got monitored twice a day for six whole months, to make sure I was attending school and not fighting. It was really embarrassing. Some lady from a probation place made me sign on a sheet twice a day, at school and at home. She followed me everywhere. What kind of a stupid job is that to give someone? My mother got so embarrassed that she acted super-nice to that lady, even made her cookies!" Skye finishes her watermelon slice and wipes her wet fingers on her tee-shirt. She picks up a taco chip and continues.

"I got this idea to get even. I'd break into Polly's house at night and scare the bejesus out of her, you know, make scary noises, jump out at her in the dark stuff. I was twelve. How smart is anyone at twelve? Except for you, the Brainiac, of course. They kept their doors unlocked, even at night. Polly said it was how her dad would be stabbed in his sleep, which was way worse than how my dad died from illness. So dumb. I sneaked out at midnight and walked the whole way in the dark. But when I got inside, I suddenly saw it was a very stupid idea, because Polly would recognize me, plus I hadn't thought about escaping. So instead I pocketed her mom's camera out in plain sight and I left. Problem was, I did a stupider thing: I flashed it at school so she'd know I had it. Her mother called the police and said I'd made 'a home invasion' when I was on probation with a curfew, being monitored by the probation lady. So then the detectives showed up at our house, and my mother totally wigged out cause her kid's in more trouble with the law. I handed over the camera, but I sassed the detective, which is contempt. So all that stuff got me 'removed from the home,' as they say. Mina was happy, I'm sure, since I'd been interfering with her own problems. It just went on from there, like exactly what Mr. Theo said. He really freaks me out."

Sophia watches the tears bead up in Skye's eyes while she continues her story.

"I ended up in juvenile detention 'cause of the pile-up of stuff, and my mother tearing out her hair, saying she couldn't handle me anymore. All they needed to hear. I kept acting worse to see how far they would go. I didn't care. They shifted me from place to place for three years. How come Mr. Theo knew? How'd he know it's hell to be dumb and scared: your mom doesn't trust you, your dad is dead, and you're in a jail with strip searches and lockdowns every time some warden loses a paper clip. But I was the sane one compared to the others. There were girls way worse off, trying every which way to kill themselves. I discovered a dead girl in the bathroom, blood all over the tiles. You can tell him sometime, that yes, losing the freedom to be a kid turns out to be quite the loss. Totally confuses you. You change, like he said, in your heart. You definitely cannot afford one: a heart. Tell him it's amazing that someone in Wacko-World gets it, the someone chasing down dumb-ass tortoises on the so-called National Highway. He totally gets 'crazy.'"

Skye is quiet. Sophia knows she is not finished, even though she barely understands what this is about. Uncle Theo is right. Skye is a broken person needing fixing. How does he know these things?

"I figured the best way to survive it all was to go Zen. It was a mistake to act like they were wrong, they were unfair. That thinking will keep you fighting to be right, and fighting them will never get you freedom. Just agree with whatever they say about you. You beat them by fooling them. Cool, right? It worked. Last year Mina got me into a day clinic, but I had to live with her. I got my high-school equivalency at home, 'the good jail,' haha. I got a job, too, cashiering, but I had curfew, which puts the damper on having friends. Not to mention, who'd be pals-y with a delinquent? That's when those therapists began, too, because at home I started cutting myself, which I'd learned about on the Inside. Look here. My tats cover up the scars."

Sophia peers at Skye's forearms, cringes and shuts her eyes. The tiny, half-moon scars in neat rows, so deliberate, make her queasy.

Skye is not done. "My mother was like having a nervous breakdown or something, all caught up in her own crap, crying and bemoaning away, like I made my dad die. She said I cut out of guilt for driving him to his grave. That really got to me, because I loved him. I remind her of him because I look like him: the red hair, why I dyed it purple. She was like the jail people, all blame. Even I began to wonder if I had pushed him over the brink, you know, by being bad. I stopped talking to her. To everyone, pretty much. Kim, my PO, says mothers don't mean what they say when they're overwrought. Nobody's perfect. In my mind I repeat Mina's accusations whenever she makes nice, not to forget the true her. We're surface okay now. I act good with everything, so she'll go to Boston. Meet someone new and remarry to forget my dad. Get her off my back." As she spoke, she pulled her frizz aside to show her roots to Sophia.

Yes, it's true. A strip of burnished rust color grows at the scalp before the magenta starts.

"Will you grow it out, or will you color it again?" Sophia asks, not knowing which is the best option.

"Don't know. Kinda liking the two-tone, on fleek look. Kim wants me to get my shit together quick. Aunt Mal wants it even faster. I'd rather just be dead. Or live in London with Aunt Mal. She trusts me. She's fun. I can always visit her, she says. She thinks I'm a card. I'm supposed to be grateful to whoever helps me get my life together, but I can't, 'cause why be grateful in advance? It didn't happen yet. Nothing's together. I don't even know where to live in the future. Yeah, you say Greece, right? Mostly I feel pretty much nothing about nothing, like just blank.

I got a job back home. That's a start, Kim says. No boyfriend. Polly was actually my last so-called friend. I just pretend I'm together to con people. So, there you have it in all its full glory: my 'sad' life story. Are you shocked? I must sound terrible to a normal, regular-type kid like you. I won't see Abbo again. He wasn't really into me. You can give him back his book for me."

"I will not give him his book back. He gave it to you. And I don't think you are 'together.'" Sophia wishes she hadn't said that. She watches big tears form again in Skye's eyes and start to drip down her cheeks. So sorry she is making Skye cry.

"Well," Sophia speaks softly, "we share something: neither of us knows where we should live in the future."

Kleio appearing at the door startles them. "Girls? I'm going out—over to Theo's for dinner. I'll have the car, so you have to stay in. Go down the hill to watch the game if you get antsy. It's called football, Skye, but it's really soccer. I'll be back about ten."

Sophia smiles at how pretty her mother looks. She hasn't seen Mama in a dress and makeup since before New York. She even got her hair done. "You look so nice, Mama!" She is caught in a wave of love that sinks to the depths of her, grateful that her mother is not like Skye's mother. "We'll be fine. You have a nice dinner."

She runs to hug her mother, who holds her tightly in return. Kleio plants a kiss on Sophia's forehead and two gentle kisses, one on each of her shoulders as she releases her. "See you later."

Sophia sees that Skye averts her gaze.

—∼∞∼—

"Theo, I want your advice, even if I intend to ignore it. What do you think about the girl?" Kleio shakes the greens soaking in a pan on his kitchen table to remove the garden soil while he starts to boil a fish. "She stopped her sass after I spoke to her. She's better, but she hardly speaks to me. Do I ignore her back? Communicate with her via Sophia? And this is really terrible: her mother threatens to come for a visit at the end of August! I don't know how that will affect Skye. I gather they do not get along. Her mother was always rather emotional, verging on hysterical. She wants to come here with two more old friends. They are dying to cheer me up, which I don't need. It's suffocating to imagine them here. I've indicated I don't want them. Was I rude? I can already guess what you will say about the girl: don't take it personally. Right? She's got her problems, and she and Sophia get along well. I heard about the tortoise. I instantly recognized your Homeric strategy, taking people on a journey to disarm them. Oh, how well I know you, Mr. Theo, after all these years!"

He comes to her and kisses the top of her head. "Do not trouble yourself about Ourania. She will be gone by the end of the summer, the better for having been here. Treat her like a fragile bird, which I believe she is. Better you focus attention on reducing stress. They say stress reactivates the cancer cells. I make small efforts with Ourania, as opportunities arise. Despite her clashes in America with its formidable legal apparatus, I see a troubled child responding in a troubled manner to a troubling situation. I believe she *wants* to right herself. And I want to see you healed quickly, *agape mou*."

My love. Kleio feels comforted. He watches over them both, and the girl. "And the visitors?"

"Everyone needs friends."

—◦◦◦—

Such a peaceful evening it turned out with Kleio, like those before she went to America, easy and amusing. After dinner he read to her from a book he is halfway through, because she would be interested. Then they listened to a tape of choral singing someone had lent him, of songs from the 1900s, songs her father also sang, learned from his parents. She sang along because she had learned them, too. They were so at ease that he considered for a moment admitting that he knew of her intention to leave Greece, but he said nothing to spare Sophaki. They felt synchronized again. To say it would disrupt the newly retrieved balance. He will wait for her to tell him. He takes out his diary.

27 July 2011. She will keep it from me until she has made up her mind definitively, to avoid a discussion. It will be an announcement.

My opinions about Ourania are evidently confirmed by what Kleio overheard. The child demands, as indicated by her tattoos and her stubbornness, her right to be herself, a good demand. Independence requires sophisticated skills for the young today which she still masters. In our own youth, the options for independence were fewer, contending foremost, as we did, with starvation and poverty. Those conditions conserve one's expectations of life. Our need for independence—freedom, Kleio labels it—was bound by family and community expectations. Ourania has numerous nebulous chains holding her down. She will need to name them to untangle herself. And Kleio's friends: what is the harm in seeing them? They will enjoy the beauty of our land, eat our food and drink our wine. They will laugh together. When they leave, they will take Ourania with them. The summer will be done. Surely Kleio will announce her plan to leave soon. Why should she go? I should like to understand. It shocks me.

Theo glances at his previous page with the schema of the women who cause him consternation, still nothing more to add but he thinks of Rina again. She is a warm soul. In her presence, he feels tethered and connected. He closes his diary. Next week offers them a good excursion. There is the *panigyri* at the monastery, a joyful gathering. Perhaps Rina will be there.

———

Skye is again at the café and orders herself to smile at the girl this time, you doofus! They're not exactly strangers now. Every time she goes in, Skye acts like she's never been there before. How dumb is that? Ask what's her friggin' name!

It is Vanessa. Okay, now tell her she is Ourania in Greece, Skye in the States.

Vanessa nods, smiles and polishes the counter. Her Greek name is Evangelia. Vanessa does not appear to be Abbo's girl, since after ten times of being here already, Skye's not seen him again. Is she stalking him, or what?

Hey! Finally! Mina answered. It's only ten days later.

July 28, 2011

Glad to hear from you, my sweet. Apologies for the delay. Very busy with the transition, but thoughts are of you, always. Did the box arrive? I hope it's what you wanted. Glad you are photographing and you like the little girl. No fights, okay? Our house is officially on the market. I hope you will decide where you intend to live. Your belongings went into storage, as staging looks better with fewer personal items visible. It's past the peak selling season, so I was concerned. I'm in a sweet two-bedroom rental within walking distance of the shop, and there is a room for you, if you want it. Kim says your hearing is set for September 10; she expects you'll be released permanently. Your service with Kleio works in your favor. Mind your P's and Q's! Fun news: Mal is organizing a reunion of our old commune, Group, in Greece near the end of your stay. We'll visit you at Kleio's. Then we go to a spa at the sea. We are waiting for Kleio to confirm. I've never been there. I'm excited. Just us girls. It is a good opportunity for you to travel on your own while we are there. Kim agrees and will not report it to the judge. You'd like that, right? Afterwards we fly with Mal to London for a few days' stay, too. Okay? Love, Mom

—✳—

There is a mangy coal-black mongrel, the size of a pony, that scares the bejesus out of Skye. Its fangs glow neon whenever she tries to pass it on the high road to a cemetery she'd like to explore that peeks between the poplars. Old monuments with morbid potential; it intrigues her. Gotta find some ghoulish statues and crypts to photograph, not just animals.

"C'mon, Sophia! Come with me! You don't need a stupid siesta. Be a pal. Help me out. Try speaking Dog, a new language for you."

Sophia thinks she knows the dog in question, so of course, she'll help Skye pass by it safely.

They meander slowly up the road because it's 115 degrees, an oven. The air just sits on you, a dead weight. Watch out for killer bees droning around like MiG-25 Interceptors, even if they look half dead from the heat, too.

Oh-ho. Behold the Dog!

Seeing Skye, the gigundo creature bares its saliva-dripping fangs, stands its ground in the middle of the road, head and tail lowered. Ears flare. A low growl escalates into a warning bark. Drool.

"Hey! It's Mavri! *Ella tho, Mavri!*" Sophia bends on one knee to its eye level. At the sound of Sophia's voice, ferocious Mavri morphs into a frisky puppy, lifts her head, yelps and raises her tail in a wild waggle. Her fangs recede into a wide grin. She prances over like she wants to play, bumps her snout into Sophia's outstretched palm. She presses her flank into Sophia's side, tail gone completely crazy.

Mavri belongs to the widow *Kyria Mimika,* farther up, Sophia explains. She rubs Mavri under her chin and coos Greek words. The mongrel fawns all over her; her slobbery tongue licks Sophia's hand, then—plop! Down she goes at Sophia's feet, a cloud of dust rises up, sprawls out, jaw in the dirt, and sighs. They walk past her, easily. Her round eyes follow them up the road.

"What are you anyway, Mowgli, Commander of Wolves? I don't believe you, kiddo. Hey, listen to this: *first*, it takes Mina two weeks to answer me. *Then* she announces she's coming right here! Here! To your house! Is nothing sacred? She can't be on my turf!"

"Wait!"

"Turf? Property. I think of here as my turf. She gets me so M-A-D! She's coming to visit your mother with Aunt Mal and someone else. Remember that photo album where they were all palsy-walsy? I can't stop her. You'll meet my Aunt Mal anyway. But I hate that my own mother is moving in on my life!"

"Are you sure? I haven't heard about this. Mama is still recuperating. She can't entertain visitors."

Skye's feeling like her life is gonna end if her mother shows up. Like everything she's done to calm down and be human is gonna evaporate. She is afraid she'll get pulled back to feeling what she felt before, that raging volcano erupting whenever. She hardly remembers it as the easiness of being here has lengthened. "Be sure and tell Mr. Theo that I'm good about being Ourania. I wanted him to know that I like it. It's like I'm not sad, boring American Skye, but a dudette who got living in a foreign country *down*. Hah! It's really just his hocus-pocus, mumbo-jumbo—his naming theory. Like, if you make one good change, one more good will happen. But if one bad thing happens, like Mina-the-bitch coming here, it will all cave. Know what I mean?"

"I have no idea, Skye. When will I ever understand you? You talk too fast. I lose the words I didn't understand. Mama said my English would improve with you here, but it's worse. Awkward!"

Skye shrugs. They've reached the small church, out of breath and sweating. The only shade is under trees in the cemetery that shelter above-ground tombs resembling caskets. It is very quiet. Hardly a bird burbles. They sit on a tomb in the shade. Skye is going to scope out the creepiest monument she can find and cranes her neck.

Sophia says this is a very popular cemetery with the old people. So popular that they bring back bodies of the ones who went to nursing homes in Athens. They really fill up the plots. It is easy to live here even if you are old, even if you do not drive, or never go to the doctor. "If I ever left, I would miss every old person here."

"Here? Really? This is quite the disappointment as cemeteries go. It's too damned cheery. Look!" she points to a row of white crosses along the tops of the tombs. The tombs are covered with photographs and lanterns, pots of green basil going to flower with spikey, purple blooms. Bouquets of bright flowers, real and plastic, fill vases, a regular party going on. Some tombs are topped with fake boulders; others have miniature porticos.

But none with anything creepy. "I guess the dead folks are inside these casket-looking things."

"Well, what did you expect?" Twerpie, interrupted, asks. She's been rambling on about everything she would miss if she left, and Skye stopped listening after she heard about the oldsters in black, sitting in a line on the balustrade waiting for their pension checks, the vegetable truck, the fish truck, the bread truck. Geesh! She even included the mounted loudspeakers on the trucks! If Sophia ever left, she would miss the danged loudspeakers? This kid does not want to leave.

"Really? The loudspeakers, too? Okay." The lack of creepiness, the downright joy of this place, is such a downer.

"Hey, Sophia, let's go back. Too damn hot and there's nothing here. Anyway, so I was sayin'—after I read my mom's e-mail, who walks in but Abbo! He had a whole bunch of his own photographs. They were pretty good: graffiti on the cliffs, ripped political posters kind of stuff. He asked if I'd go shoot with him, so I got on his Moto. Again. We went to a beach I didn't know, opposite direction from St. Christopher's, off the National Highway. Way off. A scary, bumpy path straight down to the sea! I thought I'd die. The beach was stony so I photographed stones. He said the word 'beautiful' in Greek. *Omorphi*. He said I am *omorphoula*. I know it was a line, but kinda nice hearing it, actually. He's leaving in a week. It's getting too hot here. He goes to university in Uppsala. So where is that? I didn't ask him 'cause I figured you'd tell me: Greece or Sweden? I knew I'd sound dumb if I asked him."

"Sweden, Skye! Gee whiz. Didn't they teach you geography?"

"You didn't hear about my primo education as a criminal? Geesh. He'd really think I was a primo A-hole."

"Maybe he'll invite you to Uppsala. Then you can learn where it is. Bring a *gourouni* with you on the plane. Buy it a seat next to you. It might leave behind its ka-ka on the seat."

"Uh-uh. I doubt it. Not gonna happen. Because he started getting physical, and I stopped him. Tried to explain my 'issues' without going into great ... um ... detail, but he didn't get it. He just backed off, got cold. Guys don't like it if you don't, like, cooperate. Awkward. We just rode back without talking. He left me at the car. Said bye and drove away. He's a player all right."

"Wait! Skye! I understand *just nothing* of what you said. You exasperate me!"

"Chill. It's okay, kiddo, you don't have to. I know I did the right thing. I became a tortoise, acted like a rock, but it was right—this time. Here's a selfie of him and me. I want to remember him. Not *him* exactly, but remember that a *guy* was actually nice to me for no reason. Treated me like a person up until his hormones kicked in, like Kim said they always do. A guy just talking to me is pretty much what I can handle now. Don't mean to throw shade on him. Just want to save that feeling of being liked. In case it ever happens again, I'll recognize it."

Sophia cocks her head. "This English is the hardest to understand of all so far!"

—⁓⁓—

Well, look at this, Kleio thinks, opening up her computer. Mal got Gwen Smith to write, too. Mal's continuing campaign to save the reunion. Mal really *really* wants it.

Three decades ago, when she last knew Gwen, she liked their resident egghead. She's apparently stayed the academic course. Seemingly shy and naïve back in those days, but unusually wise in her way, a sincere, authentic person. Had a bouncy, blonde ponytail to go with that school-girl innocence. Mal reported that Gwen just received a Distinguished Fellow Chair where she teaches and has accumulated a slew of honorary doctorates. She has an international reputation, another who left political action behind. Kleio sits down with a cup of coffee, intrigued. She wouldn't mind seeing Gwen again.

July 27, 2011

To: Kleio Platon
From: Gwen Smith

How to begin? With the truth: it's a genuine thrill just to think of seeing you again! I've plumbed Mal for all the news she's gotten about you in the last two months, and I'm so impressed. What courage to adopt a baby and take her to Greece to live. How fortunate is that little girl with you as her mother. And now, you recuperate from cancer surgery. I am so sorry that you had to experience that. So many friends have faced it, and have done super well, too. Your conquering spirit and positivity were always your strengths, and the little one needs you, so go to it: heal quickly!

I love Mal's idea—to reunite in Greece. I traveled there about six years ago to do some research. Just Google me if you'd like to read about it. Since then I've expanded to more artistic endeavors. I'm writing a book-length poem, and I'm in collaboration on a second, super-huge art installation.

Kleio, what a spectacular opportunity! A perfect time to catch up on the intervening years before we need walkers, not only for us, but we can talk about the state of the world since we attempted to light it on fire. Do you notice the same issues in play: equality for women, managing world destruction, overthrowing dictatorships, hyper-capitalism and the little guy? Group's concerns remain relevant. I'd love to hear your latest theories and spout off about mine. And it will be fascinating because today we will find more difference of thought among us. Aren't you the teeniest bit curious? Come on, Kleio. Curiosity is your middle name!

Mal suggested that you were afraid we'd revive our Maoist-style house meetings, all that advice we ladled out about how to improve in life (as if we knew!). And I know Mal has something to share with us that I'm dying to know. I imagine you want peace and quiet as you heal. But consider what we can add to boost you along: love. You are very much loved by us all, then and now. We were so fun together. Group, even with its limitations, encouraged me to take chances, go out on a limb to explore, still keeping me enchanted with life. It was all of us acting as one—the strength and power of a group—that encouraged me to stay true to myself and to be proactive in my interests and goals. We developed character. We grew more thoughtful, compassionate and intuitive. I was in the briefest time, but it was enough to support who I was and where I was going. Perhaps, more important, we dissolved at just the right moment. Imagine if we had followed through with our idea to live together indefinitely! I've often thought that staying together much longer would have been self-destructive. We would have eventually narrowed our horizons, modified our personal goals and imposed uniformity. We did the right thing to dissolve then and go our own ways.

Consider it an act of generosity to reconnect with friends. It is a joy when I encounter my past students to see them matured, focused and contributing. It warms me, knowing that our crossing paths mattered. That is, when all is said and done, human kindness at work. Please let us make this a gesture of thanks to one another.

"Geesh!" Kleio says out loud. Gwen deserves her chair and those honors. She's written a stirring ode to hope. Mal's deadline is the end of July. Why would she not thank her friends for what they gave her, the courage to take her own path?

———

They have resumed their weekly dinners, which pleases Theo. He has new-laid eggs to poach. Possibly, his experiment in apricot brandy will be ready to try. She will bring the greens. Mostly he hopes the renewed conviviality will lead to frank talk. They have been moving in that direction all summer, after the hiatus of her illness, her departure and return. She has let herself in, he knows from the creak of the downstairs door, her footsteps on the stairs.

"Good evening, Theo. Well, I hope? This time I brought dandelions. My mother used to dig them from our yard and steam them, as we do here on Mount Parnon, but they were big. New World big."

She goes to where he cracks eggs into a bowl and kisses his cheek. "I have salad too, with cucumbers from the garden. Sophia and Ourania send you this bread they made together."

Theo takes the bread from her and admires its heft. "Perhaps more useful as a doorstop?" He chuckles.

"Sophia has zeal for bread-making, even when it's hot as Hades. She gave Ourania a lesson this morning. Sophia says to tell you it improves with honey on it."

Kleio leaves her bags on the counter and sits at the table, hands in her lap, her eyes darting. He reads her so easily: something is on her mind; she's in that state of speaking quickly of obvious things. He already knows the subject.

"Sophia admitted to me that she told you about our move to the States. She was very upset with me for keeping it from you. She is right, of course. I hadn't considered that I had blocked her usual outlet for talk about her annoying mother. I apologized to her. It is true, Theo. We shall leave in spring. Rent out the house for next summer. Who knows, maybe sell it after that."

Theo joins her at the table "So Sophaki did not exaggerate, as I had hoped. I must say, it surprised me, and even now, I hardly believe it from your lips." He wants to hide his emotions without even knowing what they are. "Why, Kleio?"

"Well, I am rather surprised myself. I couldn't even voice it until I had accepted it fully. I am convinced it's the best resolution for Sophie's future."

She speaks slowly, brushing aside her curls where they tend to fall in her eyes. "I can't pretend that another metastasis will never come. To deny it is selfish. Not that I fear it. While I was in treatment during the spring, it came to me that I am mortal, Theo. I went into that last operation with the honesty to know I will not be here indefinitely. For that matter, I am open to dying. It is natural and inevitable. To move is to provide for Sophia, having adopted her so late in my life. I had big discussions with my sister about Sophia's future, if I should die before she is settled in her life. Should she live with her godparents, Anthi and Georges in Geneva, or live with you? Neither, my sister said, and I agree. Anthi and George may adore Sophia, but they chose not to be parents. You and I know that raising a child relies on a wealth of details about that child and about oneself that is learned mutually over time. Their ideas for her would come from old information and memories of their own childhoods in different families. They are not a good match for Sophia, who is being raised by an American mother."

Theo is surprised at the subtlety Kleio describes in what is called upon to raise a child. He remembers the continual clashes with his wife about how to raise their daughter.

"And you, Theo, who raised a daughter, would find the responsibility for another worrisome. You and I, we are in the same cancer boat. We both carry the potential for relapse within us. It haunts us. It was cancer that brought us together, so long ago. We share that trauma. I once wondered how you managed it so much better than I, in its aftermath. You impressed me with your power to go ahead without despair, as if it had been but a detour. The removal of the tumor severed your nerves and muscles, and I remember how hard you struggled then with the canes. How you exercised and swam, your gratitude to live by the sea. I would watch you out there in the water, swimming calmly. You never complained. You had so much more wisdom than I, and indeed, you still do. And you know Sophia better than anyone besides me. You love her. But Sophia was never the path you chose. She is my path, my choice. Yours is another. I even believe I may know it, from the day we went up the mountain to Kyria Rina's."

Theo feels himself blush and turns his head because she is studying his face.

"At first, I was surprised to see Kyria Rina's eyes hold yours longer than a cook's might. I even caught her fingers grazing your shoulder. She stood too close to you and remained too near you, and you did not move away. I saw love, Theo. If I read correctly, she is your path, and I am happy—for you both—should it develop so. It makes it easier for me to leave you, knowing you will not lack someone close to you, who loves you. You and I, we've had a quite extraordinary friendship these last ten years, have we not?"

Theo smiles at last and looks into Kleio's eyes, which are filled with tears, her face muscles holding back crying. "Yes," he says, "I quite agree—a most extraordinary friendship." He takes her in his arms. "And with you gone, you and Sophaki who are central to my life and my happiness, I may be less reticent to move toward Rina. I find this state of affairs inspires both happiness and sadness." Theo feels his throat constrict with emotion. She stays in his arms.

"If you intend to be angry with me, Theo, that I withheld my plan for the future from you, kindly remember: you did the same. Thus we have no need for apologies to one another."

Theo reddens. She is right, of course. He holds her close and they are silent, listening to the other's breathing.

Then she pulls away. "For Sophia, my sister Melissa is the key. We are linked by blood and history. We are different personalities, but we have synchronism closer than anyone else Sophia will find. My sister and her family are the right place for her."

He embraces her again, for she cries openly now. He has no words in response.

She adds, "Imagine that in the future I died, and you knew my wish was that Sophia go to Melissa. You would send the grieving child to be disoriented and fearful in a new country, without the ones she loves. Better to establish her now in her new home with me beside her. She will make new friends, change schools, know our family better, learn the new culture while we are strong and happy and together. It makes sense, doesn't it?"

Theo nods.

"Of course, I do not want to leave! I love my home. I love you. But we must change; nothing stays the same. Heraclitus, right? Going together, it will be easier for us to say goodbye to our life here."

The dinner proceeds with Kleio welling up with tears at different thoughts, and Theo barely eating.

—⁓⁓—

So dark, so silent. It must be 3 AM. Skye hears her own rapid breathing even out after a nightmare she is certain woke her, but which she does not remember. She's been having nightmares a lot. She's got the whole pattern down: afterward, out to the balcony with a candle, calm down and focus on reality. Done it so often, she's discovered a pattern in how this world calms down too. First thing is that around midnight the town's humanoid activities end. Lights out. Fewer headlights zoom up the coast. The roaring motorcycles fade away. Next, up here on the mountain, the bazillion creatures making the background noise—dogs, roosters, crickets, locusts, owls—quiet down. By 3 AM noise has petered out to practically total silence for, like, half an hour. Since it is 3 AM, pretty soon she'll see the tiny triangles of light twinkle in the bay, the night fishing boats. Soon after that, the creatures up here will be back at it, starting their ruckus. A dog will bark. They will all bark. When the sun comes around the bay about 5 AM and lights up the sky, the town will be up and act like it never went to sleep. She's got it, the whole routine of slow down, full stop and start up happening before the dawn gets everything up to full speed.

Tonight Mr. Theo was in her mind as she awoke from the nightmare. She has a feeling of wanting to talk directly to him, without Miss Translator continually interrupting with her "wait!" Why him, and what would she even say, specifically? Is it about Abbo? Nope. No regret there. She didn't put out for him. End of discussion. Glad Kim had insisted on "the sex talk" before Skye left. Man, she couldn't shake Kim off that topic no matter how she tried. If she could talk to Kim she would, but there's the problem of the bad transmission. Kim told her she is still twelve, emotionally speaking. That she comes by that delay honestly. Kim said, give yourself time to catch up to your peers who've been out and about, dating and carrying on all the years you couldn't. Kim said, first just make some friends.

No, her disappointment is about herself, not Abbo. She needs to talk private. She is pretty sure Mr. Theo wouldn't judge her. But the language barrier. It's a plate glass wall.

So there's Kleio. She speaks English, and she's a reasonable adult. She's been getting lighter, more humorous, more "in the room." It's even fun when they go down to the town for suppers, the three of them, when it's too hot in the house. Even with air conditioning, you sweat. Kleio says, "Well, girls, what do you say? Fine dining at Kostas tonight?"

Fun. They sit outside in the dark with the sea breeze kicking in. They watch the skinny stray cats prowling under the tables, hungry, fighting over scraps. Fun to drop food on the floor when Kleio turns away. She and Soph both do it. It's lively at Kostas, tables always packed. Everyone talking at the top of their voices. Kleio's friends stroll by the restaurant, wave, shout, come up and grab a chair, don't care about interrupting. Kleio introduces her like she's a normal person. If they speak English, they ask how-does-she-like-Greece types of questions. Where's she from? Oh, they have relatives in Massachusetts, or someone they know does. It's a miniature of a big world, Kostas. How she sees it. Funny now to find you know words for some foods you even eat—salad, beans, beets, stuffed peppers, squashes. Coca Cola, aka Coka. Whatever. Even putting on some pounds.

And that silly game with Sophia. Now they can't stop it: feed all the new vocabulary to the *gourouni*. It's getting old, but it makes her laugh to see Sophia crack up every single time. Sorta like her and Polly would do, just look at each other and *think* the same word, then crack up. Words that never got old. Sophia is the age of her and Polly. Sophia makes her think about Polly and about having friends. She and Polly did not always hate each other.

Thinking about the times before her legal troubles is like in knitting, when you drop a stitch and you have to unravel back to the mistake and fix it, and then you can keep going again. Knitting in Detention wasn't a half-bad class.

"Skye, you're out here? It's so late." Kleio in her nightgown shivers and sits down next to her. "I couldn't sleep. I saw the candle. Are you okay?"

Skye could snap, Ya think? But she pauses like some therapist had recommended, which she never tried doing. To recalibrate. Like she's a General Positioning System computer, setting up the new direction.

"Yeah. Things on my mind, I guess. I had another nightmare and woke up wanting to talk to Mr. Theo. Of all people. But I can't, you know. Unless the kid comes with me. Some stuff's not so appropriate for Little Big Ears. So I got a dilemma, you could say..."

"Can I help? No translator required." Kleio's voice is smiley and kind. She yawns.

"I dunno."

How trustworthy is this friend of her mother's? Squelch the smart-aleck retort. Anyway, she can't think of one, so she must have recalibrated. "You could listen? So late? Now? And not tell Mina? That would be the deal."

Kleio yawns again. "Well, I'm never going to tell Mina, you can bet on that. So deal. We weren't that close. A little too hysterical for me. I'd get three words out, and she'd be off and running. Sure, I could listen, now that I'm awake... Wait!" She says it just like Sophia. She goes inside to get them a blanket.

She returns with a puffy quilt to cover them and sits close. Both face the blackness beyond them that is the sea at night. Kleio extends an arm so that Skye can lean into her. Tentatively, she does, but her mind goes blank. Total shock to sit so close to someone, no idea what to say. She inhales. How would she talk to Kim sitting across a table?

"Like, it's about that I met this guy when I first got here? He was nice and all, for a while. But yesterday, he tried getting physical, and I'm not into that. 'Cause you know, I've had a long period of, um, inactivity? So, I'm sort of actually awkward? Not too experienced. Scared of guy stuff. Not just sex. But, like, how to just talk to them. What they even want from talking to you. I guess I would've asked Mr. Theo, how do you have a guy just as a friend? You know, just the amount of closeness you're up for. Say no and not lose them. Know what I mean? Not that anyone is raping me, but I was wondering. Because when I leave here, I'm gonna do some things different. First off, I'm not going to live with Mina-the-bitch in Boston, I decided. I'll have some money from the sale of our house. I won't have to work right away. I should go to school, but I don't want to. I just want to have a place to live my own life, on my own terms. Like you do here. That's what I'm thinking about. I guess. Somehow I thought Mr. Theo could hear me out. He likes to dispense advice."

Kleio chuckled. "True. So true. Goodness. That is some heavy-duty thinking." A minute passes in which she says nothing.

"You know, Skye, you surprised me. I have to say you've been great with Sophia. I appreciate how you are with her. She is very engaged and looks up to you. You set her a good example. It gives me an idea. What about being an *au pair* in another country? Even a nanny in the States, but somewhere your mother isn't? New York City? Rent an apartment with another nanny, maybe a group of nannies to pay the rent? That is something 'not school,' but not 'nothing' either—be where the action is, and where you could keep up your photography. Take a New School class in the Village. Don't you think? I like the work you've been doing. A very original vision, especially of the animals. You might enjoy studying photography formally, at some future point."

Skye is imagining an apartment in Manhattan, sharing it with some girls and working. Taking classes at night. Nice.

"If I were you, I guess I'd start with girlfriends first, because that inevitably leads to guys. How it usually works. You learn from them. You get the guts to experiment." Kleio yawns more. "But I think I have to sleep. We can always talk more tomorrow."

Skye stands up as Kleio leaves, thinking to run down the mountain into the dark. A little too much information to take in. Kleio is so quick, rapid fire.

Sophia is certain she dreamed about America, but that she and Skye lived in a jail. She lies in bed, too sleepy to move, wondering who is talking with her mother on the balcony. Is it her birth mother? Does she secretly visit Mama at night for reports? The lady—*She*—who abandoned her as an infant, maybe comes here from time to time to ask about her. Is that crazy? But if they leave Greece, chances are she will never see *Her*. She drags Rositsa out from where she was kicked during the night, down by her feet.

Rositsa, listen to me now! This is important. Since I am a mixture of Her and Him, we know they will only recognize me if they already saw a mixture of themselves by having another kid, my sister—and kept her. If I have a sister, we will look similar. Mama thinks they were very poor and showed their love by giving up their Own Flesh and Blood for me to have a better life. They were happy to do this for me. I shouldn't leave Greece, because they might come for vacation and walk hand in hand on the beach and see me swimming. They would call out, "Hey! Little Girl! You look just like us!" in their strange language. And I would recognize them. But if I go to America, we will never meet on the beach and wonder in our own languages if I came from them. A crime, isn't it?

—∿∿—

Skye stands on the balcony, wrapped in the quilt, peering at the sea. The little lights glimmer from the fishing boats. The sun will rise soon. What about photographing creatures like her, the ones who wake at dawn? She gathers her camera and waits for the first steamy orange glow to pop up in the east. Ta-*da*! Boom-boom-*boom!* She thinks there should be orchestral music when it shows up, like in a film. Ta-da! Out she runs.

—∿∿—

"Hey, sleepyhead! Wake up! Gotta show you something!" It's 7 AM, the legal hour to wake the kid. Sophia gave her a rule that Skye must never enter her bedroom. What's the kid gonna do? Toss her out? Hearing a "what?" she opens the door. Sophia is awake. Skye sits on the side of the bed, and Sophia sits up, yawns and says, "I said—you can't ever come in here!"

"Chill, kiddo. Look. I took these just now, while the sun was rising. Look at how weird the light is! Freaking cool, right? It's all about the light. The goat just woke up in that pen up the hill under that old house. There was just this one shaft of light.

Doesn't he look like he just saw a ghost? It was me. And this. By that cactus-type tree? Huge butterflies hovering over the flowers! See how their wings sparkle in the light! I'm so excited. Then I spotted these really bad-ass spiders making webs that glisten on the leaves. Look! The webs are lit up! And these guys? Any idea what they are? Caterpillars in war paint? So many of them creep together like a caterpillar army. Look at the great cast shadows! Good, huh?"

Sophia admires the pictures, rubbing her eyes. She likes them all and studies them again.

"Hey, what's that, kiddo? A sketch pad? Let me see what you drew. Hey. That's me! In a forest with animals! You little smart-ass! Haha. Let me fix up the animals to look like what I really have. You drew them all wrong."

They work, passing the pad back and forth. Sophia wants to be the one to add the colors.

"Well, I'm kinda interested in going to this shindig," Skye announces from the back seat of Mr. Theo's jeep the evening they head deep into Mount Parnon on rutted roads and hairpin curves. "I brought my lens for when it gets dark. I'm going for creepy—zombies, corpses, deranged monks in gowns cavorting around tombs in the cemetery. I'm hoping for that, anyway."

"Well don't count on it," Kleio says from the front seat. "A *panigyri* brings people together in a *joyful* way. God likes *happiness*. Right, Mr. Theo?"

No one translates her words for him. Skye's decided it's because he secretly understands everything anyway, just plays dumb to get people going. She's pretty sure he has Extra-Sensory Perception.

"This is one old monastery," Kleio continues. "Four hundred years old. It was so hidden and hard to reach that the Turks never destroyed it. The monks were able to teach the banned Greek language and religion to any child fearless enough to reach it at night, guided only by moonlight. Little kids braved wolves and snakes just to learn their language and culture."

"See?" Sophia pipes up. "That's creepy."

"Hey, you don't *know* from creepy, kiddo."

Mr. Theo, taking the turnoff from Lithoi to the mountain behind it, says—and Sophia translates—"If you will permit me, Ourania, I shall tell you the story of the Seven Sleeping Youths of Ephesus celebrated at the *panigyri,* so you can know why they are still honored so many centuries later. This story you may find 'creepy.'"

"You know me—I'm all ears. So what's Ephesus?"

"A city in Turkey today, but it is there from prehistoric times and many foreign rulers. It contains, if I am not mistaken, an ancient burial ground for Roman gladiators. Maybe someday you will visit it as part of your 'creepy' search. But the event I describe began after the Romans, in the second century AD. The rulers of Ephesus were pagans who feared the Christians. They buried seven young boys alive in a cave to punish them for refusing to renounce their Christian faith. Then, two hundred years later, the world had become largely Christian, but there were now religious arguments and conflicting opinions about Jesus and his teachings. The simple people of Ephesus were so confused by the religious disputation and very frustrated. So, to clarify things once and for all, the Christian emperor went to the cave and wakened the seven boys from their long sleep to talk to them. The boys reassured him that what he believed about Jesus was right. They went back inside the cave to die for good. Certainly creepy, I would guess, but not impossible."

Sophia's coda: "Well, that is what Uncle Theo says, anyway. I wouldn't care ever to meet anyone who came back to life after two hundred years. Too creepy for me!"

"Gimme a break! No way! Mr. Theo doesn't really believe that! He's got some weirdo ideas, but this one definitely eats it."

"Ourania believes this is impossible?" he asks from the front seat, seemingly amazed.

She watches his face in the rear-view mirror, waits for the smile to play on his lips. He's messing with her. "Duh-uh?"

"Can you accept this—that death is a long sleep, and sleep is a short death?" He pauses.

"I got nothin'. Guess so."

"Good. By the time Christianity had become the religion of the empire, disputes arose about the veracity of Jesus' resurrection. How could a person return from the dead? Do you know about that, Ourania? That Jesus spoke with his followers three days after he was buried? Remember that, because the youths echo the appearance after death. They awoke from their short sleep of two hundred years. They showed the Christian world that their faith had made them live, confirmed by no less than the emperor himself. The boys then fell into a long sleep of peaceful death. So you will not see them tonight."

Skye tries not to laugh. "Really, Mr. Theo? I can't even. I'm supposed to swallow this? Whole?"

She knows by now that his weird stories are aimed directly at her. He finds a connection to her life. And she loves it. She always loved stories at bedtime with her mom. To egg him on, she says the phrase advised by Kleio, "Who am I to disagree?" Sure enough, it's his cue to continue. It has become their own game that she loves because it is all about her. Not that she would admit it.

"Ourania, if you will permit me, I see a parallel between the community of Christians whose disputes did not permit the boys to die, only to sleep, and those who suffer the traumatic loss of someone they love. By disputing the truth of death, the person who died cannot rest in peace."

"And?"

"An example is a girl who lost her father. Her father would have wanted her to accept the loss of him, so he could sleep peacefully. He, like all adults, knew that everyone dies eventually, so acceptance is what her father expected of her. When she can do this, accept the loss, she will know what love is. She will know his love for her resides within her, unextinguished, guiding her life. She allows the knowledge of his love and his goodness from when he was alive to diminish her pain of loss. She keeps him in mind, but she lets him sleep in peace, and in so doing she lives happier."

Sophia, the translator, makes a face at Skye that reads, I don't get this one.

Skye gets it, though. So he was getting to *that*: her father and her anger at his death. "Tell him I get it. Tell him I say thank you."

They drive on in silence, everyone seeming to turn inward. Skye's thoughts are amorphous and are not shouted down and destroyed by the loud bullying voices usually roaring in her head.

Night falls suddenly. The sky is a huge dome of stars. The only illumination is from their headlights on the rocky road, and the faint glow of moon flitting behind trees and cliffs. Already there is mystery. She feels safe with these people, her friends who are present for her, who accept her, tell her things she likes to know. She wishes they could ride together forever like this, in this jeep, winding upwards, into potholes and over washboard ruts.

The road ends abruptly at the monastery.

A nighttime world is in full whirl up here, crowds of people and a cacophony of voices and musical instruments. Parking by the road, a jumble of vehicles and bodies moving in the dark, her reverie is jarred. What happened? Skye feels unprepared and vulnerable, ready to rail at something, but what?

They head toward the hubbub coming from the grounds next to the church that looms ghostly white in the darkness. Next to it is a central space illuminated by lightbulbs strung from poles and in tall pines. Silhouettes move about to sit at tables around the space. Maybe five hundred people, she estimates. The aroma of roasting lamb and rosemary fills the air, the bitter smell of cooking flesh and grease she hates. She may have to retch.

A cluster of musicians sit in a semicircle under a tree tuning up, their music stands set in an arc before them. Ear-splitting strands of snaky music emerge and sink into random screeches as they come into synch.

Several too-loud amps are adjusted, emitting throbs and screeches that vibrate inside her and extend to her arms and legs. There is no escape from the terrible loud noise. She hates the assault of sound. Is this prelude for corpses and zombies? The dead boys actually come to life? She follows Sophia through the crowd. People appear who exclaim loudly, greet and kiss Mr. Theo and Kleio and admire Sophia. Skye is introduced and regarded. She squirms. Still, people are friendly, like this event is greater than the individuals there, some kind of normal. Which it is definitely not, to her. No way. Laughter and shouting grow deafening to outdo the instruments whose screechy tune-ups are still blasted through the amps.

She is riveted by the musicians and their strange instruments. They start and stop melodies led by clarinet-type whines. This is too eerie, to be on top of a mountain at a site hidden for centuries in the darkness, surrounded by hundreds of hyped-up strangers, anticipating something that will happen—and all around her the endless strangeness of sounds. The atmosphere is electric.

She increasingly feels the lack of edges anywhere, physical or within, as if her insides are on the outside of her. She is lightheaded. Everything is black beyond the glow of the overhead lights in trees. Okay Skye, stop the drama. Just cool it. Get a grip. Control the fear. You've been in worse unknown situations. And this is nothing like Detention.

She feels herself expanding with the music throbbing in earnest now, sounds that writhe like snakes. An insinuating saxophone, hollow and reedy, vibrates in her.

A monk and two women in long robes greet them warmly, escort them to a table and leave them with others who smile greetings of recognition and keep eating. She can't hear because of the music, but she wouldn't understand the talk anyway. She knows there is a smile frozen on her face. White moths flit madly, circling the overhead light bulbs.

The air is humid, mitigated by breezes that sweep in from various angles. Ghosts? Souls? They are so up high on the mountain, she feels the altitude, like a headache. Maybe she is attending an ancient ritual repeated over eons. Maybe there are the ghosts of those who were here before her making themselves seen. Those dead boys... Kleio says she is being called and she leaves the table. Mr. Theo is engaged with someone next to him. Everyone knows everyone; people are continually introduced, remembered, hugged and regarded. Sophia is distracted, knows them all.

Aproned old women and young boys appear with plates loaded with food for them, kabob spits with cubes of meat, salad, a mound of rice, green beans, olives and peppers, crusty bread.

Someone asks Sophia what Skye will drink. *Bira? Krasi?* Sophia says bring her Coka. Skye believes she has heightened comprehension without knowing a word.

Sophia catches her eye and smiles. "Are you okay? You look scared."

Skye nods. "I can't eat. And it's meat anyway." She gives Sophia her plate of food then picks an olive off Sophia's plate.

"Eat it. It's not poisoned!"

The musicians are seriously into their music and play louder. It's a complicated rhythm that seems to draw people from the tables in droves to the center space where they form large circles. Everyone joins hands, and they fall instantly into the same steps moving slowly in long circular lines that seem not actually to advance but move nonetheless. And look who leads the longest line, a priest! He wears a pillbox on his head and a black robe, has a cropped beard, glasses. He dances, arm upraised, gripping a white cloth held between him and the woman who dances next to him; he hops and slaps his shoe in counterpoint, moves onward. People follow him linked together—old people, fat people, little children, handsome men, pretty girls, parents, even monks. It frightens Skye that they all know what to do. And they do it together.

Sophia, now possibly hypnotized, stands up and beckons Skye to follow, but Skye refuses. She doesn't dare. She might be lost. Don't go! Sophia sits again and taps her fingers. Skye stares at the complicated steps they do with their feet to the equally complicated rhythm. It looks like everyone is limping in unison, not dancing. She fears being hypnotized.

Mr. Theo leaves them to visit a different table. People with outstretched arms welcome him.

"It's gonna be boring if you don't dance," Sophia shouts in her ear.

"Uh-uh. You go on. I'll be okay here. I'll watch."

Sophia waves at two girls her age approaching. They speak animatedly and leave together to join everyone jumping and moving in the dark.

Skye is on her own, still alive, still watching, feeling braver. She remembers her camera. How intrusive would it be? Would she be arrested? No, others are photographing this witch's coven. A strong wind blowing steady transforms the overhead bulbs into blinking strobe lights. The dancers hop and skip in unison, shout at times, hold hands, form several intertwining circles. It is such a complex rhythm. Skye drums seventeen beats on the table before the phrase repeats.

A middle-aged woman with long reddish hair appears and joins the musicians to sing. Her voice is strong and nasal, sounding like those voices that come from minarets that Skye has seen on TV. People clap for her. She sings one line, a statement, and two clarinet-like instruments repeat the snaky melody—oddly comforting, the repeat, as if to verify what she said. The singer sings another line. They repeat it, decorate it. One of those weird instruments holds an unrelenting, unchanging bass note underneath the melodic tune that accompanies the woman. There is no pause or rest. A man beats a small drum; a violinist embellishes the melody while another riffs around on a bulbous guitar-like instrument. Skye hears no resolution in the melody, as if it means to continue forever.

This could be the place where the ancient women went mad in a dancing frenzy, non-stop in the summer nights, then went on to attack their husbands and sons in the farms below. Sophia told her that story. Maenads, mania, manic, she had explained, wanting Skye to understand the origin of the words. Yes, you could either go crazy or be cleansed by this music and dance.

Sophia is back to check on her. What happened to Kleio and Mr. Theo? Skye asks, fearing they've been swallowed up.

Sophia points to them. Under a far tree in the shadows, Mr. Theo has an arm around the woman from the restaurant they visited when she first arrived. What a long time ago that was. Kleio is off in a different direction in an animated group, under a circle of light bulbs. Sophia keeps tabs on her important people, Skye thinks, as if they would vanish without her vigilance. Skye feels for this little kid, also living with loss—in her case it is her birth parents.

"Soph—it's not creepy, right? It's just people, right? Getting together like God wants? Like your mom said? To be happy?"

When they can hear themselves between songs, Sophia wants Skye to know everyone. She points out by name people from the town, several mayors, the lotto ticket seller, the most popular boy in the high school with his girlfriend and his parents, five priests from their own town and from other churches sitting together, her nice teacher from last year with husband and their new baby, so cute. Her classmates, Besjana and Florian, Besjana's parents, Florian's parents. It is Sophia's world, however much she complained to Skye about being an outsider. She is an insider who does not want to live in the unknown.

Sophia again urges her to dance. "Come. I'll teach you."

"Nah-uh. I'd rather watch out for witches and stuff. I'd rather walk around and take pictures."

"As you wish, but I'm going to dance." Sophia quickly stands, eyes the line and spots the place to break in to hold hands with Florian.

She likes him. Little Sophia has a crush on little old Florian, another world expert. They are made for each other. What is it with these Greek kids she has come to know—all of them experts on something? Wanting you to know.

This new dance is terminally slow with a pounding odd-numbered down-beat. The bodies hold stiff above the waist, sway slightly to one side then turn to the other: the limping hop, the graceful slide, the steps, the repeat, everyone in unison. Weird. But great to photograph. At home everyone dances for himself, for self-expression or self-fulfillment, whatever. Here they hold hands, stick together. Like glue. Since a million years ago, according to Mr. Theo. Look at that, Skye! You're seeing deeper into life. It's the photography doing that.

She will capture the thoughts she's been having through the photographs she will take. What they do—this dancing—is intimate, and she wants to show it. Skye smiles, feels proud of her understanding. She's in a place where people celebrate death and life and death again, repeating on forever. She is happy. Just like Kleio said: *Because God likes happiness. Whatever He is.*

In two weeks, Group will arrive. There's gonna be a terrible collision in her brain, a total car crash, a total semi smash to see her mother again, Skye thinks as she and Sophia head up the road for the second time to the upper church. Man, it's so hot here. A collision of Disturbing, Rueful and Furor is churning inside her. "Why are we doing this, again, Sophia? It's a bazillion degrees! And I'm panting like Fang-Dog, if he's still there."

Skye spots him lying in the middle of the road ahead. "He looks dead." As they pass by him, he moves his eyeball to watch them.

"She," Sophia corrects. "Because I remembered something creepy for you to photograph. It is farther up on a path above the church. You'll see."

Turns out Sophia's brought her to see four miniature house-shaped boxes of turquoise-painted tin and glass set upon pedestals along the path. In the boxes are flowers, photographs, crosses, and each with a flame burning in a glass of olive oil.

Sophia says, "'Little churches' to remember four teenagers who died up here in a motorcycle crash, years before I was born."

"Oh yeah, I shoulda known: more dying boys." But she's thinking there is an invisible person haunting Greece who tends to candles and burning flames, memories and memorials, no matter the time of day or how remote. Someone does it so that no one will forget.

Sophia says, "Skye, I think you should know this. My mother and I are moving to the States in the spring."

"Geesh." Skye sits down on a boulder to let the news sink in. "I guess I just assumed your life here, which you know is probably perfect, would always go on like it does now. I'm stunned."

Sophia sits next to her, fans herself with her hand and explains the reason: so that she can get to know the other part of who she is, an American. "You might not know it, but it's my citizenship. My mother says since I've done so well at being Greek, it's time to do well at being an American, too."

Skye starts taking a lot of photographs of the memorials, all the while feeling up-turned, not saying much.

Walking back down to the house, easily skirting Fang-Dog who is actually snoring, Sophia confides her main regret about leaving Europe. Her birth parents will never find her now.

Skye says, "Well, if the bimbos really had wanted to find you, they would have contacted Kleio by now. So just forget about them."

Uh oh. She feels her gut clench to see Sophia's horror-stricken face. She hears her bitterness ringing loud and clear in her tone, reserved for her own mother. *Uh oh.* She's never thought about what abandonment might feel like to Sophia. Shoulda kept my trap shut. Shoulda done better with the kid, abandoned through no fault of her own.

She feels queasy. Try putting yourself in the other person's shoes, Kim counseled time and again, and she has had a colossal epic fail. For the first time in ages, she feels bad about what came out of her mouth. The thoughtlessness and meanness of her words punch her in the stomach.

She has to hug Sophia. "I'm really sorry."

Two days later they are hanging with Mr. Theo in town. Everyone chose the same green ice-cream bars, pistachio. They sit on the stoop outside the grocery store to eat them, greeting the people going in and out. Even Skye. Even Mr. Theo, who she's never seen sit down on the stoop before. Usually he stands with his crutches and watches them, but this time he hands her his crutches and sits himself on the top step, licking the ice cream before it melts into his beard. Everyone's feeling pretty good.

He says, "Girls, here is an idea. When the American friends come to see Kleio, why don't you both go to Delphi? Go have an adventure yourselves."

Sophia's eyes widen. Skye is blank.

Sophia stands to jump off the stoop, then jumps up and down in front of the market. "That's such a good idea! You'd love it, Skye! Delphi is full of really creepy stories!"

Mr. Theo describes the Pythia, a lady whose brain was addled by geyser gases from a pit in the ground where the priests of Apollo kept her. They interpreted her mangled words to advise visitors about their future.

Sophia adds that she went to Delphi with her class, and it is really beautiful. "People go to see the sanctuaries and the view at sunrise. It's easy to imagine the Pythia saying mystical words." She'd love to go again. They could take the public buses, like her class did. She knows the way. It's easy. She'll ask her mother if they can.

Skye says she's interested. It would make space from Mina, for one thing. And maybe she'd ask this druggie lady some questions, too. She has a shitload of questions going on in her mind. "Does she still do her thing?"

"Oh yes," Mr. Theo is fairly certain. "The Pythia continues to give oracles and make predictions. But it is done a little differently now, for modern times. Now, you must be present at sunrise to open your eyes at just the right moment, and you will feel her presence all around you. Then you can ask her anything you want. And she will answer. If you will permit me, Ourania, I will tell you about an ancient prediction that actually came true in modern times, despite the disbelief of many who say it was far too fantastical and completely impossible. That it defied logic."

———

"Why do they need a whole big Welcoming Committee? Why can't I just go out for a walk? I'll see them eventually," Skye says.

Kleio responds firmly, "They just do."

Meanwhile Sophia is peering through the poplar trees like she's got Superman's X-ray vision. She's in a yellow sundress for the occasion, and flitting about in the leaves of the trees, she looks like an exotic bird with golden plumage. She shouts that she thinks she sees the taxi.

"Look at me—they're gonna faint when they see me!" Skye's wearing an ef'n dress that Kleio and Sophia bought her. It has cutouts so her tats on her shoulders show through, so not that bad. They said she should look nice to see her mother. And Mal. And the other lady, what's-her-name with the beagle ears hairdo. It shows respect, they said. But at least it's black. She'd insisted she'd only wear black for what to her is a sad occasion. Her mother's arrival means coming to the end of her stay. Plus she dreads seeing Mina-the-bitch. She has no idea how to act with her.

Her stomach rumbles. Dread? Her hands shake. She's cold. She's hot. Or not. Can hardly breathe. She may ef'n faint. The Bitch is gonna be here any minute. Does she really have to see her? Must she really go back to the States with her? Can't she and Sophia go to Delphi right now?

"Kleio, how do I know I can trust your twerpy daughter to know what she's doing? Are you sure the bus goes from Nafplio?

Maybe you should drive us there. Are you sure Soph knows how to transfer to Delphi? What about the giant semis ready to crush puny buses on the National Highway?"

Kleio laughs. "Skye, you'll be safe and well. Be happy! My twerpy daughter will be in charge. If you miss the connection, go have a frappé at the corner and wait for the next bus. You'll discover that the National Highway will be wide enough for big trucks in both directions."

"Well, anyway, I'm psyched to see where this weird priestess lady got high off geyser gases. Maybe the geyser still puffs out fumes."

Sophia joins them. "I saw the taxi. It's going to be here in about ten minutes, I estimate."

Kleio says she too is nervous, like Skye. Not about their going to Delphi on their own, but about seeing her old friends. "A bit like America coming to you, before you go to it. I'm also excited."

Sophia says she wants to meet the mother of Skye who is the Bitch and the Aunt Mal who sounds so nice. And the other one whose name she keeps forgetting. "When you invited them to come, you said it was to make a bridge for me. I want to see the bridge."

Skye smiles at the kid. Pretty nice that Kleio thought of Sophia's fear of leaving Greece. A chill mother—not that she'd ever say it. The Twerp doesn't know how lucky she is.

"Hey, Skye, do you know that Mama spoke to my friends' parents about them visiting us in the States next year? Mama will pay Besjana's ticket to travel with Florian. She's never been on a plane. Mama said first Besjana has to mail us an essay in English with one hundred percent—that means no mistakes. Then she'll set the date of the visit. So it looks like I will see my friends again."

Kleio says they plan to return to Greece for the Christmas of 2013.

"That's because Uncle Theo said, sorry, he will never visit America. He's heard too much about its 'messes and stupidities' to want to witness them in person. If the mountain won't come to them, they must go to the mountain. That is what he said. He is the mountain."

"That is the thing about friendship, Soph. It can keep on going. So can I come with you in 2013 when you guys come for Christmas? So I can see him, too?" She sees Kleio and Sophia make eye contact, knows she just shocked the bejesus out of them.

Skye tells them that Mina and Aunt Mal are excited to see her photography. She feels proud of her pictures. She's already said both those things a hundred times, but who cares? Saying the words makes both truer.

Kleio offered to help her make a portfolio before she leaves.

"Man, I'm jumping out of my skin. I feel so different from when I came. June 14 was a bazillion years ago." She cannot give the emotion words. She *feels* it. *Feels*. That in itself is different. Will Aunt Mal notice? Kleio has noticed and hugged her. Several times now. And she didn't even die of asphyxiation. All this stupid hugging going on around here!

She has her moments of excitement about the changes coming up—but let's not overdo it, people. Not excited about everything. Not excitement as a way of life. She's gonna ask Aunt Mal about *au pair*ing for another year, like a gap year, to fill in some gaps, like Kleio said. She has realized it, believe it or not, that she now has chops as an *au pair* in Wacko-World and will get references from Kleio and Mr. Theo. Another wacko-world like England, Scotland or Ireland would be good, where people at least know English and there's more wildlife to photograph. She plans to ask that dumb priestess in Delphi, Pythia—if she feels Pythia's presence—what the chances are for success. Pythia Lady was quite the genius, apparently.

—∿—

"They're here!" Sophia shouts, pointing to the dispersing dust cloud that reveals a car with its overheated motor rumbling.

The driver who Kleio sent to pick them up took the unpaved, rock-strewn, pitted back road to arrive at the edge of the path of poplars, closer to the house.

"I bet they're all carsick now," Kleio says as she stands up.

A small woman with white hair gets out from the back seat, brushes her skirt flat, stretches and looks around as Kleio dashes from the balcony to meet them. Sophia and Skye follow behind.

Kleio shouts, "Mal!" and the two women embrace.

"My mama is crying," Sophia tells Skye, who's watching the scene in disbelief.

"Well, I'm not," says Skye. "Let's get this dang thing over with."

They approach the women emerging from the car. Kleio hugs Mina and Gwen. Everyone talks at once, laughing and crying: you haven't changed, you look so beautiful, so happy to see you, can't believe we're really here, it's been so long, a good trip, it's hot!

"My mama's crying, but she is happy," Sophia whispers.

"Well, she should be. They came all this way just for her." Skye is overwhelmed by shyness and stands still, not sure where to look.

"Oh my goodness! It's Skye! And you are Sophia!" Mal holds out arms to embrace them both. She hugs them hard, laughing. "Look at you! Both of you beautiful children! I'm so happy to see you! Look how gorgeous you are!"

Skye smiles a shy hello, notices the tears in Mal's eyes.

"See?" Kleio laughs. "You got what you wanted, Mal. Group is alive and well in the next generation."

Mina approaches Skye—nervously, Skye is quick to notice.

"Hello, my darling. You look terrific. You are glowing!"

Skye allows Mina to kiss the top of her head.

"I missed you," Mina adds. She has tears in her eyes, too, doesn't know what to do with her hands. Skye does not move to embrace her.

Skye recognizes Mina's indecision about what to do, but instead of the contempt it usually inspires, Skye feels sad. She misses her mother. She has missed her for years, in fact. But she's not about to say it. Instead she gives her mother a quick hug. They stand in silence. Awkward. Everyone has been watching them.

"Here's the kid," Skye tells Mina, standing back so her mother can see. "Sophia."

"My goodness! What a beautiful child you are! Kleio, your daughter is adorable!" She embraces Sophia and kisses her cheek.

Odd to observe her mother's most minute hand gestures, body movement, flick of the hair—odd to feel Mina's nervousness shining through her excitement. Odd to feel sympathy. She puts her arm around her mother's waist. "Come on, Mina, you gotta see where we live. The Palace. It's very chill."

Kleio introduces the girls to Gwen.

"Oh yeah. I know you from the photographs." Skye smiles. She still thinks Gwen resembles a beagle. Sad eyes. Long, floppy hair, like ears. Okay, prettier than a beagle. But still.

———

"What about this one?" Mal asks as everyone studies Skye's photographs spread out on the kitchen table. Sophia has remarked how dramatic they look all together.

Mal picks up the photograph to study it more keenly. "This is truly striking, the way you've composed it. It seems to say much more than cliffs and clouds."

Skye studies it with her. She had angled the contour of mountain cliff to intersect the picture frame at a sharp diagonal. The tip of the cliff meets the top of the photograph. The picture was really about the clouds, big, billowy, blowy clouds that seem about to charge headlong into the granite wall against a sky of Aegean blue.

"Yup. That's me, I guess. But I'm doing different stuff now, using a different perspective."

—⁓—

Delphi at Sunrise

Hey, Pythia Lady or whatever the hell your name is. Seer? Mind reader? Whatever.

They say you've been around a pretty long time with a lot of experience from people asking questions. And that your job is you give answers. I bet people do the opposite of what they should to get what they want. So they come here totally desperate. Then you talk in riddles since they're probably not going to listen to real advice 'cause no one listens anyway. Right? Well, I don't want advice. And no riddles. I really tried to change my so-called attitude, and now I'm leaving Wacko-World, aka Greece, so I want answers. Just be straight up with me.

One: do you think I should text Abbo? In case he's been thinking to invite me to Uppsala or something? Or ask him to meet me in London? Does texting to Sweden work? You know, it's pretty nice here where you live, Delphi and all. By the way, it was Sophia who got me up to talk to you at sunrise, so here I am sitting on a rock with flowers blooming and a golden sky where the sun's gonna come up, and I thought I'd tell you it's pretty much on fleek. And you should do something nice for her because she's pretty scared to move to the States. She's wacko— because she's Greek, I guess. Goes with the territory. But some nice poplars and flowers you have here all over the place. Miss Walking Encyclopedia says the red ones are poppies. I guess they're not heroin poppies. Maybe not, 'cause this is Delphi, not Afghanistan, right? So, in case you've never been anywhere outside of Greece, you should know it rocks here. Really. I'd come back, even.

So to continue my questions, if you don't mind. Two: will I stay friends with the Platons after, when they move to America? You know, I told Sophie she could look for her birth parents. She doesn't have to wait around for them to show up.

Three: will I get a job to au pair *in London and see Aunt Mal more? Probably, right? Since it's my plan, and like I said, I'm doing what I can to get there.*

So, four: do you see me being a photographer as my career? I think it's kinda chancy, but maybe, right? I'm glad things might be okay with me and Mina-NOT-the-bitch-anymore. All she is is some poor lady who had to raise a messed-up kid when my dad died and she was a mess, too. We have that in common. Sophie yells at me: Just be nice to her! Is that really so hard? She is my mom after all, and she paid for this trip.

Anyway, moving right along. Five: I want to know if Mr. Theo will marry that lady, Rina. What do you think? He'll need someone on his level after Kleio leaves. Rina looks nice. She's pretty. Not too old, either.

About this one, six, maybe the most important: what about Aunt Mal? She's the one I worry about most. She's really happy right now with her girlfriends, that's obvious, but I can tell she's kinda undecided about herself. Said she might volunteer to hold babies in a hospital. That is a weird thing they do in England. Ladies just walk in and hold babies. Would you believe it? Geesh. Maybe some babies need it, though. I guess they like it. All those years I was in free fall, dropping out of the sky, heading toward drowning in the sea? From that, I'd say they'd like it. So, you can tell that dude who you probably even know up in the sky that my teacher was an idiot. Icarus was not at all conceited. He was trying to fly away from what was bothering him on earth. So he made a mistake. It's all it was. He should just wax his wings and try flying again. Maybe it'll be fun. That's my advice to him. Doubt he'll listen.

So that's sort of it. Shouldn't you give me some sign you heard me? Where the hell around here would a sign even be?

Acknowledgments

THANK YOU TO THE COLUMBIA UNIVERSITY PROFESSORS WHO taught critical thinking, and to the public school educators who believed in me. It was at a time when it was difficult to believe in anything.

Heartfelt thanks to C. P. Lesley, Courtney J. Hall, Gabrielle Mathieu, Denise Richardson, and Gloria Rabinowitz, who generously read countless drafts, asked good questions, and offered insights and knowledge. Thanks to Jill Marsh at Triskele Books for a very helpful early read and to all the members of Five Directions Press for their help in editing and production.

Daniel Stern and Geraldine Grossman: words do not express the depth of my gratitude.

Warmly thanked are friends and family who are there with kindness and patience.

The Author

ARIADNE APOSTOLOU LIVES IN PENNSYLVANIA AND IS AT WORK ON a new novel. She holds degrees in classical art and archaeology and museum studies. Five Directions Press published *Seeking Sophia,* her first novel, in 2013; it follows the life of Kleio Platon, the fourth member of Group, and her decision to adopt a child.

Coming of age in the turbulent 1970s—where she spent years immersed in student protests, urban communes, and radical politics—Kleio Platon has never been drawn to the conventional goals of marriage and motherhood. But after a few devastating months strip her of her boyfriend, her health, and her splashy international job, Kleio realizes the downside to being a black sheep. As she struggles to rebuild her life and make peace with her past, Kleio clings to advice discovered in a fortune cookie: "Plant a tree. Build a house. Raise a child. Write a book. Wisdom streams from these endeavors."

Wisdom. In the language of Kleio's grandparents, Sophia—which is also the name of the abandoned child whose adoption may hold the key that unlocks, for Kleio, the true meaning of life.

But old habits die hard. Can Kleio find the strength to commit the ultimate rebellion: putting down roots?

"This is a writer who can do big picture and microscopic detail, depending on how it serves the story. I thoroughly enjoyed Kleio's journey, the vivid characters, the riotous description of scenery and the perfectly structured narrative through which the reader feels both wiser and more naive."

—*Words with JAM*

http://www.fivedirectionspress.com/seeking-sophia

Karen Alexander lives in California and has it all: teenage children who allow her to be seen in public with them now and then, a successful architect husband who still kind of fits into his *I Hate Maggie Thatcher* T-shirt, and a teaching career she loves, especially in the school holidays. And she has Carol—her official Best Pal since their days of platform shoes, flicked-out hair, lip gloss shoplifted from Woolworths, Ally's Tartan Army, and dancing to ABBA and "The Hustle" at the local disco.

Thirty-five years later, they worry more about a good foundation to cover the wrinkles, a reliable hairdresser to cover the grey, stylish but comfortable shoes, shapewear that gives them the semblance of a shape, and husbands who fall asleep on the couch.

Back in Scotland for a funeral and a cringe-worthy sixtieth birthday party, Karen runs into her teenage crush, Bobby Henderson, the former local punk rocker and all-round bad boy who broke Karen's sixteen-year-old heart by not noticing her. When he walks into the party in his leather jacket and winks at her, Karen's heart skips a beat like it was 1978. Is the first cut really the deepest? Has Karen spent the last thirty years with the wrong guy?

Can you rewind the tape of love, and if you can, should you?

http://www.fivedirectionspress.com/rewind

THIS BOOK WAS TYPESET USING ATHELAS, A BODY FONT INSPIRED by British literary classics, with headings in Avenir, a display font selected to convey the optimistic, future-oriented spirit of these novellas. The type ornaments come from Type Embellishments One LET, also chosen for their modern feel and, in the case of the title page, their evocation of compasses and, therefore, journeys.